Alfred Herbert Palmer

The Life of Joseph Wolf

Animal Painter

Alfred Herbert Palmer

The Life of Joseph Wolf
Animal Painter

ISBN/EAN: 9783337230395

Printed in Europe, USA, Canada, Australia, Japan

Cover: Foto ©Raphael Reischuk / pixelio.de

More available books at **www.hansebooks.com**

THE

LIFE OF

Joseph Wolf

ANIMAL PAINTER

By A. H. Palmer

(Author of *The Life of Samuel Palmer*)

ILLUSTRATED

"WE SEE DISTINCTLY ONLY WHAT WE KNOW THOROUGHLY."

Published by *Longmans, Green, & Co.*

LONDON AND NEW YORK

1895

PREFACE

IT was in the pretty house which Mr. H. E. Dresser, the accomplished ornithologist, had built himself in the midst of the Kentish orchards, that I first saw his old friend Mr. Joseph Wolf.

One day his host and hostess, having an engagement, asked me to walk over for a chat with their guest. It proved to be no ordinary visit, for I found him fascinating and interesting to a degree so remarkable, that I resolved, then and there, if no one else told the story of his life, to attempt it myself. Time passed on, and when, after many explorations of his portfolios, I had formed some estimate of Wolf's power, his ideal, and his life-long diligence in searching for knowledge, there arose a strange, strong longing to make these things more widely known—the feeling and poetry, the scholarly, unmercenary learning, and the consummate manipulative skill, all so loyally ministering to truth.

Nevertheless, the story of a perfectly uneventful life, even without the shadows of adversity to give variety to its sunshine, must often be dull reading;

but if the reader bears in mind the valiant struggle of
the little, untaught farmer's boy, the passionate love
of wild animals, and the steadfast, self-denying loyalty
to an artistic ideal in after-life, perhaps he will grant
that such a career was worth some record.

As to the result of that career, men eminent in
science have agreed with men eminent in art; but no
one person can realize the full scope of such attainments. The zoologist, the artist, the poet, will appreciate these attainments each from his own point of
view. If my short record should be the cause of the
best of Wolf's work, and what he has accomplished in
each of its phases, becoming better recognised, it will
not be futile.

Speaking of a study I had been examining one
day, Wolf said, " The thing you have put down there
" I would swear to." It is not of all his works that he
will speak thus. Some which, apparently, are very
accurate and very beautiful, he will not swear to,
either because he is not quite sure that they are absolutely true, or because the truth is not told as happily
as he can tell it. In choosing from many hundreds
of drawings and sketches the illustrations of this
volume, I have confined myself to those which have
come up to this standard of the artist's. The originals
are as true as he could make them, although, in some
cases, the scenes are imaginary; but what I have said
as to the inevitable inadequacy of any translations
whatsoever of Wolf's work, I must repeat here em-

phatically. To form an adequate idea of its merit, the work itself must, in every case, be studied.

If we (the artist and I) have inadvertently chosen any work for reproduction as to the ownership of the copyright of which there may be a doubt, we trust that our full apology will be accepted.

To the Duke of Argyll my thanks are due for his Grace's kind permission to include the original charcoal sketch of a Golden Eagle subject which was burnt at Inveraray.[1]

I am greatly indebted to the Secretaries of the Zoological Society of London and The British Ornithologists' Union for their courtesy in granting leave to reproduce some of Mr. Wolf's auto-lithographs in *The Proceedings* and *The Ibis*.

I am also indebted to Messrs. H. E. Dresser, G. B. Eyre, Alfred Healey, Robert J. Howard, and J. H. Lea, for the privilege of giving representations of their drawings ; while to Mr. D. G. Elliot I owe permission to add two sketches drawn for his well-known Monographs of The Cats and The Pheasants.

I must thank Messrs. Longmans & Co. not only for allowing me to include the sketches of Elephants, but for the liberality and thoughtful solicitude with which they have done their part. To them was entrusted the publication of the first work Joseph Wolf did in this country, and it is a happy circumstance that they

---

[1] The Duke was so good as to inform me that a copy of the picture was made by one of his sons before its destruction.

should publish also the story of his life and labours while he is yet among us.

To Mr. Dresser I owe much besides the loan of his drawings. But for him I might never have met Joseph Wolf; and with constant kindness he has spared no pains to further my object.

A. H. PALMER.

CARN TOWAN, SENNEN, LAND'S END;
September 1895.

CONTENTS

CHAPTER I

WOLF's Kindred and Birthplace, page 1. Childhood, 3. Unusual susceptibility to the beauty of Nature, 5. His schooling, 5. He turns against farming, 6. His first artistic attempts and discouragements, 7. The first Gun, 7. The Ravines of the Moselle, 9. Home-made Brushes, 10. His great powers of observation, 12. He snares Birds of Prey for models, 15. He leaves home and becomes a Lithographer's Apprentice, 17.

CHAPTER II

WOLF's apprentice life, 18. Returns home and paints the Bird Miniatures, Landscapes and Portraits, 21-24. Wine gauging, 25. He leaves home again, and calls on Dr. Rüppell, 25. His first encouragement, 26. Dr. Kaup, 27. A Commission from Professor Schlegel, 28. He escapes military service, 29. Removes to Leyden, 30. *Traité de Fauconnerie*, 31. He settles at Darmstadt, 33. Illustrates Rüppell's *Birds of North East Africa*, and contributes some Illustrations to the *Fauna Japonica*, 34. He attends his first Art School, 35. Sport in the Forests and the use he made of it, 36 37. He studies Pterylography, 38. He studies anatomical detail, 40. He studies Blackgame, 42. The Woodcock sketches, 43. Kern's commission, 44. The Darmstadt Oil-pictures, 46. He leaves Darmstadt and joins the Antwerp Academy, 49. Is invited to London and declines, 50. He leaves Germany, 51.

CHAPTER III

WOLF begins work at the British Museum for Gray's *Genera of Birds*, 53. His early friendships, 56. Science versus Art, 58. His power of revivifying preserved specimens, 61. He works for other artists, 63. Distinguished employers, 65. The Pre-Raphaelites' opinion, 67.

John Gould, 69. Wolf works for Gould, 72. Gould and Severtzoff, 75. A Great Auk's Egg, 76. Wolf visits Norway with Gould and George Parker Bidder, 77. Gould's opinion of Wolf, 80. Wolf's first Academy Picture hung, 80. He goes to Knowsley Hall, 82. The Menagerie, 83. He visits Sutherlandshire and studies Ptarmigan, 88. Visits Guisachan and studies the Golden Eagle, 91. His dislike to "Grand Visits," 93. *The Proceedings* of The Zoological Society, 94. The importance of Backgrounds, 101. *The Transactions* of The Zoological Society, 102. *The Ibis*, 105. Naturalists and Art, 107. *The Zoological Sketches*, 109. Elliot's *Monographs*, 112. Dresser's *Birds of Europe*, 115.

CHAPTER IV

WOLF begins to work for the Publishers and visits A. E. Knox, 116. *The Poets of the Woods* and *Feathered Favourites*, 117. Anderson's *Lake N Gami*, 119. Livingstone's *Missionary Travels*, 123. Drayson's *Sporting Scenes amongst the Kaffirs*, 124. More Academy Pictures, 125. "Jerfalcons striking a Kite," 126. Eagles more picturesque than Falcons, 128. Feathers and Flight, 129-31. The Sketches for Oswell, 133. Wolf's hatred of so-called "Sport" and of Sporting Subjects, 137. "The Aggressor shall not succeed," 140. Wolf removes to Berners Street, 142. His Aviaries, 143. His annual holidays, 147. His snow subjects, 149. He visits Handa and the Bass Rock, 151. His work for Routledge's *Poets*, 153. Gosse's *Romance of Natural History*, 156. Tennent's *Sketches of the Natural History of Ceylon*, 159. Johns' *British Birds*, 161. Baldwin's *African Hunting*, 165. Wood's *Natural History*, 167. Wallace's *Malay Archipelago* and Campbell's *Indian Journal*, 169. Wolf's work for the Illustrated Periodicals, 169.

CHAPTER V

WOLF's Large Charcoal Drawings, 173. The German Athenæum Subjects, 174. His humorous Designs, 180. He frequents the Zoological Gardens and his safeguard maxims in using them, 182-4. He rarely sketches animals in motion, 186. Professor Owen's *Monograph of the Gorilla*, 188. An Experiment with a Fox, 190. Wolf is introduced to Darwin, 192. "The Laughing Monkey," 193. Wolf's independence of thought, 196. Darwin and the Bullfinch, 197. *The Life and Habits of Wild Animals* and its reception by the Press, 198. Wood-engraving and Mystery, 202. Wood-engraving and Process-work, 204. "The Night Attack," 209. "Families of Lions," 211

Wolf's Mistakes, 212. Commissions, 213. Cui bono? 214. He reaches his Prime, 215. Joins the Institute of Painters in Water-colours, and exhibits "Broken Fetters," 216. His reasons for not exhibiting often, 218. He removes to The Avenue, Fulham Road, and designs " Inquisitive Neighbours," 220. His Clay Models, 221. He paints the Queen's Bullfinch, 223.

CHAPTER VI

WOLF leaves Fulham for Primrose Hill Studios, 225. His personal appearance, 226. The Studio Blackbirds, 227. His Garden, 228. His love of spring-time, 229. The Studio, 230. The great Box-portfolios and their contents, 231. The Subjects on the Easels, 234. A Notable Critic, 235. What Wolf has most suffered from, 235. Instances of his rapidity, 237. " A Row in the Jungle," 238. Scanty material to work from, 240. A notable Sofa and its contents, 241. The Cabinet of Sketches from Life, 245. Wolf's simple bachelor life, 247. His vigorous Conversation, 248. His opinion of con-temporary Zoological Art, 248. The Zoological Draughtsman's Back-grounds, 251. Wolf's favourite subjects and best works, 252. " Arctic Summer," 254. His colour harmonies, 255. German or English? 257. Nothing like Smoking, 258. His love for Children, 259. He pays the Author a Country Visit, 260. His skill with the Rifle, 262. His knowledge of birds' notes and great keenness of sight and hearing, 263. Backgrounds and Accessories, 265. His knowledge of detail is troublesome, 266. Charcoal his favourite material, 269. His water-colour method, 271. His Eclecticism, 274. His un-mercenary Ideal, 277. To compare him with other artists impossible, 279. Mr. Dresser's opinion, 283. Professor Newton's opinion, 284. Mr. Thorburn's opinion, 286. Mr. Charles Whymper's opinion, 286.

APPENDIX, 290

LIST OF ILLUSTRATIONS

PLATES

JOSEPH WOLF AGED SEVENTY-TWO   .   *Frontispiece*

Photogravure from a photograph by the Author.

AGE .   .   .   .   *To face p.* 1

An old Stag lagging behind the other Deer. From the charcoal drawing in the possession of Mr. G. B. Eyre. 1872.

PANYPTILA SANCTI-JEROMÆ   .   .   .   .   ,,   5

A new species of Swift from Guatemala. The nest is composed entirely of the seeds of a certain plant cemented tog ther, and hung from the under surface of an overhanging rock by the saliva of the bird. The structure is twenty-six inches long by six inches in diameter. From the auto-lithograph in *The Proceedings of the Zoological Society.* 1853. XXIII.

THE SHOE-BILLED STORK (*Balæniceps rex*) .   .   .   ,,   11

A gigantic grallatorial Bird found only on the Upper Nile. Total length 67 inches. From the auto-lithograph in *The Proceedings of the Zoological Society.* 1851. Aves. XXXV.

FISHING IN THE SHALLOWS .   .   .   .   .   ,,   18

White-headed Eagle (*Haliaëtus leucocephalus*) and Salmon. From the charcoal drawing in the Artist's possession.

ACCIPITER COLLARIS .   .   .   .   ,,   22

"An undescribed species of Hawk from New Granada." From the auto-lithograph in *The Ibis.* 1860. VI.

CAPRIMULGUS VEXILLARIUS .   .   .   .   .   ,,   30

Africa. From the auto-lithograph in *The Ibis.* 1864. II.

NASITERNA PUSIO (natural size) . . . . . *To face p.* 36
   A new Parrot from the Saloman Islands. From the auto-
   lithograph in *The Proceedings of the Zoological Society*.
   1865. XXXV.

CAPRIMULGUS TAMARICIS 44
   Dead Sea. From the auto-lithograph in *The Ibis*, 1866, II.

SPIZAËTUS NANUS . . . ., 48
   New species. Borneo. From the auto-lithograph in *The
   Ibis*, 1868, I.

SOLITARY . . . ., 52
   Rough-legged Buzzard (*Archibuteo lagopus*). From a charcoal drawing in the Author's possession.

ELEONORA'S FALCON *(Hypotriorchis eleonorae)* . . 58
   Madagascar and adjacent islands. From the auto-lithograph
   in *The Ibis*, 1869, XVI.

ASTUR GRICEICEPS . . . ., 62
   Celebes. From the auto-lithograph in *The Ibis*, 1864, V.

GERMAIN'S POLYPLECTRON (*Polyplectron germaini*) ., 69
   Cochin China. From the auto-lithograph in *The Ibis*, 1866.

BUBO FASCIOLATUS . . . ., 76
   An African Horned Owl (not quite adult) ; never previously
   brought to Europe. From the auto-lithograph in *The Proceedings of the Zoological Society*. 1863, XXXIII.

LEUCOPTERNIS PRINCEPS . . . ., 80
   A new accipitrine bird from mountains in Costa Rica. From
   the auto-lithograph in *The Proceedings of the Zoological
   Society*. 1865, XXIV.

TREGELAPHUS SPEKII . . . ., 85
   East Africa. From the auto-lithograph in *The Proceedings
   of the Zoological Society*. 1864, XII.

PITHECIA MONACHUS . . . ., 92
   From the auto-lithograph in *The Proceedings of the Zoological
   Society*. 1862, XXXVII.

DACTYLOPSILA TRIVIRGATA ♀ 97
   Aru Islands. From the auto-lithograph in *The Proceedings
   of the Zoological Society*. 1858, Mammalia, LXIII.

DEAD AYE AYE *(Chiromys madagascariensis)* . 103
   Outline of a specimen which had lived in the gardens of the
   Zoological Society, illustrating the Artist's method of re-
   cording the measurements of dead animals. The reproduction is from a chalk drawing in the Author's possession,
   of the natural size ; that is, from nostril to tip of tail in a
   straight line twenty-six inches.

THE EASTERN RED-FOOTED HOBBY *(Erythropus amurensis)*. ♂ ♀ Juv. Natal . . . . *To face p.* 106

From the auto-lithograph in *The Ibis.* 1868. Plate II.

FELIS MACROSCELOIDES . . . . . . 　,,　 111

Nepal, India. From the auto-lithograph in *The Proceeding of the Zoological Society.* 1853. Mammalia. XXXVIII.

REEVES' PHEASANT *(Phasianus reevesi)*. . . . 　,,　 114

From the original charcoal sketch for the lithograph in Mr. D. G. Elliot's *Monograph of the Phasianidæ.* With his permission. In the Artist's possession.

THE PANTHER *(Felis pardus)*. . . . . . 　,,　 116

The larger and lighter variety found in India and Morocco. From the original charcoal sketch for the lithograph in Mr. D. G. Elliot's *Monograph of the Felidæ.* With his permission. In the Artist's possession.

THE PALLID HARRIER *(Circus swainsoni)* . . . 　,,　 122

From the original sketch in charcoal-grey for the lithograph in Mr. H. E. Dresser's *Birds of Europe.* In his possession. 1877.

THE MARSH HARRIER *(Circus æruginosus)* . . . 　,,　 124

From the original sketch in charcoal grey for the lithograph in Mr. H. E. Dresser's *Birds of Europe.* In his possession. 1877.

GOLDEN EAGLE *(Aquila chrysaetus)* . . . . 　,,　 128

From a charcoal study for a picture commissioned by the Duke of Argyll. With his Grace's permission. In the Artist's possession.

"SPORT" . . . . 　,,　 135

From a charcoal sketch in the Artist's possession. 1875.

A MONGOOSE *(Herpestes smithii ?)* . . . . 　,,　 138

India. From an auto-lithograph in *The Proceedings of the Zoological Society.*

THE SILVER MARMOSET *(Mico sericeus)* . . 　 146

Brazil. From the auto-lithograph in *The Proceedings of the Zoological Society.* 1868. XXIV. Drawn from life.

A STORM IN THE ALPS . . . . . . 　,,　 149

From the charcoal drawing in the possession of Mr. Alfred Healey. 27 × 21. 1877.

MORNING, A SEQUEL . . . . . 　,,　 171

From the charcoal drawing in the Artist's possession.

TAME AND WILD . . . . 　,,　 175

From the charcoal drawing in the Artist's possession. 1872.

SURPRISE . . . . *To face p.* 176

From the charcoal drawing in the Artist's possession. 1874.

PEACE AND WAR . . . . ,, 179

From the charcoal drawing in the Artist's possession. 1874.

A LECTURE ON EMBRYOLOGY . . . . . ,, 180

" Came the first Egg from an Owl, or came the first Owl from
an Egg ? " From the charcoal drawing in the Artist's possession. 1877.

THE BASHFUL MONKEY . . . ., 186

This lithograph, though drawn from life for *The Proceedings
of the Zoological Society,* was not published. It represents
a species of *Cebus* from South America.

MONTEIRO'S GALAGO (*Galago monteiri*) . . . ,. 193

Angola. Length 28 inches. The ears of the Galagos are
large, " quite bare, and have the unique peculiarity that they
can be partially folded upon themselves at such times as
their owners please, so as to be nearly flat upon the sides
of the head." Lydekker. From the auto-lithograph in *The
Proceedings of the Zoological Society.* 1863. XXVIII.

BARTLETT'S SPIDER MONKEY (*Ateles bartletti*) . . ,. 198

River Amazons. From the auto-lithograph in *The Proceedings of the Zoological Society.* 1867. XLVII.

ALLEN'S GALAGO (*Galago alleni*) . . . . ., 202

Camaroons River, West Africa. From the auto-lithograph
in *The Proceedings of the Zoological Society.* 1863. XXXII.

THE WHITE-CHEEKED SAPAJOU (*Cebus leucogenys*) . ., 208

A new species of *Cebus* from Brazil. From the auto-
lithograph in *The Proceedings of the Zoological Society.*
1865. XLV.

A NIGHT ATTACK . . . ., 210

Pine Marten and Ring Dove. From a chalk drawing in the
Artist's possession.

INQUISITIVE NEIGHBOURS . . . . . . ,, 221

From the charcoal drawing in the Artist's possession. 1875.

A BEAR WITH HONEYCOMB . . . . . ., 222

From a model exhibited at the Royal Academy in 1876. In
the Artist's possession.

THE JAPANESE BEAR (*Ursus japonicus*) . . . ,, 225

From the auto-lithograph in *The Proceedings of the Zoological
Society.* 1852. XXXII.

A PEREGRINE TIERCEL (*Falco peregrinus*) . . . *To face p.* 231
From a charcoal sketch in the Author's possession. 1876.

PTEROMYS GRANDIS . . . . ,, 234
A "Flying Rat," four feet long. Formosa. The camphor tree
in which the nest was placed having been felled, the young
were captured. The parents at first escaped, but, having
returned, were secured also. From the auto-lithograph in
The Proceedings of the Zoological Society. 1862. XLV.

THE SIAMANG (*Hylobates syndactylus*) . . . . ,, 236
From a water-colour sketch from life, painted in the Gardens
of the Société d'Acclimatation, Paris. In the Artist's possession.

THE SIAMANG (swinging) . . . ,, 240
See above.

THE SIAMANG (sitting) . . ,, 244
See above.

OSPREYS (*Pandion haliaetus*) . . . . . ,, 249
From a charcoal drawing in the Artist's possession. 1869.

EQUALS . . . . ,, 255
From the charcoal drawing in the possession of Mr. J. H.
Lea. 1877.

A MIDNIGHT RAMBLE . . . . ,, 267
From the charcoal sketch in the possession of Mr. Robert
J. Howard. 1856.

CAPTIVITY . . . . ,, 268 .
From a charcoal sketch in the Artist's possession.

ILLUSTRATIONS IN THE TEXT

PAGE

A BLACKCOCK AS HE FELL 65
From a pencil sketch from nature at Inveraray. In the Artist's possession.

SKETCHES OF FLYING OSPREYS 132, 133
Illustrating the Artist's remarks touching laborious and easy flight. In
his possession.

JOSEPH WOLF IN THE FIFTIES . . . 141
From a photograph.

PAGE

MODE OF TYING AN ELEPHANT 160
  Original sketch for the woodcut in *The Natural History of Ceylon*, by
  Sir James Emerson Tennent. 1861. By permission of Messrs. Long-
  mans & Co. In the Artist's possession.

HIS STRUGGLES FOR FREEDOM 161
  See " Mode of Tying an Elephant." In the Artist's possession.

A WILD CAT (*Felis catus*) 172
  From a pencil sketch from life in the Artist's possession.

FIRST SKETCH FOR 'A LECTURE ON EMBRYOLOGY' . 181
  In the Artist's possession.

THE LAUGHING MONKEY (*Cynopithecus niger*) 195
  A duplicate version of a sketch, from life, for *The Expressions of the
  Emotions in Man and Animals.* In the Artist's possession. 1871.

HEAD OF OVIS AMMON 224
  From a chalk sketch in the Artist's possession.

SKETCH OF OVIS POLI IN SNOW . . . 239
  In the Artist's possession.

PÈRE DAVID'S DEER (*Cervus davidianus*) 260
  Northern China. From a charcoal sketch in the Artist's possession.

LION CUBS 289
  From a pencil sketch from life in the Artist's possession.

TURTLE DOVES 303
  From a sketch in the Artist's possession.

Errata

Page	37,	line	8,	*for* animals *read* mammals
	112	,,	9	*for* Elliott *read* Elliot
	113	,,	20	,,	,,
	114	,,	7, 25	,,	,,
	179	,,	7	,,	,,
	198	,,	17	,,	,,
	243	,,	4	,,	,,

Joseph Wolf

CHAPTER I

EARLY in the present century, when the province of Rhenish Prussia had been recently formed, and the country was settling down to a state of unwonted peace, one Anton Wolf lived in the little village of Möerz, in the district of Mayfeld, not far from the road connecting Trèves with Coblenz. The village was about fifteen miles distant from this city, but only two from the market town of Münstermayfeld—just remote enough, in fact, to enjoy some of the blessings of remoteness. As for antiquity, if any of the inhabitants cared for such a thing, a neighbourhood where stern old Rome had left her handiwork would have been interesting enough and to spare.

Anton Wolf was a reserved, well-to-do man (farming his own land), who, as Headman of the place, had some degree of authority. Among a number of his small duties were such as the reading to the villagers, summoned by the church bell to the public bakehouse, any new government regulation, or signing the book of the *gendarmes* at stated and sometimes untimely hours.

The Headman's house was distinguished from the others by the Prussian Eagle on a large metal plate, and was a substantial, slate-roofed, stone dwelling of two stories. I have seen a sketch representing it as bosomed in trees, with a sleepy, old-world look about it, enhanced by a flock of pigeons which wheel about over the steep gables, and bask in rows upon the ridges. Tiles there were none in the place, and very few of the houses were thatched, for such an inflammable method of roofing was discouraged by a careful government. Indeed, if an economical man mended his thatch he was straightway fined. It was a place that seemed, from all appearances, to have quietly settled down to slumber. Each burly village stay-at-home was content with his quiet life, though, perhaps, he may have growled a little if the Headman billeted a Prussian artilleryman or trooper upon him, when the duties of a squadron or a battery brought it towards the frontier.

As for Anton Wolf himself, his ambition climbed no higher than good prices and good seasons. Since the days when he had been drafted off with a heavy flint-lock to withstand Napoleon (before the death of his little daughter), his troubles had been few— nothing much more serious, indeed, than increasing taxation.

Touching the five strong boys which were borne
him by Elizabeth his wife, his main desire was that
they should become comfortable, saving men like
himself, worthy to plough the paternal acres.

Of these five surviving children I have to follow
the fortunes of Joseph, the eldest, who was born on
the 21st of January, 1820, and soon grew to be a fair,
sturdy child, evidently destined to inherit the big
bones of his ancestors.

Among the earliest things which he noticed, next
to a Black Forest clock, a ponderous oak table where
the family fed with their labourers, and the spinning-
wheel at which his mother laboured, was her flower
garden. Her fragrant, old-fashioned blossoms were
the pride of her life, and it soon became her little
son's delight to watch her as she tended them, or to
toddle about by himself, prying for the earliest shoots
of the tulips, and hyacinths, and daffodils in the
spring.

A notable event was his first sheep-washing, for
it was always a real, old-fashioned, village holiday,
merrily kept at Catenass on the lovely banks of
the Moselle two miles away. The child's joy at the
bustle and excitement of the journey, and at the first
sight of a river and a fish, he remembers still.

After a while he began to enjoy the other pleasures of a primitive life, and he loved to watch the
rape-threshing by men mounted on the ponderous
farm horses ; or to run at the heels of the field-

labourers, who were well versed, of course, in poacher's wood-craft.

It is evident that an unusual susceptibility to the witchery of nature began to show itself very early. At an age when the average village child thinks only of what he can tease and what he can eat, little Wolf was exulting in the teeming life which came with the spring. The re-appearance of favourite flowers and familiar birds, mourned all the winter as dead and gone, thrilled him in a way which neither he nor any one else who has felt it can express in words. It was also evident that, coupled with the overpowering love of nature, there was a power of observation altogether phenomenal.

As a very little child, the Nightingale's song raised a longing to know what great, beautiful bird sang "so wild and well." So one day he crept along till he was able to see the little insignificant brown thing, not even as large as a Thrush, with arched back and drooping tail, singing right merrily. He was bitterly disappointed ; and he says, " It was too small " for me. I thought 'What an ugly little brute you " 'are!'" But when a pair of Goldfinches set up their housekeeping in the garden, he spent hours in watching them and wondering at their exceeding beauty and brilliancy.

Such as these are the incidents he can recall of his childhood. He tells how greedily he listened for the Buzzards' cries as they soared high up in the air ;

PANYPTILA SANCTI-JEROMI.

how he longed and waited for the cheerful laugh of
the Green Woodpecker ; and how the monotonous
note of the Turtle Dove always filled him with unac-
countable melancholy. He remembers, too, how he
grieved to say good-bye to the last Swallow.

It was not a brush, or a pencil, that first found its
way into Joseph Wolf's small fist, but a pair of
scissors. With these he cut out paper silhouettes of
birds and animals of his own design, to paste on a
window ; where they were much admired by a sym-
pathetic tax-gatherer.

Before this time the boy had gone to school at
the neighbouring village of Metternich. Here, in
a small library belonging to the schoolmaster, he
soon scented out an old work on natural history ; one
of that class, he says, where the Orang-utan is
represented as sedately walking with a stick.[1] At
that school, however, science was at a discount, and
little Wolf had to content himself with many a wistful
glance at the outside of the volume he longed to
pounce upon.

His observant habits and superior skill in drawing
maps told favourably with the master ; but to the
scholars, a boy who refrained from bird's-nesting on
principle and who was willing to fight any one of

---

[1] At the Zoological Society's, at Hanover Square, there is a careful
early drawing by Wolf of an Orang-utan living in the Gardens, support-
ing itself upon a stick. This, he says, was simply a trick the animal had
learnt, and would not be natural to a wild specimen. " Representations
of its walking with a stick," says Wallace, " are entirely imaginary."

them in defence of a nest-full of young birds was a
puzzle.

Among the boys, Whitethroats were called
"Grass-sparrows," and as a war of extermination was
carried on against "Sparrows" all and singular, they
adjourned one day to enjoy the slow torture of a nest-
full. The ingenious cruelty so infuriated little Wolf
that he betook himself to his fists, and then to the
master, who severely punished the chief torturer.
This incident naturally led to a stormy time, and but
for the protection of a warm-hearted big cousin it
would have gone ill with him.

The farmer took advantage of the holidays, and
of the hard weather when the Wolves were abroad
(troublesome enough at times), to set his boy to
work ; but it was becoming pretty evident that Joseph
was no true chip of the heavy old block. Although
he loved grafting, and took good care to plant plenty
of cherry trees, he hated the horse-tending, and
would be off in the snow, if he could, all round the
villages, to search for the tracks of the Marten-cats.
He loathed sauerkraut ; and lived contentedly (as he
says he could live now) on bread and butter. With
a morsel of the evil-savoured Limburg cheese he
could be driven anywhere ; and, indeed, his mother
once offered him five groschen to eat a piece of that
abomination, and he failed to do so.

His father, besides being a very reserved man, not
given to enthusiasm of any kind, thought all things

vain which had nothing to do with the farm, or with
village affairs ; and when Joseph snatched a few
hours for scribbling the outlines of birds from recollection, the only notice he got was a very doubtful
" Humph !", though his mother thought the attempts
pretty. " Just as the country people in England,"
he says, " when they see a strapping artist at work
" on his picture, think he might be doing something " more useful." Old Anton in fact, associating
only with people of his own class, was very pre-
judiced ; and his son remembers, even now, the
paternal rage if he was caught when he was busy
with his caterpillars, or piping a lesson to a pet
Bullfinch.

A full measure of the love of firearms with which
most boys are born burned in Wolf's heart. He had
occasionally abstracted from his father's keeping some
great key (such as the key of the church), sounded
the depth of the barrel with a stick, and filed a small
touch-hole: with the addition of a little gunpowder
and a match, the key then became a notable piece of
ordnance, to be unlimbered in secret and fired in tre-
pidation. At last there came that day of ecstasy when
the boy was allowed to furbish up the old gun he had
so often devoured with hungry eye ; a long, single-
barrel, flint-lock, rejoicing in that fanciful, carved
stock which would so much offend the eye of Purdey
or Grant. Now, at last, the poultry and pigeons
could be protected from the Goshawks, and the

mystery of some of those perplexing notes and cries of
the woods and fields might be solved.   So, when the
boy returned from a tramp to Münstermayfeld with a
few cheap water-colours in his pocket, a new flint or
two, and some ammunition, he felt that the world was
not a bad sort of place after all.

Besides models for his sketches, he shot some fat
Fieldfares, with the view of selling them to an old
huckster in order to secure a supply of powder and
shot.   This dame seems to have been a bit of a
character.   She was a notable busybody, and as she
went her rounds among the farms, buying butter
and eggs and poultry for the Coblenz market, she
collected gossip and toothsome scandal.   One day,
when she paid Frau Wolf her usual visit, Joseph
(then about fourteen years old) came in to sell his
Fieldfares.   His mother mentioned his strange wish
to become, of all absurd things, an artist.   He, the
eldest son of the Headman himself, a lad who would
never lack to jingle the thalers in his pocket, or to
smoke a quiet pipe, like his father and grandfather
before him—he, an artist!   The old huckster sympa-
thized and shook her head as she gazed at the fair,
well-grown lad, clad in his blouse, peaked cap, and
heavy boots ; and then she repeated impressively an
old country saying, " Seven artists, seven shooters,
" seven fishermen, and seven bird-catchers cannot
" support one idle man."   They were ominous words,
and not very much to the mother's liking, for she

loved her first-born dearly, and petted him, and knew that he returned her love.

Having provided himself with colours, Wolf was no longer content to scribble pencil outlines. There happened to be at the farm a few of the illustrated volumes of the last century; and of these he set himself to paint the wood-cuts. Wherever furniture was represented, he appealed to the cake of Vandyke brown with startling effect. He says, " I spoilt the " whole of the books, and I ought to have been kicked " at that time."

Fortunately the country was very favourable for the observation of birds. Four or five hundred yards above the farm it became flat and open, though the fields were small. In the other direction it trended down into a valley, increasing in beauty and interest to the naturalist as it approached the Moselle. Each little tributary wound its way through a well-wooded ravine, so secluded that even a she Wolf could rear her young there, now and then; and birds without number thronged the steep hangers. Golden Orioles, White-spotted Bluethroats and Hoopoes always appeared in the spring, and there was many a bird which here is accounted rare. In addition to other quadrupeds (such as Otters, Foxes, Stoats, Weasels, and Pole-cats), Stone-martens occurred; a circumstance which suggested to the boy an original scheme. Long ago he had learnt the rudiments of trapping from one of his father's labourers who was skilful in setting gins and horsehair snares, and he determined to turn his knowledge to account. Having managed to secure a fine Stone-marten or two, he chose the longest and most elastic hairs from the tails, and tied them neatly into some Crow and Thrush quills. Thus he furnished himself with a set of brushes incomparably better than the limp, camel-hair things he had bought with his first colours. They were so good that he became ambitious; and casting about for something to copy, he pitched on an elaborate line engraving of Louisa, Queen of Prussia. He sat down with a tiny brush and Indian ink, determined to reproduce that engraving line for line. He says, "There was nobody to tell me "it was impossible, and I felt very unhappy because "I couldn't do it. But fancy trying to do such a "thing!" The natural deftness and patience which led to such incidents as these (for it is not every boy who could impress the tails of Marten-cats into the service of art), led to better results when more sensible copies were chosen. He had reared from the nest a Long-eared Owl; [1] and finding it very beautiful he set himself to draw it. In order to get the proportions right he kept at a distance, and for detail went closer, thus showing signs of gumption not to be expected from a farmer's boy. About this time he discovered that an Eagle Owl was kept in an hotel yard at Münstermayfeld, and he went off at once to make a

---

[1] He speaks of all the Birds of Prey as good sitters, and of the Owls as pre-eminently so—the very opposite of a Titmouse, or a Monkey.

THE SHOE BILLED STORK.

sketch. This expedition he kept quiet at home, and, indeed, he had the sense to say nothing whatever about his drawing at Möerz. It is a reticence which, ever since that time, he has observed in the presence of people ignorant of art. Before the Philistines he keeps silent; but ever watchful to add to his store of their observations on art and artists.

A few migratory Storks sometimes pitched near the village, and on one of these occasions young Wolf crept up with his gun and succeeded in winging a bird. Then he amputated the broken wing, and for some time the Stork paraded the farm, unconscious of the multiplication of his portrait.

By this time the cousin who had protected little Wolf from the revenge of his schoolfellows had grown up; and as he rented the rough shooting of this and a neighbouring commune, he allowed the boy to bring the old gun and to join him in his rambles. He was somewhat astonished at the use which was made of it, for Wolf thought nothing of the amount of the bag; but at the sight of a strange bird, or the sound of an unknown note, he would be off, regardless of time or place. It was a curious circumstance connected with these field-days, that the cousin's clay pipe was frequently bitten in two as his gun went off, from which I should imagine that it was a notable kicker.

For some time, there had apparently been a good understanding between Wolf and many animals, especially wild animals. In spite of the gun, they seemed to understand that he did not really thirst for their blood, but merely wished to know all about them. His patience and gentleness of disposition may have had something to do with this, besides a certain skill in the language which every animal uses in its intercourse with an especial human friend, in those rare cases where it finds itself understood. His eyesight, outward and inward, was literally of the keenest possible description ; and as he looked at everything which interested him with intense purpose and zest, his power of observation grew very great— an habitual, unlaboured watchfulness worthy of a wild animal. His purpose was not only to study the habits of mammals and birds, but to paint the animals so faithfully and fearlessly as to do them justice. He knew nothing of what was before him—nothing of the scope, or history, or heart-breaking difficulty of other branches of art ; and it is well for him and for us that he did not, or he might have resigned himself to study the points of the Möerz pig.

Some of the incidents of a farm life in that particular district furthered his object. Thus the occasional dash of a Goshawk upon the poultry or pigeons was not an unmixed evil ; for the boy and his younger brothers, by means of the gun, or a gin laid on the fowl which the bird had killed,[1] usually

---

[1] There is a spirited and very highly finished little panel picture by Wolf of this subject, painted in Germany when the incidents were fresh. The trap has been baited with a rabbit.

managed to secure at once an arch-robber and a splendid subject for a drawing. He treasured up in his memory such incidents as the visit of an Eagle Owl to the tree where some of the fowls roosted, or the more dreaded visit of a Stone-marten, which (if luck favoured) was treed by the dogs, and shot as it was dimly seen against the night sky. As for Foxes, there was common cause against them in a place where their murder was a manly virtue, and the only view halloo was that of the Magpies. The enemy's approach was often signalled by these birds ; which, in return for their service, were beloved and protected by everybody. Then the gun or the gin squared all the poultry accounts. Moreover, when a vixen's earth was found, the young men would some-times dig out the cubs and take them round to the farms in a basket, each rejoicing hen-wife giving a reward of eggs. The eggs were fried, and with plenty of cheap wine an unholy wake was held over the poor cubs which would have sorely angered an English M.F.H. Sometimes, when they thought they could manage it, the lads would clap into a basket a sharp-nosed, sandy puppy, and cheat the women out of their eggs.

As Wolf's skill with his brushes grew greater, his love of the Birds of Prey kept pace with his love of painting. This district lay in the course of the annual passage ; and in the spring an occasional Honey Buzzard appeared ; in the winter, Rough-

legged Buzzards from the north. Sometimes both
Black and Red Kites were to be seen flying towards
the south-west, returning with the genial weather.
Goshawks, Sparrow-hawks, Hobbies, Merlins, and
Kestrils also occurred frequently; but the idea of
shooting such courageous and beautiful visitors as
these, except in actual defence of the poultry, was
out of the question. Wolf wished to draw from the
living birds in all their wild perfection, and at first
sight it seems as if he might have wished on till the
present time.

It was a local custom that, at times, the sheep
belonging to the farmers were drafted together into
one large flock, and placed under the care of a shepherd; each farmer having a right to contribute according to his acreage. The shepherd's duty was to feed
off with the sheep all the available pasture; and the
fields being small, the flock might perhaps be dispersed over the property of half a dozen men, besides
the "commune" property on the hills, which was
distinct from private land. If the stubbles of any
particular farmer happened to be sown with clover, or
there was any other reason for excluding the sheep,
he set up there a stake topped with a wisp of straw,
as a notice to the shepherd. Wolf frequently saw
Hawks and Falcons sitting on these stakes (for the
country just here was very open and treeless), and he
began to think over the chances of catching them.[1]

[1] At that time, he had probably never heard of the pole trap.

He was familiar with the use of snares, and by dint of great patience and ingenuity, he succeeded in contriving some springes sufficiently powerful, which, in conjunction with short perches, he attached to the stakes in the forbidden fields. He was soon rewarded for his labour ; and made the round of his springes, in the evening to forestall the Foxes, and in the morning to release the Little Owls which sometimes got caught. Once even a Buzzard was secured, and by sheer power of wing gradually loosened and then flew away with the whole apparatus. Another time, a fine old male Sparrow-hawk was held fast merely by the hind claw. Merlins and Kestrils were the most common captures ; and Wolf used to give some of the latter a forked tail with a pair of scissors. There was a colony of Kestrils on a high tower at Münstermayfeld, and there he often saw the forked tails of those he had caught, three or four miles away.

In this successful method of capturing birds of prey, he claims to be original and alone. He has never heard of any other person in Germany who used springes in this way.

He was seldom without a living model now ; and how he conquered the difficulties of making use of it, may well puzzle us. That he did conquer, is testified by numberless sketches and drawings. One day he had a Kestril sitting for its portrait on a chair-back, and he himself was working away, hardly daring to

move. Suddenly the farmer entered, and the spell
being broken, the bird dashed through the glass of
the nearest window. Whereupon the young painter
received a swinging box on the ear, delivered, I dare
say, with the emphatic epithet of " *Vogel narr.*" In
spite of such discouragements, sometimes when he
could steal the time from the farm, he would set
out on foot to Neuwied (a four hours' journey), to
gloat over Prince Maximilian's fine collection of South
American birds.[1]

Loving guns and gunnery, Wolf took care to be
present at the *Vögelschiessen* held among the neighbouring peasants and foresters. A wooden bird with
an iron rod passing through it was fixed at the top of
a tall pole, and shot at with heavy small-bore rifles
till the very last splinter was knocked off.

Notwithstanding the delights of his art, and wood-
craft, and gunnery (all more or less stolen pleasures),
the monotonous drudgery of the farm life palled on
the boy more and more. He says, " I was looking
" out for something different, and couldn't find what
" I liked." He was troubled, too, by the growing
consciousness that to succeed as a painter of birds,
more training would be needful than he could ever
get among people who looked upon him as a mere
bird-catcher, and preferred the weight of their horny
hands to the weight of argument, if they found

---

[1] Mr. Dresser tells me that the collection was afterwards purchased
for New York by Mr. D. G. Elliott.

him neglecting the horses to scribble pictures of vermin.

Now at that time lithography had advanced far towards perfection, and was in high repute. From Munich, Düsseldorf, and Paris, lithographs of the pictures at the chief continental galleries were circulating even in the country, and the boy began to think that the trade of a lithographer might possibly help him on the road he had chosen. He says, "Lithography was something betwixt and between. "It was supposed at that time to be a good thriving "business." Again and again he approached his father on the subject, who consented, at last, that he should desert the plough, and provided sufficient money not only for binding him apprentice to Gebrüder Becker at Coblenz, for three years, but for lodgings in that city. It is satisfactory to know not only that this amount was repaid with interest, but that the whole family were afterwards indebted pecuniarily to one upon whom they had probably looked as likely to turn out a troublesome prodigal.

Thus ended the first era in the life of Joseph Wolf. Simply and solely by the light of his own genius and the force of his own character he had removed the obstacles and had conquered the inertia that have been responsible for many "a mute inglorious Milton."

C

CHAPTER II

JOSEPH WOLF, when he found himself one of Gebrüder Beckers' three or four apprentices at Coblenz, was sixteen years old, and much too broad-shouldered to be safely derided as a country bumpkin. If he had been an ordinary lad, simply seeking excitement and relief from monotony, he would have found that he had gone from bad to worse. Certainly, for a day or two, he enjoyed the fun of learning to write backwards; but that soon palled, and the laborious copying of commonplaces which followed was depressing work. He says, " Nobody would tell me anything, and I felt they were all duffers." But it was impossible that he should ply his tools for long without the discovery that he was no mere beginner; and in spare moments he made some original sketches which pleased his employers not a little. " When they found that I " had ideas," he says, " and could compose, they let " me alone, and I had no more drudgery to do. Even " when I left off working, and began to cudgel my " brains for an idea, the firm said nothing." He told

FISHING IN THE SHALLOWS.

them he was "searching for an idea," and they had
the sense to believe him. They turned him to
account by causing him to make designs of flowers,
fruit, or landscapes, which sometimes took the form of
bottle labels ; and he thinks that if Christmas cards
had been invented he would have been condemned to
do nothing else. Among the labels were some which
were required by the proprietor of an " Eagle Phar-
macy," who wished for an appropriate device.
Here was a chance for Wolf ; and he drew a whole
stone-full of Eagles, all in different positions. He
would have nothing to do with the cards and billiards
of the other apprentices, and even ignored the
military bands on the parade ; but the instant his
day's work was done, he was off like a rifle-bullet to
the banks of the Rhine. There he hunted among the
willows for birds, and moths, and caterpillars ; or tried
to catch the Bluethroats with Nightingale nets in the
early spring.

He discovered in the city a large wholesale tradesman who had kindred tastes, and who owned a good
collection of stuffed birds. Here it was that Wolf
saw, for the first time, an illustrated ornithological
book. It was a work by Susemihl, and he says " I
" couldn't make the book out. According to my
" knowledge, the plates were not the right thing." [1]

[1] He afterwards did six full-page designs and several others of Falcons,
Owls, and other birds for what appears to be a later edition of the same
work, namely Johann and Eduard Susemihl's *Abbildungen der Vögel
Europas*. No better example could be given of what kind of illustra-

Save for the few old volumes on which he had exhausted his Vandyke brown, books were little known in his family. No scion of the house, save himself, had ever been guilty of the slightest inclination to tempt the dangers of any art or science. Yet, in spite of this, let loose as he was among half a hundred seductive shops, one of his first purchases was Schlegel's translation of Shakespeare, which he greedily devoured, astonished, he says, at the great mind of the author.

As far as art was concerned, Wolf thinks that the three years of his apprenticeship were quite thrown away; and with many lads, fresh from a farm life, it is certain they would have been worse than thrown away, by turning them out neat, stereotyped journeymen, warranted absolutely free from originality.

The qualities for which Wolf's work became so pre-eminent are not such as are usually evolved from the drawing of bottle-labels, or the dull routine of a lithographic draughtsman's office ; but yet he was quite uninjured in any way. Indeed, it is likely that in the case of such an enthusiast—so passionate a lover of nature, a training in patience, and method, and exactness was more to the purpose than the best training of a first-rate art-school would have been. The apprentice work increased

tions Wolf's work superseded at that period (the forties), and how he superseded them.

by contrast the attractiveness of his favourite subjects,
crystallized his undefined hopes, and did not di-
vert his energy to other alluring branches of art. It
will be presently seen how greatly he was afterwards
beholden to the sound knowledge of lithography.

When the three years were over, Wolf returned
for a time to his father's · farm, where he was
regarded in a very different way from the obstinate
" bird fool " of the old days. He was now a competent tradesman. He could write backwards neatly,
and draw you, out of his own head, a noble bottle-
label ; feats which made even the old Headman
himself put on his spectacles. If the lad still insisted
in spending a little time in painting owls and vermin
—why, after all, it didn't matter much now. They
might come in for tradesman's bill-heads, or something really useful.

As for those ravines of the Moselle, teeming with
bird life, and ringing with many a pretty call and
song, what a paradise they were, after the dingy lanes
and the ceaseless, mercantile buzz of Coblenz ! The
lad spent day after day in these favourite haunts of
his by the river, storing his memory with the life
history of the birds and beasts. He took his gun
with him of course ; partly because he knew that a
great deal of important knowledge could not be got
without it, and partly, I think, because he loved it
pretty keenly. One day he flushed a large bird, and
a relentless pot shot knocked a lovely Hazel Grouse

off the tree where it had settled. It was a rare species on the north bank of the river, and the pleasure of that shot lives yet, though the shooter has burnt, since then, a good deal of powder. Another day, near home, he had released a Little Owl from one of his springes, when a splendid Goshawk intercepted its headlong flight towards the woods. It battled on its back with pitiful screams, but by the time Wolf had got to his gun, the deadly foot had gripped home, and the Hawk glided away to his dinner. Always very interested in the exploits of this bird, he relates how he was once out shooting near Mörz, and put up from some turnips a Short-eared Owl. Almost immediately, a Goshawk swept from his look-out on a neighbouring tree, struck the Owl in mid air, and carried it off. " People who have never been in a " country where Goshawks are common," says Wolf, " hardly know what brutes they are." Incidents such as these, and many others, kept the lad's pencil hard at work.

He had taken up his painting with a will when he came home ; and he began now to make a series of miniature bird studies in water-colours. These miniatures are so extraordinary that I am at a loss how to describe them without incurring the accusation of exaggerating most grossly. It must be remembered that they were the work of a youth still in his teens,[1]

---

[1] In my former sketch of Wolf's life, among many other inaccuracies, the date of these drawings is fixed some years earlier.

ACCIPITER COLLARIS.

who, save for the three years lithographic practice
from which he had just escaped, was entirely self-
taught. They were done without books from which to
learn the scientific detail, or crib the attitudes. There
was not the smallest encouragement—nothing but the
distractions of a small farm-house, with hostile critics
whose ignorance of natural history was hardly less
profound than their ignorance of art. In spite of all
this, we find that after the earliest attempts of all
each of these tiny studies is a portrait so true to
nature, so brilliant and life-like, that astonishment
stifles all criticism.

In answer to my question when I first sat wondering before these drawings and found that they
would even bear the use of a strong lens, the painter
said, "The reason I did them so small was that I had
"got then into the way of working minutely, and
"could not cover a larger space to my satisfaction—
"not so as to get *the quality of the surface.* Rough
"paper and the ordinary water-colour method would
"not have suited me." Here, at all events, he was
evidently paying the penalty (if it were a penalty), of
his lithographic minutiæ. Long before this he had
noticed not only that there was a considerable
difference between the summer and winter plumage
of the common Sparrows, but that their backs were
marked very definitely in stripes. He says, "I used
"to labour to get those stripes right, as if everything
"depended upon it." How much did depend upon

this craving for truth, upon the labour unspeakable to show the soft sleekness and delicate, dainty precision of marking which distinguish a perfect specimen of a wild bird, he did not realize at that time. It would seem, from what we know of zoological art, past and present, that such an overpowering solicitude for truth in this all-important respect, and the sound, scientific knowledge of the feather tracts which follows, are not too common even now.

As for these miniatures I think they have been as much admired, and that by artists, as anything Wolf has done.

I have seen some laborious pencil and Indianink drawings of landscapes in the neighbourhood of Möerz, which were produced at this time, showing the same solicitude to draw faithfully from nature. The work is very elaborate, but the surface to be covered being larger than it was in the bird subjects, the elaboration is misapplied, and is not focussed.

It was, of course, quite natural that Wolf should try his hand at portraiture, and I believe he painted at this time several little water-colour likenesses of people in the neighbourhood; one or two being commissions. Small oil portraits of his father and mother hang in a brother's house to this day.

Joseph Wolf had now been a year at home, and no doubt his father (naturally thinking it high time his son should earn his living), considered it a time of sheer idleness. But sooner than even appear to be

idle, the lad accepted from the excise authorities
a temporary engagement which he calls "wine
revising"; that is to say he became for the time a
gauger whose duty it was to visit the various wine-
producing villages, going from house to house with
the Headman, with power to search for concealed
liquor, if any were suspected. Having completed this
unpleasant work, he sent in his report, put his
sketch-book of miniatures in his pocket, and trudged
off into the world to seek his fortune as a journeyman
lithographer.

Although there were several lithographic houses
at Frankfort, he failed to find employment at any.
Nevertheless, one of the proprietors, having seen the
sketch-book, said, "Don't you forget to go to Dr.
" Rüppell here at the Museum before you leave." "So
" I went," says Wolf. "He was a serious old fellow
" with rather a forbidding exterior. When I came in
" —a young lad—he looked at me as if he had no idea
" what I wanted to see him for. I said, 'I am a litho-
" 'grapher, and have been about to the different estab-
" 'lishments to look out for work, and at one of them
" 'they told me to show you this book.' Of course
" the moment he opened it he brightened up, and
" got very amiable all at once. 'I hope you will be
" 'able to remain near Frankfort,' he said, 'for I am
" 'about to publish a work on the Birds of Abyssinia,'

---

[1] *Systematische Uebersicht der Vögel Nord-Ost-Afrika's*, nebst von
Dr. Eduard Rüppell. Frankfurt a. M. 1845.

" ' and I should like you to do the illustrations for me.
" ' Wherever, on your travels, you remain to work, let
" ' me know, and you shall do the drawings there.
" ' When you go to Darmstadt, you go to Dr. Kaup.' "

It was the first piece of pure encouragement that
the lad had ever experienced : and it was sweetened
by the fact that it was not the lithographic knowledge,
but the knowledge of birds, so much despised at
home, which had brought success at last.

In the course of this interview, Wolf described
a new note which he had heard for the first time,
near Frankfort. " You are a good observer." said
Rüppell. " That is the Serin Finch." This species,
which now nests near the city,[1] had gradually extended northwards from southern Europe.

Bidding the Doctor adieu, Wolf turned off with a
lighter heart towards Darmstadt. Here he not only
found employment as a lithographer (besides doing
some overtime work for the Frankfort Museum.
which Dr. Rüppell sent him), but he was able to
make himself independent of that trade as a means of
livelihood. He was far from deserting it altogether,
and the dry knowledge his apprenticeship had given
him was to bear good fruit.

There are few who find themselves dropped with
hardly a disappointment or rebuff into that precise
niche in life which fits them to a hair's-breadth.

---

[1] See Mr. R. Bowdler Sharpe's *Handbook to the Birds of Great
Britain*.

The charm which, in Wolf's case, worked this wonder was, once again, the little sketch-book. Dr. Kaup, to whom Rüppell had given him an introduction, was also a well-known naturalist, and the Director of the Darmstadt Museum, to which most of the rare or curious objects of natural history collected in that neighbourhood found their way. Kaup rejoiced over the miniatures with a great joy, and even conceived a scheme, which never came to anything, for a work on ornithology to be written by himself and illustrated by his new friend. He introduced the lad to some living Peregrines, and requested his help in stuffing and setting up a Sparrow-hawk. Wolf went to work with some diffidence, as he expected to find in the Doctor ornithological science severely personified. His astonishment was boundless when he discovered that this professed naturalist knew next to nothing of the distribution of the feather tracts, and that he had to arrange the feathers himself. In telling me this incident he went on to say, "Those "fellows know very little. To put a bird right, they "smooth it down with their hands, and tie paper "round it very tightly, but this gives a totally false "impression. The feathers are naturally full of "spring, and lie lightly." [1]

---

[1] This method of "putting a bird right" flourishes still, as will be seen from the following quotation from Browne's *Practical Taxidermy:* "Game "birds stuffed as 'dead game' and hung in oval medallions [?] form suit- "able ornaments for the billiard room or hall if treated in an æsthetic "manner. Not, however, in the manner I lately saw perpetrated by a

Wolf was not a man to rest on his oars, so he settled down to his trade, and worked away at his "compositions" for the firm which employed him, with the cheerful industry which became so strong a point in his character. This industry was more than the mere daily habit of mounting the treadmill common to business men ; and it had nothing mercenary or sordid about it. It was an insatiable appetite for work—a zest and an avidity which always consume obstacles, and achieve (with the help of a fine physique), something out of the common way.

Meanwhile, taking the sketch-book with him, Dr. Kaup had left for Leyden to attend a conference of ornithologists. The designs of the Birds of Prey had their effect, and in a few days Wolf received letters from Dr. Kaup and also from Professor Schlegel giving him a commission for some life-size drawings of the young and adult Goshawk, intended to form part of the illustrations for Professor Schlegel's and A. H. Wulverhorst's *Traité de Fauconnerie.* These he proceeded to do in his overtime.

In spite of Dr. Kaup's enthusiastic recommendation, backed by the little sketches, Wolf's fate was

"leading London taxidermist--a game bird hanging in a prominent posi-
"tion, as if dead, from a nail, enclosed in an elaborate mount, the bird so
"beautifully sleek and smooth that, although it was head downwards, *not*
"*a feather was out of place!* All was *plastered* down, and gravity and
"nature were utterly set at defiance. A little consideration, and a visit
"to the nearest poulterer's shop, would have prevented such a palpable
"error."

not quite settled even yet. When he was twenty
years old (that is in 1840), he had to appear at
Maien before the authorities for drafting army recruits. It is obvious how much depended on the
result ; for though so keen a shot would no doubt have
taken kindly to his rifle, he might have returned from
his term of service (if he returned at all), with the
edge of his artistic enthusiasm hopelessly dulled.
In any case, the loss of time would have been
ruinous. To make matters worse, he was as sound as
a bell, upright as a corporal, and had the sight of a
hawk ; just the very lad the recruiting sergeant
wishes for, and the very last to dream of malingering.
Fortunately at that peaceful time very few recruits
were wanted, and it was easy to get off. Still more
fortunately he knew the surgeon well. When his friend
asked him with a smile, " What shall we say about
you ? " the young fellow answered, naturally enough,
that he had nothing whatever to plead. Nevertheless, by means of the kindly but particularly inappro-
priate fiction of a weak chest, he was let off with
" garrison duty," which then involved service only in
case of war. Thus released, he hurried back to his
work at Darmstadt.

Although the first drawings for the *Traité de
Fauconnerie* were done, as we have seen, in overtime,
the commission was of an importance too great to be
deemed secondary to the humdrum work of a lithographic office—work of which Wolf saw that he

could be independent at last.   Accordingly, he gave
his employers notice and removed for a time to
Leyden.

Schlegel gave him, as a pet, a fine old Peregrine
tiercel (from which he drew many pencil studies), and
generally made much of him.   This does not appear,
however, to have been the first interview, for Mr.
Dresser sends me the following interesting anecdote :—

"Professor Schlegel told me, many years ago, when I was
"spending a few days with him at Leyden, that his first acquaintance
"with Wolf was when he invited the latter to Holland.   Wolf came
"as a young, fresh-looking lad to see him, and told Schlegel that he
"would like to see some waders and marsh birds ; so Schlegel took
"him out in a punt covered with bushes, in which he was wont
"to watch the birds.   On arriving among them, he asked Wolf
"where his note-book and pencil were, but the answer was that
"he did not require them.   After spending some time watching the
"birds, they returned to Leyden, and Schlegel asked Wolf to supper,
"for which purpose they adjourned to a restaurant ; and, after supper,
"Wolf asked for paper and pencil, and made some excellent sketches
"of birds he had that day seen for the first time.   Schlegel told me
"that he was astounded at the accuracy of the attitudes, as given
"by Wolf ; and at once realized that he excelled any other natural
"history painter he had hitherto known.   Schlegel, before I left
"Leyden, made me a present of Wolf's original of one of the plates
"in the *Fauna Japonica*, which I think I showed you."

Many years afterwards Schlegel forcibly endorsed
the opinion he had formed.   Wolf, on the occasion of
one of his trips to Germany, paid a visit to his friend
at Leyden, and found him at the Museum.   When the
Professor saw him coming he exclaimed in a loud
voice, " Here comes the first man in his branch of art ! "

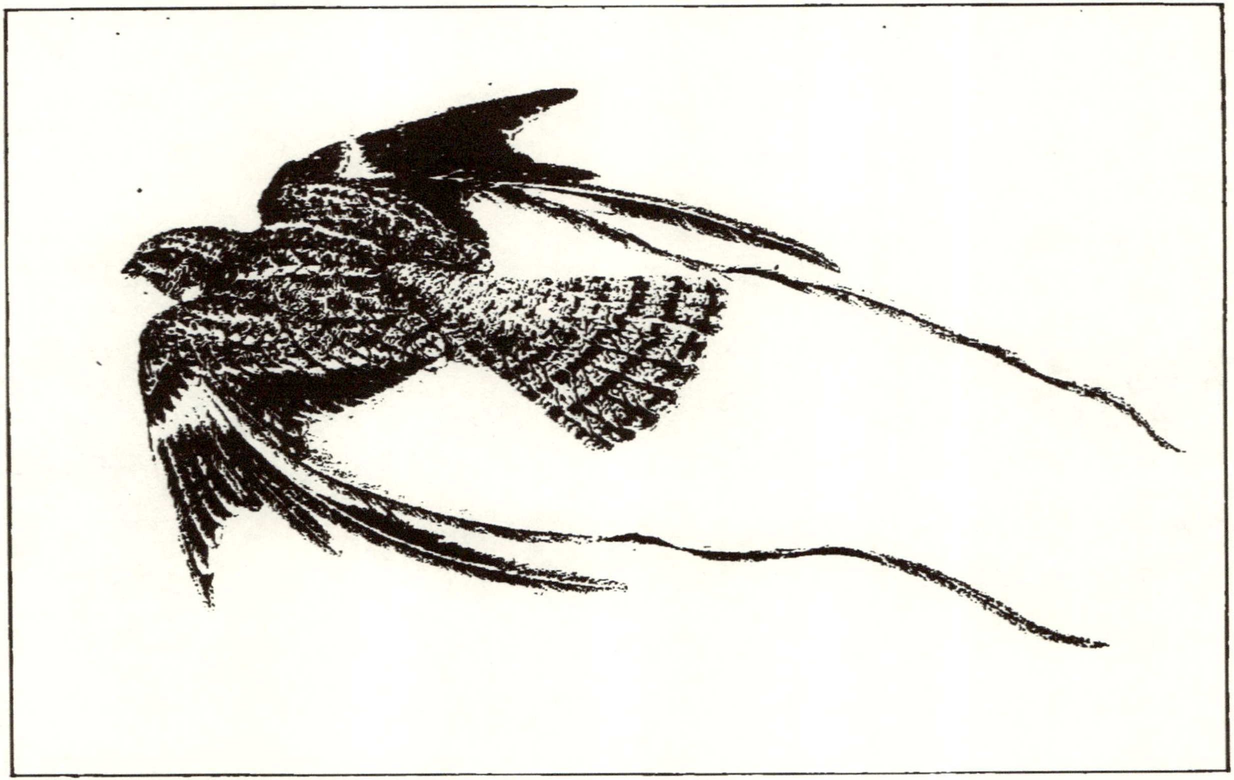

Caprimulgus vexillarius.

This high opinion was reciprocated, for Wolf thinks that, of all persons he has met, his friend was one of the nicest, and one of the best all-round men of science.

After this early and congenial commission, Wolf was, as he expresses it, "an independent artist. My head was above water at last." His talent and knowledge, being no longer hidden under the anxious mien of a quiet-spoken, journeyman lithographer, he was treated accordingly.

Herman Schlegel's and A. H. Wulverhorst's *Traité de Fauconnerie* [1] is a mighty volume with which many a good falconer, bent on a comfortable read, must have had an angry tussle ; and over which the authors, as they say, spared no pains. The publication, indeed, appears to have been spread over no less than nine years.

After a most elaborate but uninviting title-page and some other lithographs (representing the Heron hawking of the Loo Club), Wolf's work begins with the fifth plate ; a Greenland Falcon hooded and on the fist. It is followed by twelve other Falcons on ten plates, drawn in the artist's most careful and conscientious style, with all the elaboration of that period of his art. For the backgrounds (and very bad they are), other artists are responsible ; and this, jointly with the fact that the birds themselves are somewhat

---

[1] *Traité de Fauconnerie* par H. Schlegel et A. H. Verster de Wulverhorst. Leiden et Düsseldorf. Arnz et Comp. 1844-1853.

stiff and formal in their attitudes and treatment,
detracts from their artistic merit.

The authors, in their preface, speak of the artist
as follows : " Quant aux figures des oiseaux de chasse,
" elles ont été faites sur le vivant par M. Wolf, jeune
" peintre d'animaux qui a, sans contredit, surpassé
" tous ses devanciers par une étude profonde de la
" nature."

It may be added that it is said in the Badminton
Library *Falconry*, " The illustrations,[1] from the pencil
of Wolf, are in themselves an education in falconry."
He says of them himself, that, as far as scientific
detail goes, they are perfectly correct, but that he has
learned, since then, " to do Falcons in a different way
—a better way." But, as we shall see, he does not
consider them as susceptible to artistic treatment as
the Eagles.

Nearly perfect, even then, in his knowledge of
wild Falcons, he has since learnt a great deal of
the detail of a sport which Mr. G. E. Freeman calls
" a gallant, venerable *friend*, whom our forefathers
" loved with all their hearts."

Freeman himself, to whom (jointly with Captain
Salvin, that keenest of keen hands), sport is indebted
for a most interesting and enthusiastically written

---

[1] One, if not more, of these was exhibited at the Sports and Arts
Exhibition at the Grosvenor Gallery, without any reference in the cata-
logue to its origin, or to the fact that it was a lithograph. Mr. Wolf
has no doubt that it was taken for an inferior chalk drawing.

book,[1] speaks of its illustrations as coming "from the excellent and well-known pencil of Mr. Wolf." Of these the most notable is the "Female Goshawk and Hare."

Although most of the exciting flights Wolf has witnessed have been those of wild birds, yet he is fully awake to the fascinations of falconry, and his name is probably as well known to some of the members of the Old Hawking Club as that of Adrian Mollen.

It was once my good fortune to listen to a conversation between our friend and a keen Anglo-Indian falconer, which dealt with Sacres, Luggurs, and especially with the Shahins, besides the notable career of certain of these birds. Wolf's real interest was evident; and it was also evident that he knew much of the respective merits of the different species, not only from an artistic, but from a sportsman's point of view.

After a profitable and pleasant time at Leyden, Wolf had a bad attack of ague, with which he battled for a month, but at last was driven back to his old quarters at Darmstadt. There he settled down to begin the most serious studies of his life. He wrote to Dr. Rüppell, and having received from him the box of skins, was soon engaged on the lithographs

[1] *Falconry, its Claims, History, and Practice.* By Gage Earle Freeman, M.A., and Francis Henry Salvin, Captain West York Rifles, to which are added Remarks on training the Otter and Cormorant by Captain Salvin. London, Longmans, Green & Co. 1859.

D

(fifty in number) for *The Birds of North-East Africa*. Of this early work, consisting as it did almost entirely of drawings of widely-differing species from specimens more or less badly preserved, we must not be too critical. The attitudes, here and there, are stiff; and, as a whole, the backgrounds are weak. A few are good; but they are wanting in freedom and the look of nature. The feet are not so learnedly drawn as we find them in subsequent work, and the lithographic draughtsmanship, pure and simple, depends more on its colouring than afterwards.[1]

The acquaintance with such men as Rüppell, Kaup, and Schlegel, and their keen admiration for his work led, of course, to plenty of employment. Among other commissions there came one from C. H. Temminck, then a very old man in failing health. Wolf also undertook to draw upon the stone ten of the *Accipitres*, and the same number of birds of other orders, out of the 119 species illustrated in Temminck and Schlegel's *Birds of Japan*, forming part of Siebold's *Fauna japonica*, completed and published in 1850. Some of these lithographs are well worth study, such, for instance, as *Strix fuscescens*.

It was at this time that Wolf began to attend his

---

[1] I am indebted to Mr. H. E. Dresser for the following translation of a passage in Rüppell's preface :—" The fortunate chance of becoming " acquainted with a very talented young natural-history artist, Wolf of " Darmstadt, gave me the opportunity of having fifty birds which occur " in North-East Africa figured ; and which are either unknown, or of " which, up to now, only descriptions have been published ; and this has " been carried out in the most satisfactory manner."

first art-school ; and it is certain that many men whose career had begun so happily—whose hands were full of work after their own heart, with no fear of rivalry, would have done nothing of the kind. But he had already made some money, and he determined to invest it in his own way. He copied portraits and other pictures in the Darmstadt Gallery (including a few for the King of Bavaria), and he also painted a portrait or two on his own account. But all this time he was still at work at his birds, whenever he got the chance.

At the art-school he set himself to draw outlines from the Antique ; for he knew by a kind of intuition the value and difficulty of such training, if conscientiously battled with. Indeed, I have heard him express his wonder that outline, which he considers the most difficult thing of any which an artist has to conquer, should be chosen as the first course in elementary schools. He went at his outlines with such a will that he had a good deal of spare time on his hands, and soon got into the good graces of a landscape-painter named Seegur, who acted as inspector, or something of the kind. Seegur shook his head, nevertheless, when a lively sketch of a trapped Fox appeared one day on the back of an outline Venus. Besides this Antique work, Wolf also began to apply himself to oil-painting ; but he says that had all this school discipline come earlier, his animal subjects would have been "knocked out of his head."

D 2

Among the friends he made at Darmstadt was
one Baur, an *Ober Forst Rath*, or Upper Forest
Councillor. From his youth to a ripe old age, this
veteran sportsman had continued, with "a fierce perseverance," to slay Roe Deer with a rifle. Wolf says
Baur proved a good friend to him. "He had no
"artistic taste, but he saw that I represented animals
"as he knew them himself." He was also pleased with
the young artist's keenness not only with the rifle, but
to learn every detail touching the habits of the wild
animals of the forest. Through old Baur's favour,
Wolf was often allowed to join him at the shooting
parties, and even to practise a little still-hunting on his
own account.

He had picked up at a pawnbroker's a capital gun,
lately the property of a certain spendthrift Baron.
With this and his rifle he had some fine sport, the bag
including Wild Boars, Red,[1] Roe, and Fallow Deer,
and Hares ; not to mention Black-cock and other
winged game.[2] Yet he did not suffer even such sport

---

[1] These Red Deer are so much larger than the Scotch specimens
that the first time Wolf shot a Highland stag he was astonished at its
smallness.

[2] Mr. Robert J. Howard of Blackburn possesses, among other works
of Wolf's, a water-colour drawing of an adult male Hobby, touching
which he was good enough to tell me this, "When I bought the drawing,
"Mr. Wolf said that he was not at all anxious to part with it ; he kept it
"for auld lang syne. I wished to know the history of the bullet holes in
"the tree on which the bird stands. Mr. Wolf wrote this, which I have
"pasted on the back of the picture. 'The Hobby is represented perched
"'on the dead top of an old fir tree which stood on the outskirts of a
"'plantation some hundred yards or so from the path by which we
"'sportsmen emerged from the wood on our way home. The tree-top

NASITURNA PUSIO.

as this to usurp for one moment the first place in his mind. His own particular "fierce perseverance" was shown by the making of a large series of outlines of the dead animals at the end of the day, which were laid on paper and pencilled round. From these data he was able to compile a scale of careful comparative measurements which he drafted into a couple of books, one for birds and the other for mammals. On inspection I found these books were as neatly kept as ledgers. In the first, fifty-eight measurements of each species are subdivided under such headings as "Spread wings from above," and from below; "Foot"; "Tail," &c. In the second, fifty-four measurements are subdivided in the same manner.

Of many of the birds he also made a painstaking plan to scale, showing the tail and wings extended. The plan is equally divided by a central line, and shows half the bird as seen from below, and half from above. The exact positions, shapes, and areas of the various tracts of feathers, besides the individual shape of each kind of feather and the shapes of the markings, are all sedulously given. These diagrams are sometimes accompanied by an outline of the head, and most of them by a full-size drawing of the tarsus and foot, done without regard to time and labour, and

---

"'was a favourite perch for the different Birds of Prey, and for Turtle "'Doves, &c., and by way of emptying our rifles we would take long "'shots at any bird sitting there and presenting so tempting a target. "'Hence the idea of the bullet holes in the tree, as shown in the drawing. —J. WOLF.'"

giving the exact shape and positions of the scales and
scutellæ.[1] In some cases there is even a third
diagram representing a plan of the same bird, with
the wings half extended and the tail feathers closed ;
showing also in outline the boundary lines of the
tracts of feathers on the body.

The making of a set of measurements and
diagrams such as these, if only of one species, would
give more knowledge than a good deal of time spent
peering into the glass cases of a museum ; but when
species after species was thus elaborately analyzed,
measured, and drawn, it may be imagined whence that
mastery came to which I shall allude, especially as the
practice was continued to a time when the draughtsmanship became absolutely faultless. Of the Birds
of Prey (always his favourites), Wolf was particularly
careful to secure records in this manner.

The systematic study of the arrangement of the
plumage (upon which the beautiful precision of the
markings of the wild bird so much depends), Wolf
says he was the first to introduce into England, and
he also says that the time of its introduction by him
may be traced in Gould's works. It will be seen at
the conclusion of this book that Professor Newton,
speaking of Wolf's knowledge of pterylography and
its great effect upon his work, thought that he must
have seen Nitzsch's treatise upon that subject, and

---

[1] Two of these drawings (unfortunately lithographed by another hand)
were reproduced in *The Zoologist* for August 1880.

unlike other ornithological artists, have profited by
it. This, however, is not the case. The labours of
Nitzsch, like those of Sundevall, were unknown to
him ; and like all his knowledge, the knowledge of
pterylography was entirely self-acquired, without re-
course to books, without the help of teachers, and
without the advantages of wealth or wealthy friends.
It was not till many years afterwards that the translation of C. J. Sundevall's treatise *On the Wings of
Birds* came in his way, or that he became aware
how this indefatigable Swedish naturalist had been
laboriously studying the external characters of birds,
with the view of building up his system of classifi-
cation, at the time he himself was patiently studying
them in Germany.

Had the works of Nitzsch and Sundevall fallen
into Wolf's hands at this time they would have interested him deeply ; for he was labouring with his
pencil, to an extent of which even many of his
warmest admirers know little, in the same field ;
continually harping, as he harps to this day, on the
paramount importance of a systematic study of the
beautiful "*surface*" of mammals and birds—on the
importance of the closest attention to the distribution
of the tracts of a bird's feathers, and the growth
of a mammal's coat.

It is hard to imagine any person who loved his
gun, however much he loved his art, cumbering
himself with a gigantic roll of "continuous cartoon"

paper ; or going out in the winter to shoot one or two
Fieldfares or Redwings, which had to be carried
carefully home, measured, analyzed, and drawn, as I
have described.   It is a good instance of that Darwin-
like love of the truth that is humbly and patiently
built up little by little.   " It wasn't sport," says Wolf,
" that took me out shooting.   I wanted to learn.   If
" you study animals, even at the zoological gardens,
" you learn much more than by looking at them along
" the barrel of a gun."   To the gun, nevertheless, he
owed more than he is, perhaps, willing to acknowledge.   His powder was straight, and almost every
shot added to his portfolio at least one study or
diagram ; sometimes a whole series, as in the case of
a Crane or two he shot at Darmstadt.   Besides these
dead models, he had usually several living sitters,
including a Goshawk and a Great Plover, from which
he also frequently sketched.   As to a Quail he had
studied at Möerz, it grew so tame that it used to sit
on the toe of his boot while he drew it.

Besides what I have named, there were other
researches.   I have found in his portfolios series after
series of studies of the superficial and anatomical
detail of animals ; such, for instance, as the species
of Deer which were met with in the forests, each of
which was minutely analyzed, measured, and described
—so minutely that there is a perfect gallery of drawings of the horns alone.   When a vixen was dug out
by the foresters and knocked on the head, she was

immortalized in a dozen or more little analytical drawings, and consequently committed to memory, inch by inch.

It must not be imagined that Wolf devoted himself to the study of zoology only. I was astonished, one day, to find in one of his presses two formidable volumes. The one contained a large number of elaborate tracings of the human bones and muscles from engravings ; and the other, tracings of the same kind of the bones and muscles of the Horse. These were all accompanied by neatly written lists of the names (including the processes and attachments), and comparative measurements. The care and painstaking were those you would expect to see in the ledgers of some merchant prince. There was not an erasure, or an illegibility, or a blur. It was work done *con amore*. I have also seen numbers of landscape studies of this period, in pencil and watercolours ; besides many others of foregrounds and trees. Most of these were drawn direct from nature in the neighbourhood of Darmstadt ; and with the same indefatigable, conscientious care—the same determination to learn as much as possible, that is shown by the zoological work. Some of the foreground studies, by their handling and repletion of detail, suggest rather strongly the influence of Albert Dürer, but at that time Wolf knew nothing of his work.

The desire to learn was so strong that, in bad

weather, the student elaborated certain pencil copies
from old prints and lithographs of foreground foliage.
In fact the word "elaborated" hardly conveys the
laboriousness of this work. It was work in facsimile.
As a kind of relief or reward at the end of each copy,
he perched a bird or an insect on one of the bushes or
rocks.

Wolf was now steadily applying himself to the
drawing of trees and foreground foliage ; and he probably enjoyed sitting down for a good tussle with a
bit of complex ramification, or with a tangled thicket
of brambles, nearly as much as he enjoyed the difficulties of drawing animals. He saw that these animals
depended for much of their beauty, their concealment,
and the interest of their habits, upon the nature and
colouring of their surroundings, and he set himself
to learn those surroundings.

Near Darmstadt he found a small avenue of
fantastic and stunted firs, which he says he used to
delight in drawing. The use he made of them is
evident in many subsequent designs.

From his friends among the foresters he learnt
much woodcraft, besides some useful wrinkles in
shooting.[1] One of them showed him a good hiding-
place in the Odenwald, whence to see the assembly
of the Black Grouse. Here he dug a hole, screened

---

[1] To a lover of guns, Wolf is an interesting companion. He will talk
by the hour of the minutiæ of bullet-casting ; of rapid and slow twists,
the proper use of the sling, and other things on which the man who is
once thoroughly bitten with an affection for firearms burns to discourse.

it with fir boughs, and armed with his binoculars,
crept into hiding just before day-break. He says
"There is great enjoyment in watching these birds
"day after day. When they fight, the combs of the
"males are inflated, so that they look as big as straw-
"berries. These combs are chiefly developed in the
"breeding season, and are therefore not much known
"to sportsmen. Nor do sportsmen know the size of
"the comb of a Red Grouse ; which, when courting
"is going on in the spring, is three-quarters of an inch
"high." A series of careful recollections were afterwards made of the fighting birds. The results of this
watching, day after day, were not only stored in one of
those memories whose storage-room seemed infinite,
but were also added to the corpulent portfolios.

It was at this period, that Wolf made a few little
studies that I think he looks upon with as much
satisfaction as any he has done. He was energizing
away at some very pleasant country quarters (the
village of Grassellenbach), where he had the whole
wing of a farm-house to himself and capital cookery,
for the sum of one shilling a day. Some wood-cutters,
as they felled a neighbouring oak-copse, saw a Woodcock fly off her eggs. The forester on duty told Wolf
that the bird had returned, in spite of the destruction
of the cover. Sketch-book in hand, and trembling
all over with excitement, the artist crept up, sat down
"by inches," and worked, as he says, "like blazes,"
till he had secured careful drawings from several

points of view. If not altogether unique, such a chance was rare enough to shake a man's nerves who realized the beauty of the sight, and what the sketches were worth in days when "snap-shot" photographs were unknown. The power to turn out careful studies under such circumstances arose partly from a habit of intense concentration when the time came for it, and partly from the perfect knowledge of the distribution of the feather tracts. "It would otherwise," says the artist, "have been impossible. The light stripes on " the backs of the birds of this genus are each com- " posed of two lines of parti-coloured feathers; the " light webs of which, joined together, form the stripes " when the plumage is in perfect order. There are " hundreds of sportsmen who have killed no end of " Woodcocks who don't know anything about that. " They don't know the beauty of them. Professed " ornithological artists have made the mistake of " representing the stripe as formed of one line of " feathers."

It was natural that Wolf should be anxious to turn to some practical account the knowledge derived from the long twilight watches and exciting days in the forest; and towards the end of his residence in Darmstadt he was fortunate in receiving a commission from one Kern, a publisher in that city, to draw on stone a series of natural history and sporting subjects, in conjunction with an artist named Frisch; a kind of blank cheque which allowed him free scope

CAPRIMULGUS TAMARICIS.

for invention. These designs (which are dated 1846 and 1847), were the first commissions in which he was allowed free scope ; and they prove that the imagination which was afterwards so strong was, even then, fairly sturdy. The subjects include the various game-birds in their haunts, Badgers at play, Wood-cock-shooting ; wildfowl, and like designs. The Blackgame Lek shows a vigorous fight between two cocks ; and in the distance may be seen a man watching them, as Wolf had so often done himself.

In one of these designs we see, for the first time, a favourite whim of his—the flouting of the aggressor. A marauding Fox has sprung at a fine cock Caper-caillie, and is rewarded with a mouthful of tail-feathers. Of this kind of episode we shall afterwards find plenty of examples.

The Woodcock-shooting shows the artist's usual way of handling sporting subjects. The shooter is at least a gunshot distant, and the birds so near in the twilight sky that the broken leg and floating feathers appeal to our sympathy, as they are intended to do. The composition strikes me as unfortunate, but that of the Badger design is the reverse. Here, a whole family scuffle and play together in a glade of a dense pine-forest, by the rather pronounced light of the full moon. Thirty years later the artist would have suppressed much of the detail both of the animals and the landscape ; but even here we find, to a certain extent, a quality which afterwards became one of his strongholds—the quality of the "lost and found," or mystery, or suggestiveness, allied to that all-important item of artistic knowledge, the knowing what to omit.

The lithographs I have described appear to me to possess, among their other good qualities, originality. Seeing how little Wolf knew of contemporary art of any kind, how conventional much of the sporting and zoological art was at that time, originality is not, perhaps, so great a merit as it might have been. He saw his subjects vividly in a mind not confused by a thousand recollections of this school or that ; and he tried to draw what he saw with his natural naïveté. There was this disadvantage, that he had little or nothing to "crib" from. He could not help himself to a head here, an attitude there, or the whole composition of a group somewhere else, as his plagiarists have so often done at his expense. He was a pioneer, and had to fight his way, as it were, and pay his footing.

The Darmstadt period of Wolf's art, as we may call it, is represented in oil-colour by a series of little panel pictures which in their crispness of touch and elaborate finish would suggest Dutch influences, if we did not positively know that the painter was altogether uninfluenced by any school. One of the most elaborate of these pictures (perhaps too elaborate), represents a quantity of Wild Duck and Widgeon thronging in the old channel of the Rhine.

The chief figure is that of a fine Mallard, which, with extended wings, is scrambling out of the half-frozen water upon a small bank of snow beneath a thicket of reeds.

Another picture shows us a covey of Partridges, dusting, basking, and playing in a patch of sunlight, with so perfect an abandonment of happiness that the subject is charming. That the actions of the birds are thoroughly natural it is unnecessary to say. They are the result of actual observation.

A third and much smaller subject represents one of the experiences of Wolf's trapping days; for a large Goshawk, its foot fast in a gin, struggles for freedom with the full strength of wings and body, looking round with furious eyes at the trapper who is evidently approaching. The dead Rabbit which is the cause of the beautiful criminal's destruction lies on the snow, and the distant woods whence he came loom mistily against a yellow, wintry sky. This is one of those little artistic achievements which must always be coveted by the lover of zoological art, both on account of its interest, and the extreme faithfulness of the work, although it is very early work.

Without this ocular demonstration of Wolf's capabilities as an oil-painter at this period, I should not have believed that the time at the Darmstadt art school could have been so profitable.

The work and the sport I have described are only a fraction of the fruit of this period of his life; work ranging from an auto-lithograph "diploma card" of the Natural History Society of the Grand Duchy of Hessen, alive with mammals and birds, to highly-finished studies from nature. It was a time full of sunshine, when the mental attributes to which Wolf was to owe his success in life, were slowly ripening. Among these attributes was one which proved of far greater value to him than many others. With increasing success and knowledge, there grew up a power of discounting them, as it were. It was a power of estimating their relative values and amount compared with what might still be achieved—of self-appraisement. It was Wolf's determined resolution to be accurate, thorough, and true, even in the least of his zoological studies ; and it was to this resolution, to the invincible patience with which he built up his knowledge of the detail of species after species, and to his hearty sympathy with wild animals, that his ultimate unequalled success in the most difficult part of his profession was due.

Solicitude and patience in the conquest of elements has generally been a sign of a logical mind, and often a sign of genius. Wolf knew perfectly well that he had much to learn in art which could only be learnt in the schools, and though everything seemed to drag him in a contrary direction, he determined to begin over again.

Early in 1847 he broke off a career which I always like to think of ; happy, congenial, and suc-

$\frac{1}{3}$

SPIZAËTUS NANUS.

cessful in the highest degree, to take his place, as
he puts it, "among the small-boys at the Antwerp
Academy." He voluntarily deserted work such as
that he had been doing for Kern, where he had a
free hand and could follow his bent; fired his farewell
shot at Roe Deer and Black-game; and after four
pleasant years at Darmstadt, betook himself to school
again.

He soon passed into the life-class; and there he
settled down with his usual determined application—
every nerve strained, and every sense on the *qui vive*,
to make the most of his time. He says he wished to
study *painting*; but as there was no school for animal-
painting, he had to paint what he could, that is to say,
from human models. "If I had remained at Antwerp
"I should have been led away into a different groove
"altogether—perhaps figure and landscape. I felt
"loth to part with my natural history, and yet I was
"led to believe, by all my surroundings, that figure and
"landscape were the only worthy kinds of art." He
knew also that he was liable to be influenced, not only
by the personality of the professors, but by the
example of the students; so he took refuge in the
zoological gardens.

Perhaps, for a short time, lured by some mental
ignis fatuus, he may have intended to throw in his
lot with the figure-painters, without altogether deserting his first love.

Now it came to pass that, about this time, Dr.

E

Kaup went over to England, on ornithology intent.
As far as Wolf was concerned, the first-fruits of this
visit soon appeared in the form of a commission from
John Gould, then well known on the Continent, for
a small water-colour drawing. The subject (almost a
miniature), was " Partridges dusting," and this was
probably the first of our friend's works in colour
which had been seen in England. But English
ornithologists were getting to know that a young
German had arisen who had done some fine work for
Professor Schlegel ; and when Dr. Kaup was at the
British Museum he was questioned as to the whereabouts of the artist who had drawn the Falcons in the
Traité. The result of this was that Wolf received a
letter, which, on translation, proved to be an invitation
to London. The late Mr. D. W. Mitchell asked for
his help in completing the illustrations of an important work on the Genera of Birds, then in the course
of completion by that indefatigable ornithologist Mr.
George Robert Gray. Wolf said to himself, " Wait a
" bit ! I must study here nine months more at least,
" before I leave." So he declined the invitation, and
set his palette in peace.

I have seen some of the oil life-studies which he
did at Antwerp, and they seem to me to show considerable promise. At all events, he had completely
overcome the early inability to cover a large surface.

It may occur to us to wonder why, in the course
of his career at the schools of Darmstadt and

Antwerp, he was not smitten with the desire to seek
his fortune as a zoological artist at Berlin. That it
was not so is an example of the smallness of the pegs
on which great matters sometimes hang, and also an
example of prejudice. He says, " It is very curious
" that I never had any inclination to go to Berlin. It
" was simply because the Berliners I had met were
" men I did not care for—talkative, laying down the
" law &c. I might have had to fight some duels if I
" had gone there. But if the Franco-Prussian War
" had broken out earlier, and Germany had got to be
" what she is now, I might probably have remained
" there—might have gone to Berlin, where there is
" also an appreciation of careful work."

Fate, who had plucked the little "bird-fool" from
the farmyard, and filled him with loathing at the
mere smell of Limburg cheese and sauerkraut, was
not going to have all her work undone by the
Antwerp professors. Just in the nick of time (namely
in 1848), " Sceptre and Crown did tumble down,"
and all over Europe, says Wolf, "the artists hung
" up their palettes and took to rifle-shooting. I made
" up my mind to see what London was like, so here
" we are." He packed up his studies and firearms,
and embarked with his belongings, all and singular,
in a London steamer; thus bringing to an end the
second era in his life.

CHAPTER III

IT was one of those February days when the London soot falls in the shape of a cold, black drizzle upon a million umbrellas and a sea of slime—a day when the bespattered wayfarer falls out with what he chooses to call his native air, that Joseph Wolf got his first glimpse of British architecture; and he was not impressed by it. Of our tongue he was utterly ignorant; but he was burly and canny enough to escape a fleecing by the river-side, and to keep an unflustered eye on his gun-cases and trunks.

When he had joined the Antwerp Academy he had made up his mind to master the mystery of flesh-painting and solid colour quite at leisure; and now we find the student bumping in an unsavoury four-wheeler towards a very different career from that he had pictured to himself!

At The Museum he was cordially welcomed by Mr. Mitchell (who was able to converse with him in French), and was straightway carried off to take possession of some temporary quarters at No. 14 Howland Street, Fitzroy Square. This was a far

SOLITARY.

better neighbourhood than it is now; and, finding it
to his mind, Wolf afterwards settled down per-
manently in the parlours of No. 17.

Mr. Mitchell was determined to counteract the
depressing effect of the weather, and on the very first
evening, he made up a little party for the theatre ;
including Mr. Trübner the publisher (then with
Messrs. Longmans), who acted as interpreter.

Next day Wolf was installed in the Insect Room,
and began his work for Gray's *Genera of Birds*,[1] auto-
lithographs which are certainly notable, though purely
scientific.

Mr. Mitchell, in his " Postscript by the Illustrator," writes as follows :—

"It is perhaps scarcely necessary to state that the illustrations of
"this Book have no claim to be considered as works of art. My con-
"stant object has been to represent as closely as possible those charac-
"teristic variations of form which are relied upon by ornithologists
"as the distinctive marks of generic separation. When I accepted
"the office of Secretary to the Zoological Society and found myself
"no longer able to devote to the completion of the series of plates
"the time which the work demanded, I was fortunate enough to
"obtain the assistance of Mr. Wolf of Coblenz;[2] and I have the
"pleasure of believing that, as I thus secured the best available
"talent in Europe as a substitute for my own pencil, my friends will
"have no cause for regret that the latter part of the work has been
"entrusted to another hand.—Montague Street, August 29, 1849."

---

[1] *The Genera of Birds*, Comprising their Generic Characters, a notice
of the Habit of each Species, and an extensive list of Species, referred to
the several Genera. By George Robert Gray, F.L.S. Illustrated by
David William Mitchell, B.A., F.L.S. &c. Secretary to the Zoological
Society of London. In 3 volumes, 1844 1849. Longmans.

[2] He did not then know Wolf's native place.

If we turn over the three volumes, after reading this, and compare the illustrations by the veteran naturalist with those by the young, self-taught artist of twenty-seven, we shall at once see a difference, and shall agree pretty cordially that the friends of the former had little cause to regret his relinquishing the work. It will be unnecessary to warn those who wish to study these drawings, that only eleven or so of the hundred and eighty-five coloured plates are of Wolf's doing, and fifty-nine out of the hundred and forty-eight plates of detail. It will be equally unnecessary to recommend a comparison of such a performance as Plate No. 7 (*Aquilinæ*) with the sound workmanship and artistic feeling of Wolf's *Cacatuinæ* (Plate 105, Vol. 2) *Corvinæ* (Vol. 2), (Plate 76, Vol. 2); or *Charadrinæ* (Plate 145, Vol. 3).

Even if the volumes be turned over very rapidly, the difference will strike the eye; for each of the heads (no less than 345 in number), in Wolf's plates is a *portrait*, instinct with life and individuality. This is the case whether it is the head of a tiny Humming Bird, or of a large species such as a Flamingo or Swan; and it is especially noteworthy that while Mr. Mitchell often copied conscientiously the "distortions of the bird-stuffer," Wolf, in no single instance, even suggests a stuffed specimen. It is in this power of re-vivifying a dried skin, and not merely revivifying, but showing the most characteristic and beautiful attitude and expression of the living bird or animal,

that he stood alone then, and appears to stand alone
now.

Such of the feet and detail of wings as he drew
upon stone with his own hands are also excellent;
but, unfortunately, in most of the plates which contain
the best portraits, these details appear to have been
delivered over to "Hulmandel and Walton's new
Process"; a process which we will hope died an
early death.

As a piece of unwavering devotion to nature, of
unmercenary industry, and of skill in differentiating
specific character, these bird portraits of Wolf's are
remarkable. Of this work he says, "If I hadn't felt
the importance of it, I couldn't have done it." It is
evident now, how directly profitable the self-imposed
labours at Darmstadt—the constant watchfulness and
elaborate records of measurements, had already become. Without the industrious habits and the enthusiasm which had long ago formed themselves into a
second nature, he might have qualified himself to provide "figures" for this book, but he could not have
adorned it to such a degree. It was well for him that
this, his first undertaking in England, was connected
with a work prepared in so painstaking and able a
manner. Professor Newton, in his most interesting
article on Ornithology in the *Encyclopædia Britannica*,
says of it :—

  "The enormous labour required for this work seems scarcely to
"have been appreciated; though it remains to this day one of the

"most useful books in an ornithologist's library . . . . to have con-
" ceived the idea of executing a work on so grand a scale as this
". . . . was itself a mark of genius . . . ."

By constantly drawing at The Museum the young
German became acquainted with a good many men
of science ; and he took to some of them at once.
Professor Westwood, for instance, used to talk to him
in French, at a time when his knowledge of English
was chiefly confined to certain exercises in *The Vicar
of Wakefield* which his master set him.   In addition
to this well-known entomologist, he of course made
the acquaintance of many other scientific men ; and
on the occasion of one of the country excursions of
The Entomological Society he met, for the first time,
William Yarrell ; who so far unbent, as to sing a comic
song, to feast with the rest of them on strawberries
and cream, and even to join in a little rifle practice.

One day, soon after Wolf's arrival in England, he
was introduced, at the Zoological Gardens, to a man
small in stature, but by no means small in mind, who
was engaged on some dissecting.   This was Mr.
Bartlett, now known far and wide, in a hale and
vigorous old age, as the Superintendent of the Zoological Gardens, and for his most extensive zoological
knowledge.   He asked Wolf to visit him, and the
invitation being accepted, the artist found that his
new friend was a naturalist, living in College Street,
Camden Town, where he was often to be found
skinning birds, or busy in the interesting work of his

profession. The acquaintance, in spite of the early difficulty of communication, ripened ; and it has lasted ever since ; each of the men appreciating the other's energy and talent.

It was at the Gardens, too, that Wolf first made friends with Mr. H. E. Dresser, then (in the fifties), a lad beginning the study of natural history. As they became intimate, the artist would often turn up on Sunday at Mr. Dresser's home at Norwood, fully enjoying the comfort there, and absence of cere-mony.

I regret to say that a few of the men of science Wolf came across filled him with wonder, just as Dr. Kaup had done in setting up the Sparrow-hawk. He says, " Some of the ornithologists don't recognise " nature—don't know a bird when they see it flying. " A specimen must be well dried before they recognise " it." He found also (which to him was much more serious), that his instincts and knowledge as an artist were at a discount among many of his new friends, thoroughly able men and good fellows as they were ; and it grated upon him. "Among the naturalists," he complains, "there are some who are very keen " about scientific correctness, but who have no artis-" tic feeling. If a thing is artistic they mistrust it " There must be nothing right in perspective. There " must be nothing but a map of the animal, and in " a side view. They are like those other naturalists " who only know a bird when they handle the skin.

" It is impossible, for instance, for a mere museum
" man to know the true colour of the eyes."

Few who are not thoroughly familiar with the
technical training, to say nothing of the talent, necessary to form an accomplished artist; who have never
fruitlessly endeavoured to sound the depth of the
general ignorance about art, even in the case of many
highly educated men, will be able to read between the
lines of these complaints. The learned naturalist
would very properly smile at an outsider who scouted
the idea that any special training was needed in
the writer of one of those admirable monographs or
papers which show such accuracy and patient re-
search. Yet, strange to say, when he comes to the
illustrations he often considers himself much more
competent to decide on their handling than a man
who has spent the best years of his life, not only in
the study of all branches of art, but of zoological art
particularly.

And woe be to this unhappy man if he follows out
the refinements he has been many years in mastering,
or obeys the laws of perspective or chiaroscuro. The
result of this state of things may be seen in many a
scientific work; but it has not always been the case.
A few ornithologists, for instance, have proved themselves most appreciative and kindly employers of the
artists upon whom, as they know, they depend so
much for the interest and value of their labours.
But Science and Art, though ostensibly united under

ELEONORA'S FALCON.

the auspices of a government department, have, in
certain branches, been well nigh divorced from each
other.[1]   The fault is not on one side ; and the more
we apply ourselves to study the subject,[2] the more
shall we incline to the opinion that Art has been very
greatly to blame.   Artists have sneered at Science,
and have treated her simplest laws with open ridicule.
They have considered themselves far above such
things as the trammels of draughtsmanship ; or even
the superficial knowledge of elementary human anatomy.   They have looked down from the sublime
pinnacles of landscape art with openly avowed contempt upon the man who has devoted himself to any
but the regulation animals and " the regulation nest of
a Chaffinch with Hedge Sparrow's eggs."   They have
eagerly turned aside to welcome " Impressionism "
into their very midst ; and have shaken their tresses
not only at " the objects of natural history," but at
Nature.

There is little doubt that both Science and Art
have suffered and will suffer from this mutual hostility
or contempt.   If the time should ever come when

[1] This is exemplified by a very amusing article in *The Field*, once or
twice a year, on the Sporting subjects at the picture galleries ; an article
full of vigour and sense, by a thoroughly competent naturalist, who fights
a good fight, all the year round, against the nauseous popular-natural-
history anecdote and the marvel-monger.

[2] It has been a source of the greatest regret to me that I had not
studied the subject as I ought when I wrote the sketch of Wolf's life some
years ago.   Had I done so I should not have written as I did.   It is a
subject of which it is essential to consider both sides ; but unfortunately
it is easy to lose all patience in considering either.

they are really united, the closer that union becomes
the more valuable will be those works in which both
have to take a part.

At the time Wolf came over, English ornithologists had standards of several kinds by which to
judge representations of birds and mammals. A few
of these standards were high ; but, for the most part,
and even in the great encyclopædias brought out
regardless of cost under the auspices of the élite of
Science, some of the zoological illustrations showed
every conceivable elaboration of vileness that could be
foisted upon nature by outrageous artistic empiricism.[1]
Among the ornithological artists then in repute there
can hardly be mentioned one who could be depended
on for an accurate and life-like representation of a
specimen to which he had been unable to get access
while it was living, or at all events in the flesh. Of
Bewick, Professor Newton writes :—

" Fully admitting the extraordinary execution of the engravings,
" every ornithologist may perceive that as portraits of the Birds,
" they are of very unequal merit. Some of the figures were drawn
" from stuffed specimens, and accordingly perpetuate all the imper-
" fections of the originals ; others represent species with the appear-

Speaking of *Allen's Naturalists' Library*, a reviewer in *The Daily
Graphic* says : " As illustrative of the relative advance of knowledge in
" these matters, [butterflies and monkeys] it is interesting to note that
" while the old series of plates in ' Butterflies' remain intact with a few
" additions, those, without exception, in the old ' Jardine' volume on
" monkeys have been discarded, and an entirely new series substituted.
" Th others, ' with appropriate inscriptions' says Dr. Sharpe, would have
" formed a very good instalment of a Series of ' Comic Natural History'
" volumes, as they were, in fact, nothing but a set of extraordinary carica-
" tures of monkeys."

" ance of which the artist was not familiar, and these are either
" wanting in expression or are caricatures ; [Note. This is especially
" observable in the figures of the Birds of Prey. Newton] but those
" that were drawn from live Birds, or represent species which he
" knew in life, are worthy of all praise."

The same writer, speaking of a French ornithological work, continues :—

" The plates in this last are by Barraband, for many years re-
" garded as the perfection of ornithological artists, and indeed the
" figures, when they happen to have been drawn from the life, are not
" bad ; but his skill was quite unable to vivify the preserved specimens
" contained in museums, and when he had only these as subjects,
" he simply copied the distortions of the ' bird-stuffer.' "

As I have said, it was in this respect, even thus
early in his career, that Wolf's art was unique. He
was an unconscious co-worker with Nitzsch and
Sundevall, but not a disciple. By means of his
devotion to the study of external characters (not
neglecting anatomy), and the logical evolution of
principles from well classified facts, he had, at last,
become capable of revivifying species, either birds
or mammals, of which he had never seen more than
the skin, or a specimen preserved in spirits ; and I
should say that hardly an instance can be found in
which he was led far astray by a preserved specimen.

Mr. Mitchell, then, had had his choice ; and he
found that he had cause to congratulate himself on
the result. As will be seen, he ultimately brought
our friend plenty of work, besides the illustrations for
the *Genera*. Some time afterwards he had to deliver

a series of lectures on ornithology, and he commissioned Wolf to furnish the illustrations, in the form of
large water-colours eight feet by five.   Among these
subjects were Cranes : a Goshawk striking a Rabbit ;
and "a lot of Ducks dashing into the water, with a
Peregrine whipping past."   Wolf worked his hardest
at these designs while the lectures lasted, finishing
two or three a week, out of a total of a dozen.   They
were very freely executed, partly with a sponge, and
partly with large brushes.[1]   A well-known picture-
dealer had to strain them on canvas ; and scenting
money with the keen picture-dealer nose, he gave
the painter two boards, with a commission for small
replicas of the Peregrine and the Goshawk subjects.
" Those boards," says Wolf, many years afterwards,
" are knocking about my studio still, and very dirty
" they are.   I had always an aversion to do anything
" for a dealer, and I would sooner have died of
" starvation than have run to one."   It is fortunate
for Wolf that he was never driven to one with the
scourge of that direst form of necessity which has
blasted many a painter, bitterly striving after higher
things than pot-boilers.

Much as he got to like some of the scientific men,
Wolf was resolutely determined not to become a mere
scientific draughtsman.   He naturally felt that he
had more in common with members of his own profession, and soon numbered a good many among his

---

[1] These drawings afterwards became the property of Professor Owen.

ASTUR GRICEICEPS.

friends. At The Museum he had already made the acquaintance of that accomplished lithographer G. H. Ford ; a man who, in spite of his skill in representing reptiles and fish, utterly failed in the revivifying of preserved specimens of other orders; such for instance is the *Chiroptera*. He saw with pleasure how Ford would patiently labour for weeks over a drawing ; and of course he appreciated the thorough-going nature of the workmanship that so aroused Darwin's enthusiasm ; [1] but he saw also where Ford stopped short.

Up to the present time he had known comparatively little of the ways of artists, and he was surprised to find how eager some of them were to get him to put in their animals.

The following incident shows how completely ignorant he was of this system of borrowing. One day he had just finished a great flight of gulls in one of his friends' drawings, and was resting, very tired, when a visitor was announced. The visitor gazed at the drawing, and then said, " There is no other man " who can put in gulls like you, H——." " H—— said " nothing, but *I* said ' Good-bye,' and it *was* ' Good-" ' bye' for any more gulls and things." In after years Wolf became familiar with this kind of thing, and even found artists, here and there, (such as his friend Thomas Woolner, R.A.) ready and even anxious to acknowledge his help in a substantial way.

---

[1] *Life and Letters of Charles Darwin.*

He has also become familiar with flattery in its
sincerest form ; but sometimes he is apt to growl
when he encounters a particularly strenuous attempt at
copying some bird or beast of his.   He says " I have
" seen some of my gulls flying about in fellows'
" pictures at the Academy," and says it with a laugh
which proves that he takes it, after all, as he takes
most things—pretty easily.   There are certain exceptions, however, and he boils over at the recollection
of one particular instance, because his designs, after
being handed over to the publisher, appeared as the
work of a man who professed the most sublime contempt for natural history.

The tide of his fortunes which had turned almost
imperceptibly in Dr. Rüppell's study some eight years
before, now flowed swiftly.   Long before Wolf was
by any means perfect in his knowledge of English, he
became acquainted with Mr. William Russell (a well-
known accountant), who brought Sir Edwin Landseer
to see him.   His studies were pinned thickly to the
walls ; and finding the room thus papered, Sir Edwin
was keenly interested.   This was the first of a series of
visits to Wolf by Sir Edwin and his brother Thomas,
who both formed a very high opinion of him.

Mrs. Russell was a Campbell and related to the
Duke of Argyll, who was then, as Wolf puts it,
" mad for birds."   The artist was introduced to the
Duke, who became a patron in the best sense of that
perverted word ; kind, appreciative, and keenly inter-

ested. In *The Reign of Law*, published as long afterwards as 1867, there are several most careful diagrams by Wolf, illustrating the "machinery of flight," and a kindly acknowledgment of their authorship.

The pencil sketch, a small reproduction of which I have given, was made from a Blackcock which he shot at Inveraray, and is interesting from the fact that it was done in ten minutes.

SKETCH OF A BLACKCOCK AS HE FELL

Through Mr. Russell he was also introduced to the Sutherland family, and to the Duke of Westminster; who, like the Duke of Argyll, became an occasional visitor at No. 17, Howland Street.

If the wiseacres of Möerz, who shook their heads at the *Vögelfanger's* folly, could have known all this, and if they could have counted the guineas that gently

F

trickled into his exchequer, they would probably have
said that they had always predicted his success—
had seen from the very first that there was something
uncommon about the boy.

Success in art, to say nothing of other professions,
has always depended to a certain extent upon the
prestige acquired by patronage. Now Wolf had, all
along, looked upon patronage, in its usual sense, with
dislike ; and, fortunately, he had contrived to keep
himself free from it. What many men, therefore,
would have regarded as the gayest feather in their
caps he, rightly or wrongly, ranked second to the
unaffected approval of a brother artist.

Perhaps, of all his artistic laurels as apart from
those bestowed on him by Science, the most honour-
able are represented by the admiration of the Pre-
Raphaelite " Brotherhood " for his work ; and so
young a painter who could number its members among
his champions had good cause to congratulate himself.
Wolf's art, in fact, was entirely free from the conventionality and mendacity against which the Brotherhood girded ; and the attribute which probably
appealed to their sympathy was his evident determination to do every work as perfectly, conscientiously,
truthfully, and patiently as it could possibly be done—
to maintain an unswerving faithfulness to nature.
Moreover, he was no believer in dogmas, or systems,
or schools ; and would have refused to follow any
artist, or the Brotherhood itself, further than his own

reason allowed him. He says, "I always hated what
" they call ' style ' in art. The moment you get into
" that you become unnatural."

At the suggestion of Mr. F. G. Stephens, when I
was publishing my former sketch of Wolf's life, I
wrote to the late Mr. Woolner, and to Mr. W. M.
Rossetti, with the view of learning from each of them
"The Brotherhood's" opinion of the work in
question. They kindly permitted me to quote their
replies, which were as follows. Mr. Woolner
wrote :—

"I cannot speak in words of Wolf as highly as he deserves, and
" I am rejoiced that you seem resolved to do his splendid abili-
"ties justice. I remember fighting his battles as far back as
" 1848, when many persons were inclined to disallow his high
"originality and vivid truthfulness ; and I doubt, even now, if
" there are a great number who appreciate his works as they ought
" to be admired."

Mr. Woolner, who was six years younger than
Wolf, remained his friend in after life, and was one
of the few (as I have said), who, while sometimes
availing themselves of his help, anxiously sought to
offer him proper remuneration.

Mr. W. M. Rossetti wrote to me as follows :—

"It is quite true that my brother admired Wolf's pictures and
" drawings heartily. Wolf began exhibiting in London soon after
"the Pre-Raphaelite movement began in English art, and all the
" Pre-Raphaelites, including my brother, were delighted with his
"acute and minute observation, and delicate precision of ren-
"dering."

Probably Wolf's greatest achievement is that

while he realized the ideal of men such as these, he more than satisfied the demands of the most accomplished and learned zoologists (who speak of him again and again as simply "unrivalled"), to say nothing of the enthusiastic praise from "the greatest hunter ever known in modern times."

Mr. J. E. Gray used to say to him, "No one can put an animal together as you can;" and Professor Newton, in the article I have quoted, refers to him as "the greatest of all animal painters." Sir Edwin Landseer, on one occasion, said of his brother artist that he must have been a bird before he became a man; and that he had never seen the *expression* of a bird rendered as Wolf did it.

It is partly due to the wide grasp I have described that Wolf's fortunes prospered, and also that he never allowed the sunshine of success to blind him. He did not lower one jot his high standard of finish and care with the increase of commissions; or even begin to affect artistic dress. He was a diligent, unaffected student still, as he has remained throughout life—his habits simplicity itself, with just a dash of homely Bohemianism about them.

He would get up very early on a spring morning and buy a nest of young Bullfinches in Covent Garden Market, or explore the seductive alleys of Leadenhall; or, later in the year, he would sow a patch of mustard and cress in a neglected corner of the back yard. Now, when his crop looked "tempt-

GERMAIN'S POLYPLECTRON.

ing," he betook himself to a poulterer's, and picked
out the finest Partridge he could find. He then laid
it tenderly on the mustard and cress, and sat down to
make a study, for the sake of the contrast of colour.
" It was a very good lesson," he says, " and I came
" to the conclusion that all these sombre-coloured
" birds looked particularly beautiful among fresh
" green."

It is impossible to turn over his portfolios without
being struck by his happy treatment of sombre-
coloured species. He took much more pleasure in
revealing the latent beauty, the gentle harmonies and
gradations of some unobtrusive species, by means of
the subtleties of his art, than in painting the members
of the more gorgeous orders.

Among the most interesting of Wolf's reminis-
cences of these early days in England are those
connected with John Gould, whose pronounced,
rugged personality he conjures up by means of many
anecdotes. It is a portrait less smooth and pleasing,
but infinitely more striking than that generally current.

I have already mentioned that he had painted a
little water-colour for the ornithologist while he was
yet in Germany. The two men were introduced to
each other after the artist had been in London about
a fortnight; Gould (long since a widower), being
about forty-four years old, and the other's senior by
sixteen years. They seem to me to have been so
totally opposite in disposition that real intimacy was

impossible. Had it not been for their common scientific enthusiasm, and for Gould's wisdom in cultivating
a man who could be immensely profitable to him,
friendship of any kind would have been difficult; for
Wolf says that Gould " was a shrewd old fellow, but
the most uncouth man I ever knew." This opinion
is endorsed by a few to whom Gould's rough manners
(and sometimes equally rough tongue) and method of
doing business are well known.

Born in 1804, Gould was the son of an under-
gardener, who, fourteen years later, was fortunate
enough to secure a situation in the Royal Gardens at
Windsor. Here, says Mr. Sharpe,[1] the boy "picked
" many a bunch of dandelions for Queen Charlotte's
" dandelion tea," and effectually taught himself the
elements of taxidermy, which, it is said, he turned to
account by stuffing birds for the Eton boys. Leaving
an under-gardener's situation in Yorkshire, he returned in 1827 to London, and secured an appointment at The Zoological Society. " He is remembered
" in these early days," writes Mr. Sharpe, " as a man
" of singular energy with a good knowledge of the
" art of mounting animals." As an example of this
knowledge Mr. Dresser tells me that Gould stuffed
for King George IV. the first Giraffe that ever came
over to England.

In 1829 Gould married, and to his wife's zeal and
self-sacrificing devotion it is evident that he owed

Analytical Index to the Works of John Gould. Sotheran 1893.

much of his after success. His own industry, enthusiasm, and perseverance were beyond praise; but
without this timely help, and the ceaseless labour of
a long-suffering slave, one Prince (called by courtesy a
" Secretary "), the result might have been different.

How Gould prospered, everyone knows. We are
told that when he left England for Australia he had
made 7,000*l.* by his publications; and afterwards his
subscription list at one time amounted to 143,000*l.*[1]

As for a bargain, artistic or otherwise, no one
could drive a keener.

It was chiefly Wolf's knowledge of scientific detail,
and his willingness to impart it, which attracted Gould
in the first instance, and also his singular facility in
designing good attitudes and groups; matters of
which Gould knew little or nothing.[2]

Wolf says that Gould never knew very much

---

[1] His subscribers, as contained in a prospectus dated January 1, 1866,
amounted to a total of 1008, divided as follows: Monarchs, 12 (The
Queen and Prince Consort each taking an entire set of ten works);
Imperial, Serene, and Royal Highnesses, 11; English Dukes and
Duchesses, 16; Marquises and Marchionesses, 6; Earls, 30; Counts,
Countesses, and Barons, 5; Viscounts, 10; Bishop (Worcester), 1;
Lords, 36; Honourables, 31; Baronets, &c., 61; Institutions and
Libraries, 107; Miscellaneous, 682. The subscribers, as divided among
the ten works, were as follows: *Birds of Great Britain* (@ £78 15 0) 397;
Century of Himalayan Birds, 328; *Birds of Europe* (@ £76 8 0) 282;
Birds of Australia (@ £115 0 0) 238; *Birds of Asia*, 207; Monograph
of the Ramphastidæ, 213; Trogonidæ, 167; Odontophorinæ, 135;
Trochilidæ, 296; Mammals of Australia (@ £41 0 0) 146.

[2] I am quite aware that his name is attached to hundreds of his
plates; and that these plates are spoken of by authors who evidently
have no professional knowledge of art, not only as if they were Gould's
handiwork, but as being unsurpassed and unsurpassable.

about the feather tracts, and nothing of composition. He liked to over-colour his things, and he used to say, " There are sure to be some specimens brighter than we do them."

In after years, when Gould lived at Great Russell Street, he kept in readiness a box of fourpenny cigars, and a number of sheets of drawing-paper *tacked* upon a board; for he was a very notable man for small economies. When Wolf called, the board, a piece of charcoal, and a cigar were produced, with a request for a sketch or two—not at all as a matter of business, but just in a friendly way. " I wish," said Wolf on one of these occasions, " that you had told me before " what species you would like done, because I have " studies of many." " Ah," said Gould, "you will manage it." Our friend always did manage it; and part of the result was a series of life-size charcoal drawings, together with a few water-colours, for *The Birds of Great Britain*, which were drawn upon the stone by a lithographic draughtsman, and vigorously coloured. The series (as far as Wolf is concerned), includes twenty-five of the Birds of Prey, fourteen Ducks and other water-fowl, and sixteen other species : fifty-five in all, or thereabouts. I have looked through his copy of this book with him, with the advantage of his comments ; and though the plates for which he did the sketches can generally be picked out easily by their superiority to the others in composition and action, the seeing them once more after a long period,

in the full blaze of their colouring, somewhat disturbed
him. He growled over his pipe, as I turned over,
such comments as these. Of the Woodcock, " *Much*
" too red, and he must go and put in those blue-bells
" and things too! I can't be answerable for the
" colouring. Everything gets vulgarized." Of the
Hoopoe, " Look at that dreadful water he has put in
there !" Stella's Duck was " Dreadfully hard, and
stripey and streaky." He was quite right. The
lithographic draughtsmanship and the colouring, of
which Gould was so excessively proud, are of a very
popular kind indeed.

Whatever drawings Wolf contributed to other
works of Gould's will be mentioned in the Appendix.

Touching the illustrations of Gould's works
Professor Newton's criticism (as is generally the case
on artistic matters) is very much to the point :—

" The earlier of these works were illustrated by Mrs. Gould, and the
" figures in them are fairly good ; but those in the later, except when
" (as he occasionally did) he [Gould] secured the services of Mr. Wolf,
" are not so much to be commended. There is, it is true, a smooth-
" ness and finish about them not often seen elsewhere ; but as though
" to avoid the exaggerations of Audubon, Gould usually adopted the
" tamest of attitudes in which to represent his subjects, whereby
" expression as well as vivacity is wanting. Moreover, both in drawing
" and colouring, there is frequently much that is untrue to nature, so
" that it has not uncommonly happened for them to fail in the chief
" object of all zoological plates, that of affording some means of
" recognising specimens on comparison."

Gould was indefatigable in his search after new
skins in the dealers' shops. If he found one, says

Wolf, "he would not betray his excitement but would
"say, 'I think I have that; but I wish you would lend
"'it to me to compare.'" If the dealer complied, a
sketch was immediately made and the skin was
returned. On these occasions, and in later years when
Wolf lived in Berners Street, Gould used to bring the
new skin, help himself to a cigar, and walk restlessly
about the room while the sketch was made; or sometimes a water-colour drawing. Wolf says that
"Gould was the most restless fellow, who would
"never sit down except when he was fishing at
"Maidenhead, when he would sit for hours."

I have heard from a friend who knew Gould and
his character intimately, some most amusing stories of
his craving for new or rare skins of birds which he
did not possess; and of his efforts (sometimes successful, sometimes ingeniously baffled) to borrow them for
very indefinite periods. Wolf says, " I had the skin of
"a splendid young male Norwegian Falcon; very
"dark—extremely so. It got into Gould's box, and
"never found its way out again."

The following anecdote is perhaps the most
characteristic of any. Dr. Severtzoff, who was then
engaged on the ornithology of Central Asia, came to
England with a letter of introduction to another well-
known ornithologist, who told me the story. This
gentleman, who shall be called "G." and who knew
Gould intimately, offered the use of some empty
cabinets in his rooms for the reception of the Doctor's

collection of skins, which, as it included many new and very rare species from Turkestan, was of great value and interest. The offer was gladly accepted, and that evening the more important birds were stowed away.

Next morning it occurred to G. that perhaps the skins might be interfered with. Knowing that Severtzoff would not want to refer to them himself, and having to leave for the day, he took the precaution of locking the cabinets, and put the key in his pocket. On his return, he found the Doctor awaiting him, who said he had an amusing tale to tell. He had arrived at the house the morning after the skins had been put away, and was proceeding to unpack some other boxes when Mr. Gould called, who sent up his name with the message that he particularly wanted to see Dr. Severtzoff if he was in the house :—" He did come up," said the Doctor with his strong foreign accent, " and he did talk to me, and did flatter me in " every way. He did tell me that I was a naturalist " greater than Cuvier or Linnæus, and I did begin to " think what little bit of cheese I shall drop from my " bill. He then did tell me he hear that I have with " me all my rare birds of Turkestan, and that it was " in the interests of science necessary that he should " borrow and examine them. I did tell him that the " birds were in the house, and he express himself most " charmed, and did ask me if I would at once let him " look at them. I then did go to the cabinets, but I

"found that you, clever man! had taken away the key.
"I then say to Mr. Gould that Mr. G. have taken the
"key away. That minute his face change. He go
"straight down the stairs, and at every step he say—
"*Damn* Mr. G.!'"

One day Gould was calling on Wolf in order to get
a sketch made and said, "Well, Wolf, I am going to
"have my hair cut, and when I come back, I can take
"the drawing away." On his return he exclaimed,
"Look here, what I've got!" and produced from his
handkerchief an egg of the Great Auk! "Where did
you find that?" said the astounded artist. "In the
"German Bazaar. Whittaker [a naturalist] asked
"what he thought a good price, [naming a small sum]
"so I gave him a cheque, and here's the egg."[1]

The existence of the rarity soon became known
among the collectors, one of whom called on Gould at
Great Russell Street. The egg was produced with
the remark that it was probably the last of the species
that would ever be for sale; and what was then an
enormous price was asked for it. The collector
having, at last, consented to the terms, Gould said :—
"Wait a bit, sir! This being probably the last Great
"Auk's egg which may be forthcoming, I have made
"up my mind that only a subscriber for one of my

Mr. Dresser, who well remembers the incident, says that the dealer
had already sent to Gould to say that he had the egg : but that Gould pooh-
poohed the matter, and said the specimen was probably nothing more than
a double-yolked egg of another species. He afterwards, however, went
to see it, with the result related by Wolf.

BUBO FASCIOLATUS.

" works shall have it." Even this being insufficient to
deter the enthusiast, he put down his name for *The
Birds of Great Britain*, and carried off the egg.
Wolf relates this anecdote with anything but approval
—as the exact opposite, in fact, of what he
admires.

In 1856, and therefore long before the completion
of *The Birds of Great Britain*, the two friends sailed
for Norway on board the yacht of Mr. Bidder,
formerly The Calculating Boy, and then, Mr. Dresser
tells me, an eminent consulting engineer. Landing at
Christiania, Wolf and Gould went on alone, with an
interpreter. The artist had his drawing materials and
gun ; the ornithologist his skinning-tools ; but when
they came to practical work Wolf discovered that
Gould, learned as he was in birds, knew the notes of
comparatively few.[1] For his part he was soon able
to discover the Three-toed Woodpecker, the Red-
spotted Bluethroat and others, by his knowledge of
the notes of the adults. Of this last species, Gould
writes :—

" Mr. Wolf, who accompanied me to the celebrated Snee Hætten

---

[1] This, I believe, is largely a matter of ear as well as constant practice.
For instance, I know a keen-sighted artist who formerly devoted himself
a good deal to British birds, but who is deficient in his knowledge of
their notes ; and can never, he says, acquire it to any great extent. On
the other hand, I also know an ex Royal Artillery officer, whose eyes
were so injured by an explosion that he cannot recognize any bird by
sight even at the closest quarters ; yet who is exceedingly well up in the
notes of all the species in his neighbourhood ; and, strange to say,
acquired much of his knowledge since his accident.

" range of mountains, on the 1st of July accidentally discovered some
" young birds which were just forward enough to hop out of the nest
" — a great prize to me who had never before seen the bird at this
" age in a state of nature."

As a matter of fact, but for previously identifying the
note of the parents, Wolf would not have searched for
the nest.

The Gun, sketch-book, and knife were kept well
employed ; especially at the posting station of
Hjerkin : where, in their farm-house lodgings, Gould
skinned the specimens that Wolf shot and drew.
Here they got some young Willow Ptarmigan, and
accomplished one of the chief objects of the journey,
by investigating the breeding habits of the Fieldfares ;
whose noisy colonies disturbed their rest even in the
nominal night.   Gould writes :—

" Desirous like Mr. Hewitson to see the Fieldfare in its native
" woods, I proceeded to Norway, for this and other reasons, in the
" year 1856, accompanied by Mr. Wolf. We found the bird breeding
" on the Dovrefjeld in abundance, and the only difference from
" Mr. Hewitson's description which we noticed was that all the nests
" we saw were placed among the stunted birch trees, but this was
" doubtless due to our being far above the pine-forests."

It was here that one of those little incidents
occurred that have always delighted Wolf.   He was
out one day, sketching by himself, when he disturbed
a brood of Willow Ptarmigan ; one of which, with a
rapid grab, he succeeded in catching.   Meanwhile all
the others had suddenly become utterly invisible.
When the captive saw its mother it began to call to

her, and she came close up with her beak open, but
then retired. Wishing to discover how the young
had hidden themselves, Wolf liberated the one he
held, which instantly dived under the Reindeer moss.
He then retreated, and watched with his glasses. As
the old bird called, he saw the young ones emerge
one by one from their concealment, until all were once
more visible.

The friends had a fine large bedroom, and the
simple people of the house thought that breakfast
might be laid in this room. Such a suggestion
aroused Gould's dignity (never very sleepy), and the
interpreter was summoned in haste. The hostess was
solemnly informed that breakfast must be laid elsewhere, and this being immediately done, Gould's
anger was appeased. For a time all went well ; but
presently, behind an unnoticed curtain, an old woman
burst into a fit of coughing. They had got their
breakfast in a separate room—the bedroom of the
ancient grandmother of the family. Gould flew into a
passion, but could not help laughing at the way he
had been tricked.

He was very anxious to get a young Capercaillie ;
and at one of the farms where they stayed he
offered a substantial reward. When they were on the
point of leaving some labourers presented themselves,
produced from a small piece of paper a dead Thrush,
and claimed the reward, little thinking who it was
they were trying to cheat. Gould threw the Thrush

in the spokesman's face with a laugh, in which the men heartily joined.

It was on this journey that Wolf first saw Ptarmigan in their breeding plumage ; and the cocks, he says, were nearly as dark as Black-game. Afterwards he found them equally dusky at Guisachan, Sir Dudley Marjoribanks' place in Inverness-shire.

Of the ornithologist's opinion of Wolf's artistic powers, Mr. R. Bowdler Sharpe gives an instance in his *Analytical Index* to Gould's works, as follows :—

" It was always a real pleasure to see the delight which animated " the old naturalist when, in his invalid days, I took him some " startling new form of bird such as Bulwer's Pheasant, to be figured " in his ' Birds of Asia.' On the latter occasion he exclaimed that " there was only one man in the world who could do justice to such " a splendid creature, and that was Mr. Wolf ; who, at his request, at " once designed a beautiful picture which appeared in the ' Birds of " ' Asia.' Some of the finest pictures of the Raptorial Birds in the " ' Birds of Great Britain ' were also drawn for Mr. Gould by Mr. " Wolf."

Not long after his first arrival in England (to retrace our steps for a time), Wolf had received from Gould a second commission ; and the subject he chose was *Woodcocks seeking Shelter*. It was sent to the Royal Academy of 1849, and the artist received his varnishing ticket. He was pleased to find his little picture well placed ; but he knew nothing of the rules, and went home quite ignorant that it was on "the line." Some time afterwards, he found he was indebted for this good fortune to Sir Edwin Landseer,

$\dfrac{3}{3}$

LEUCOPTERNIS PRINCEPS.

who had not only saved the picture from the chalk cross about to be put upon it by the foes of " The Objects of Natural History," but had hung it where it was. Commercially it was a hit ; for commissions for Woodcocks flowed merrily in, and years afterwards the subject appeared in startling chromo-lithography. Of these versions Wolf says, " All were Woodcocks on " their nests, you know. I didn't want to do the legs. " I had never seen them on their legs, and I wanted " to do them as well as possible, as I had actually " seen them." As for the size of the versions, he naïvely confesses there were so many of them that in time "they got to be circular, and about a foot in diameter."

It will be observed that it did not occur to him to compile, or to evolve the legs. At that time he was not familiar with the structure of the legs of living Woodcocks ; so he painted the birds sitting, as he "had actually seen them."

A Woodcock on its nest was not only one of his most successful subjects, but a great favourite with him. I have seen an elaborate version of it which must have been done not long after the original sketches were made in the Odenwald. In most of the designs a Robin is present, just as in after years he found pleasure in associating Goldfinches with Partridges in the snow. He says, " I have " been doing those Goldfinches with Partridges, " over and over again, and the Robin with the

G

" Woodcocks ; and so you go on making a fool of
" yourself."

In 1850 Mr. Mitchell introduced Wolf by letter to
old Lord Derby (the thirteenth Earl), who had made
Knowsley a bye-word with naturalists by reason of its
superb menagerie and museum. Whatever the most
lavish expenditure, the influence of the head of a
great house, untiring foreign collectors and corre-
spondents, extravagant enthusiasm, and dogged per-
tinacity could do to enrich the collections, living and
dead, had been done. There was, perhaps, nothing
to equal them at that time, and I suppose that, in
many respects, they have not been surpassed.

Wolf had never seen a copy (out of the hundred
privately printed in 1846) of Mr. J. E. Gray's *Gleanings from the Menagerie at Knowsley Hall.* If he
had, he would have been to some extent prepared for
what awaited him ; but, in any case, when he arrived
and took up his quarters in a wing of the Hall, he
must have been deeply impressed with the sights in
the menagerie.

He found his new employer very deaf, and in his
speech, he says, somewhat resembling the gobbling of
a turkey-cock. As plain English was rather a puzzle
to him still, direct communication under such circumstances was difficult. The ancient Earl was wheeled
about amongst his paddocks and aviaries in a Bath
chair ; giving his orders to the keepers,[1] or to the

One of the keepers was "Young Scott," afterwards "Jumbo's?

artists who, from time to time, had worked his will
(such as the well-known Waterhouse Hawkins, or
Edward Lear), through Thompson, who was afterwards superintendent of The Zoological Society's
Gardens. As for Thompson, having received a
general order to give Wolf every possible facility, he
did his best to act as interpreter of the broken English
on the one hand, and the gobbling on the other.

Judging by the elaborate coloured illustrations in
the *Gleanings*, the standard of zoological art was not
high at Knowsley ; and if, when he received the list
of the Antelopes and birds he was to begin with,
Wolf's object had been to outstrip his predecessors,
he would not have had a very difficult task.

He describes the menagerie as covering more
ground than the present Zoological Gardens in
London, and says that there were many Antelopes in
large paddocks, to say nothing of the Elands which
the Earl was the first to introduce into Europe. No
better idea can be formed of Lord Derby's keenness in
his favourite amusement, or of a place which must
have had a considerable indirect influence on Wolf's
subsequent work, than by reading the Earl's notes
as quoted by Mr. J. E. Gray. Of the Elands he
writes :—

"The principal item that I obtained from the expedition upon
"which I sent Mr. Burke into the Interior of South Africa was, as
"far as I know, for the first time brought alive into Europe. Of this
"interesting species I received three individuals in November 1842,
"but unfortunately only one of them was a female. . . . "

G 2

"By the way I am sorry to tell you that my Eland cow has to-
"day produced another calf and another male. Alas ! I could
"have wished much it had been of the other sex, but it is very
"strong and healthy and I hope we may in regard to it parody
"Cranmer's consolation to Henry the Eighth on Elizabeth's birth.
"'This bull promises cows hereafter.' March 1, 1845."

"I know you will be glad with me to hear that Mrs. Eland has
"at last mended her ways, and has this time produced a young
"lady ; so that now I begin to flatter myself that even without fresh
"negotiations we may look on the breed as established in this
"country. I now possess, therefore, of this kind, four males and
"two females. . . . 1845."

"My five Eland and four Wapiti make a very pretty herd, and
"as yet agree very well : but when Mr. W. gains his full head, we
"must not expect it. They will be separated before then. May 31,
"1845."

Under the head of *Oxen* he writes of *Anoa
depressicornis* :— [1]

"I like the Anoa much as a curiosity, but it is certainly horrid
"ugly, though I will make Hawkins draw it, as I know no figure
"from the life. . . . Jan. 3, 1847."

Of the American Buffalo, of which Lord Derby
had a herd, he says :—

"Did I tell you that the Bison had calved? . . . The young
"Bison is a female and very odd-looking I am told, of a yellowish
"colour. I have not yet seen it. . . . Miss *Bison* progresses vastly
"well. June 1846."

"We have had an alarm about the *Bison*, who has got out of his
"paddock and into the open park, having fairly swum over the great
"water. Very luckily he has been got back again without any
"mischief being done. July 7, 1846."

It was not only the quadrupeds that troubled the

The Wild Cow of the Malays. "An animal which has been the cause
of much controversy, as to whether it should be classed as an ox, buffalo,
or antelope." Wallace.

TREGELAPHUS SPEKII.

Earl by breeding at their own discretion, and the vexation expressed by some of his notes is amusing. For instance, he writes :—" It is rather pro-"voking our Emu will not sit, while at Wentworth "the male is wanting to sit and has no eggs. John "thinks of sending our eggs to them." Other birds were more sensible :—

"My black swans," writes the Earl, "are proceeding famously. "A pair I have on the Kennel Dam bred late in last year, and out "of six eggs hatched four cygnets, of which one died, and the "remaining three are now about four months old. They are, of "course, still with their mother, who however has now six more "eggs, and is beginning to sit again. . . . March 10, 1846." [1]

I have no space to describe many of the curiosities of Knowsley—the breeding of the herds of Llamas, Alpacas, Guanacos, Wild Asses, Zebras, and Antelopes. On every side there were objects of interest. There was a tandem in which a mule between Burchell's Zebra and an Ass was driven ; and a small cart was drawn by a double mule.[2]

[1] At that time the breeding of the Black Swan was, of course, watched with interest by naturalists. Wolf mentions that at the request of Mr. Samuel Gurney, M.P., he went down to Carshalton to make studies for a large oil picture of these birds with their brood in the snow. By degrees, he says, their domestic arrangements conformed with our spring-time.

A reproduction of this picture, or one of the sketches for it, appeared in *The Band of Hope Review* of Jan. 1, 1863, with some comments, including the following :—"Mr. Gurney informs us that during the last seven years, these Australian birds have had even sixteen broods of young ones ; sometimes *three* in one year ! In the coldest winters the eggs have been laid in a nest constructed of rushes on the snowy bank of the ice-covered stream. . . ."

[2] This little animal was only eight hands high, and was " The offspring of a mule (the produce of a male *Ass* and a *Zebra*) with a bay mare *Pony*." It was " Iron grey, with a short narrow cross band on withers, very faint

One of the most interesting of the Earl's notes gives the history of a certain notable Red Deer stag. Born at Knowsley in 1819, and regularly hunted in Surrey for some years from 1823 without the slightest injury, he was returned to his native park and lorded it over all the other deer. Being wounded by a rival, he was doctored by a keeper, and thenceforth became more or less tame. In 1842 he was painted by Mr. Richard Ansdell, who was then doing some work in the menagerie, and after a gradual decline he died at the good old age of twenty-five. For the last two or three years of his life he was often led by his old friend the keeper to the yard where he had been doctored ; and " when there, if he could find " an opportunity by the door being open, he would " often enter the kitchen and lie down like a dog " before the fire."

Wolf must have found the Museum at Knowsley scarcely less astonishing than the menagerie. Its presiding genius was then Louis Fraser, who was the " Naturalist to the Niger Expedition," and for whom his patron (no doubt more with an eye to the collections than the diplomatic service), afterwards got the appointment of " Vice-consul for the Kingdom of Dahomey."

During Wolf's visit, his old friend Dr. Kaup

indications of stripes on the sides, and more distinct dark stripes on outside of the hocks and knees. Tail bushy from the base like a Horse. Head bearing in the brown and grey."

received an invitation to Knowsley, and the Doctor's attempts to express in polite English his admiration of what he found there, not only gave Thompson plenty to do, but more than once disturbed the dignity of the footman who wheeled the Bath chair.

We find in *The Proceedings* of The Zoological Society for 1851 a communication from the Doctor in which he speaks enthusiastically of the " noble collection " which contained more than 14,000 specimens of stuffed birds, besides unnumbered skins ; a " colossal library" in which no work of importance was wanting ; and "aviaries of magnificent living birds from every zone of the world."

It was in this " Eden," as the Doctor called it, that Wolf spent two months ; and with what profit may be imagined. Here he laid the foundation of his sound knowledge of the Antelopes, and laboured to increase the learning which was gradually making him familiar with the zoology, not only of Europe, but of every country.

He had not long left Knowsley when its enthusiastic owner was gathered to his fathers. Some of the drawings (which were half imperial), were still unfinished, but the successor to the title courteously permitted the completion of the commission ; and ultimately, I believe, the whole series found its way to the Liverpool Museum.

Wolf's acquaintance with the noblemen I have named led to other visits to their country seats. He

travelled, for instance, direct from Knowsley to
Inveraray; and another time he accompanied the
present Duke of Westminster (then Earl Grosvenor)
into the west of Sutherlandshire, where he was much
struck at first by two things, the magnificent scenery,
and the complete indifference to rain among the
natives—rain to the persistence of which the surfaces
of some of his water-colour sketches bear witness to
this day. It was on one of these occasions that he
made a sketch, at the Earl's desire, for a large charcoal drawing illustrating a strange penchant for
salmon on the part of some cows. Two or three fish
had been landed and laid in a clump of bracken
behind a small bush in a meadow, where they were
afterwards sought for in vain. Gould, who was staying there at the time, hinted that one of the keepers
might be guilty; but they laid the blame upon the
cattle. It was resolved to test the correctness of this
curious theory, and one afternoon a fresh salmon was
brought from the larder and placed in the same field.
The cows soon found it out and lost no time in
feasting.

In his boyhood, and long before he ever saw a
book on ornithology, Wolf had dreamed a dream of
small fur-footed birds which he encountered on the
sides of a rugged mountain, but of which he knew not
the name. It was while he was staying one August
at Lord Grosvenor's place at Loch Stack, in the west
of Sutherlandshire, that the dream was fulfilled in

detail. In quest of the Ptarmigan he went up the
mountains of Foinaven and Arkle while the birds
were still in grey plumage. Knowing the extraordinary effect of the weather on their habits he had
chosen a fine, calm day for the climb; so that, under
the forester's guidance, he was able to shoot what
specimens he required, after he had well studied what
he saw, and proved the great difficulty of distinguish-
ing the game from its surroundings.[1]

In many of Wolf's sketches, the Ptarmigan are
crouching under rocks, or on the snow, while a
Golden Eagle glides by without seeing them; or, in
other cases, snatches a victim from the pack. The
episode occurs so often that it is evident he took an
especial interest in the marvellous power of concealment—in the contrast between the huge irresistible
robber and the small quarry which cheat the hungry
eye. Wolf says:—"It was a favourite subject. I
loved the solitude of the grand surroundings."

---

[1] Lord Walsingham, in his most interesting account of these birds,
quotes from Mr. E. T. Booth two notable instances of this difficulty :—
" After a long and futile search for the nest of the bird his dog, [Mr.
" Booth's] moving less than a yard from where he had been lying, actually
" resettled itself on the back of a sitting bird, which formed almost the
" centre of a group of men and dogs which had been reclining around it
" unawares for some length of time. . . . The same day another sitting
" hen was discovered through one of the pannier straps falling on her
" back between the legs of the pony as the lunch was being repacked,
" after a protracted search for the nest everywhere except under the
" pony." Badminton Library *Shooting*, pp. 38–41, vol. 2. The first of
these instances would appear to be a good example of the way a sitting
bird completely loses its scent. I think it is Mr. Tegetmeier who, in

It has always seemed to me that the *Tetraonidæ* are a family which was a great favourite with the artist. From the first, he enjoyed learning the habits of the species he knew ; and it is evident from the number of studies, more or less elaborate, of Ptarmigan, Grouse, Capercaillie and others, that he also enjoyed drawing them ; especially with such surroundings as the Scotch mountains or the Scandinavian forest. Capercaillie, especially, he has shown in many an interesting episode ; furiously fighting, stalked by the shooter while " playing " on the summit of a dead fir, or done to death by a Goshawk.

The opportunity of studying at leisure the habits of the Golden Eagle, especially its nesting, was, even then, not common ; but through Professor Newton's kindness Wolf was able to pay a spring visit to Black Mount, on the estate of a nobleman near Glencoe. Here, under the guidance of an old keeper, he could watch a couple of eyries day after day.

One result of these observations will be found in plates F and G of *Oötheca Wolleyana*, edited by the Professor ; lithographs of exceptional interest, as showing the eyrie and the young birds with a background of the wildest kind, whence the parents bring the result of their foraging. This book also contains a lithograph after a drawing of Wolf's which Professor Newton says was the only representation of the

pointing out the reason for this singular fact, states that the bird is scentless until she has left the nest with her brood.

adult female Jerfalcon at that time published in England.[1]

It was at the late Lord Tweedmouth's (then Sir Dudley Marjoribanks), that Wolf was able to enlarge this experience of the Golden Eagle; and while he was Sir Dudley's guest at Guisachan in Inverness-shire (a place bosomed in the kind of scenery he loved best), he watched one of the birds beating its preserves on the mountain side for several consecutive days. By this time the reader will know what Wolf's watching amounted to.

It was at Guisachan too, that he was introduced to the Osprey's home and family, and made some careful studies, which bore abundant fruit.

Sir Dudley gave his guest a commission, among others, to paint five upright oil panels nine feet high; the subjects being An Osprey's Nest; Otter and Herons; Greenland Falcon surveying the flight of some wild Swans overhead; and a Snowy Owl dashing down on some Ptarmigan.

It will be seen that Wolf was indebted to Scotland, not only for many of his best subjects, but for some

---

[1] He writes as follows :—"I have here to express my thanks to "Mr. Wolf for a beautiful picture, which he was good enough to paint for "me from one of the birds to be mentioned hereafter. A reduced copy "of it executed by Mr. Jury under the artist's immediate superintendence, "embellishes this work (tab. C) and I think cannot fail to afford pleasure "to naturalists; as, excepting Herr von Wright's figure in the *Tidskrift* "*för Jägere* . . . it is the only representation of the adult female Gyr-"falcon that has been published. Of its accuracy I need say nothing, for "that is guaranteed by the painter's name."

very interesting experiences denied to the ordinary
traveller, and even to the ordinary sportsman. But
his experiences were not always connected with
natural history ; for at one time we find him hanging
on for his life while he is driven about rugged
Sutherlandshire roads by the young Marquis of
Stafford, at a pace which threatens an effectual end
to an artistic career ; or he complacently smokes his
lordship's cigars, and defies the attempts to make him
ill on a rough coasting voyage ; or, again, he shoulders
his gun and takes his place on the moors.

Although, at this time of his life, he had plenty of
opportunities for sport, he cared very little for these
brilliant shooting parties ; and his memory went back
to old Baur, and the exciting days among his good
friends the foresters.

Nevertheless, if these visits to Scotland were not
altogether to his mind they were very profitable
indirectly. Little by little, he had acquired the power
of seeing a vast amount that either altogether escapes
the man untrained in observation, or leads him on an
utterly false scent. He knew how and where to look ;
and, above all, how to interpret truly what he saw.
Thus he may be described as possessing senses quite
different from those which the ordinary traveller
brings to bear ; and so it was, that the lovely cloud
effects over the Scotch scenery, besides the fauna, had
a great influence on much of his subsequent work.
Just as the grove of fantastic fir-trees at Darmstadt

PITHECIA MONACHUS.

left its mark on his compositions, so did the rugged outlines, and the wreathing mists of the highland mountains. Here too he sometimes found his favourite grove reproduced on a larger scale.

Now though Wolf was by no means a shy man, still less an unpolished one, he was essentially homely. His early life had been spent among the homeliest surroundings, in a district of independent people and peasant proprietorships. To his homeliness, the free life of a bachelor artist, and the career of a self-made man who owed no man anything, had added that almost inevitable Bohemianism and impatience of ceremony which, perhaps, flourish nowhere so luxuriantly as in an atmosphere of turps and varnish. Moreover, a singularly unconventional mind that had been so independent of the aristocracy of art, and had obeyed its own laws alone, instinctively, I fear, grew to rebel against aristocracies in general. So, what with one thing and another, Wolf disliked these "grand visits" as he calls them. He thoroughly and heartily appreciated his hosts' kindness, and he respected their greatness; but, by degrees, he got to resent the very crow of their Cock Grouse and Pheasants.

Two or three summers ago we were sitting, the artist and I, in the cool of a June evening on the bank of a Surrey river. Birds innumerable were deep in their sunset chorus. Far and near, they filled our ears with a grateful melody, so softened that we

could hear every note of a Willow Wren's monotonous
little chant in an alder-bush close by, and even the
splash of a fat trout, busy with his supper.　Suddenly,
close by, there clanged out the strident crow of one
of the squire's cock Pheasants.　The charm was
broken, all the associations conjured up in such a
place were dispelled like a smoke-wreath, and Wolf
burst out :—" I *hate* a Pheasant—so aristocratic you
" know, so oriental.　His call seems to say, 'I am a
" ' Pheasant ; and I am under the protection of Lord
" ' So-and-so ; and I may come into your garden and
" ' scratch it all to pieces if I like, and you mustn't
" ' touch me.'　Put that down."　" You want a few
Goshawks here," he continued, " to thin down those
Hares and Pheasants over there."　Accustomed in his
youth to a neighbourhood where the Birds of Prey
were comparatively abundant, he is somewhat given to
amuse himself with the idea of the sudden descent
of a few Goshawks upon the coverts of our English
squires.

As to the chief of the works resulting from the
industrious Scotch holidays, they abide, for the most
part, in the collections of the noblemen who commissioned them ; and have not been seen by the public.

．　　．　　．　　．　　．　　．

Few more pleasant and profitable tasks could be
undertaken by the lover of zoology than to have
to search through *The Proceedings* of The Zoological
Society of London, and few tasks more humbling.

The papers will seize upon his attention one after the other in spite of himself; and in a range of no less than thirty-two years he will find these papers frequently illustrated by the hand of such a master, that there, at all events, he will see how the union of Science and Art can be happily brought about. The reader, as he takes down volume upon volume, will wonder, perhaps, how some of these great naturalists can, in the course of a natural life, have acquired such a wealth of accurate knowledge, together with the art of communicating it in a clear, attractive, yet perfectly unassuming way. Even if he has not already formed a pretty definite opinion as to the value of the labours of the popular purveyor of anecdotal natural history, he will probably feel less inclined to say with a certain ornithological writer who omits all mention of Gray, or Dresser, or Macgillivray's *History of British Birds* from his list of desirable books :—" Without our Rev. " F. O. Morris of Nunburnholm, we should be lost " indeed ! "

If Joseph Wolf had done no other work in England than that which he did for The Zoological Society, he would have deserved a pre-eminent place in the history of that branch of art ; and from Science herself, no little gratitude.

The greater part of this work consisted of what, for brevity's sake, I shall, as before, call auto-litho-graphs—lithographs, that is, from Wolf's own hand, though some of his drawings were lithographed

(as they are always coloured), by other persons.
Almost as soon as The Society decided to illustrate
its *Proceedings* it had secured his help. After two
plates by Richter and Waterhouse Hawkins, we find
his first auto-lithograph,[1] *Ptilocercus lowii*, illustrating
a paper by Mr. J. E. Gray on a new genus of insecti-
vorous mammalia, which was read on the 8th of
February 1848, with William Yarrell in the chair. I
am bound to say that neither the animal nor the tree-
trunk on which it stands is in any way worthy of
the artist; a criticism which has very seldom to be
made. From this time to the middle of 1880, Wolf's
work appears, more or less interspersed with the
work of other artists. Sometimes, indeed, it is found
side by side with drawings, such as G. H. Ford's
reptiles, which, as far as mere draughtsmanship goes,
are faultless.

Of Wolf's auto-lithographs in *The Proceedings*
there are between 330 and 340; no less than 282,
or thereabouts, being executed from 1850 to 1865

---

[1] This lithograph, like many of Wolf's designs in *The Proceedings*,
is very badly copied by wood-engraving in an edition of Brehm's
Tierleben, published in 1876. The woodcuts have recently reappeared
in Lydekker's *Royal Natural History*. In a review of a volume of this
book in *The Field* of June 1, 1895, we read (touching the eulogy of the
"illustrations of G. Mützel and others in the preface), "Two large wood-
"cuts of the great ant-eater are given, one from the well-known deline-
"ation of Mr. Wolf. This is remarkably accurate, and, at the same time
"artistic. The other, which is signed 'G. M.,' is as absurd as can be
"conceived. . . . The illustrations, which are mostly taken from Brehm's
"*Tierleben*, may be artistic, but they do not even approach, much less
"rival, those of Wolf and Keulemans; and many of them are ludicrously
"inaccurate."

DACTYLOPSILA TRIVIRGATA.

inclusive. From about this time onwards they diminish in number, for other much more important work monopolized his time, and he most willingly relinquished the duty. Yet, even then, he did not refuse his help, upon the advent of any animal of exceptional rarity or interest.

The lithographs were frequently preceded by careful water-colour sketches painted direct from life : a series of which is still in the artist's possession. In one case there might be a beautiful mammal or bird to work from, in the perfection of health and condition ; in another, nothing but a dried skin which had lain for years unrecognised at The British Museum ; and in a third case, a specimen of some hideous rarity recking from an unsavoury barrel of spirits. Moreover, at one time (notably in the year 1867), a desire for retrenchment seems to have possessed the Publishing Committee ; and Wolf's work suffers as severely as the rest from the coarse and mechanical colouring.

Thanks to my friend's kindness, I am most fortunate in possessing, among many of his other auto-lithographs, a large series of uncoloured proofs from those in *The Proceedings* ; and in looking at the best of them, over and over again, I never fail to feel very great regret that they have not been more widely known, *in this state*, to the art-loving public who love also animal life. So perfect are some, that there is, as it were, a physical pleasure in looking at them, and they

H

convey so well the sense of colour that its absence is not noticed.

These drawings are necessarily unequal in interest and execution ; and, as the artist points out, a few of the early ones are certainly " wooden " ; but the best show to perfection his literally unrivalled knowledge, and his unrivalled skill in applying that knowledge.

Not only are the general forms, textures and surfaces rendered with perfect truth (with no further surrender of artistic " feeling " than followed as a matter of course in carrying out the behests of Science), but learned draughtsmanship and minute analytical know-ledge are found in minor details. The watchfulness of a Sundevall to detect specific character is found in conjunction with the artistic culture and high train-ing that, although they are severely curbed, are rarely led astray into mere map-making, and never into the choice of a common taxidermist's attitude. This is the more remarkable, because, as Wolf says, "You " have to put in the attitudes according to what you " have to show."

As instances of his thoroughly sound analytical knowledge, an accurate rendering of the feather tracts of the different species of birds may be men-tioned ; the little hands of the *Lemuroidæ* ; the feet of the Falcons and Hawks ; and the *expressions* of the mammals. Indeed, one of the most astonish-ing points is the faithfulness and skill with which the *exact* expression of the face of each species, whether

bird or beast, is caught, in a range embracing many
utterly different orders.

The result is the perfection of art as applied
(under most difficult restrictions), to science; and
having said this I can say no more. Wolf himself
sums up his opinion of this work in his usual simple
way. "I did it as I saw it." It is at another time
that he asks me to print upon the title-page of his
biography a favourite truth of his, "*We see distinctly
only what we know thoroughly.*" Speaking generally of his work, he said to me recently, "The great
"thing I always aimed at was the expression of
"*Life*. In animals the ear is the great organ of ex-
"pression—but Life! Life! Life!—*that* is the
"great thing!"

It must be remembered that these drawings have
passed the ordeal of the most learned and exacting
criticism, often calling forth expressions of approval
from the Secretary, and the members whose papers
they adorned. The care, a measure of the knowledge, a measure of the power of drawing are, of
course, not peculiar to Wolf, but are to be found in
the best work of some of his brother draughtsmen;
but these very men are the readiest to acknowledge
the truth, that in the *perfection* of all these qualities,
and in some qualities peculiarly their own, his works
stand utterly alone.

At a meeting held on December 12, 1865, a paper
was read by Mr. J. H. Gurney, senior, on a species of

Harrier from New Caledonia. "I propose," said the ornithologist, "to assign to this new species the "name of my friend Mr. Wolf, to whose talented "pencil all students of zoology, and especially those "who study the Birds of Prey, are so greatly "indebted." The paper was illustrated by the artist's drawing of the species; but, unfortunately, the name was incorrect. Mr. Dresser says, "*Circus wolfi*, I am "sorry to say, must sink into a synonym of *Circus* "*gouldi*; as it turned out not to be a new species."

It is interesting to ascertain how long the artist took to do such drawings on the stone as these. This we can learn in his own words. "You have no idea," he says, "how quickly I did those things. I used to "wait till I had about a dozen illustrations for *The* "*Proceedings* accumulated, with the skins, etc., and "then I set myself to do a hard day's work, and spent "an hour on each drawing with my watch in front of "me." On one occasion he did no less than twelve complete drawings on the stone in one day; the subjects, however, being single small birds. "This," he says, "was because I knew all the detail so well, "and if you know a thing you can do it quickly. I "would not rest till all the drawings were done in the "day, and then I went out for a walk, very tired, and "sometimes very giddy from the hard work. When "the proofs came home from the printer's, I had to "sit another day to do the patterns for the colours. "It was hard grinding, mind you."

Perhaps it was at the time I have mentioned as being marked by a falling off in the illustrations, the authorities had determined that, in future, the backgrounds should be plain, not coloured. Wolf attached very great importance to these backgrounds. They were well thought out and admirably drawn ; and he had often relied upon them to enhance the beauty of the animal, by means not only of the composition, but of the complementary colours. The prohibition was therefore unfortunate, if it was not rather short-sighted. He says, "The background is always of "the highest importance—the indefinite ; but there "are many people who think this quality laziness on "the part of the artist. They want everything made "out." What was really wanted was probably a well-executed and thoroughly correct elevation of the animal. As Wolf says, "The animal is '*figured*.' That is the term."

If any person thinks that Wolf's invariable solici-tude about his backgrounds is a mere fad, and that the authorities were right, let him read in the daily papers of March 14, 1895, the report of " The Living Pictures Case." Mr. Alma Tadema, R.A., . . .
"asked if he seriously maintained that one person in fifty paid any "regard to the backgrounds thought that certainly every one must "have noticed the backgrounds along with the rest of the pictures."
"Counsel tried to get Mr. Tadema to agree that a picture might "have more than one background without injuring its effect, but "Mr Tadema refused to accept this theory. 'One picture—one "'background' was his view. 'I have often altered a background in "'the course of painting a picture,' he said, 'in order to come nearer

" ' to the meaning of the idea I designed to convey, but once a back-
" ' ground has been finally decided on you cannot alter or destroy it
" ' without destroying the significance of the composition.' "

The Transactions of The Zoological Society, unlike *The Proceedings*, were published at irregular intervals. They contained :—

" Such of the more important communications made to the scientific
" meetings of the Society as, on account of the nature of the plates
" required to illustrate them, were better adapted for publication in the
" quarto form. The numerous and elaborate papers of Professor
" Owen on the Anthropoid Apes, and on the various species of
" *Dinornis*, all form part of this series." [1]

Wolf's contributions to the illustrations of these notable volumes amount, as far as I have been able to ascertain from the British Museum copy, to twenty-seven ; only a dozen or so being lithographed by himself.

To the general reader, *The Transactions* will be less attractive than *The Proceedings*, as he will have neither the ability nor the inclination to study the more abstruse papers. Some, however, are of general interest. Among the drawings, those of the Gorilla, the remarkable *Balæniceps*, and the Aye Aye should be studied. This last, a weird-looking and most interesting animal, was stated to be " one of the greatest rarities ever possessed by The Society." It was chosen as the subject of an elaborate mono-graph by Professor Owen in *The Transactions* ; but I think the finest portrait out of several drawn by Wolf is that forming the central figure of a group of

---

[1] Guide to The Society's Gardens.

DEAD AYE AYE.

Madagascar animals, an auto-lithograph illustrating
an article by Mr. Sclater in the first volume of *The
Quarterly Journal of Science*. A careful life-size
chalk sketch of the Aye Aye after death, which the
artist kindly gave me, is perhaps even more interesting than the other representations.

The last of Wolf's drawings to be found in *The
Transactions* (lithographed by Mr. Smit), were from
life, and are accompanied by a paper " On the
" Rhinoceroses now or lately living in the Society's
" Menagerie" by Mr. Sclater, who says, " The main
" object of my remarks on the present occasion is to
" illustrate the very beautiful drawings by Mr. Wolf
" now before us." The first of these represents
Rhinoceros unicornis :—

 " Of this huge animal the first specimen obtained by the Society
"was a male purchased on the 28th of May, 1834, from Captain
" Fergusson for the sum of £1050. . . . It died in November 1849
" and was dissected by Professor Owen. . . . The second male was
"got in exchange for an African elephant from the Jardin des Plantes
" in 1865 and was the original of the water-colour drawing taken by
" Mr. Wolf in 1872. He is of enormous size, and measures about
" 5′ 3″ in height at the shoulder and 10′ 6″ in length along the back
" from the top of the nose to the root of the tail."

Of his drawing of the Black Rhinoceros Wolf
says, " I had secured one day's work ; and, on coming
" next day, to my great astonishment I found the
" animal really black. They had oiled him all over !
" Luckily I had got most of the colouring the previous
" day."

The last of the four drawings is a portrait of one

of the most interesting sitters which Wolf ever had—a
female *R. lasiotis*; and it was executed in 1872, from
the only specimen then known.   Mr. Sclater quotes
from a Calcutta newspaper an account of her capture.
Found in a quicksand completely exhausted with her
efforts to escape, she was dragged out by some two
hundred men, by means of ropes made fast to her
neck, and was then tied to a tree.   Next morning the
now vigorous Rhinoceros made such efforts to escape
that her captors were frightened, and sent for help.
Accordingly a Captain Hood and another started with
eight Elephants, and after a march of sixteen hours
came up with the animal.   She proved to be rather
more than four feet high, with a smooth skin like a
pig, and two horns; and she proved also to be a
tartar.   After a general stampede of the terrified
Elephants, a rope was with difficulty made fast to the
Rhinoceros's hind leg, and secured to one of them.
At this juncture she roared, and the whole of the
Elephants fled once more, the noose, fortunately, slip-
ping.   She was, however, eventually secured between
them, and began her march to Chittagong.   Two
large rivers had to be crossed, over which the Rhinoceros was towed between Elephants, for she could
not swim, and could only just keep her head above
water by paddling like a pig.   Thousands of natives thronged the march in ; the temporary bamboo
bridges invariably falling in with the crowds which
collected upon them to watch the Rhinoceros crossing

the stream below. Arrived at the end of her journey effectually tamed, the captive was freed in an enclosure ; soon fed from the hand, and might have been led about by a string.

The Council of The Society, after some unsuccessful negotiations, purchased the animal on its arrival in England, for 1250*l.* ; and as it was ultimately found to be a distinct variety, it was named *R. lasiotis*, from the fringe of long hairs on the edges of its ears.

It was not for many years that Wolf was asked to draw another Rhinoceros ; and then the request came from so eminent a hunter that there must have been a strong reason for declining. " I was asked," says the artist, " to draw an almost extinct animal, the White " African Rhinoceros. The man who asked me said " that the only difference between that species and " other Rhinoceroses was that it had a mouth like a " cow—a broad muzzle ; whilst the others had over- " hanging, pointed lips. But I was sure that the " animal must have had other distinctions in the body, " which were not noticed, and in which the difference " was more striking. I declined to do it because I " did not know enough about the animal."

Similar in size and treatment to his auto-lithographs in *The Proceedings*, Wolf's contributions to *The Ibis* range from the first number in 1859, to 1869, and include some seventy-five drawings of new or rare species.

Illustrating a paper by Messrs. A. and E. Newton

on the Birds of St. Croix, Wolf's first drawing represents a weird-looking, curious bird—the Bare-Legged Owl (*Gymnoglaux nudipes*) in the act of capturing a lizard.   In the same volume is this note by Mr. J. H. Gurney on Pel's Owl (*Scotopelia peli*):—" Having lately been presented with a living " specimen of this extremely rare Owl by Col. " O'Connor, C.B., by whom it was recently brought " from the River Gambia, I have requested Mr. Wolf " to draw the bird from life."

This was a somewhat sinister present, for it was believed by the natives that this was a bird of peculiarly evil omen, bringing dire disaster upon the heads of those who kept it in captivity.

Among Wolf's drawings in *The Ibis* will be found some of the best examples of his Hawks and Falcons, including a very pretty family group of the Eastern Red-footed Hobby (*Erythropus amurensis*) and other beautiful species drawn with that consummate skill, and taste, and accuracy, which, by common consent of ornithologists, had earned him so great a reputation in connection with the Birds of Prey.

Mr. Dresser tells me that having, in 1869, secured the services of Mr. Keulemans in illustrating his *Birds of Europe*, that gentleman " took Wolf's place in *The Ibis*, Wolf being very glad to resign in his favour."

At first sight it may seem singular that an artist capable of turning out such perfect work as that he had been engaged upon for this periodical, and for The

THE EASTERN RED-FOOTED HOBBY.

Zoological Society, should have wished to relinquish
it. How easily and rapidly he did it we have seen ;
and it does not look like the workmanship of a
man whose heart was elsewhere. Yet such was the
case. The love of art—the desire to revel in its mys-
teries and to grapple with its most alluring difficulties,
which had drawn him away from the free, happy life
at Darmstadt to the Antwerp Academy, were still
burning. The consciousness that, for the most part,
artistic refinements were entirely thrown away on the
naturalists and perhaps resented by them as impairing
the accuracy of the drawings, disturbed him still. He
says :—" There have been very few among all my
" acquaintances among naturalists who could appre-
" ciate a drawing if it were ever so well done ; and
" sometimes the better it was done, the less they liked
" it. . . . There are naturalists who think a stuffed
" Falcon superior to the best picture which can be
" painted. How can you expect respect as an artist
" from a man like that ? The scientific work consists
" merely of *portraits* of single figures. I was never
" satisfied with this, but tried to express action and
" life—to make the animals do something by which
" you could give the picture a name. . . . You know I
" make a distinction between a picture in which there
" is an idea, and the mere representation of a bird.
" Before you are able to make mammals or birds do
" what you like (which very few can manage), you have
" to work hard. . . . I did not enjoy the zoological

" work, and always wanted to get rid of it ; but, of
" course, I did my best, whatever I did.   I even put
" up a gallery in my studio in order that nobody who
" called to see my pictures or drawings should catch
" me at the other things."   He goes on to tell me
a significant little story.   A friend of his was once
praising his work to a museum official.   " Ah !" said
the man of science, " Mr. Wolf is too much of an
" *artist* to do drawings as we like them."   " So among
" the artists," he says, " I shall be called a ' naturalist,'
" and among the naturalists, an ' artist.'   But when my
" friend told me that story I felt very proud."

I have heard him say more than once, with all
the emphasis of his most firm convictions, " Some of
" the naturalists with regard to art are perfect *babies* ;
" and that is why I did not like working for them."   I
must confess that I keenly regret this strong feeling
on Wolf's part ; the more so as I know that it is by
no means an imaginary grievance.   The reality of it has
in some cases been proved up to the hilt, and needs
not the circumstantial evidence, the inimitable little
anecdotes which he occasionally repeats, to   say
nothing of the evidence gaily paraded in many a work
on natural history, including the most recent.   It is
rare to meet with such sound criticism as that of
Professor Newton, and correspondingly common to
find indiscriminate praise lavished on illustrations of
all degrees of merit or no merit whatever, in a way
which approaches the ludicrous.

That the mutual hostility or indifference I have already alluded to should continue to intervene between Science and Art is sad ; and that the talent of such an artist as Wolf should be so curbed and fettered by the requirements of his scientific work that he keeps it rigidly distinct from that which, in the proper sense, is artistic, and finally does it, so to speak, in secret, is still more sad. When the man of science accords to the artist a small measure of that respect which he justly claims by reason of his own life-long study and devotion, a better day will dawn ; though it will have dawned too late for the one man who has united, as they have never before been joined, the best attributes of Science and Art.

We learn from Mr. Sclater that :—

" In the year 1852 the Council of The Zoological Society, impressed
" with a sense of the great value of an accurate artistic record of the
" living form and expression of the many rare species of animals
" which exist from time to time in the menagerie, resolved to com-
" mence the formation of a series of original water-colour drawings
" to illustrate the most interesting of these subjects. For this purpose
" the Council was fortunate enough to secure the services of Mr.
" Joseph Wolf, who may be fairly said to stand alone in intimate
" knowledge of the habits and forms of Mammals and Birds." [1]

Sometimes, in addition to these drawings, a study

---

[1] Preface to the *Zoological Sketches*. First Series. Graves 1861.
Perhaps it may not be generally known to admirers of Wolf's designs that
the stones of both series of *Zoological Sketches* are in existence, and that
the separate coloured plates can be got at the publishers' at a cost of 7*s.* 6*d.*
each. The following are fine examples of this phase of the artist's work :
First Series, The Bassaris ; The Greenland Falcon, The Horsfield
Kaleege ; The Mantchurian Crane. *Second Series*, The Markhore ;
The Saddle-backed Stork ; The Shoe-bill ; The Indian Wood Ibis.

was made of some animal in the Gardens which had
reached a high degree of perfection ; and of such
animals Wolf says, " I delighted to do them more
" than the others ; for sometimes, when they arrived,
" they were in a miserable state, and I hardly knew
" what to make of them.   I used to do two or three of
" these drawings in a day, if the material were good.
" All these were vignettes only ; but I took care to
" get the true character of the animal.   By that time I
" had thorough *confidence* in my work.   It is then you
" do your best."

The drawings referred to hang partly in the
Picture Gallery at the Zoological Gardens, and partly
in the Society's Lecture Room at Hanover Square.
Some of the former have suffered severely by a too
continuous exposure to bright light ; I should fear
even to sunlight ; but many remain uninjured, from
which it is possible to form an opinion.   What this
opinion is depends on the artistic training of the
critic, and his power of detecting the unobtrusive
touches of nature which give the vitality and individuality in which Wolf revels ; and partly on his love for
natural history.   What will be found in the best of
these subjects is a series of some of the most rare or
most beautiful animals in the world, brought before us
so naturally, in the full perfection of their vigour and
wild, unpersecuted life, that the art which brings them
—which so deftly conceals the fact that they are captives in London, is, for a time, forgotten.   Fifty of

FELIS MACRURA LOIDS.

these drawings were reproduced in hand-coloured lithography, by other artists, and published in parts from 1856 to 1861. A second series followed from 1861 to 1867. The letterpress, begun by Mr. Mitchell, was continued, after his death in 1859, by Mr. Sclater, from whose preface I have quoted. Although, of course, losing much of their refinement by translation, the *Zoological Sketches*, as they are called, are striking even at first sight ; some of them, perhaps, a little too striking ; and, in default of the original drawings, they are well worth much study.

Touching a very curious sky introduced by the lithographic draughtsman, Wolf said, "And then " they did the clouds you see ; one—two—three— "four! They weren't even asked for that." No one but an artist can realize what an artist suffers when a translation of some of his best work in colour is thus attempted. The first things that are sacrificed are those very qualities he values most highly. Having no means of putting himself right with the public he remains for ever in the wrong, and is praised or blamed for much with which he has had absolutely nothing to do. Probably many people thought that these coloured lithographs were the work of Wolf's own hand, clouds and all. In spite of their inferiority to the original drawings, Professor Newton writes of the *Zoological Sketches* as follows :—

"Though a comparatively small number of species of birds are " figured in this magnificent work (seventeen only in the first series

"and twenty-two in the second), it must be mentioned here, for
" these likenesses are so admirably executed as to place it in regard
" to ornithological portraiture, at the head of all others. There
" is not a plate that is unworthy of the greatest of all animal
" painters." [1]

In the same category as the *Zoological Sketches*
must be placed the elaborate monographs of the
Pheasants, the Birds of Paradise, and the *Felidæ* by
Mr. Daniel Giraud Elliott.   A Prospectus of the
Phasianidæ printed in *The Ibis* in 1869, runs as
follows :—

" Birds so showy and attractive should be worthily represented,
"and the author has the satisfaction to announce that the plates
" will be drawn from original paintings executed expressly for the
" present work by Mr. Joseph Wolf, whose characteristic delineations
" of Birds have justly earned for him a world-wide reputation.   The
" lithography will be entrusted to Mr. J. G. Keulemans, who is fast
" establishing himself as a first-rate draughtsman of animal life ; thus
" it will be seen that the author has spared no pains or expense to
" secure the best available talent in the world."

These volumes form an *édition de luxe* ; that is to
say they in every way promote the discomfort of the
would-be reader ; who, in heaving them up upon the
table, involuntarily wishes that the author's expenses
had not been quite so liberally allowed.   In the Birds
of Paradise alone there are some 112 square feet
of illustrations distributed among thirty-seven species,
and in the Pheasants 246 feet, to say nothing of the
Cats.   It is a large superficies of zoological art, to
say the least of it.   The birds, for the most part, are
life-size, and the tails are as deftly manœuvred as the

---

[1] Article " Ornithology," *Encyclopædia Britannica*, ix. ed.

ladies' trains at a Drawing-room. So many gorgeous plates of species that are often yet more gorgeous are somewhat overpowering. We turn them over with fear and trembling.

Next to the Birds of Prey, Wolf is admitted to be *facile princeps* in delineating the Gallinaceous birds, and himself considers them one of his strongest points. It is easy to see from these volumes of Pheasants that this is the case.[1]

It is almost a relief to turn from the Pheasants and Birds of Paradise to the more sombre colouring of the Cats; a most interesting tribe, whose varied expressions of cunning, intense ferocity, or well-simulated meekness are admirably rendered; whose beautiful coats and mighty muscles bring into play the artist's rare power of modelling, of foreshortening, and placing in faultless perspective the various markings.

Although it is as much to the illustrations as to the letterpress of these monographs that Mr. Elliott owed their subsequent reputation, a would-be student of Wolf's work should be warned against accepting them, any more than the *Zoological Sketches*, as

---

[1] The dedication of the *Phasianidæ* runs as follows :—" To my friend "Joseph Wolf, Esq., whose unrivalled talent has graced this work "with its chief attraction, and whose marvellous powers of delineating "animal life render him unequalled in our time." The author adds in his preface a somewhat similar eulogy, " and is sure that all "naturalists will join him in acknowledging that Mr. Wolf is the only "one who has succeeded in elevating to its proper position in art both "ornithological and mammalogical illustration."

I

thoroughly or even fairly representative ; because it is work which, under no circumstances, will bear translation with impunity even by such skilled hands, to say nothing of the addition of colouring done at a low rate of remuneration.

All possible care was certainly taken that the translations should be good ; and Mr. Elliott used frequently to take his friend in a cab to the residence of the lithographic draughtsman, that Wolf might correct, with his own hands, the drawings on the stone. A comparison with the original charcoal sketches, and that alone, will show why any attempt at translation must necessarily fail. I think it is doubtful whether the artist himself could have transferred to the stone *all* their refinement and vigour.[1] They depend on subtleties which, in all probability, no other living man could fully understand, much less translate.

The differentiating between the merits and peculiarities of Wolf's own handiwork, in whatever material, and those of the work of his translators is, to one who has received the higher education of an artist, an easy matter ; but it seems to have been a stumbling-block to some persons not so qualified, in spite of undoubted scientific attainments.

If it be a relief to turn from Mr. Elliott's Pheasants to

---

[1] Wolf, on reading this paragraph in the proof, remarked, " You can't " transfer all the vigour. It never comes back again. In the next " attempt you may get a different inspiration. Equally good, perhaps, " but not the same." He spoke thus touching all his own translations. He speaks yet more strongly of those by other hands.

REEVES' PHEASANT.

the Cats, it is still more so to sink into a chair with a volume of Mr. H. E. Dresser's *Birds of Europe* ; one of the most fascinating, comfortable, and useful books a lover of birds can covet. It takes, of course, an ornithologist to appreciate the incalculable value of a work such as this,[1] but we can all appreciate the interest of the descriptions and the vivacity and truthfulness of attitude in the fifteen designs which Wolf did for his old and intimate friend. The chief of these are to be found in the family *Falconidæ* ; and the designs were boldly sketched on a large scale in Wolf's favourite " charcoal grey ; " being afterwards lithographed by the same artists who were responsible for the lithography of Elliott's monographs. Through Mr. Dresser's kindness, I am able to reproduce two of the originals. The designs for the title-pages are also Wolf's doing, and I regret that they are so.

[1] " As a whole," writes Professor Newton, " European ornithologists " are all but unanimously grateful to Mr. Dresser for the way in which he " performed the enormous labour he had undertaken."

CHAPTER IV

IT is not clear how Joseph Wolf became generally
recognised as anything more than an eminent
specialist who had chiefly devoted himself to
illustrating books on Falconry, and to zoological
drawings. Yet the transition to the work which
followed was natural enough. At the beginning of the
fifties he began to draw in earnest for some of the
London publishers ; leading off, as far as I know, with
four auto-lithographs for Mr. A. E. Knox's *Game
Birds and Wild Fowl: their Friends and their
Foes.* This was one of the occasions on which he
formed a firm friendship with an author, which was
only ended by death. He travelled down with Mr.
Van Voorst, the publisher of this charming book, on
a visit to Knox at his fine old home near Midhurst ;
and he describes him as " a tall, gentlemanly-looking
" man, full of amusing stories—a sportsman but not
" ostentatious about it." The visitors were taken by
their host to see the pictures at Petworth House ;
" He was a funny fellow," says Wolf, " who could
" make all sorts of faces, and he imitated the old
" housekeeper who guided us."

THE PANTHER.

Among his ornithological curiosities which Knox
pointed out (such, perhaps, as his "Chelsea Hospital"
of stuffed birds which had been maimed in various
ways by shot), were some specimens which had been
set up by Gould when he was a gardener's boy; probably at the time he stuffed for the boys at Eton.

The illustrations to the *Game Birds*, although most
interesting, will hardly compare favourably with the
best of the artist's later work; and one of them is
certainly unfortunate in treatment.

Reluctantly passing over the second edition of the
same author's delightful *Ornithological Rambles in
Sussex*, in which he avails himself of "the gifted pencil
of Wolf," and not at all reluctantly omitting the
distressing copies of our friend's work in Knox's
Autumns on the Spey, we shall do well to study a
most spirited design of a Goshawk striking a Gazelle
in Burton's *Falconry in the Valley of the Indus*.

In 1853-4, chromo-lithography claimed a victim
in Wolf. *The Poets of the Woods* and *Feathered
Favourites* (published by Bosworth) are a collection of
quotations from the poets touching our British birds,
each volume illustrated with twelve reproductions
from small, circular, water-colour drawings.

This is another case, and a notable one, where the
attempt to reproduce Wolf's work in colour, amounted
for the most part to a libel, or, as he calls it, "a
fiasco"; and, to those who do not know his original

drawings, an emphatic warning is necessary to that effect.

Mr. Dresser possesses some of the originals, which came into his hands in a singular way. The publisher entrusted them to an auctioneer to sell, who promptly failed; and all trace of the man and the drawings was lost. Subsequently they appeared in one large frame at a city dealer's; who, in selling them to Mr. Dresser for a nominal sum, and in ignorance of their authorship, informed him that he had bought them over the counter of his shop, loose in an envelope.

Never did a more tasty plum fall into the mouth of a collector; for the drawings are gems, glowing in the most delicately harmonious colouring, and full of refinement in draughtsmanship; witness the little pictures of the Green Woodpecker and the Ring Doves. As for the chromo-lithographs, they are pretty, it is true; a few are very pretty; but they do not fairly represent Joseph Wolf; and the marvellous rococo borders that surround them would offend the taste of a fairly well-educated cheesemonger.

Mr. Dresser has a few drawings uniform in size and treatment with those I have mentioned; and the subject of one is parrakeets. Wolf says "I did them "because I liked them. At that time they were new. "I put them on a bunch of dark grapes, which I "believe they never touch." They appear to belong to another series of which I know nothing.

The only other instance I know of a series of circular chromo-lithographs from Wolf's drawings, is an edition of *Cock Robin*. In his portfolios other circular subjects sometimes occur, and he does not seem to have found himself hampered in any way by that rather unpleasant shape. The composition is always skilful enough to avoid any appearance of cutting down, or cramped work. He was also given at one time to rounding off the top corners of his subjects. On my objecting to this on one occasion, he naïvely admitted that he sometimes did it to escape the difficulty of filling them up ; but this, of course, was early in his career. He says, " Sometimes a subject is not fit to be done upright. " Then I do it round. What I hate most is a lozenge- " shape, or a round subject bursting out in one place " like a rotten egg." The American fashion of mixing up the design with the letterpress, he nauseates.

Possibly the artist was dispirited by the mechanical translation of his work, for next on the list after Bosworth's volumes, we find one illustrated by no less than thirteen lithographs from his own hand—lithographs far superior to any in Knox's works. *Lake N Gami* by C. J. Andersson [1] was, as far as I know, the first book of adventure and sport with which Wolf was connected. He was given free scope, the text was interesting, and he got on well with the

[1] Hurst & Blackett, 1856. The imprints of several of the lithographs, incorrectly ascribe them to Wolf, an error not found in the list of illustrations.

author, so that he enjoyed the work. Indeed, so
good were his opportunities, that on one occasion
the traveller actually crawled upon the studio floor
with his rifle, that some sketches might be made quite
truthful in detail, for his figure in "Unwelcome
Hunting Companions."

Among the most interesting illustrations are the
furious charge of a Black Rhinoceros, a night scene;
and a perfect contrast to this is a group of browsing
Koodoos.[1]   But perhaps the best of these striking
pictures of African wild animals is that representing
the approach of a herd of thirsty Elephants to a pool
already thronged with other game :—

"The accompanying plate," says the author, "represents one of
"those numerous and exciting scenes that I have witnessed at night,
"at the water, when lying in ambush for game.   There is one fact
"—a fact that has hitherto escaped the attention of the African
"sportsman   connected with this illustration that makes it particu-
"larly interesting, and which induced me to designate it 'The
"Approach of Elephants.' The animals are just appearing above the
"distant hill.   If the spring or pool, as the case may be, be of small
"extent, all the animals present will invariably retire from the water
"as soon as they are aware of the presence of the elephants, of whom
"they appear to have an instinctive dread, and will remain at a re-
"spectful distance until the giants have quenched their thirst.   Thus,
"long before I have seen or even heard the elephants, I have been
"warned of heir approach by symptoms of uneasiness displayed by

[1] Koodoos by a pool in the evening, with a few Zebras, form the subject
of a charming composition painted in water-colour for one of the artist's
many kindly and appreciative sportsman friends, who writes to him as
follows : " Mr.   is very much taken with the drawing and told me he
" tried in vain to find faults, and congratulated me on being the happy
" possessor of ' the only good picture of the most beautiful animal in the
" world : which I quite endorse."

" such animals as happened to be drinking at the time. The giraffe,
" for instance, begins to sway his long neck to and fro : the zebra
" utters subdued, plaintive cries ; the gnoo glides away with a noise-
" less step ; and even the ponderous and quarrelsome black rhino-
" ceros, when he has time for reflection, will pull up short in his
" walk to listen ; then, turning round, he listens again, and if he feel
" satisfied that his suspicions are correct, he invariably makes off,
" usually giving vent to his fear or ire by one of his vicious and
" peculiar snorts."

The subject is one after Wolf's own heart ; who,
always fond of night scenes or twilight, must have
entered enthusiastically into the pleasure of depicting
such a romantic episode.

There is a passage or two in *Tropical South
Africa* by Galton, Andersson's companion, dealing
with nocturnal sport, which so happily and exactly
suggest the kind of nocturnal subjects Wolf would
have loved to design, had he come across them, that I
will quote them :—

" It is one of the most strangely exciting positions that a sports-
" man can find himself in, to lie behind one of these screens or holes
" by the side of a path leading to a watering place so thronged with
" game as Tunobis. Herds of gnus glide along the neighbouring
" paths in almost endless files : here standing out in bold relief
" against the sky, there a moving line, just visible in the deep
" shades ; and all as noiseless as a dream. Now and then a slight
" pattering over the stones makes you start. It jars painfully on the
" strained ear, and a troop of zebras pass frolicking by. All at once
" you observe twenty or thirty yards off, two huge ears pricked up
" among the brushwood ; another few seconds and a sharp solid horn
" indicates the cautious and noiseless approach of the great
" rhinoceros. Then the rifle or gun is pushed slowly over the
" wall . . . and you keep a sharp and anxious look out through
" some cranny in your screen. . . ."

" A rhinoceros is a sulky, morose brute, and it is very ridiculous
" to watch a sedate herd of gnus bullied by one of them.   He runs
" among them and pokes about with his horn while they scamper
" and scurry away from him in great alarm.   He surely must often
" kill them.

" For my own taste I should like to spend nights perched up in
" some tree with a powerful night glass watching these night frolics
" and attacks.   I really do not much care about shooting the
" animals, though it makes a consummation to the night work, as
" the death of the fox does to a fox hunt, but it is the least pleasur
" able part of the whole.   Great fun seems to go on among the dif-
" ferent animals ; jackals are always seen and are always amusing ;
" their impudence is intolerable ; they know that you do not want
" to shoot them ; and will often sit in front of your screen and stare
" you in the face.   Sometimes, whilst straining your eyes at the
" dimly seen bushes around you, the branched stem of one gradually
" forms itself into the graceful head of some small antelope.   The
" change is like that of a dissolving view, the object being under
" your notice for a minute, yet you could not tell when it ceased to
" be a bush and became an animal. . . ."

When I read these passages to Wolf he said,
" Simply *splendid!* I have had the same sensation
" watching for deer just before the morning twilight.
" You hear the click, click, click, of the hoofs, gradu-
" ally approaching, or passing by, just as the case
" may be, until the deer gets your wind and stands
" still.   It is curious how they will stand at night even
" close to a road, perfectly still, and relying on not
" being seen.   They come very near before you see
" well enough to shoot, and then you try to get the
" broadside, and fire with your heart in your mouth,
" for fear of missing."

Wolf did not always find authors so pleasant and

THE PALLID HARRIER.

appreciative as Andersson. On leaving a publisher's
office with a gentleman whose book on hunting he
was to illustrate, he ventured to ask a question about
an animal he knew the other must have met with.
He was answered thus. "That's nothing to do with
"you. What you have to do is to get those right
"which you have in hand." When he speaks of this
kind of man Wolf repeats an old German saying,
which, being interpreted, is this: "They go to work
"with an artist like a swine with a beggar's bread-
"bag."

In 1857 appeared Livingstone's *Missionary
Travels in South Africa* ; a book defaced rather than
illustrated by a number of Wood-cuts so atrociously
engraved, and, for the most part, so utterly wanting in
good qualities, that it is very small praise to pronounce
the twelve by Wolf the best of them.[1] He had expected intellectual translation ; but he now learnt, for
the first time, what an ill-paid British wood-engraver
could achieve in that way. Thanks chiefly to that
engraver, his version of the celebrated incident of the
Lion's attack upon Livingstone is simply grotesque.
If we did not know upon whom to lay the blame, it
would seem incredible that the same artist could produce "The Approach of Elephants," "The Koodoo,"
and "Unwelcome Hunting Companions" in *Lake*

---

[1] There is no acknowledgment of their authorship, but they will be
found facing pages 13, 26, 27, 56, 71, 140, 142, 210, 242, 498, 562, and
588.

N'Gami, and only a year afterwards, such coarse and unhappy work.

Among the reasons why the Livingstone illustrations were a failure were, perhaps, firstly that the author was so ignorant of art that the subjects he proposed were the most impossible; and, secondly, that he altogether lacked the power of vivid verbal description. Wolf says, "I used to go to see " Livingstone at Sloane Street; and he would pro-" pose subjects; but there was no *handle* to what he " said. He had a thing in his mind that couldn't be " illustrated. I couldn't make pictures of what he " thought would be the best subjects. I didn't feel " the inspiration to work with Livingstone as I did " with Oswell."

Livingstone had made a sketch of what he thought was a new species of monkey; but it was so "*awful*," as Wolf calls it, that nobody could tell from the sketch, for what it was intended. This the publisher was happily dissuaded from reproducing. The artist still has in his portfolios two or three of his original sketches which were submitted to Livingstone; with questions as to particulars, and answers in the author's handwriting.

Passing over sixteen illustrations by Wolf in an edition of Æsop out of the hundred all ascribed to Tenniel on the title-page, we come to Captain Drayson's *Sporting Scenes amongst the Kaffirs*; published by Routledge in 1858. On the title-page of my copy

THE MARSH HARRIER.

it is said that this book is " Illustrated by Harrison
Weir from designs by the Author." There are, however, only eight illustrations, all of which are by
Wolf; and they had nothing whatever to do with the
author's designs. " Elephant-hunting in the Bush,"
" Sharp Practice," and " The Red Buck and the
Sporting Leopard" are the best. In the last of
these, the engraver (as we shall often find in parallel
cases) has carefully cut a light halo round the foremost Buck, that there may be no mistake about the
outline. It is curious how often this pernicious
officiousness in clearing up everything that the artist
has intentionally left doubtful, or in non-relief, or subdued occurs in wood-engraving. The determination
to cut away the wood round dark or middle-tint forms
—to sharpen everything up, seems to be a kind of
irresistible mania which seizes the engraver, just as
the opposite mania to obscure, and besmirch, by
means of his fatal *retroussage*, rages within the mind
of a printer of modern etchings.

As I have now reached the close of the first decade
of Wolf's residence in England, I will postpone, for
the present, the account of his further successes as an
illustrator.

There should be included in this ten years' work
eight oil pictures,[1] which were exhibited at the Royal
Academy after the " Woodcocks seeking shelter."

[1] These were as follows. 1850. " Autumn " [Wounded Woodcock].
" Wild Boar " [Kitcat, landscape way. A moonlight landscape, strikingly

One or two of these pictures are still in the artist's possession ; and in spite of most careful drawing and good composition they have possibly helped to give an impression to others besides myself, that oil is not the material in which he most excels, although it is as an oil-painter that he prefers to be known. The best of his works in water-colour, and particularly those in charcoal, chalk, or charcoal grey have, in fact, completely spoilt some people for his oil pictures ; and the change of material seems to me to be followed, in some instances, by a palpable change of style. There are, however, numbers of his best works in oil which I have never seen.

" The Proud Bird of the Mountain " bears a quotation from Grahame's *Birds of Scotland*, where Wolf found descriptions of his favourite birds and favourite scenery. From his well-worn copy he has taken many a subject ; and in *The Poets of the Woods*, already mentioned, there are eight quotations from Grahame. Some exceedingly careful studies were made for the Eagle's plumage ruffled by the storm.

A large picture called " Jerfalcons striking a

poetic . " Winter " 'A dying partridge. Upright about 24" high]. 1851. " The Falcon's Nest " Upright and 3 or 4 feet high. Purchased by the Duke of Argyll and afterwards burnt at Inveraray". 1853. " The Happy Mother," " The Mourner " A Dove with destroyed nest. Circular and " in diameter . " The Proud Bird of the Mountain " 'Golden Eagle in a snow-storm. A quotation from Grahame's *Birds of Scotland*. Upright. Purchased by the Duke of Westminster'. 1856. " Jerfalcons striking a Kite. As only one more oil picture was ever exhibited at the Academy, I quote it, to make the list complete. 1863. " Wapiti Deer and Scenery at Power court Park."

Kite" failed to sell at the Academy. It was afterwards bought by a well-to-do gentleman-farmer, and
finally found its way into the collection of Lord
Lilford. The picture was reproduced in *The Field*
of January 10, 1890, and was exhibited at the Sports
and Arts Exhibition in the same year, under the
title "Kite Hawking with Northern Falcons on a
Suffolk Heath." Wolf says, however, " I never
thought of a Suffolk Heath at all." The birds are
all life-size, and the actions of the Falcons are very
vigorous. Mr. Harting, in his interesting article in
The Field describing this glorious sport, speaks of this
work as " one of the finest bird pictures ever painted
by Joseph Wolf." This may be the opinion of
a falconer and naturalist, but it is not one in which
every artist would coincide. The picture has points
of affinity with a group of Wolf's works which he says
were purposely treated ornithologically, and it does
not show the full strength of his power of composition.
A few of them, representing Falcons, appeared in the
Sports and Arts Exhibition ; but he was very sorry
to see them exhibited, and describes them as " The
hardest things I have ever done." I have always
feared that some people have known him chiefly by
such works as these ; by his hard, semi-scientific
pictures. If this is the case, if they have lacked
the knowledge necessary in order to appreciate the
draughtsmanship, the truth and vivacity of attitude, and
the skill with which the markings obey the perspective

and modelling—merits which, by common consent of the best judges, place Wolf at the very head of draughtsmen of the Birds of Prey—they will have formed a totally false conclusion. They will not suspect that the same painter who has produced these hard and rather severely treated pictures of birds, naturally revels in artistic qualities and subtleties which are very different.

It is indeed unfortunate that while many of his less successful achievements are widely known, and translations or parodies of others in which all the qualities he most valued are wanting, his best and really representative works are known only to the purchasers and their friends, and to the few who were privileged to see them on the easel.

He holds that the hardness of some of the subjects I have alluded to is chiefly due to the unpicturesque nature of Falcons, and says that the Eagles are far more picturesque and consequently easier to paint.

"Look at a Falcon's feather, and look at an "Eagle's feather," he says. "An Eagle's feather is a "beautiful honest brown, light grey and white at the "base; whilst the Falcon's has a certain number of "cross markings to its entire length, which have to be "given, in order to *make* it a Falcon's feather. Then "the spottiness throughout the bird does not admit of "broad handling. This is what misled you once into "saying that some of my Falcon subjects were hard

GOLDEN EAGLE.
(*A Sketch for a Picture.*)

"and tight.[1] It is easy to paint an Eagle soft and
"feathery. None of the spotted Falcons, Peregrine,
"Norwegian, or Iceland, are picturesque birds. One
"can't handle them broadly. A Goshawk is more
"picturesque than the Falcons, and the Sparrow-hawk
"than the Peregrine."

"Then people say, 'He knows how to paint
"feathers.'[2] There is no sense whatever in this—
"none whatever. They have no idea of the differ-
"ence in feathers. For instance, an Owl's feather is
"a soft, fluffy thing, whilst a Falcon's is hard. One
"floats in the air, and another falls to the ground so
"that you can hear it. The tail of a Woodpecker is
"as stiff as a piece of whalebone. The feather of an
"Owl is a ghost—you can hear nothing. But when
"an Eagle or a Lammergeyer folds up its wings, they
"rattle like cardboard."

"When I came to the smaller birds like Jays and
"Bullfinches I enjoyed doing their feathers. They
"are split feathers, and they almost dissolve them-
"selves into hairs. You do not see any outline to
"them. In the Owls they would not appear so very
"soft if the feathers were plain; but the markings
"are zig-zag and zig-zag, and dots, and all sorts of
"small marks, which make the whole bird look beau-
"tifully blended and soft in appearance." Speaking

---

[1] He forgets that he himself has made the admission of a certain
hardness in a few pictures.

[2] At the end of this volume will be found Professor Newton's testimony as to Wolf's skill in "pterylosis."

K

of another artist Wolf continued:—" His feathers
" used to be too wide. That amounts to something,
" if you only get six in when you ought to have a
" dozen. When I began to study, I used to measure
" the feathers with a pair of compasses, and I had no
" difficulty then in getting the right number into their
" place. After you have been doing it in this way,
" *carefully*, for a time, it comes quite natural to you.
" For instance, in drawing an Eagle's tail spread, I
" had no occasion to count the twelve feathers. They
" came right by themselves."

From feathers it is an easy transition to flight, and
the representation of motion in birds. Here, also,
every word Wolf has to tell us carries the greatest
weight, if only by reason of the immense study he has
given to the question. He says:—" In the flight of
" birds you cannot give the relative rapidity of the
" movement of their wings. They always look soar-
" ing with the wings open. This is right with Eagles
" and Falcons and soaring species; but with Par-
" tridges and others in which the wings flutter, it looks
" wrong if they are drawn in a hard way. It can only
" be done in the way the spokes of a moving wheel
" are indicated." Now it does not take the student of
his work long to discover that whatever species of
bird he represents in the act of flying, seems to *fly*,
and further, that it flies in its absolutely natural
manner. The Vultures in " Morning " (the dead Lion
subject), do not approach in the same manner as the

Hooded Crows in " Hunted Down "; and the Ptarmigan dashing up before the Alpine blizzard are
perfectly distinct from the Wild Geese which scurry
overhead in the wildest terror and confusion at the
report of the fatal shot. In nature we have rarely
a doubt about the species which flies rapidly by
us. The outlines of the head, the tail feathers, and
primaries are clear cut against the sky ; and, if the bird
is near enough, we scarcely need the characteristics of
the flight to help us. How Wolf transfers all this to
his canvas, how he secures the sense of various kinds
of motion so successfully, the soaring, the fluttering,
the laborious, the easy, it is hard to say ; but that he
does secure it, can, I think, be proved.

There are certain artists who treat their birds so
" artistically " that it is sometimes an effort, if not an
impossibility, to distinguish the species (which to me is
the most objectionable form of artistic affectation : the
affectation which is more repulsive, and sickening than
any other in the world), and pterylography is utterly
unknown to them. The feathers, indeed, look as
if they had purposely been brushed the wrong way to
give " breadth." There are others whose elaborate
drawings leave no more doubt as to the identity of
the species than the well-wired, well-smoothed, staring
specimens in the second-rate naturalists' shops. It
seems to me that Wolf has hit the happy and intensely
difficult middle course, completely avoiding these two
errors. That is to say he gives the impression of

life (as he has always striven to do), and with the look of life, the look of motion. How has he done it? " *I* cannot tell you how I did it, at all," he replies. " It is so subtle that you cannot explain. Of course " a laborious flier would have his head forward and " down like the Gallinaceous birds. Then they work " heavily with their wings, and their hind quarters

LABORIOUS FLIGHT

" seem heavy and down a little—not a horizontal line. " For instance the flight of an Osprey rising from " the water with a weight would appear laborious. " Without the weight he would fly in a more hori- " zontal position."

My sketch of the ten years' work, imperfect as it is, would be deficient if it did not include a series of

eleven or more designs in chalk,[1] done for the great hunter, Mr. William C. Oswell, to illustrate his African adventures. Wolf thoroughly enjoyed this work, and about two years ago he spoke to me of Oswell as follows :—" He could describe to you scenes so pictu-
" resquely that you could draw them at once. I
" never heard anybody describe more clearly, or who

EASY FLIGHT

" was more capable of explaining a situation. You
" could see that it was all truth, and you could see
" picture after picture. He did not mind telling you
" if he missed clean. As he was telling the story, I
" composed it in my mind, as I thought it would come

[1] They have been reproduced in the Badminton Library *Big Game Shooting*.

"best, and he generally said 'Capital!' He paid me
"a visit about six years ago. He _was_ a nice fellow,
"upon my word! The nicest of all that kind of
"fellows I have met, and a most gentlemanly man.
"He was very much astonished when he saw me at
"work; but Livingstone was too ignorant of art to
"be astonished at anything. Oswell saw I was inte-
"rested in guns, and he lent me his 10-bore Purdey,
"with the stock all scratched with wait-a-bit thorns.
"I had it in my studio for some time."

If the reader refers to the Badminton volumes on
Big Game Shooting, he will find a piece of testimony
touching Oswell's descriptive powers similar to that
I have quoted. Preceding his intensely interesting
chapters on South Africa, is a short notice of the
hunter; and, in his own introduction to his narrative,
he pays a warm tribute to Wolf's genius.

In the former, Sir Samuel Baker says :—

"One man alone was left who could describe from personal experi-
"ence the vast tracts of Southern Africa and the countless multitudes
"of wild animals which existed fifty years ago. . . . This man, thus
"solitary in this generation, was William Cotton Oswell. . . . No
"one could describe a scene more graphically, or with greater vigour;
"he could tell his stories with so vivid a descriptive power that the
"effect was mentally pictorial; and his listeners could feel thoroughly
"assured that not one word of his description contained a particle of
"exaggeration.

". . . . He was accepted at that time as the Nimrod of
"South Africa, 'par excellence,' and although his retiring nature
"tended to self-effacement, all those who knew him, either by name
"or personal acquaintance, regarded him as without a rival; . . .

'Sport.'

" the greatest hunter ever known in modern times, the truest friend,
" and the most thorough example of an English gentleman."

This magnificent man writes as follows :—

" I have often been asked to write the stories of the illustrations
" given in the chapters on South Africa, but I have hitherto declined,
" on the plea that the British public had had quite enough of Africa.
" . . . As I now stand mid-way between seventy and eighty, I
" trusted that I might, in the ordinary course of nature, escape
" such an undertaking ; but in the end of '91, the best shot, sports-
" man and writer that ever made Africa his field—I refer to my good
" friend Sir Samuel Baker—urged me to put my experiences on
" paper. . . .

" The illustrations are taken from a set of drawings in my pos-
" session by the best artist of wild animal life I have ever known—
" Joseph Wolf. After describing the scene, I stood by him as he
" drew, occasionally offering a suggestion or venturing on two or
" three scrawling lines of my own, and the wonderful talent of the
" man produced pictures so like the reality in all essential points,
" that I marvel still at his power, and feel that I owe him most grate-
" ful thanks for daily pleasure. . . . Many of the scenes it would have
" been impossible to depict at the moment of their occurrence, so
" that even if the chief human actor had been a draughtsman he
" must have trusted to his memory. Happily I was able to give my
" impressions into the hands of a genius who let them run out at the
" ends of his fingers. They are rather startling, I know, when looked
" at in the space of five minutes, but it must be remembered that they
" have to be spread over five years and that these are the few acci-
" dents among numberless uneventful days. I was once asked to bring
" these sketches to a house where I was dining. During dinner the
" servants placed them round the drawing-room and on coming
" upstairs I found two young men examining them intently.
" ' What's all this ? ' one asked. ' I don't know,' the other replied.
" ' Oh, I see now,' the first continued, ' a second Baron Munchausen ;
" ' don't you think so ? ' he inquired, appealing to me. We were
" strangers to each other, so I corroborated his bright and certainly
" pardonable solution ; but they are true nevertheless. I have

"kept them down to the truth. Indeed, two of them fall short
" of it."

Whatever their artistic merit may be, or the rank
they hold among Wolf's works, the sketches which
were at once so life-like and deliberately true as to
give such a man as Oswell daily pleasure for many
years—which were done under his eye and under the
direct inspiration of his marvellous descriptive powers,
are (even in the little process blocks) of great interest.
Such a hunter and such an artist will never again
work in conjunction.

Gordon Cumming was a sportsman of a different
stamp, and Wolf severely censures the slaughter
which made the reputation of such hunters. He did
not illustrate Cumming's books ; but drew, nevertheless, a series of large designs for his lectures. But so
much did he revolt against the bloodshed described
by Cumming, that one day, when he felt particularly
angry, he caught up a bit of charcoal and made the
sketch a reproduction of which the reader will see.
It was intended as a kind of counterblast or protest
against the popular notion of sport, and the general
tendency of Cumming's anecdotes. These are the
words in which Wolf imagines that writer would have
described the incident :—" On coming into the neigh-
" bourhood of our waggons, our dogs gave tongue in
" a clump of bushes. I walked on, and there was a
" savage Lioness ! I knocked her over with my first
" barrel ; and then I found that she had cubs, which

" were instantly torn to pieces and greedily devoured
" by our hungry dogs."

Sport, in its aspect of needless butchery, Wolf
loathed at all times, and even for sport as practised by Oswell and Sir Samuel Baker (whose forbearance so disgusted his American hunters), he grew
to have less and less toleration. As years went
on, and he became more familiar with the life-history,
the beauty, and the languages of wild animals, his
love for them increased, till the time came when he
hung up his guns and rifles, and would kill no
longer.

Like most men of strong character he can hate
most vehemently, and there are few things that he
hates more intensely than the sporting picture pure
and simple. He says :—" I *hate* sporting subjects.
" The ordinary sporting things, where the proper cut
" of a shooting-coat seems the chief object, are *detest-*
" *able*. Whenever wild animals come into contact
" with man they are in fear of death, and appear ill at
" ease. How would an unarmed man look, painted
" with a Tiger confronting him ? "

In the artist's own sporting subjects (in which, I
must confess, I take great delight), the sportsman is
distant and the game is close—so close, in most
instances, as to appeal to our sympathy by the pathos
of death and mutilation. As a further protest, he
drew a pair of subjects suggested by a passage in
Grahame's *Birds of Scotland.* In the first of these a

large covey revel in the early sunshine of a fine first
of September, in all the plenitude of their vigour
and beauty. The sequel shows a few survivors at
twilight, calling in vain for their dead brethren, while
the eyes of one wounded bird are closing for the last
time.

Wolf not only thinks our innate craving for sport
and the insatiable desire to kill, a relic of a savage
condition, out of keeping with the exalted culture and
civilization we claim, but he girds at the superficial
character of the average sportsman's knowledge of
animals, and in this he keeps step with Knox. He
says, " They have no *desire* to know about a thing.
Their only desire is to kill it."

He fairly boils over (as he can do, now and then,
to some purpose) at the accounts of indiscriminate
big-game shooting, either to feed the enormous
retinue of the wealthy sportsman, or, worse still,
when hundreds of magnificent beasts are left to rot,
and still shot down, till species after species is exter-
minated. The man who " sports" in this way he
compares unfavourably with a Marten-cat in a hen-
house, which kills on till there is nothing left alive.
Touching a young man who was about to betake himself on a " shooting trip" to Africa, he growled, when
he was gone, " I hope that when they have to go
" somewhere by boat, a Hippopotamus will upset
" them, and that they will have to swim ashore,
" leaving all their rifles at the bottom of the Zambesi.

A Mongoose.

" It has become a recognised thing even in novels,
" that when a fellow is disappointed in love, he goes
" out to America or Africa to shoot big game." He
goes even further than detestation of sport, and refuses
to believe many of the stories touching the innate
ferocity of certain species, and of their unprovoked
attacks. Of man's unprovoked attacks on certain
species he learnt a notable instance from Mr. Bartlett,
who told him that sailors have been known to land
on islands densely peopled with Penguins ; to kill
or stun a sufficient quantity with sticks ; and then to
set fire to their oily bodies, " for a lark." He says,
" When a schoolboy sees an unfortunate Owl in his
" power, turning its eyes upon him in fear of death,
" he takes it for ferocity and stones the bird."

He admits, of course, that maternal affection
entirely alters a pacific disposition. There is a
reason, he says, for the occasional ferocity of some
animals. " You are too near the nest." He tells
how a mother Partridge will attack a Crow, and
a farm-yard hen beat off a Kite, in defence of
their respective chickens ; both of which incidents
he has sketched with others of the kind. " It is a
" grand law in nature, parental affection. It is princi-
" pally maternal affection which keeps the world
" together, you know.[1] If anybody has a mind to
" think (or you may say the heart to think), he will

---

[1] Of Wolf's keen appreciation and reciprocation of his mother's affection for him, and of her great influence over him, an old friend of his has
told me.

" never interfere with a mother when she is defend-
" ing her young."

In fact to sum it all up Wolf adds, " Then comes
" man, the most destructive and carnivorous animal
" in the world. Look at the Tiger. He is nothing
" compared with man.[1] Wild animals are more in
" fear than ferocious." Knowing also the dire severity
of the struggle for very existence among them, he
sees nothing so cruel in the depredations of the
Tiger, and for that matter nothing more ridiculous in
the strut of a Turkey-cock, than he can see, any day,
in the actions of his fellow-men.

Even among wild animals themselves, he deprecates the inevitable aggression of the strong upon
the weak. He repeats both by word and by brush,
" The aggressor *shall* not succeed " ; and he delights
to frustrate him in his pictures. He has loved wild
animals since he toddled about his mother's garden.
He deeply sympathizes with them and their perse-
cuted lives ; and though, to a certain extent, he once
gave way to the all-powerful instinct of sport in the
single form of shooting, he has completely changed.
He still cherishes his guns, and keeps them always in
his sight ; but he loves his wild friends better, and it

" A young terrier or kitten," writes Francis Galton in his book on
South Africa, " seems the most harmless and mildest of creatures, until he
" has been brought into contact with rats and learnt the luxury and taste
" of blood, and many an instance may be found along the distant coasts
" of the wide world where a year or two has converted the Saxon youth,
" who left his mother all innocence and trust, into as diabolical and reck-
" less a character as ever stabbed with a bowie-knife."

has come to this, at last, that if he sees a shooter at work, he exults if he misses.

.   .   .   .   .   .

It is not always easy to discern any well-marked eras in a life which, in the ordinary sense, is quite uneventful. It runs on its course, in outward appear-

JOSEPH WOLF IN THE FIFTIES

ance, like a slow, sober river; the reaches varied with sun and shade, but never tumultuous and never stagnant. The ripples of its shallows are evident enough, but the strength and direction of the deeper current are hidden. Nevertheless, in the case of an artist,

a removal from quarters where he has made a great
reputation forms a kind of era in his life. As the
studies on the walls are taken down, one by one, the
place seems to shrink to half its size. The cob-
webbed corners yield up treasures long since forgotten ; and thrifty old spiders, who have outlived an
occasional " spring cleaning," sidle away to pastures
new. It is melancholy work ; but the painful effort
by which the poor Bohemian evolves some semblance
of order in his new home diverts his mind from the
dusty comforts he had got to love so well.

When Joseph Wolf was introduced by his solitary
English acquaintance into his first Howland Street
lodgings, probably few besides the ornithologists and
falconers had ever heard of him. In the more
abstruse branches of art, and in men, he was comparatively inexperienced ; and his fingers were only
familiar (but not too familiar) with the thaler of the
Fatherland.

When Joseph Wolf, in 1860, lit his first pipe in
his new studio at 59 Berners Street, he had friends
enough for a prodigious house-warming. Besides
being looked up to as absolutely " unrivalled "—as
" the best available talent in Europe," by the most
distinguished men in Science, he was known to many
other people of great influence and taste, just as he
most wished to be known ; as an accomplished and
learned artist in oil and water-colour ; and so the
seductive crackle of the British bank-note (with which

dulcet sound William Hunt was sometimes to be
beguiled when all other arguments had failed), was
familiar music.

His new home was much more convenient than
the old one, and he found himself master of three
comfortable rooms with the offices thereto. There
was a large north window, but no skylight ; and he
thinks it was due to this moderation in the lighting
of his studio, that his Berners Street works generally
gained by the light of exhibitions.

One of his first cares was to provide his favourite
hobby with suitable stabling. At that time it was
cage-birds, and so he gradually surrounded himself
with aviaries.

From the very first, and long before he had defied
the whole school in defence of the nestlings, he had so
peculiar a love of birds that it apparently led to reciprocation. There is nothing at all extraordinary in
this ; for, over and over again, it has been proved not
only that animals will respond in a remarkable degree
to the kind treatment of a man who has learnt their
language and taught them his,[1] but that wild birds

---

[1] I was talking to a well-known authoress (whose sympathy with
animals and eagerness to respond to their advances somewhat resembles
Wolf's) on the subject of this responsiveness. She said it was singular
that, in the case of such wild birds as Sparrows, their familiarity and confidence never got beyond a certain point. They would crowd round for
their accustomed meal day after day, but any incautious movement
scattered them. But these birds, it must be remembered, were birds of
experience, and already accustomed to the fierce fight for existence.
Had they never known hunger and thirst, or danger, they would probably
have behaved differently. Wolf himself says, "A single sparrow you

intelligently treated, will even rival in tameness those reared from the nest.

After he had set up his aviaries, he soon got to be on the best of terms with the inhabitants. The Whitethroats would take their meal-worms from his hand; and in time they got to associate it with their dinner. When he was painting in oil they used to fly down upon his palette, hop upon the brush-handles, and peer between his fingers for the insects they were used to find there. But his greatest triumph was in the management of his Nightingales. When they were let out they would crowd upon the meal-worm box, so that their big master had to push his hand among them to lift up the rags in which the larvæ were bred. He says, "They were no more afraid of my hand "than a kitten was. . . . I have had a Nightingale "sitting on my boot and singing, so tame they "get."

At this time the artist did some drawings for a professor of Dublin University, who called one day when a Nightingale was singing magnificently in its closely papered cage. Never having heard the song before, the learned man asked what bird it was, and when Wolf told him, he said he was disappointed. He had gathered from what he had read that it was much more wonderful! "If ninety-nine people out of a "hundred," says Wolf, "hear a Nightingale singing in

"might get tame enough, but when there are so many of them there are "too many eyes."

" the day-time, they don't know it. They think a
" Nightingale's song must be at night." [1]

He had in his studio a big bath for his birds, and
describes the morning squabbles to get sole possession
of it as most amusing.   First a Chaffinch (who was the
tyrant of the aviary), flew down and bathed in solitary
pomp.   Then followed, perhaps, a Bullfinch or a Goldfinch ; and afterwards a couple of Nightingales,
sparring together.   By and bye, when the bathers were
all wet and draggled, they would flutter across the
carpet, and dry themselves by twos and threes on the
fender-rail before the fire.

Having once to draw some Redstarts, Wolf put
upon the table two or three stuffed specimens from a
museum, set upon small wooden stands.   This threw
a tame Robin into a fluster ; and, on being released
from his cage, he first flew down and sang to them,
but finding out his mistake, he got very angry, and
began to knock the impostors over.

It is not often that an artist's studio rings with the
songs of Nightingales and Blackcaps ; and it is still less

---

[1] It is singular that a song which is the quintessence of joyousness
should have been so often described as melancholy, plaintive, and even
doleful.   " A melancholy Bird?   Oh, idle thought ! "

" It is curious," writes Mr. Harting in his *Summer Migrants,* " how
" wide-spread is the belief that the Nightingale warbles only at eve.   The
" reason, no doubt, is that amidst the general chorus by day its song is
" less noticed or attended to."

This author does not include among our nocturnal songsters the
Hedge Sparrow and the Blackbird.   Few things are more impressive than
a chorus (near and distant) of two or three of these last magnificent singers
at a still, warm midnight, as I have heard it.

often that he consults them on matters artistic ; but on one occasion Wolf found them rather flattering critics. He had finished, and finished very highly, an oil picture of a Peregrine. He says, " I had a " large cagefull of birds at that time, and when the " picture was done I thought I would try its effect " upon them. So I showed it to them, and at " first only one took any notice. Then all of them " saw it, and there was quite a commotion among " them. The Serin Finch lay all along the perch, " and the Chaffinch hid himself down by the board " at the bottom."

On another occasion he had an exceedingly realistic life-size study of an Alpine Hare standing on the floor at the foot of an easel, when a friend came in with a couple of Bassett Hounds. Both of them made a rush at the Hare, and were grievously puzzled when they discovered their mistake. Wolf says " It " is not as difficult a thing to astonish animals with a " picture as people suppose, if it is tolerably well " done." Whether he tried any experiments of this kind on a lovely Silver Marmoset which came on a visit from the Zoological Gardens I do not know. His drawing of this little animal is one of the best in *The Proceedings.*

Year by year he had assiduously kept up his com- munication with his kindred, although there was not very much in common between them, and they knew next to nothing of his work and its success. Nearly

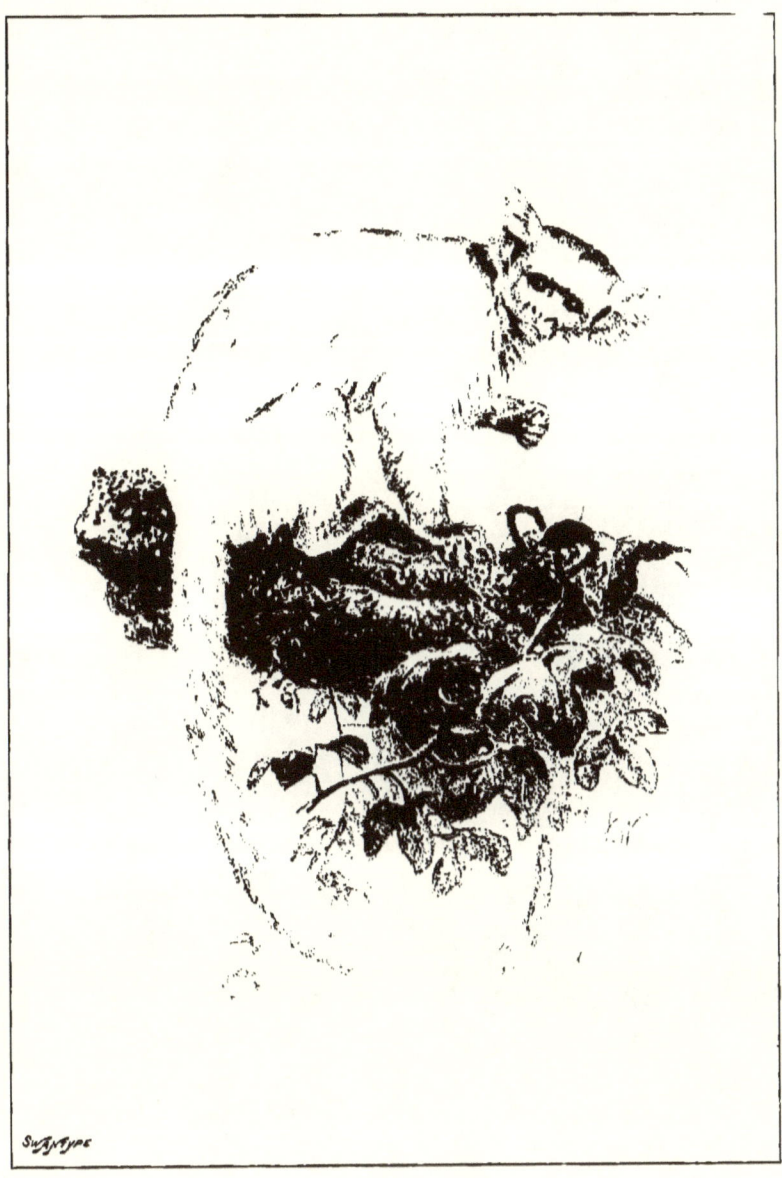

THE SILVER MARMOSET.

every summer he travelled, formerly by a Rhine steamer and then by rail, to visit his native village. There, everything was somewhat modernized, but still sleepy and peaceful, in spite of the advent of the iron road, here and there. " One of my brothers," says Wolf, " only once got into a railway train, to go from one "village to another, and was astonished to find how "quickly he got there."

The old people of the place were glad enough to see the young man from London, with outward and visible signs upon him of great prosperity ; and how many men would have yielded to the temptation to boast of that prosperity ! Wolf took exactly the opposite course. Simple at heart, he relapsed quite naturally into simple village ways ; and wandered about with his butterfly net or opera-glasses. As for his work in England, he kept very quiet about it ; for he says that he knew nobody in the whole neighbourhood, from the parson to the labourer, would understand it. His brothers had a hazy sort of notion that it was Joseph's bird-painting that had worked such wonders ; and when they approached him on the subject of building a second house, close to the old one, and found him quite willing to advance the money without security, there, at all events, was a pretty convincing bit of evidence that whatever trade he made his money by he was a substantial tradesman.

The big cousin had long since departed to happier hunting grounds ; and the old farmer had also been

gathered to his fathers, full of years.   Jacob, one of his
sons, had married, and was settled in a remote farm-
house on the hill-tops south of the Moselle, overlooking a splendid woodland prospect.   It was here
that the artist preferred spending the greater part of
his hard-earned holidays at harvest-time.   He says,
" You don't see the beauty of the landscape in your
" native place till you have been away from it.   But
" when you come back, you say, ' Oh ! how beautiful ! I
" never saw that before !'   Nevertheless, I had always
" dreamed, when I was a lad, of much wilder scenery
" than that of Möerz."

    He used to get up at sunrise, and go out with his
glasses to watch the birds.   He says, " I saw the
" broods of Carrion Crows, Magpies, and Kestrils
" actually playing—enjoying the moment.   You could
" see that it was pure enjoyment, as if they felt the
" poetry of the scene."

    No bird detective can doubt the truth of this ; and
no one who has turned his telescope upon the throngs
of Jackdaws and Gulls on the sands of a remote
estuary on a hot September day, or upon a party of
Magpies in the South Devon hedges, can have failed
to be struck with the signs of exuberant joy.   They
are thoroughly at ease and at peace ; replete, but not
too lazy for some burst of birdy horseplay, accompanied by a sudden babel of the wildest and quaintest
notes you can imagine.   This is very different, as
our friend is so fond of showing, from the terrified

dash of the sportsman's game; a race for life before
the muzzle of the gun.

Those familiar with Wolf's works will easily call to
mind a number in which snow is represented. A pair
of Goldfinches sit in "Adversity," with the flakes
falling thickly around them; or a couple of sour old
Boars flounder past one another in the forest, too
equal in prowess to adventure a midnight duel; or,
again, a group of Chamois huddle under the thick
mantle of dwarf firs, while the Alpine storm rages,
and the Ptarmigan dash up to the same shelter. The
snow is often rendered with a true poet's feeling.
Sometimes it faintly blushes at the sun's kiss, thousands of feet above the sea; or sparkles in the moonlight which dances among the mysterious, tangled
shadows of a forest; and sometimes it hides itself
coldly in the cloud and mist of a dreary, Scandinavian
solitude. It will be noticed, too, that the snow has
nearly always the tracks of animals upon it; not
aimless tracks, but as significant as they are in nature.
" I was always very fond of footmarks in snow," says
Wolf. " They tell a story. . . . Then I always saw so
" much more brilliance and light with the sun on the
" snow, and it made me feel cheerful. Then, too, there
" is the beautiful rounding of the animals by the
" reflection up from beneath of the snow. Altogether
" they look so well, and it does not interfere with the
" colouring."

The material for all this, and the much more

important knowledge without which all mere material is useless, the artist has accumulated slowly ; and it need scarcely be said that it was not accumulated in London. I have told of his delight in the wildest highlands of Scotland ; and it is probable that, as he toiled up the mountains, he had as keen an eye to the snow, and cloud, and mist—their contrasts and affinities, as he had to the Ptarmigan or Eagles. Some of the most careful of his snow studies were made in Switzerland, where he spent a month for the purpose ; and they were chiefly intended to record " the relative tones of warm and cold."

Wolf also loves a perfectly undisturbed surface of snow, because he says that upon it " there is always a mystery." As I shall perhaps have occasion to reiterate, this is a quality in art, as in nature, which strongly appeals to him. Complaining that the employer for whom he had to do some drawings of birds on wood had said that they must be " plainly seen," he adds in disgust, " There are a great many " artists now who do not understand the value of " mystery in art." We shall find this quality realized very perfectly in numbers of his works, especially in some of his northern landscapes. These, for some inscrutable reason, carry the mind far away to those more awful solitudes where the White Bear sniffs round the bones of many a valiant mariner ; or the frozen dead lie under their shroud, hidden for ever.

A Storm in the Alps.

In addition to his visits to his kindred and other occasional journeyings, Wolf kept up his acquaintance with Sutherlandshire. At the Duke of Westminster's desire he spent three days on the Island of Handa (being fetched off at night), for the purpose of making sketches as material for one of a series of drawings. The Island is known to ornithologists as the rugged nursery of many species of sea-birds, and the haunt of a pair or two of Peregrines. Wolf was delighted with what he saw; and how much he contrived to see in that short time (in spite of a dense sea-fog which caught him unawares), we should hardly be able to credit.

I asked him if he took his gun, and he said "No. "I had found out that if you take a gun with you you "don't work. Your mind is occupied with watching "for something to shoot." Although unarmed, he had a constant companion which was invaluable to him; a pair of powerful Ross opera-glasses. These, as an aid to a keen vision which little escaped, and the careful habits of the habitual stalker of living animals, revealed, as it were, a new fauna.[1]

[1] The value of a small pair of really first-rate twelve-lens opera-glasses of great magnifying power, carried ready focussed for *instant* use, no lover of nature can over-estimate. Such an instrument should not exceed six or seven ounces in weight in brass, and is somewhat rare. I have found it in absolute perfection at the great optician's Dallmeyer's. If furnished with a lanyard and a small curb-hook, it can be carried in the pocket, or be suspended instantaneously from the armhole of the waistcoat, where it will be out of the way and out of danger. As Francis Galton points out, "opera-glasses are invaluable "as night glasses; for, by their aid, the sight of man is raised nearly

The drawings commissioned by the Duke were in charcoal, about six feet high, and comprised the following subjects. "The Island of Handa." "Sea-gulls." "Herons and Otter." "Young Ospreys feeding." "Ptarmigan on Foinaven"; and "The Peregrine's nest." This last is a particularly spirited and original composition. The hungry scramble of the young birds towards their mother above shows to perfection the immature plumage, which is in the state just before the time when the eyesses are removed from the nest.

There were sundry other journeys made for a certain definite purpose; one, for instance, to the breeding haunts of the Gannets on the Bass Rock. The result of this trip was a good crop of sketches, besides the last of the drawings just mentioned. Wolf went with a brother artist, and for a week or so worked diligently, being greatly pleased to find the Peregrines on the Rock besides the rightful owners, some marked specimens of which (we read in *The Ibis*[1]) had been known to breed there for forty years. A visit to Lord Powerscourt's wild estate in Ireland should be included in the special journeys; a visit made in order to secure studies from the Wapiti living in the Park, from which the picture was painted which was exhibited in 1863. It was in London that

---

"to a par with that of night-roving animals." Let those who doubt this, try the glasses I have named upon a Barn Owl after dusk.

1866. "Dr. R. O. Cunningham on the Solan Goose."

a sketch was made of his Lordship's gigantic and notorious Red Deer head, well known (says Wolf) to be spurious even then.

Returning for a while to the subject of Wolf's book illustrations, we find that he always refers to his relations with the Brothers Dalziel as satisfactory; and their name will be seen on many wood-cuts after his work which are as successful as we could expect any translations to be of such very difficult originals. By a good rate of remuneration (when they had the power to control it) and, like the Whympers, by pains-taking translation, they encouraged him when encouragement was useful, and rarely if ever drove him to despair like some of the rank and file of the wood engravers who attempted his work.

In 1858, and before he had left Howland Street, he had taken part in illustrating a very pleasing edition of Thomson's *Seasons*. He also contributed rather more than forty designs to a series of modern poets published by Routledge, which appeared in the next decade; namely, Wordsworth, Montgomery, Eliza Cook, Sacred Poetry, and Robert Buchanan's *North Coast*. There may, however, be others of which I am not aware. These volumes are distinguished by their singularly ugly exteriors, and by the tasteful care with which the text and the wood-cuts are printed and engraved—wood-cuts after the best known artists of the day. In Wolf's case, indeed, the engraving is sometimes as careful as any I have seen applied to his work, and some delicacies of tone and drawing have survived.

Taking these volumes in the order I have named, we shall find in *The Seasons* three designs worthy of especial attention : a Tiger stalking some Antelope ; a covey of Partridges ; and a horseman attacked by Wolves in a dreary pass of the Apennines or Pyrenees ; a weird, moonlight tragedy full of imagination. The Wordsworth designs are less satisfactory, and contain two (the Hares and gambolling Lambs), which I can never bring myself even to tolerate. To me it is a relief to turn from these to the Kite's Eyrie in " The Deserted Cottage." Here, again, we get a glimpse of the artist's favourite mountainous landscape, with a few old firs clinging in despair to the precipice which gave them a wretched birth.

In the *Montgomery*, our friend divides his attention between such subjects as browsing Giraffes, or the slaughter of a Zebu by a Tiger, and simple English themes such as the nesting of our common birds. In the pretty illustration of " The Wild Pink," where, in the poem, the " blythe Swallow" builds on " yonder ledge of quarried stone," Wolf plants the " pert Sparrows " thereupon, but boldly substitutes a House Martin clinging to its nest beneath ; evidently being pretty confident that the general reader of poetry will be none the wiser. His love for butterflies (which sometimes crops up in unexpected places) is shown by the introduction of a fine Peacock, basking on the wall close to the nest.[1]

Passing over the *Sacred Poetry* (but commending it to the reader), we find in Eliza Cook's *Poems* a fine design illustrating the lines on the Ruins of Babylon, where an Eagle Owl screams at a couple of sleeping Jackals and arouses them. In the next we have the artist at his best. This represents a rookery in a fierce March gale. The birds (with which we are on a level), are rudely interrupted in their nesting, and balance themselves, swinging and swaying to and fro, while their plumage is roughened by the wind which drowns their "loud caw caw."

This is not Wolf's only rookery, for (not to mention the little one in Johns' *British Birds*), he contributed a very pleasing version under the title of " Rebuilding," to *The Illustrated London News* for April 8, 1871 ; the operations, both in the mansion below and trees above, going on as peacefully as in the other version they are disturbed.

One other book, *Lyrics of Ancient Palestine*, must be added to the short list I have given, for the sake

---

[1] If we wish for a foil to the illustrations I have named we may find a very perfect one in the *Montgomery*, by W. Harvey ; a good example of a kind of illustration once common enough and probably admired enough, and not extinct even now. It is one of the illustrations of " Greenland " and gives the impression of some thirty badly stuffed and very doubtful made-up specimens of birds having been pinned quite indiscriminately to a sheet. The apostle of this school of bird caricaturists (we cannot call them ornithologists, or artists) is perhaps Giacomelli.

of a solitary design of singular originality, " Samson's Riddle." The Lion's skeleton lies on its side beneath some bushes ; grim, and terrible, and perfect. The swarm of bees boils up through the staring ribs with such truth to nature that we can hear the loud hum with which they laboured the livelong day, till " out of the eater came forth meat."

While admiring the foliage with which Wolf surrounds his animals, as we find it in these and other volumes, and the skill with which it is at once subordinated, and yet made essential to the principal object, we may not notice the occasional occurrence of the flowers or leaves of the large white convolvulus. They appear like the butterfly, the spray of ivy, the bending reeds, and the acuminate or lanceolate foliage, because they are an especial favourite. Over and over again we meet with the white convolvulus among the studies in Wolf's portfolios ; and wherever he has settled down in London, plants of this or some other variety have been found climbing aloft.

In 1861 Mr. P. H. Gosse brought out his *Romance of Natural History*. Now Wolf says this :—" People " have a fantastical belief in natural history—in any- " thing that is fantastical and marvellous. If you tell " them the real truth they are not interested. If you " explain what appears marvellous to them, they no " longer care for it. Hence the origin of books like " Du Chaillu's. . . . I wish I had not given way to

" some authors by doing things as they wanted them
" —untrue, like the Gorilla throttling a negro with his
" hind foot ; dragging him up a tree and strangling
" him.   Such untruth is awful! . . .   In the case of
" animal life far in the world where I have never been,
" *to a certain extent* I have been obliged to believe
" what I have been told.   I believed it if what I knew
" and what I could see at the different Zoological
" Gardens, did not contradict it.   But, as I have said
" before, there are very few people who can interpret
" *truly* what they see in nature."

The Gorilla subject is an illustration in *The Romance*, and happens to be one of those in which,
perhaps, the *primâ facie* improbability does not offend
Wolf's love of truth more than what he considers to be
an exaggerated estimate of a wild animal's ferocity.
In spite of this, and in spite of what he says, I think
it is in accordance with the fitness of things that he
should have been the author of most of the illustrations of this work.   While despising the chimerical
and fantastic side of natural history, and rebelling
vigorously against its untruthfulness, he, once again,
shows the nice balance of his mind and at the same
time reveals his nature by revelling in the romance
that is so real, in the poetry and glamour so unspeakably beautiful in Nature and her children.   We
should know little of his best work if we failed to see
its poetry ; and when was true poetry far distant from
romance ?

As has so often been the case with large-hearted and large-minded men, Wolf's mind is swayed not only by his intellect but by his affections. Simply altering the name, I cannot do better than apply to him the words I wrote of another artist. " Unless we " can believe that a man's mind may be divided into " two sharply-defined kingdoms or polities, the one " ruled by his impulses, affections, and imagination, " the other by his intellect and reasoning power ; each " kingdom being distinct, and sometimes able to act " independently of the other, it is impossible to recon- " cile all we meet with " in studying Joseph Wolf and his work.

For instance. In Winwood Reade's _Savage Africa_ Wolf gives us a design the _primâ facie_ improbability of which is quite as great as that of the Gorilla and Negro. Speaking of " A Flood in Sene- " gambia " (the title of the wood-cut), Reade mentions that he had the story second-hand, and that :—

" On this island [a few feet square] there were lying, huddled to- "gether, two Lions, a Leopard, some Monkeys and Hyænas, two "Antelopes and a Wild Boar. All of these they killed without difficulty. " None of them took to the water. The Leopard only made an effort " to escape by running up a tree. This is certainly an improbable "story ; but to those who know how danger will stifle ferocity in wild " beasts, it will not appear impossible."

This is a typical case. The one subject, an improbable and hearsay version of the ferocity and malice of a wild animal, Wolf detests. The other, also hearsay, and also improbable, he loves, because the animals are in pitiful straits, and their natural ferocity is extinguished by their peril, so that they appeal to our sympathy.

While he has never wilfully turned away from what he believes to be true (except when compelled to do so by the exigencies of illustrating), Wolf knows, full well, the rashness of asserting anything to be impossible ; and he is not so little-minded as to allow his innate reverence for truth to hobble him in the narrow paddock of possibility as fenced in by ignorance.

His reason and his affections have kept one another within bounds ; with the result that his art is neither dull, prosaic, and matter-of-fact ; nor, contrari-wise, fantastical and mendacious. It is *true*, and yet often, in the highest degree, poetic and romantic.

Gosse mentioned three ways of studying natural history, " Dr. Dryasdust's," the Field Observer's, and the Poet's, but omits Joseph Wolf's, though more excellent than all. This is possible only in the excep-tional man ; for it unites a poet's imagination, keen susceptibility, and mental culture, with a naturalist's powers of close observation, and his sound inductive knowledge, leading up to the discovery of those immutable laws to which the strange, microscopic antics of a Rotifer anchored to an atom of pond-weed, are no less obedient than the body of the microscopist himself.

In Sir James Emerson Tennent's *Sketches of the*

Natural History of Ceylon, published in 1861, will be
found a good many of Wolf's designs.   They can
easily be distinguished ; and among the best of them
are those representing newly-captured wild Elephants
and their behaviour.   The original sketches in ink
outline are far superior to the wood-cuts, and are
good examples of the vigorous artistic shorthand of a

MODE OF TYING AN ELEPHANT

man whose knowledge of his subject is thoroughly
sound.   This is a work which every lover of natural
history should try not only to place upon his shelves
but to read carefully.

In this and the preceding year, Wolf also illustrated, either wholly or in part, some half-dozen books
of sport, adventure and other subjects, none of which
call for any particular comment.

In 1862 another excellent work illustrated by Wolf was published, of quite a different kind. The Society for Promoting Christian Knowledge, by keeping Johns' *British Birds in their Haunts* in print for thirty-three years, have done their best to make it known to the public; and it deserves to be known. The descriptive matter is free from wearisome

His Struggles for Freedom

facetiousness such as that of Morris, and is pleasant reading; while it suffices for purposes of identification.

The whole of the 190 illustrations were drawn on the wood by Wolf. He says, "Some of them I took "a liking to, and took pains with; but many were "done merely for the money." More than once I have

M

heard him regret that the meagre price forced him
to do the drawings rapidly (even as rapidly as half a
dozen in a day), and secondly that many of them
were simply " murdered " in the engraving.   " In that
" way," he complains, " having to do a thing cheaply,
" many a work is spoilt.   The artist has not got his
" heart in it then.   If you know that the employer not
" only knows nothing, but *cares* nothing for the kind
" of thing you are doing, it influences you very much."

It needs but a glance, or, at the most, a comparison with a few of Wolf's auto-lithographs of birds,
to show how these drawings must have suffered ; but
we shall find, nevertheless, that, in early copies,[1] the
result is often very good.   Probably with ample
time, ample payment, and the best possible engraving,
the wood-cuts would have been little miniatures fully
equal in truth and minuteness of finish and more than
equal in artistic beauty, to those which were painted
many years ago at Möerz.   The illustrations of the
Birds of Prey and the Wildfowl seem to me particularly happy ; and while the latter have been
editorially alluded to in *The Field* as the best extant,
the former speak for themselves as the work of a
master of the scientific detail and the characters of the
order.

It has been my good fortune to go carefully
through this book with the artist ; and some of his
remarks may be of interest to the reader.   To begin

[1] The latest editions are worthless.

with, he himself is satisfied, for various reasons, with
the representations of the Birds of Prey, the Crested
Tit, Tree Sparrow, Linnet, Bullfinch, Carrion Crow,
Magpie, Lesser Spotted Woodpecker, Wryneck,
Wren, Ptarmigan, Bustard, Woodcock, Coot, White-
fronted Goose, Mallard, Lesser Tern, and a few
others. He says one of his faults then was that he
sometimes made the heads too big; and he points out
this defect in the Goldfinch, Yellow Hammer ("eye
too far behind"), Woodlark, Spotted Flycatcher and
Jay. The Song Thrush, he says, looks as if he were
going to break a blood-vessel, and the Starling as if
he were going to be sick. Of the Cuckoo he remarks
that it never utters its note with an open beak as he,
and half a hundred others have represented it, but
produces it from the crop, like the Pigeons and
Hoopoes. The Blackbird is not good because the
beak is too far away from the eye. Of the Pied
Wagtail, "The cows are bad. I did not brace myself
"up. That might have been the third or fourth I had
"done that day." The Long-eared Owl he likes,
because it is a portrait of a pet bird he used to keep.
Among the actions he explains, is the crouching
attitude of the Skylark, which sees the bird of prey
behind; while the Pheasants are disturbed by poachers
below. Always a friend to the friendless, he says he
likes the Greenfinch because it is generally so despised; but points out that to show its full beauty it
ought to be painted in a copper beech.

M 2

On my asking him why the Ducks appeared to be more finished than some of the other species, he replied that it is owing to the smoothness of their feathers. He merely had to put in the markings as he would on a bit of paper.

If the Kite in Wordsworth's "Deserted Cottage" be compared with the Common Kite in Johns' *British Birds*, it will be seen that, save for the heads, the attitudes are nearly the same. It is obvious that, as the latter design had to be done hurriedly, there was a considerable temptation to make it more or less a replica of its predecessor. Yet we find that no two feathers are alike. Each bird is full of individuality and character of its own. Any touch of conventionality would have destroyed these qualities, and brought about a suspicious similarity between the two. This is a point which should be borne in mind in the study of this painter's works. "It was far easier," says Wolf, "not to look at any-" thing else, not to think of anything else. That is the "only way in which you can keep that kind of thing "original." Even in those drawings which were done for *The Proceedings* of the Zoological Society, where similar species recur, there is always sufficient, besides the mere markings, to keep them distinct. There is so strong an individuality as to amount to a portrait of the *specimen*; and this in spite of the fact that, in some cases the only available model was a dried skin.

So completely are Wolf's bird designs creations as opposed to compilations, that in no single instance has he resorted to the expedient of propping up or suspending a specimen in the given attitude, to draw from.

No epitome of Wolf's work as an illustrator should omit three auto-lithographs out of the six by him in W. C. Baldwin's *African Hunting.*[1] "An African Serenade" is imaginative to a degree which is difficult to describe, because it deals, like several of the other illustrations, with that romantic side of nature, that thrills the mind, but is quite indescribable. On the far side of a wide pool the fires of a kraal flare and crackle in the midst of the black darkness—darkness which seems almost tangible. Round the fires the scared oxen are huddled ; for in the foreground a troop of hungry lions, indistinctly seen, pour out roar after roar which seem to make the air quiver and the water ripple. On the distant margin of the pool, and just discernible in the fire-light, a few curs impotently defy the awful voices. All else (and herein lies the subtlety) is left to darkness, for the reader to fill up as he will. This design was chosen for one of the most impudent pieces of piracy among the many perpetrated on Wolf's work. It is the frontispiece of a book published in 1868 under the title of *Cats and Dogs,* and has been altered so little

---

[1] Bentley 1863. In the first edition of this book all mention of Wolf's work is omitted from the List of Illustrations ; and, on the title-page both his names are wrongly given.

that I have known a child of nine greet it as the original.

Partaking in some degree of the same qualities as those of " An African Serenade," and thrilling as well as delighting the mind, " Night Shooting" takes its place among the smallest and the best of Wolf's auto-lithographs. A Rhinoceros has already dropped in its tracks to the hunter's rifle on the margin of the pool ; besides one or two other dimly seen animals. A huge Lion comes prowling round them, and, shot through the heart, vaults, with a great roar, high into the air, where he is seen against a faintly luminous sky. I have had this little lithograph hanging up, amongst works of other veteran artists, for several years ; and it seems to me (like all Wolf's works on my walls), to gain in beauty and suggestiveness literally every day. Some people who have seen it have remarked on the improbability of the greatness of the leap (forgetting the very low horizon), and a few have been touched by the singular poetry of the subject.

In the two designs I have just described (and in many others), the artist proves himself as notable a master of the Indefinite, and the glamour that lurks in the Indefinite, as, in other works, he shows an equal power over the Definite, even to the verge of photographic minuteness. A third design is noteworthy as being the idealization of an African river-scene and as showing how Wolf will sometimes give his imagination plenty of rein. The myriads of Flamingoes which

rise on the horizon in a dense cloud, and stand in
pretty groups under the tangled reeds, emphasize the
solid, repulsive hideousness of the Crocodiles and
Hippopotami, which are drawn with great realism
and care.

We must pass by Wolf's illustrations in Mr. H. W.
Bates' *Naturalist on the River Amazons* with a mere
glance; but it was one of those works where artist and
author were in harmony. Bates, in those wild regions
which he described with such manly and self-denying
accuracy, was keenly alive to the romantic splendour
of nature and to the stupendous interest of nature's
laws. Never shedding unnecessary blood, his unpre-
tentiousness and humility were just such as would
appeal to Wolf.

The Rev. J. G. Wood's larger *Natural History*
was in every way so well adapted to appeal to the
dabblers in popular science, and the lovers of marvellous anecdotes of animals, that it has, I think,
remained in print to the present time; and belongs to
that large class of books upon whose title-pages certain
publishers prefer not to print the date. In early
copies, thanks to the Dalziels' wisdom and liberality,
will be found some excellent translations of our friend's
designs—happy designs, because (knowing nothing
of the anecdotes) he was allowed to unite scientific
accuracy with artistic qualities in his own way.

If a concise piece of evidence were wanted of Wolf's
all-round ability in zoological art, as a draughtsman of

mammals, birds, and reptiles ; and as a skilled artist capable of facing great difficulties of composition, it would be found in the frontispieces of the first and second volumes of this book, and in the capital design in the third of "African Crocodiles at home." Although the species which are represented are so widely different, there are no signs of greater facility in drawing one order of animals than another.   In the first volume (Mammalia) there are twenty-eight of Wolf's designs, besides the frontispiece, and in the second, twenty.   At first sight the frontispiece of the third suggests his handiwork ; but, like many more illustrations in this book and others in which they worked together, it was done by his friend Mr. J. B. Zwecker.   At this time they lived in the same house ; and though ten years Wolf's senior, Zwecker (a native of Frankfort) was glad to avail himself of his countryman's help, and of several introductions to publishers.   It is said that his early studies had been devoted chiefly to the Horse, and that a certain "horsiness" may be discovered in his Antelopes.   Nevertheless, his work appears to me clever, conscientious, and often both spirited and original.

A friend who knows, perhaps, as much as any man of Wolf's large-heartedness and kindliness of disposition has told me how Zwecker, when he was dying, was indebted to his countryman's help and sympathy. He died, and was buried with the money Wolf gave for that purpose.

Some of the Birds of Prey in the *Natural History* were done in Wolf's studio by Mr. J. Browne, a regular pupil of his.

Among the books to which he contributed illustrations at this period (including Mr. A. R. Wallace's most notable *Malay Archipelago*), Col. Campbell's *Indian Journal* must certainly be included, if only for the sake of the frontispiece, which, in my opinion, is Wolf's finest Tiger. The great, supple brute crouches in dense shade beneath a rock, covered with tangled, flaunting creepers. He stares out fixedly into the sunshine with contracted pupils, and save for the tip of the tail which wags gently and so betrays his excitement, he bides his time. I speak of the tail as actually moving, and it does appear to move. The sleekness and beauty of marking are so happily superimposed upon the tremendous muscular development; the modelling and perspective are so faultless, that this auto-lithograph must always stand alone among the artist's work. Touching the other subjects, Col. Campbell says :—

"I think much credit is due to the talented artist Wolf, for "having, with no other materials to work upon than my rough "sketches, aided by my descriptions, managed to produce such ad- "mirable portraits of the Sambur, Bison, and Ibex, three animals "with which he was previously unacquainted, but which any Indian "sportsman will at once recognise. The Tiger, being an old friend, "he has treated as such, and, I think, done him ample justice."

Of Wolf's connection with the illustrated periodicals I have no inclination to say much. It was a good sign that his work often appeared in them ; but how his drawings were engraved years ago, long before the days of any "mechanical process" save the most mechanical of any, the process of the cheap engraver, it is well not to enquire.   I have seen many wood-cuts from *The Illustrated London News, Once a Week,* and other papers, that have little besides his initials to associate them with Wolf's work.   This is another instance in which he appeared before the public at a great disadvantage.   How great, we can see in an instant by comparing with the engravings any black and white drawing of his, or even an auto-lithograph done at that time.

It can hardly be imagined that the "J. W." which appears in the corner of a glaring chromo-lithograph, or some sickly, vapid piece of colour-printing can be the hall-mark we are accustomed to find on the purest metal.

There were, of course, some exceptions.   For instance, it was in *The Illustrated London News* that one of the artist's most vigorous African subjects appeared.   A magnificent Lion has seized a mongrel from a caravan which has halted for the night ; and as he is fired at from the waggon over a pool, he launches himself with a few enormous leaps towards the spectator and into the darkness.   Some curs, with their tails between their legs, bewail their comrade ; and, by the glare of a flash of lightning added to the glint of fire-light, the whole picture—the

MORNING.

plunging oxen, and the confusion of the camp—is clearly but momentarily seen.

The sequel to this grim episode of African travel might have been doubtful if the artist had never drawn the companion subject which the reader will see. The hurried snap-shot told ; and in the beautiful morning twilight, far away from the scene of his last foray, the Lion lies, while the Vultures glide up one by one from the horizon, and settle cautiously round him, till they are sure that his sleep has no waking.

A search among old numbers of *The Illustrated London News, Once a Week, The Leisure Hour, The Sunday at Home*, and other periodicals will bring to light a good many engravings after Wolf, all more or less wanting in the chief beauties of his workmanship ; and some of them, such as *Pheasant Shooting*, in *The Illustrated*, parodies so egregious that they can hardly have failed to do him actual harm. Under these circumstances, it is not extraordinary that when the victim saw an engraving after his work in a shop-window, he crossed over the road to avoid it.

In *The Sunday at Home* there appeared under the title of "A Tropical Bathing Place," the identical engraving, line for line, which afterwards took its place in an important and beautiful work to be presently noticed. Its first appearance was distinguished by colour-printing of the most alarming kind ; a gratuitous stab at the artist's reputation among

those who knew not his unspeakable loathing and
disgust at such crudities.

A large proportion of the engravings after Wolf in
The Illustrated represented the new or rare animals
which were added, from time to time, to the Gardens
of The Zoological Society.

A WILD CAT

CHAPTER V

IN the two preceding chapters I have briefly re-
viewed the scientific and illustrative sides of
Joseph Wolf's work; which was done on wood
or stone as the case might be, either by himself or
translated by engravers and lithographic draughtsmen in a way which he rarely found very satisfactory.
Even the scientific work of this kind that he did
himself was done, it seems, against the grain. He
would not stake his reputation as an *artist* (a reputation which he cherishes), on this phase of his art;
though, as a conscientious endeavour after truth, he is
quite ready to "swear to it." As for his illustrations,
though he regards them with more toleration, I think
he is rather indifferent. He rarely, if ever, found
men like Oswell, with whom he could work in perfect
harmony, and he could never brook the insulting
manner which a few authors thought fit to assume
towards him.

It is far otherwise with his large drawings in
charcoal, charcoal-grey, or chalk (a considerable number
of which were produced within the period we shall now

have to consider), together with his more important
achievements in water-colour and oil.   It is unfortunate
that the finest of these have not been seen and are not
likely to be seen by the public, for it is on them that
his fame as an artist should indisputably rest.   Upon
the best of them, any competent critic would doubtless
agree that it would rest securely for all time.

He says of his scientific work for *The Proceedings*
and *The Ibis*, "I did it as I saw it."—as he saw it, that
is, with the bodily eye.   He might with equal truth
say the same of the designs some of which I shall
describe or allude to ; for before the charcoal touched
the paper, they presented themselves clearly to that
inner vision which is so distinct and so real in the
imaginative man.

Some of the most striking of his work, because
of its complete freedom from restraint, and because of
the use of his favourite material, charcoal, was done
in connection with The German Athenæum.   This
Society was founded about 1869, and had a very
unambitious origin.   The members, numbering perhaps
a dozen or a dozen and a half, included Wolf and
others, who used to meet together in a quiet way in
Hanway Street.   There was a Scientific evening, a
Lecture evening, a "Composition" evening, and a
Musical evening ; the science and music and art being
washed down with wine and beer in moderation,
amidst clouds of tobacco-smoke.   Owing to the advent
of several good musicians, their special evening soon

TAME AND WILD.

assumed grand proportions, and the others were not far behind. At last the subject given out for the next "composition" was "Farewell to Hanway Street," and Wolf's version represented one of the members, Dr. Strübing, grave and spectacled, with a fine large umbrella under his arm, turning out the gas for the last time.

Having thus outgrown the old room, the Society migrated to permanent quarters in Mortimer Street, where the monthly "Composition" evenings soon rivalled those devoted to music. The subjects were often suggested by a lover of antithesis, which in some cases appears to have presented no difficulties to Wolf, though in others it forced him to design two separate subjects, as in the case of "Prosperity and Adversity." To bring these into contrast, he painted companion water-colours. In the first, two Goldfinches are shown in the midst of an abundance of hemp-seed, vigorously quarrelling. In the second, hunger and cold have settled their grievances, and they sit close together on a dead thistle, while the snow falls around them. Sometimes, says Wolf, the subjects were so foggy that the artists could make nothing of them. It was otherwise with "Strength and Weakness," which he brings into striking contrast by a playful fight between two huge Rhinoceroses in the jungle, close to an Indian Axis Deer, and two tiny fawns in the foreground. "Tame and Wild" shows a fight in earnest. A bull Buffalo, roaming across the prairie

with the herd, meets near a farmstead an unexpected
adversary in a powerful domestic bull, who leaves his
harem and dashes into a shallow pool to drive off the
stranger. Touching this subject the artist says, " To
" please the public it is necessary to show sympathy
" with domestic animals, but I would rather show it
" the other way—with wild animals, and I prefer to
" represent them unpersecuted by man. . . . Man
" has no business to be near wild animals."

In " Repose and Restlessness," a few fat, lazy Sheep
are dozing in the sun, while, in a thicket of tall thistles,
a large flock of Goldfinches flutter, and hop, and spar,
with restless small-bird energy, to the evident astonishment of an inquisitive lamb. The criticism has been
made in my hearing by one of those artists who cannot
look at a work of art without throwing back their
locks and gesticulating with their right thumb, that
there are too many Goldfinches ; that the subject would
be improved by cutting down, and so on. To this it may
be answered that Wolf's object has been exactly fulfilled through enhancing the feeling of repose, and
conveying the idea of extreme restlessness to the eye,
by the flutter of a large flock of little birds, although a
flock of Goldfinches of such numbers may, in certain
districts, be rare.

One of the best of this series is " Surprise," where
two Hares, foraging over the snow, encounter a wild-
looking scare-crow, which seems to be solemnly warning them with uplifted arms. It is a still, frosty night,

SURPRISE.

yet some snow is dropping from these arms; for crouched against the stake that supports the figure is a Fox, quivering with hungry excitement.

"Joy and Sorrow" is another of the Athenæum sketches. A group of Cranes are disporting themselves after their manner beneath the cloudy skies of Lapland. Some of them caper in an ungainly dance among the cotton-grass, while others hail, noisily, an approaching detachment of their friends. One solitary bird, plunged into sorrow, mourns over his dead mate lying on her nest.

"Youth and Age" shows us an old Red Deer stag teased with impunity by some calves, and butted at because his horns are in velvet. "Old Age," said the artist as I turned over the drawing, "didn't want to be worried ; and quite right too."

"The Fiddler and the Wolves" is a striking moonlight subject, though a grim one. A poor musician, trudging through the forest from town to town, finds himself belated and surrounded. Despair suggests the old experiment of the effect of music on wild beasts. Never was such music! The wails of the tortured fiddle are answered by a dreary, dreadful, long-drawn howl. One of the brutes puts up his hackles viciously, and another sits down fairly puzzled by the strange sounds. The fiddler's hat blows off, and then, suddenly, a string cracks. Still the wretched man plays on, till but one string is left. This is the time chosen by the artist. Another moment and the

N

last string may break; the Wolves be choking over the clothes and licking the blood from the snow. The realism of the draughtsmanship of the animals' expressions and actions gives a painful excitement; and our attention rapidly changes to and fro between the disabled fiddle and the menacing eyes upon which it is ill to look.

A contrast to this episode is "Grave and Gay," in which a Long-eared Owl dozes in shadow, while some butterflies frisk about near him in the sunshine. That he might study the living insects, Wolf got some Swallow-tail chrysalids; and he found the transformation so interesting that his old enthusiasm revived after a forty years' interval, and set him to work in earnest. He has now a considerable collection of European butterflies, many of which he has bred; and he has taken great delight in studying their combinations of colours. Like all he has done, this collecting has been done as well as possible. The insects are pinned and set quite up to an entomologist's standard. Mr. Charles Whymper tells me that not content with taking his net with him on his annual visit to the Continent, and "like a boy chasing with ardour the Swal- "low-tail and Camberwell beauty, Wolf made his "own rearing-boxes with carefully arranged lamp and "thermometer, to keep all at the right temperature, "and was most successful in getting perfect specimens "from Indian and American chrysalids."

The war of 1870 brought anxiety and sorrow, as

PEACE AND WAR.

well as exultation, to the members of The German
Athenæum. Wolf became the treasurer of a fund in
aid of the German widows and orphans, and was
rewarded for his hearty labours in the cause by being
able to send out about 2,000*l.*

Soon after the war was over he spent a fortnight
in Paris with his friend Mr. D. G. Elliott, and they
paid a visit to one of the battle-fields. As a result, he
added to the series of antithetical designs, on his
return, "Peace and War," an upright subject shaped
like a grave-stone. A Turtle Dove mopes on a branch,
mourning sore over her shattered nest. Just below
her, and embedded in a clump of forget-me-nots and
bluebells, lies a soldier's helmet illuminated by a ray
of sunlight in which some butterflies take their pleasure. The mourning of some bird over a destroyed
nest is a favourite subject, and there are other versions.

The butterflies are intended to typify a bright
future beyond the grave, and were suggested by a circumstance which happened some years before. I am
indebted to Mr. A. Thorburn for the anecdote. Wolf
had not been able to attend his father's funeral, but
when he next went to Möerz he, of course, visited
the grave. While he was there, a Red Admiral
butterfly suddenly settled on the grave-stone and
sunned itself. The incident struck him much ; for the
butterfly seemed, he said, like an emblem of the resurrection.

The only other design of Wolf's connected with the

N 2

war of which I am aware was commissioned by *The Graphic*, and shows a trained Peregrine Falcon striking a Homer Pigeon which is carrying messages from Paris. It is one of those incidents touching which the artist is entirely sceptical.

A good many examples of the humorous side of Wolf's art were from time to time exhibited at The German Athenæum. Apart from their quiet fun, there is sometimes a touch of well-directed satire to be found here and there. These subjects of his are never silly and never broad or vulgar ; for of vulgarity in any form Wolf and his art are the antipodes—antipodes so absolute that if I were to try my hardest to recall a single instance of vulgarity I should try utterly in vain.

Among many such subjects, I have chosen for reproduction " A Lecture on Embryology," which bears for its inscription an old saying, " Highly learned makes a fool." In this design Wolf girds gently at certain men of science he has met ; " Dry sticks," as a great ornithologist calls them, " who work with their noses a few inches from their desk." The Owl is supposed to be propounding to his audience the vital question " Came the first Egg from an Owl, or came the first Owl from an Egg ? "—a question Wolf himself is perhaps not prepared to answer offhand. Innumerable little embryos dangle in spirits behind the lecturer.

Other instances of Wolf's humorous designs include a version of the Eagle and Tortoise fable

A Lecture on Embryology.

(where the reptile is not beyond the suspicion of
taking the visage and the form of a corpulent fellow-
member of The Athenæum), and various versions of
" Using a Donkey to catch a Goose."   Here, the Fox,

FIRST SKETCH FOR "A LECTURE ON EMBRYOLOGY"

whose vast cunning Wolf never tires in illustrating,
stalks a flock of Geese on a common behind a phleg-
matic Ass, wrapped up in his own reflections.

In this phase of Wolf's art should be included his
designs to *Reynard the Fox*, which were etched by

other hands. It may not strike us at first, in looking at the original sketches, that they are a most notable example of the artist's power of making animals "do what he likes," as he expresses it. Regarded in this light they become a most interesting study; and even if we prefer to see wild animals in a state of nature, and unhumanized, we shall have our admiration filched from us by some of the attitudes and expressions.

There is even another point. The essential essence of Wolf's representations of wild animals, that which distinguishes them pre-eminently, is the total absence of the human element—the human expression. "Men," he says, "have no business to be near wild animals"; a simple observation on the face of it, but weighty if applied to his art. Here, in these sketches (to say nothing of certain other works of his), is a positive, unanswerable piece of evidence that, when he chooses, he can humanize his animals in expression, in action, in feeling, and every other way, to the greatest degree; his skill enabling him to preserve, at the same time, the animal characteristics so perfectly, that the Hare, the Fox, Wolf, Lion, or Badger (as the case may be), are full of individuality. The question naturally arises, has any other animal painter ever existed who could simultaneously touch these points?

It is obvious that in a great deal of his scientific work, such as his drawings for *The Proceedings* of The Zoological Society, *The Ibis*, and Elliott's *Monographs*,

besides certain of his book illustrations, Wolf had
found the Society's Menagerie indispensable. "When
"I first began," he says, "I had no ideas except
"of European animals, but when I came to see the
"splendid species in the different Zoological Gardens,
"I changed my opinion."[1] The Gardens in Regent's
Park soon became his studio and recreation-ground.
But there were many dangers lurking in the study
of animals kept in confinement, to say nothing of
the constant distractions. It takes a man some
practice to be able to concentrate his attention on
such difficult points as the anatomy and actions of half
a dozen active Ratels, trotting round and round and
round again, or climbing up the wire; and to catch
the unamiable expression of a misanthropic cat, when
he is jostled by a crowd to whom an "artist chap" is
a perennial wonder, always worth an extra shove or
two.

As a delicate hint to these people he tried the
simple plan of stopping short, and drawing a Donkey's
head or a Goose on the margin of his paper. He had
found that a Monkey's head was too amusing, and
defeated his object; but a Donkey never failed to make
the people retire "after they had digested the meaning
of it"; not all at once, he says, but gradually.

As to the dangers which threatened him, his chief

---

[1] "When I came over," he says, "there were perhaps only one or two
"artists studying the animals at The Zoological Gardens. Now the whole
"place is crammed with them."

protection lay in the following maxims, various versions of which he reiterates to this day :—

"We only see distinctly what we know thoroughly."

"You must be able to interpret *truly* what you see, and that only comes of intimate knowledge."

"Not everything in nature is fit to be done. Only "a very small percentage. People make a mistake in "supposing that what is done from nature must be "right. A figure-painter would not take the first man "or woman he met in the street as a model. Only "very few are suitable."

"All nature consists of individualities, and only the most perfect are fit to use."

These opinions have no less an authority than Lord Byron to back them, who wrote :—

"The poetry of nature alone, *exactly* as she appears, is not "sufficient to bear him [the great artist] out. The very sky of his "painting is not the *portrait* of the sky of nature : it is a composition "of different *skies*, observed at different times, and not the whole "copied from any *particular* day. And why? Because nature is "not lavish of her beauties : they are widely scattered, and occa- "sionally displayed, to be selected with care, and gathered with "difficulty."[1]

In addition to those useful convictions of his I have quoted, Wolf was aware that even the finest menagerie animals are not always to be depended on as correctly representing the same species in a wild state. In close confinement the muscles are comparatively undeveloped ; while, sometimes, parts of the coat,

[1] Pamphlet on Pope.

such as the Lion's mane, grow to an unnatural
length.[1]

"First of all you have to study when a bird is in a
"fit and perfect condition to be drawn from properly.
"That you must learn first, or else you will get into all
"sorts of messes, and you will get Zoological-Gardens
"birds. . . . To find all the real arrangement of the
"feathers (which you very rarely see at The Zoological
"Gardens), you must see a wild bird. When you once
"learn it you can do it rapidly." A good deal, of
course, is involved in what Wolf means by "seeing"
a wild bird and "learning" the "real arrangement."
What he actually did, long before he ever heard of the
labours of Nitzsch [2] or Sundevall, was to spend years
in the closest study of the external characters of birds,
besides mastering their habits. Consequently, he says,
when at last he read Sundevall's writings, he found in
them nothing that was new to him.

His labours in The Gardens were carried on at all
times and seasons, and were not confined to summer,
or even to daylight. At one time he was to be seen
standing in the snow, elaborating with frozen fingers
and his favourite split brush a Vulture's head. At
another, he was patiently watching, by candle-light, the
movements of strictly nocturnal animals, such as the
Galagos, and Lemurs, and the Aye Aye. Then you

---

[1] See Sir Samuel Baker's *Wild Beasts and their Ways*.

[2] I am indebted to Professor Newton's kindness for an explanation of
the meaning and great import of "Pterylosis." Of Nitzsch we may read
in the article on Ornithology in *The Encyclopædia Britannica*.

found him vis-à-vis with a small South American monkey whose intensely human face is troubled, and hastily averted when the artist glances at it. Much finesse is required to secure that monkey's expression (the expression of a man of business whose affairs are not prospering); and finally, in deep disgust and displeasure it creeps into a corner, and hides its head, furtively peeping when its persecutor's eyes are turned down upon his paper.

For the most part Wolf has rarely troubled himself to sketch animals in motion; and in looking over his innumerable studies from life, even the most rapid, it will at once strike us that the greater part of the animals are either in quiet action or in repose. If we call to mind Mr. Dresser's most interesting anecdote of the first interview with Professor Schlegel, we shall see the reason for this.

With a phenomenal power of observation and memory for detail, it has sufficed for Wolf to watch moving animals closely without distracting his attention by pencil and paper. Speaking of the Lemurs he said to me recently, " Those things are in action only " at night, and you can't draw them while they are " moving about. The fact is, you must know the *struc-* " *ture* of the animal, and then you must learn to make " it do what you like. That is hard work. You " must not see the animal when you want to do him " in action. You must become an ' Impressionist ' " then, and do your work from the impression you

THE BASHFUL MONKEY.

"formed when you saw the animal in motion, and
"from knowledge, for you can't have a right im-
"pression unless you know. Then, by your knowledge
"of its structure, you ought to be able to do rapidly
"what you saw. Then you come again to what I
"want you to put on our title-page. 'You only see
"what you know.' I recollect I told another zoological
"artist that, and he kept repeating it. 'Very true!'
"he said. You look at things with the *intention* of
"remembering. When the things are flying about
"your ears, how can you sketch? You *look* at them.
"The artists who only study in academies (first from
"the Antique, and then from the Life), have not the
"slightest idea how *I* had to study. They have always
"said to me, 'How *did* you manage to do that?'"

Again, "When I go to The Zoological Gardens, I
"*can* look at the animals like other people; but if it
"occurs to me that I should like to draw them, they
"appear to me entirely different. The artist does not
"see the animals as other people see them. The more
"you know the things the better you see them."

Wolf paid frequent visits (not altogether of a dis-
interested nature), to certain fine animals with whom
he was accustomed to have a chat, and who knew him
well; and he did not forget a friendly shake of the paw
with a young Lion whose portrait is one of the most
successful water-colour studies he has done. But,
usually, he has found the little Monkey no exception to
the rule that animals dislike being continuously looked

at. Once, for example, forgetful of all else, he was studying a Tiger's stripes, when the owner, equally forgetful of the bars, charged at him with an indignant roar. "He let the other people pass," says Wolf, "but "my constantly looking at him he didn't like. It must "be a kind of mesmeric power which irritates the "animal."

Wolf's labours were not confined to living or healthy specimens; and many a dying or dead rarity has been restored to vigorous life by his pencil, before it was further immortalized by the Prosector.

He possesses among his relics a copy of Professor Owen's monograph of the Gorilla (for *The Transactions*), thus inscribed, "To the 'Artist' from the "'Author.'" "I was glad," says the latter, "to receive "the aid of the graphic skill of Mr. Joseph Wolf in "securing the characteristic outline views given in "Plate XLVI." The "outline views," unlike the two fine drawings of the adults, are rather ghastly; being made from a hideous baby Gorilla exhumed from a cask of spirits with his "external characters" in a somewhat dilapidated condition.

These drawings were made in 1864, at a time when everything connected with the great ape was still shrouded in mystery and romance. "The first "authentic information which I received of its exist-"ence," writes the Professor, "was by a letter from "Dr. Sharpe, dated Gaboon River, West Africa, "April 24, 1847, enclosing a sketch of the cranium.

" . . . In December 1847 I received from Bristol
"two skulls of the full-grown male. . . ."

In *The Proceedings*, thirteen years later (1877),
we read that " Mr. Sclater " exhibited " the very beautiful chalk drawing by Mr. Wolf " from a photograph
of another baby Gorilla. The drawing is a large one
in charcoal, and hangs at Hanover Square.

Wolf has not much faith in travellers' adventures
unless they are men of the stamp of Andersson and
Oswell, who were not ashamed to confess to a clean
miss ; and he laughs quietly to himself over the marvellous shooting, and the marvellous ferocity of the beasts
which are always killed by " a well-planted shot." Few
things please him better than to read such remarks as
those of Winwood Reade in *Savage Africa*, on Du
Chaillu's stories ; or to tell you of the singular circumstance that most of the skins of the Gorilla killed in
the fearful breast-beating charge, have the wounds in
the back.[1]

His long-standing friendship with the Staff, and with
Mr. Bartlett (besides the fact that he is a Fellow of
the Society), gave him advantages in his work at the
Gardens. He witnessed or heard all about many exciting incidents of which the public knew nothing. Now
and then, too, an experiment could be tried to prove
or disprove some doubtful habit. For example, Wolf

---

[1] In *The Royal Natural History* we read that these wounds were
caused not by Du Chaillu, but by the weighted spears which the natives
set for the animal.

was once of opinion that all animals laid back their ears
before biting.   To test this, he and a friend, hardening
their hearts, took a live Rabbit in a bag, and paid a visit
to the Common Fox.   On the release of the prey, the
Fox made a quick snap at the hind quarters as it
rushed by.   " Then he worked forwards towards the
" neck by a series of bites, but the whole time kept his
" ears well forward.   He looked *Satanic* —beastly, you
" know ! "

Possibly the difference in the position of the ears
depends on the dangerous or harmless character of the
prey or enemy.   In biting the Rabbit, the Fox knew
that there was no danger of any kind, and further-
more, his attention was no doubt distracted a little by
the spectators in front of him.   In biting a Dog, on
the other hand, the ears might be laid back out of
harm's way, as Darwin says is the case with all animals which fight with their teeth.[1]

" A Deer," says Wolf, " in defending itself will lay
" back its ears.   Even Roe Deer, the most harmless
" and soft-looking creatures, look furious when they
" do this—a caricature of themselves.   When you put
" it on canvas, where it perpetually stares at you, it
" gets unbearable.   Altogether, you have to take care
" not to introduce extreme expressions, which in
" reality only last a moment."

While the incident of the Fox and Rabbit was still
fresh in his memory, Wolf made a large charcoal

[1] *Expression of the Emotions*, chap. iv., p. 111.

sketch, exactly embodying what he had seen; but with a different background. It is characteristic that, on my finding this sketch one day, and asking his leave to reproduce it, he should have demurred. All animal suffering is so repugnant to him, and he so keenly sympathizes with the sufferer, that the incident has haunted him. He has drawn the animals of prey at their work times out of number, though always with the keenest sympathy for the victim; but this particularly realistic and careful sketch was rolled up and hidden away, till, years afterwards, I accidentally discovered it.

For the melancholy effects of the London atmosphere on the plumage and coats of the outdoor captives in the Gardens, it needed not Wolf's knowledge to allow. He said to me once, " There is a " White-headed Eagle at the Gardens now; but, " would you believe it! there is no real white about " him. All London soot, and quite dark."

It was not only for the sake of the animals that he loved to haunt The Zoological Gardens, but largely for the sake of the flowers. Of late years, when the gardening became more elaborate, he might often be seen, placidly smoking, while he chatted with the men at their work, or dwelt with loving eyes on some clump of convolvulus or evening primrose, or magnificent gigantic hemlock. The Lions might roar their loudest without diverting his attention from a study of a fine piece of foliage. Indeed his sketchbooks contain occasional gleanings from trees in the Park outside.

Another never-failing attraction was that fascinating Insect House, where the life-history of so many splendid species may be studied. Of this place he has, to this day, never tired ; and of its surplus riches in the shape of pupæ he has sometimes availed himself, breeding the huge tropical moths as enthusiastically as a schoolboy.

Another favourite and very profitable place of resort for our friend was Kew Gardens ; and there, as is proved by his sketches, he accumulated much of the material which he used in the foliage of his foreign compositions.

To what extent his imagination came into play in the use he made of this material it is scarcely necessary to refer. He quaintly observes, " If you have " two twigs, you know, you have enough for the rest " of your life." An observation of great significance, if rightly understood.

To have been in any way associated with Charles Darwin is an event in a man's life. Early in 1871 Darwin was preparing the materials for his *Expressions of the Emotions in Man and Animals* (published in the following year), and mentioned to Mr. Bartlett his wish to have some work done at The Gardens which required unusual care. The Superintendent spoke of Wolf's accuracy and closeness of observation in high terms, and in due course introduced the two

men to each other. Darwin, with a view to that section of his fifth chapter dealing with " Astonishment" and " Terror" in Monkeys, caused a living fresh-water Turtle to be placed in one of the cages. Wolf's account of the incident is this :—" One of the " Turtles was put into a covered basket, and the " keeper was asked to place it carefully under a heap " of straw which was in the cage. Whilst that was " being done, the Monkeys suspected something and " kept looking down from on high. Clever fellows! I " shall never forget that. The keeper then retired, " and presently the heap of straw began to move. " The Turtle came out, and instead of showing fear, " the Monkeys crept nearer. Then the Black Crested " Ape [*Cynopithecus niger*], came and looked at it, " and walked in front of the Turtle as it crept after " him. Finally he went and sat on the Turtle." Darwin was much amused, and asked for a drawing of the incident.

At this time, Wolf began to suffer from the chronic rheumatism which has troubled his later years ; and therefore he was delayed in completing Darwin's commissions. After a while he received the following letter :—

Down, Beckenham, Kent : March 3, 1871.

DEAR SIR,—You said that you would be so kind as to endeavour to make a sketch for a wood-cut of a monkey's face when laughing, as the keepers express it. The Barbary ape would have been incomparably the best, but is dead. I found, however, in the Zoological Gardens a species that does fairly well, viz. the *Cyno-*

pithecus niger of Celebes, though it unfortunately has permanent transverse wrinkles on the face.   It can be easily caught, and Mr. Bartlett
said could be put in a separate cage to be drawn.   There ought to
be a drawing of the face when tranquil and the mouth closed ; and
another of the same size and in the same position, whilst laughing.
When Sutton the keeper allows this monkey to play with his hair, it
chuckles or laughs, and keeps moderately still.   The face then
becomes a good deal wrinkled, and as far as I could see under dis-
advantageous circumstances, the skin is especially raised and wrinkled
under the lower eyelids.   When I asked Mr. Bartlett whether he
thought you could possibly draw the laughter of so restless an
animal, he answered that "Mr. Wolf has got an eye like photographic paper, it will seize on anything !"

I enclose the size of my page for any figures.

Also a drawing of a leopard which (excepting that the mouth is
here more widely opened) shows fairly well the appearance of a cat
when savage, and not at all frightened, as I have occasionally though
rarely seen.

I hope to get a photograph of Herring's picture of a savage
horse and another of a pleased one.   Your willingness to assist me
as far as lies in your power has relieved me from much difficulty.

Dear Sir. Yours very faithfully, CH. DARWIN.

Wolf afterwards received other letters referring, in
Darwin's habitually courteous terms, to eleven sketches
of Dogs, Cats, and Monkeys he had sent him.   Two of
the latter were rather badly engraved in *The Expressions ;* both being heads of *Cynopithecus niger.* I have
reproduced one of the series of sketches (made from the
living animal) which was retained by the artist, representing the " Laughing Monkey."

" I have already had occasion to remark," says Darwin, " on the
" curious manner in which two or three species of Macacus and the
" *Cynopithecus niger* draw back their ears and utter a slight jabbering
" noise, when they are pleased by being caressed.   With the Cyno-
" pithecus (fig. 17), the corners of the mouth are at the same time

" drawn backwards and upwards, so that the teeth are exposed.
" Hence this expression would never be recognised by a stranger
" as one of pleasure. The crest of long hairs on the forehead is
" depressed, and apparently the whole skin of the head drawn back-
" wards. The eyebrows are then raised a little, and the eyes assume

THE LAUGHING MONKEY

" a staring appearance. The lower eyelids also become slightly
" wrinkled ; but this wrinkling is not conspicuous, owing to the
" permanent transverse furrows on the face."

On showing the reproduction of his sketch of this
Monkey to Wolf, he said, " I never believed that that
" fellow was laughing, although Darwin said he was. I

"am not one of those who place absolute belief in all
" authority." This I have no doubt the reader will
have discovered for himself. Wolf's mind, so to speak,
is to some extent rationalistic ; and, as I have pointed
out, not only are there many incidents in natural history
he has had to depict which he scouts as unreliable (such
as a cat suckling a mouse),[1] but he would not allow the
opinion even of a great naturalist to convince him,
simply because it was so. It might be said of him
what has been said of Freeman the historian, " . . .
" he is sometimes surprised to find how entirely he had
" thought things out for himself, and that he could not
" attribute his opinions to the direct influence of any
" one man, however eminent." It is the old story of
the self-made man who has spent a laborious life in the
making ; whose slowly-acquired knowledge may be
compared with the pure metal produced first of all
by the miner's patient toil, and then by careful refining,
rather than with the current coin smoothed by a
thousand hands and still handed on. This strong independence of thought and belief is a great characteristic
of Wolf. In times of old it might have made him
a leader of men, as, in his own day, it enabled
him to fight his way upwards from the farm-yard, to
inaugurate with his own hands and mind the greatest
renaissance in zoological art that has ever been known.

He says, " I haven't got that sense of excessive
" veneration for great men. I don't believe in it.

[1] *Once a Week.*

" When you get to know them you find that they are
" fallible. Some of the great scientific men have been
" very unhappy creatures ; soured, if they were ever so
" successful. Some are haughty and unapproachable,
" and those I never went near."

He is fond of a certain story bearing on hero-
worship, which I will repeat in his own words. " A
" young student *walked* from a distant university to
" Weimar to see Goethe ; who, thinking it a nuisance
" to be interviewed, stood upright for the front view,
" and when he had taken in that, for the side and the
" back. 'Well done, *Herr Geheimerrath !* How
" much will that be ? ' said the student, putting his
" fingers into his waistcoat pocket. Goethe saw that
" he had made a mistake."

Darwin occasionally called upon Wolf in Berners
Street, who says that his visitor " was not like many
" great men who would put you down with a look or a
" sentence. A child might have talked to that man.
" He was wonderful in that respect."

Now among the artist's birds at that time was a
particularly tame piping Bullfinch, which had learned,
among many accomplishments, to distinguish the note
of his master's bell from the others. At the first tinkle,
he would fly to a chair-back near the door of the studio,
where he would sit and bow and pipe to a favourite
visitor, but would attack any person he mistrusted.
One day Darwin called ; and the Bullfinch, not liking
the look of his long white beard, flew straight at it,

"pulling with all his little might, while the old man laughed and chuckled."

We have now reached a time when, by means of the reviews of what is called a "gift-book," Joseph Wolf was brought suddenly and prominently before the public ; but in some of these reviews, just as if he were making his *début* as an artist !

Mr. Edward Whymper says that, years before, when he first turned over his friend's portfolios, he had been as much "astonished and delighted by the origi-
" nality of his conceptions, as by the profound know-
" ledge which was displayed in his studies of almost
" every branch of animal life ; and but a short time
" elapsed before I endeavoured to induce him to execute
" a series of designs which should give some idea of
" the wealth of his stores and the range of his pencil."

Mr. D. G. Elliott, cordially admiring Wolf's work not merely from a scientific point of view, but on account of its artistic beauty, was delighted to undertake the descriptive letter-press. The descriptions were written after the designs were made, and the artist had nothing whatever to do with them, but took his own time and followed his own bent ; retaining the originals.

At the end of 1873 the book was published by Macmillan, under the title of *The Life and Habits of Wild Animals*, and it met with a perfect ovation from the press. Indeed, there cannot have been far short of fifty highly eulogistic notices. A score or so that I

THE VARIEGATED SPIDER MONKEY.

have read are unanimously enthusiastic ; a few are
exceptionally discriminating and appreciative, and
several are somewhat ludicrous. The authorship of
The Genera of Birds, for instance, is attributed to Asa
Gray by one reviewer ; who, since he rejoiced exceed-
ingly over Giocomelli's illustrations to Michelet's *Bird*,
has seen nothing else to compare with Wolf's designs !
Another alludes to a wounded Hare and Hooded
Crows as a subject where " a Rabbit becomes the prey
of half-a-dozen Hawks " ; an Eagle Owl and Rabbit
are described as " a Hare bolting into its hole under-
" neath a tree-root to escape from the impending talons
" of an Eagle " ; and a Lynx in ambush above some
Goats is " ready to drop down from a tree on to the
Deer below " !

One of the best of the other class of critiques is
that in *The Field*, which runs as follows :—

"On perusing some of the notices which have already appeared
" of this work, we have been struck with nothing so much as the way
" in which the respective reviewers have introduced Mr. Wolf to the
" public, as if he were a new aspirant for academic honours,
" apparently overlooking the fact that he has been working in our
" midst for the last thirty years, during which time, in depicting
" animal life, his pencil has been one of the busiest.

"At a time when the hearts of Englishmen are still mourning the
" loss of their great painter, it may seem invidious to draw com-
" parisons between Landseer and Joseph Wolf ; but from a careful
" study of their respective works we have long since been of opinion
" that, of the two, Mr. Wolf has proved himself immeasurably
" superior. Not only has he worked in a much larger field, depict-
" ing by turns the animals and birds of all countries, but his ac-
" quaintance with the habits and actions of wild animals, from

" personal observation, has enabled him to trace their forms upon
" canvas with a fidelity to nature which, in our opinion, has never
" been excelled.   In artistic and scientific circles this has long been
" admitted ; and if, as it would seem, Mr. Wolf is not so well known
" to the general public as he deserves to be, we can only surmise that
" it is because he has never had time to exhibit. . . . Lest we may
" be thought to be according undue praise, we shall invite the
" attention of the reader to some of the numerous productions of his
" pencil, which, viewed with the critical eye of the naturalist, must
" always be regarded with favour. . . . We have said nothing about
" the many large works which have passed from the easel to the private
" cabinets of those who know well how to appreciate them, because,
" although we have had the privilege of seeing many of them, the
" public have had no opportunity, as with the exhibited works of
" other artists, to judge of their merits. . . ." [1]

We have here a view of Wolf's work as expressed
by a skilled hand writing for naturalists and country
gentlemen. I will add a few words written by the
critic of *The Art Journal*[2] for another class of
readers :—

" Rarely, if ever, have we seen animal life more forcibly and
" beautifully depicted than in this really splendid volume. As a
" painter of the untamed beasts of the forest and the wild feathered
" tribes of the air, Mr. Wolf has long made himself conspicuously
" known in this country, and in this series of illustrations he seems
" to have put forth all the power of his art to produce a variety of
" pictures of the most attractive kind. They are far more than the
" mere representations of certain phases of natural history ; they are
" highly picturesque scenes in which the animal or the bird [*sic*]
" is a principal actor."

In *The Times*[3] we read :—

" These drawings well exhibit the marvellous skill with which he
" [Wolf] depicts not only the outward forms, the fur and hair and

[1] Jan. 3, 1874.　　　　　　　　　[2] Jan. 18, 1874.
[3] December, 1873.

" feathers of the animal kingdom, but the very soul and character of
" the wild creatures which inhabit them. ['That,' said Wolf as I
" read him this passage, 'is what I have always been striving to do.'
" Anybody can say 'This is a Tiger,' 'This is a Dove.'] The
" subjects of his pictures are chosen with artistic skill, and each one
" of them testifies to a close study and accurate knowledge of the
" habits of birds and beasts. . . . As we close this exquisite volume,
" we cannot help thinking what pleasure it would have given to Sir
" Edwin Landseer to turn over its pages."

It was thus, without an exception, that Wolf's
workmanship in the *Wild Animals* was received by
the Press. Also without an exception, the share the
Whympers had in the result is spoken of with the
highest praise, and not unjustly. *The Art Journal*
says :—

" To Messrs. Whympers' engravings, too high praise cannot be
" given. Long as our experience has been of wood engraving as
" practised both in England and on the Continent, we remember
" never to have seen work surpassing these examples for tone and
" colour, softness and brilliancy. Solid, but without the hardness of
" some of the best modern French wood-cuts, . . . they combine free-
" dom of handling with the greatest delicacy of execution. There is
" scarcely one of the whole number which is not a fine example of
" the art."

The engravings, in fact, certainly go as far towards
the faithful rendering of the artist's work as was then
possible under the best conditions. How far this is,
can only be gauged by a careful comparison of the
original drawings (still in the artist's possession), with
the wood-cuts ; and in making this comparison many
times, I have not been blind to the exquisite technical
qualities and the skill shown in the latter.

I have pointed out that the quality of mystery

which forms so important a factor in the romance of
nature exists in many of Wolf's works, and in some of
the originals of the *Wild Animals* it is particularly
attractive. Here, of course, lay a good, substantial
stone of stumbling for the engravers. As we look at
the drawings, we gradually forget the existence of the
paper, and the chalk, and even the great manipulative
skill. We have donned an invisible coat, and we are
alone in the ancient forest, or the moonlight (or now
and then in the sultry tropical glare), with nature's wildest children. Our eyes, as it were, get *gradually* accustomed to the conditions and surroundings. The
romance, or the terror, or the splendour of the scenes
grows upon us little by little, and intensifies slowly.

Now, speaking of the engravings, one reviewer
praises their " marvellous distinctness," another is delighted with their " clearness," and a third complacently
observes, "*Every plate tells its story without any
obscurity.*" Here, neatly expressed in eight words,
we have the chief cause of the difference between the
best of the drawings and the engravings, and of the
unmistakable inferiority of some of the latter. One or
two are undoubtedly superior to the originals, as
Wolf points out ; but, in a certain proportion, the
beautiful semi-obscurity of nature—the atmosphere
which intervenes between the near and the distant,
giving to each its relative value and reality, have been
injured. Whatever the artist intentionally left as
doubt or suggestion (in moonlight, for instance, or the

ALLEN'S GALAGO.

gloom of the forest), has become unequivocal fact, and every fact is, to a certain degree, emphasized. It is, as it were, an absolutely faultless recital on a faultless piano, compared with the notes of some siren or mer-maiden of old, so remote that the mariner's imagination strove almost painfully to link together the fragments of the uncertain melody.

In Wolf's own words, " Engravers cut out all the " mystery—that which makes the picture. I assure " you that when I received the first proofs of the *Wild* "*Animals*, though I had done the drawings on the " wood myself. I found that the original scheme of light " and shade was gone altogether, and I had to concoct " a different arrangement. I had put in work which " was not understood."

It is much to be regretted that in doing these drawings on the wood, and all else destined for the engravers (even such engravers as the Whympers), Wolf did not study the kind of manipulation best suited to translation, and settle in his mind before he took up his pencil how many of those mental and technical refinements he revelled in would inevitably have to be sacrificed by any process of reproduction. He made the then common mistake of supposing the existence of some of his own peculiar knowledge in the engraver ; and of imagining that the engraver's tools could render faithfully, even in the most highly-skilled hands, his delicate gradations, melodious light and shade, and extraordinary niceties of modelling and draughtsmanship. For all the suffering brought about by this want of experience in adapting his work, he had no consolation.

I am not so ignorant and presumptuous as to dare to depreciate the beautiful art of wood-engraving ; or so blind as to do otherwise than most cordially admire much of the exquisite handiwork of the Whympers, and some of the élite of the engravers. Nor am I blind to the sparkle, richness, and vigour which, except in the *old-fashioned* etching, is found nowhere so captivating as in the best wood-cuts by the best hands. Still the fact remains that, partly through the want of calculation and forethought on the part of the painter in adapting his work, and through the engraver's inevitable want of training in the more abstruse refinements of original art (sometimes from his persistence in tradition, and to a certain extent from the nature of the tools he employs, not to mention other causes), wood-engraving, as applied to such work as the best of Wolf's and its kind, has failed on the whole to render it truthfully. It has not failed in a slight degree. It has failed so signally that, again and again the artist has suffered torture.

In spite of the violent denial often flung at like statements, and the hap-hazard railing of many a pre-judiced painter, it may, nevertheless, be safely main-tained that first-rate " process " work, judiciously follow-ing equally first-rate photography by artistic and skilful men, has succeeded and succeeds every day just where wood-engraving has been found, over and over again, to fail. I do not deny that it often fails where engraving succeeds.

Process work has the misfortune to be cheap, and it also has the misfortune to be (to a certain extent) mechanical. Therefore, according to the words of the prophets, it is unspeakably vile. They shut their eyes to all that even the best wood-engraving has failed to do, and to that which the worst has done execrably— to all that the best process has achieved ; and, with praiseworthy logic, compare the workmanship of the finest and costliest wood-engraving in the world, with a third-rate process block made from a fourth-rate photograph, at a shilling or so a square inch.

Copies of the original edition of the *Wild Animals* are rather scarce ; but with few of Wolf's illustrations have publishers made more free. The copyright has passed from hand to hand, and I am told that the designs have been reproduced in Germany, France, Russia, and Switzerland. The whole twenty have been republished side by side with another artist's compositions, under the curious title of *Wild Animals and Birds.*[1] Not only have Elliott's descriptions of Wolf's designs been excluded from this volume ; but others have been substituted which are ludicrously malapropos. For example, in " The Hairbreadth

[1] Cassell, 1882. In this volume will also be found reprints from the engravings of the Polar Bear and Snowy Owls, and the Wild Cat and Ring Dove alluded to presently ; besides " The Home of the Herons,' and Wolf's favourite subject, A Golden Eagle and Ptarmigan.

Escape," the Rabbit striving its utmost to reach shelter is described as a Hare; while "the companion Hare flies into its burrow"! The original titles of some of the designs have also been altered. Thus the lazy Jaguar, dozing in the midday heat as close to the cool water as he can get—so close that the tip of his tail occasionally touches it in his sleep, is no longer enjoying "The Siesta," but is "The Jaguar on the Watch"; a manifest absurdity stultifying the whole gist and essence of the design.

"Rival Monarchs" I have met with in a School Board "Reader." Others of the series have been cut down to fit the pages of a new *Natural History*; and I think Wolf would not be surprised to find any of these subjects (as he did one of his Tigers) ornamenting a biscuit-tin on a friend's breakfast-table.

Twelve of the designs illustrate the dangers to which animals are naturally exposed by duels and persecutions among themselves; and in six of these the aggressor palpably fails in his purpose, or is understood to do so. Save in one instance, the common phase of wild animal illustration, the phase of sport, is entirely omitted; and in that instance the sportsman is shown in helpless peril.[1] Throughout all, the romantic side of natural history is agreeably prominent; a fact by no means lost sight of in the letterpress.

I think that three out of the twenty subjects stand

[1] The incident will be found in Lloyd's *Field Sports of Northern Europe*.

apart from the others from their interest, admirable
execution or pathos; namely, "A Hairbreadth
Escape," "Maternal Courage," and "Hunted Down."
In the first of these a magnificent Eagle Owl has struck
at one of the Rabbits which have been gambolling on
the moonlit snow, but merely succeeds in grasping
beneath a root which forms part of the entrance to the
burrow, the skin of the hind quarters. The squealing
quarry struggles for safety, as a frightened Rabbit can
struggle, but the bird, with outstretched wings, main-
tains its hold. Contrary to the description, says the
artist, it would have succeeded after all, but for the
sudden appearance of a Fox, which has been attracted
by the Rabbit's cry, and diverts the Owl's attention.

In "Maternal Courage" the attack of a hungry
Lammergeyer upon a Chamois kid is defeated by the
brave mother. The robber has been severely handled.
His feathers garnish her horns, and float away over
the precipice, while he clings for a moment to a rock,
and then sails off to smooth his torn plumage and seek
a less risky meal.

"Hunted Down" is full of the quiet pathos so
characteristic of the artist's best work. A dreary, snow-
covered plain meets, in a solitary gleam of light on the
horizon, a leaden sky; while the wind sweeps across
the waste, spitefully flinging the snow against every
obstruction. A Hare, hard hit earlier in the day by
some reckless shot, has limped on more and more
painfully, till she crouches down by a few dead weeds

to wait for the end.   There is death already in the eyes
and the staring coat, and the end will soon come.   By
evil chance there crosses her track a foraging party
of Hooded Crows ; and the foremost, with famished,
vigilant eyes, shout out a bloodthirsty view-halloo.

In turning over these designs with their author,
once or twice, I have found that the stories he intended
to tell are not always correctly interpreted in Mr.
Elliott's letterpress.   For instance, in " The Shadow
Dance" it is not the moon, but the early morning sun
that throws the tempting images of the Rabbits on the
bank.   The Fox, says the artist, far too clever to take
any shadow for the substance, looks round the furze-
bush at the animals themselves ; but the result is very
doubtful.   Again, though it seems a certainty that
the Lynx in " The Ambuscade " will dine off a tender
kid, the artist is of a different opinion.   He said with
a smile, " He has not succeeded yet.   ' There's many
a slip 'twixt the cup and the lip.' "

His present opinion of the preceding subject,
" The King of Beasts," is, I am glad to say, one of
thorough disapproval.   He sees well enough now that
it is theatrical, and he says also that the engraved
lines are too close together.   This design, and " The
Gleaners of the Sea," are the least satisfactory of
a series otherwise in every way notable.   " Catching
a Tartar " is very different.   It is not only full of
poetic feeling, but represents a most interesting incident
in natural history.   A Barn Owl, more hungry than

The White-Cheeked Sapajou.

discreet, falls a victim to a Weasel which he has carried
off. The subject is based, says Wolf, on an anecdote
he heard in Germany, and a version of it is to be
found also in Bell's *British Quadrupeds.*[1]

In the volume already alluded to (*Wild Animals
and Birds*), the Weasel is described as a Polecat which
has ventured "to attack the peaceful Owl." This
bird, "roused from its monotony by the fangs of the
"carnivore, flies into the night, bearing with it . . . its
"assailant."[2]

There are two other subjects (originally published
elsewhere) which, from their uniformity in size and
shape with the series just described, may be classed
with them ; and the original drawings are too good
to be passed over. In the first, a huge White Bear,
sated by a hearty meal, sleeps heavily upon a ledge of
ice. Some hungry Snowy Owls, anxious to pick up
the fragments, screw up their courage till they are
almost within range of the mighty paws.

The second design is called "The Night Attack,"
and is one of those rare instances where moonlight
has been represented by art with some truth to nature ;
that is, with regard to the amount of detail which is
shown. There is not too much shown, and a natural

[1] First edition, p. 145.

[2] It is hardly necessary to point out that any person who knows the
relative sizes of the Barn Owl and Polecat and those of the Polecat and
Weasel (to say nothing of other points), but does not know how Wolf's
designs have been handled in this book, will be puzzled at the singular
description.

result is that what we do see gains enormously in poetry and truth ; giving a protracted pleasure which can never be derived from detective art that reveals every mystery and ransacks every shade. A marauding Wild Cat, in the perfection of fur and of vigour, roaming about by the light of the full moon to seek his supper, has sighted a Ring Dove's nest aloft in a pine ; and reasoning by deduction, he thinks it worth while to see whether the maker of the nest is at home. He climbs silently, and makes a sudden but vain attack upon the intended victim. She, flying off her eggs in terror, leaves one of her tail-feathers behind her, and once again the aggressor is foiled ; lashing his bushy tail with rage. This is one of those subjects which depend upon the "lost and found" for their charm. The Ring Dove's outline, like the Cat's, merges imperceptibly into the background, and we discover such portion of the detail as the artist wishes to reveal, only by looking for it. Look as we will, we cannot discover it all. "Because," says Wolf, "it is not there." The subject was also drawn with a Pine Marten in the place of the Cat.

In addition to these two admirable designs, there is an early version of "The Struggle" (a tussle between a Tiger and a Crocodile), which always seems to me to be a fine bit of work, though very slight. A pair of Jaguars and their cubs have come down to the water to slake their thirst, and the paw of the male has been seized by a huge Alligator. It is a case of "pull devil,

A Night Attack.

pull baker," and every fibre of the Jaguar's enormous muscles quivers in a contest which is still uncertain.

Touching this subject, and some others in which he has represented certain species of the *Felidæ* as associating together in complete families, Wolf holds that he was wrong. He says, " Why don't people " think ? Why must they still believe in *families* of " Lions ? . . . I do not know any quadruped where the " male has anything to do with bringing up the offspring. " This is one great fact in natural history. In nature " everything goes to utility. What fools a lot of Tom " Cats would look if every one of them were to bring " a mouse to the kittens. Of what use is the buck " Hare to bring up the leverets, the bull to bring up " the calf, or the stallion the foal ? It will be found " that as long as the Lioness is suckling her cubs the " Lion keeps away ; the Lioness, in fact, would not " allow him to come near them ; but afterwards, she is " not faithful to one Lion, and consequently several are " after her. Hence the troups of Lions one hears about. " Men are too much inclined to think that there must " be fathers, mothers and children."

He is quick to point out any inaccuracy in his work, such as he imagines the representation of the Jaguar's family to be, and other subjects of the kind, and tells you that he did so and so because he knew no better at that time. In this case, however, the point seems to be open to doubt, for we have the authority of Sir Samuel Baker that Tigers, at all events, are to be met

with in families.[1] Oswell, too, speaking of the dis-
inclination of Lions to attack men, says :—" When the
" cubs are very small the male will show fight, to give
" the Lioness a chance of making off with them, but
" this is rather a demonstration than real business." [2]
" The Lioness," says Wolf, " has several mates, and
" the young are not the offspring of one father. The
" old Lions will sometimes play with the half-grown
" cubs, but it has nothing to do with parental
" affection."

The willingness to admit error or ignorance is, as
I have already remarked, one of Wolf's characteristics. Touching an illustration of his to Montgomery's
Pelican Island he said, " Poor little chicks ! I have
" never seen Pelican chicks, you know, but I suppose
" they are something like them."

Again, he blames himself for having fallen into the
error in some of his drawings of Gorillas, of representing them as pot-bellied.

In the Lecture-room of The Zoological Society at
Hanover Square, among the other works of the artist
is a very careful chalk drawing of an adult Chimpanzee,

" It is frequently the custom of tigers to remain together in a family,
" the male, female, and a couple of half or three parts grown young ones.
" We cannot positively determine whether the male always remains with
" his family under such circumstances or whether he merely visits them
" periodically : I am inclined to the latter opinion, as I think the female
" may be attractive during her season, which induces the male to prolong
" his visit, although at other periods he may be leading an independent
" life." *Wild Beasts and Their Ways*, vol. i. p. 174.

Badminton *Big Game Shooting*, vol. i. p. 94.

executed in 1883 from a specimen living in The Gardens. On my remarking that the drawing was rather stiff (a very unusual fault with his work), Wolf said: "The drawing was done in exact profile, and "exactly natural size, in order to record the correct "measures. For years and years I had never seen an "old Chimpanzee—only young ones. I knew that "young children have big stomachs which they after- "wards lose. I forgot that it is the same with apes, "and in my early drawings I made the mistake of "representing the adults with large stomachs. Then "I saw this adult Chimpanzee, with full development "of limb and quite slim and elegant in shape."

An artist's calibre and sympathies cannot always be gauged by the subjects he paints as commissions, but when he settles down to work *con amore*, to work that he can brood over, the case is different. Our friend would be content to stand or fall by such drawings as the originals of the *Wild Animals*, but of the other class of work he says this :—"Whenever you work at a "commission you are always haunted by the thought, "'What will the man say to it? Will he like this or "that?' He has composed the subject in his own "mind, and it is a thousand to one that it is different "from one's own way."

"While I am labouring at an eye or a feather, "to get it quite true to nature, I suddenly think, "'Perhaps he would like it much better if it were "done in an off-hand, dashing way"; and I am sure "that if I paint beyond his comprehension, he will not "like the picture at all." Again, touching the indefinite or blurred appearance indicating the rapid movement of a bird's wings which I asked him about in a certain work, he said, "I tried hard to get it, but nobody would care for it."

This is not the first instance to be found in Joseph Wolf's sayings of a melancholy *cui bono*. He asks what is the use of labour, and knowledge, and years of study, if nobody—publisher, critic, or public, understands the result; and having asked it, he redoubles his care, and adds every possible item to his knowledge, with a great deal more than the humility of most students. He looks round him and sees that the greatest fame in zoological art and the highest prices have not always followed upon that fidelity to nature which concerns itself about the absolute correctness of an eye or a feather. Day after day he has faced the direct temptation to adapt his work to popular comprehension; to hide his knowledge under a bushel, and thus instantly to make himself master of the popular purse. He has faced it as his bitterest enemy, and has conquered.

The words of his I have quoted above deserve a little consideration, for they are a commentary on the unhappy fact that the manly struggle involved in honest workmanship goes for nothing against the popular delight in a sort of slapdash, sprawling sleight of hand, with an impudent signature as an important feature of it.

Joseph Wolf, at the time he drew the *Wild Animals* series, may be said to have reached his prime ; and he had reached it so quietly that neither himself nor anybody else knew when he did so. It was like the prime of some great oak ; for, as far as I can ascertain, he has been singularly free from that rapid falling off which has marked some artists' work ; due of course to failure of judgment, as well as perversion and failure of sight.

At the present time, in his seventy-fifth year, he says, " I think that with regard to sight I could paint " a better picture now than I could at forty. I saw too " much, you know. As Landseer said to a young " artist, ' You young fellows will never paint a decent " picture till your eye-sight begins to fail.'"

In spite of this opinion he has had the rare wisdom to hold his hand. Though, physically, full of vigour still —keen of sight, and hearing, and perception, he shows no touch of the unhappy infatuation which has tempted many a veteran artist steadily to paint away the reputation of his prime, in order, as it really seems, that he may be complimented upon being able to paint at all.

Wolf's position at his zenith was thus summed up by Mr. Edward Whymper in his preface to the *Wild Animals* :—

" As a painter, Mr. Wolf is highly esteemed among artists, but " his works are seldom exhibited, as they generally pass directly

"from his studio into the hands of the best judges and largest
"collectors in the kingdom. Upon this account he is, as a painter, not
"so generally known as many artists of less eminence ; but the
"solidity of the position he has attained is sufficiently evidenced by
"the eagerness with which his pictures are secured for the most
"princely collections in the country, and his success is the more
"remarkable since he owes nothing to notoriety."

The year after this was written, namely in 1874,
Wolf became a Member of The Institute of Painters
in Water Colours,[1] and exhibited there "Broken
Fetters," an upright subject representing a Golden
Eagle escaping from captivity to his snow-capped
mountains, with the fragment of the chain still attached
to his leg.[2] The drawing was done in a week, and
the Eagle was most carefully painted. In the review
of The Institute exhibition *The Observer* remarks :—

"There are no less than seven new Members, who have not, as
"usual, been selected from a list of candidates, but have been
"specially invited to exhibit their works. Of these works, however,
"a good drawing by Mr. Wolf, the well-known animal painter, . . .
"is the only contribution we observe which makes much mark."
"Another remarkable drawing in The Institute," writes the critic of
The Times, "is a magnificent Golden Eagle soaring aloft, with the
"broken chain dangling from his strong talons, by J. Wolf, the most
"vigorous living painter of wild animal life."

The Athenæum says this :—

"Mr. J. Wolf has long ago recommended himself to admiring
"eyes ; his *Broken Fetters* (148), an eagle soaring near a mountain
"top, which is surrounded by mists and denser vapours, while the
"bird's feet are trammelled by the ropes which formerly kept it
"captive, shows at once his great powers and the unfavourable cir-
"cumstances under which he practises his art, for he must needs

[1] He has lately resigned.
[2] This drawing was purchased by Lord Eldon.

"make a subject where, but for popular notions, none would be
"wanted. The result of making a subject here is to injure the in-
"spiration of the picture. But the bird, apart from this, is a most
"vigorous piece of design ; one can hardly think of anything more
"intense than the action of the wings, the eager thrusting of the
"neck, as the creature hovers above its home."

The melancholy sequel to "Broken Fetters" was
drawn in charcoal some time afterwards. The Eagle
has reached his old haunts, and settles for a moment,
that he may gaze down into the ravine which still
shelters, perhaps, the beloved eyrie. He spreads his
wings again ; but the chain has caught in a fork of the
tree, and after the fierce death struggle, he hangs head
downwards, swaying in the wind.

Wolf's election as a Member of The Institute did
not tend, as might have been supposed, to his becoming
a prolific exhibitor. It is one of those points on which
I must venture to differ with my friend that he prefers
his oil pictures to his water-colours. He says, " I wish
"I had stuck to oil as I began, and never listened to
"some friends in the Water-Colour Society and joined
"them." His sympathy is certainly more with oil-
painting than with water-colour. "Water-colour is
"thin and weak compared with oil." Nevertheless, I
have seen water-colours of his so strong that at the first
glance I actually mistook them for oil, but I have never
seen one which struck me as weak.

Another deterrent was this. When he told one
of his employers that he should like to exhibit such and
such a work at The Institute, the gentleman would

probably say, "And what is 'The Institute'?" If he went there to see how his purchase looked, he found it, perhaps, conspicuous for singularity of subject, among "heaps of coast scenes and landscapes piled up to the skies." Speaking at another time of the fewness of the works which he has exhibited anywhere, Wolf gives the chief reason. "The prejudice of artists against natural "history has stood in my way more than anything in "England. It was before a committee of that class "of men, that I should have had to appear with my "works if I had exhibited. I couldn't do it, and I "didn't do it." I look upon this feeling of Wolf's with the same regret that troubles me when he states his case against the naturalists, and for the same reason; that the grievance is not imaginary. It is based upon actual incidents and actual statements which have come to his knowledge. It is of little avail to go into the question. Suffice it to say that the artists among whom Wolf is accounted a mere "naturalist," have never seen many of his finest works. Had they seen them, I cannot help thinking they would have changed their opinion. The subject has an amusing side. "I had "a world of trouble," says our friend, "to get the very "printers and lithographers to pay *common respect* to "my things. Because they were 'natural history,' "they looked upon them as if they were for children's "picture-books."

I have not been able to give more than the land-marks of the history of Wolf's work during the fourteen years of his residence in Berners Street. He has kept no journal or record in any shape, and has forgotten much that was worthy to be remembered. He may say, as he does, "What a record it would be!" but, nevertheless, I regret the want of it deeply. An artist's works are the children of his imagination, if they have any definite parentage at all. They reflect the conscious and often the unconscious bent of his mind, and the depth of his mind. Naturally, he himself can see more in them than the critic, however learned and discriminating ; and the artist alone can recall the incidents of their birth and growth. Then too, they are often the outcome of a struggle more or less intense to realize some ideal ; to touch, or enthral, or to teach— to tell some story, the incidents of which are naturally best known to the teller. It always strikes me as sad that so many works are exhibited, collected, dispersed by the hammer, and forgotten, without an inkling beyond the critic's technical description (often given in terms only intelligible to artists), or the auctioneer's hap-hazard puff, of what they represented in the painter's own mind. What does the astute dealer know or care about the emotions and struggles, sleepless nights, and miserable days ? Even the title sometimes changes with the ownership of the picture ; and the very point of the story it was intended to indicate (if it is told unobtrusively) is often completely stultified.

It may be imagined, from what I have told of this fourteen years of Wolf's life, that a man who some-

times went on working till he was giddy, whose natural
industry forbade all waste of time, whose every touch
was the result of knowledge and thought—it may be
imagined what he would accomplish, and how he would
ripen and mature.

A sort of migratory impulse seizes us sometimes,
as irresistible as that which drives the Swallow and
Nightingale from our shores. In 1874 Joseph Wolf
determined to leave Berners Street, and he chose The
Avenue, Fulham Road, as his next head-quarters,
where a small colony of artists was established, with
everything adapted to their habits and liking.

Visitors to his studio, soon after he took possession,
would have found him, pliers and wire in hand, sitting
before a pile of little bones and a charcoal sketch.
He had another Ring Dove subject in progress, and
was carefully setting up a complete skeleton of the
bird in the chosen action. " You have no idea," he
says, " how it explains the attitudes if the legs and feet
are in the right place." The title of this drawing
is " Inquisitive Neighbours." Two Squirrels, frolicking round and round the stem of a pine, pop suddenly
on a Ring Dove sitting on her eggs. She is indignant
at the invasion of her particular tree, and loosens her
wings in order to give full effect to a good buffet.[1]

---

[1] To country people, a boxing match between a couple of Ring Doves
in the spring is doubtless familiar ; but some have no idea of the force and
vigour of the blows they shower on one another with their wings, or of
the noise thus occasioned. I have seen a fight of this kind last a long time.

INQUISITIVE NEIGHBOURS.

The first sketch of this subject hangs, through the artist's kindness, on my walls ; and I have often seen the third version (a water-colour), which lacks, I think, some of the vigour of the sketch. The bird is as fine a piece of colour and drawing as one could wish to see ; but perhaps it is the elaboration of the surrounding foliage that gives the impression of a redundancy of minute finish. I have reproduced the second version, a careful charcoal drawing.

In preferring the first sketch, I must plead guilty to doing so in many other instances, particularly in Wolf's case. The first sketches are dashed off with an impulse, and are the first-fruits of the imagination. As the impulse is often a kind of inspiration, they are done with enthusiasm. They may contain many faults, but, nevertheless, often represent the artist's ripest powers, for he is on his mettle, and they do not show the reserve or forbearance brought about by considering whether they will sell, or be severely criticised, or be hung beyond human ken. Sketches, in fact, though they are often the amateur's most effectual offensive weapon, are the true artist's shorthand. Every scratch, or dot, or smudge has its own peculiar significance, and is essential to the coherency and sense of the whole composition.

At the Academy exhibitions of 1876 and 1877 Wolf was represented by casts from three little models ; a Wild Boar ; a Bear licking his lips over a honeycomb ; and " Suspicion," a Lioness with two cubs, alarmed by some danger in front of them. Although he was not altogether unpractised in the art of modelling (for he had found out its value in solving problems of light and shade, and cast shadows), one would hardly expect to find such a complete mastery over means and material as is represented by these three miniature animals. Not only are the anatomy and actions first-rate, but the texture of the different coats is admirably given. " It " is very difficult," says Wolf, " for anybody who has " begun modelling to leave it. It is so fascinating to " a *painter*, simply because it is far more simple than " painting. You have no local colour, or light and shade "—no perspective, no atmosphere, and so on. In fact, " comparing the painter with the sculptor, the painter " must know all that the sculptor knows (or ought to " know), and a great deal more."

I believe that very few casts from these models were disposed of, but it seems a pity that the moulds should have been idle for so many years. Casts in bronze shown in some good gallery would surely have commanded a great sale. It also seems a pity that, with the exception of an Owl which was never exhibited and another Wild Boar's head, Wolf should have done so little finished work in clay. The Owl is four times life-size, and a very careful piece of work. I once ventured to suggest that the eyes were too big. " Yes," said Wolf, " when you know that the eye is big you are apt to make it too big." The temptation to exaggerate is very seductive in art, and literature, and

A Bear with Honeycomb.

conversation ; but it is very rarely that Wolf yields to
it in any form, though no one is keener in seizing the
point of view which brings characteristics sufficiently
into prominence. I have noticed his love of truth crop
up in many ways ; and have myself often been brought
down from some too enthusiastic description of animals
or insects to the regions of actual fact, by a smile or
a question.

The 24th of May 1878 was likely to have made an
impression on our friend's memory, for he was commissioned by The Marquis of Lorne and The Princess
Louise to paint them a birthday present for the Queen.
The subject was a pet Bullfinch of Her Majesty's, and
if this had not been a bird with which the painter was
thoroughly familiar, he might have found it nervous
work, and have been tempted to compile a Bullfinch
from sketches. As it was, he made a succession of
visits to Buckingham Palace, and laboured in his
usual way to make the drawing a true *portrait*, as well
as a graceful composition. Judging from the original
study (itself highly finished) which recently hung in his
studio, the result must have been most satisfactory.

I will conclude this chapter with the following note
from Lord Lorne about this drawing, quoted with his
Lordship's kind permission :—

Kensington Palace : May 20, 1878.

DEAR MR. WOLF,—We are much obliged to you for the care
and trouble you have taken to have the charming picture of the Bullfinch ready in such good time. If you should want to do anything
more to it, or if the Queen would like any slight alteration, it can

always be got back for a short time. It seems to me perfect as it is.

I am glad that Mr. Dresser does not think the getting of the Hazel Grouse would be very difficult in Scandinavia. I am most anxious to get them, and having failed both at Paris and Berlin, should much like to be put into communication with any friend of Mr. Dresser's who might be able to procure them. I am almost sure they would do among the large woods at Inveraray if the birds are brought from a Northern country. I return Mr. Dresser's letter. I remain with many thanks yours faithfully.

J. Wolf, Esq. LORNE.

Lord Lorne has been so good as to inform me that he was, unfortunately, not successful in this attempt to acclimatize the Hazel Grouse

OVIS AMMON

THE JAPANESE BEAR.

CHAPTER VI

JOSEPH WOLF found it a long journey from the Fulham Road to his models in Regent's Park, and knowing that a little swarm of artists was comfortably hived in Primrose Hill Studios, he began to contemplate a third migration. The Studios were so near the northern entrance of The Zoological Gardens that, on a quiet summer's night, an imaginative tenant might think himself far away in foreign lands, till some rattling hansom dispelled the illusion. This propinquity settled the question; so in 1878 our friend removed to No. 2 ; and there he has dwelt ever since, till by virtue of seniority, both of years and occupation, he has become the patriarch of the colony. He has acquired, too, a certain affection for the place ; and though, at last, he has had to pile away his bird-cages, and will no more listen to the songs of his Warblers and Bullfinches, he has been able, as we shall see, to give another hobby a little rein.

To describe our friend "at home" is not an easy matter ; but it is only by mentally accompanying me to his studio, that the reader will be able to see him at his best, or to realize the profusion of intensely interesting things which it contains.

In answer to the tinkle of the bell at No. 2 Primrose Hill Studios, a tall, broad-chested old gentleman appears, pipe in hand, at a door which is fringed with climbing convolvulus and ivy. Happily there is nothing " artistic" about him, unless it be a knitted " Tam o' Shanter" cap. His hale, upright figure is clothed in the well-cut vestments of a quietly disposed Londoner (to whom eccentricity would be as unnatural as slovenliness), and his short, grey beard and moustache are neatly trimmed. A pair of very large round spectacles rests on a nose which has the strong angular bend of the Eagle's beak about it, but nothing of the semicircular Jewish curve. The wide nostrils appear to be drawn back so as to cause upon the cheeks the furrows to which the expression of the face is partly due. Behind the spectacles are very kindly, true-looking, grey eyes, in which a merry twinkle is not unknown.

Following my friend down a short passage, I find myself in a lofty and well-designed studio, which, in spite of its size, is pre-eminently cosy—easily warmed in the winter, and as I find now, cool even on the sunniest summer's day. On the blinds flying back, I can see at once that there is much to attract the attention on every side ; but to begin with I discover, fast asleep upon a Leopard skin, two very fat, very nondescript, and very tiny puppies. This is not their

true home, but their dissipated little mother long
ago discovered that their brothers and sisters were
always welcomed by her big friend, and she leaves them
here out at nurse as it were.

Wolf is anxious to give me the latest news of the
studios, and he tells it in remarkably well-chosen
English idioms. There is no gesticulation, no shoulder-
shrugging. The manner, like the words, is even
quieter than that of many a Briton. Some brave
Blackbirds have nested for several years in the ivy at
the back, and this year, again, have hatched their
young successfully. It is a secret (undoubtedly known
to many cats), but he is as glad to tell me all about
the nest as if it were at least a Golden Eagle's eyrie.
As for those cats, they were so troublesome last year
that he tells me he used to call the young birds every
evening, catch them one by one with a butterfly net,
and cage them till the morning. He wishes to point
out to me the site of the nest, and before he opens a
back door leading to the garden, he mixes a saucer of
bread and milk which I imagine is intended for the
puppies. But directly we get into the open air I see,
upon the neighbouring roofs and walls, an excited little
troop of Starlings awaiting their early luncheon. He
speaks of the precocity of the London Blackbirds ; and
we find, on comparing notes, that they are in full song
here long before they find their voices in the Surrey
wilds. He loves them greatly, and considers them the
noblest of the Thrushes.

The garden surprises me. When Wolf first came here, he tells me, it was a forlorn back yard where even the ivy looked sulky and disappointed in life. There was just one solitary carnation ; and this, as his mother's favourite flower, somehow or other recalled those remote days spent with her so happily at home. So, thinking to himself that he would revive the old memories still more, he set to work in earnest. The yard was common to two of the studios, but Wolf has lavished upon his neighbour's share, as well as his own, so much time and pains, that he has conquered the disadvantages. Of his feline enemies, a dingy, tailless specimen accosted him one day, purring and rubbing against his legs so vigorously that he had not the heart to drive her away. Since then she has disputed with the Starlings, and the Blackbirds, and a tame Toad that lives in a corner, their several claims to the master's attention. Some of the refinements of the florist's art are going on. Seeds and seedlings engross my host's spare time, and try even his patience. Hand-glasses, cocoa-fibre, and thermometers, would point out the nature of his favourite hobby, even without the piles of florists' catalogues indoors. " To have a hobby," he says, " is the only expression of happiness. The " man who has not got a hobby is to be pitied." " It " is quite as much pleasure to me," he continues, as he slides off the lid from one of his frames, " to see " the seeds sprout and come up nicely, as to see the " flowers open. It is the principle that the anticipa-

"tion is sweeter than the possession." You would think he had that passage of Dudley Warner's in his mind :—" To own a bit of ground, to scratch it with a " hoe, to plant seeds, and watch their renewal of life, " —this is the commonest delight of the race, the most " satisfactory thing a man can do."

It is, in fact, the renewal of *life*—the reawakening of all nature in the spring, that especially rejoices Wolf, as (in spite of the renewal of " Pusley "), it rejoiced Dudley Warner. He says, " The first awakening of " spring is signalled to my studio by a South American " bird at The Zoological Gardens—Cariama, I think.[1] " It is a long-legged species which lives on the prairies " where their strong voice is the means of keeping the " birds together." This spring note fills him with pleasant recollections of very early days, when he used to listen anxiously for the laugh of the Green Wood-pecker and the cry of the Buzzard. Other recollec-tions of spring are sometimes called into existence in the country, he tells me, by the piping of children's willow whistles ; a sound which seems to him by no means devoid of poetry, simply because it carries his mind back to the time when, himself intent on whistles, he waited for the rising sap.

When he has shown me his favourite flowers, he turns to another part of the garden. " People say " we can't grow roses here in London. Now here's a " rose—and what a rose it is, by Jove !" pointing to one

[1] *Cariama cristata.*

shamefaced little blossom on a weazen bush, that
" looks as planted by Despair."

Re-entering the studio, we pass by a large glass
case standing beneath a mighty Moose's head (a
present sent by Mr. D. G. Elliott from America), which
stares out upon the room as a kind of presiding genius.
The case contains (besides the little models already
described), part of the artist's collection of fire-arms.
They have evidently been kept in order by a keen
connoisseur ; though they date from the far-distant time
when their owner superintended their building with as
much care as he set about a picture ; and when he loved
a good autumnal tramp over the heather or turnips.
Among the guns and shooting paraphernalia he has
elsewhere is one of the ponderous small-bores which
were used so effectively in the *Vögelschiessen*, many
years ago.

Besides the Moose there are many other heads of
Deer and Antelope round the walls, ranging in size from
the Wapiti downwards.   Opposite the garden door, in
a long line across the room, hang the original drawings of the *Wild Animals*, which, in this fine light,
look their very best.   As time presses, I am compelled
to pass onwards, bearing with me the impression,
firstly, that drawings so hard to interpret and so
dependent on suggestiveness must have vexed the soul
of the engravers : and secondly that, considering their
price, it is extraordinary they have remained so long
unsold.

A PEREGRINE TIERCEL.

Round the room there stand a number of huge and cavernous box-portfolios, which contain so many of Wolf's sketches and studies that not to-day nor for many a day shall I exhaust them. The artist himself has his doubts about some of the contents ; and if the whereabouts of a sketch is once forgotten, long-continued burrowing in these seductive depths becomes necessary in order to recover it ; sometimes even that being unsuccessful. One of these searches, to an admirer of Wolf's works, is intensely exciting, for there is no knowing what will turn up next. Even his never-failing pipe is mislaid and forgotten, and many are the exclamations of astonishment as long-lost sketches meet the eyes of their maker once again. Now a little batch of chalk life-studies appears ; and then a lovely life-size charcoal design of a Peregrine tiercel ; the first idea of a picture exhibited at the Sports and Arts Exhibition.[1]

Continuing the search I come, perhaps, to a drawing in the same material by Mr. Carl Haag, the result of an exchange,[2] and groping right at the bottom

[1] Any reproduction will fail to convey the beauty of this sketch ; the skill of the modelling ; the grace of the attitude ; and the mastery of the draughtsmanship. Like many of the artist's sketches, it is done on thin paper (often whity-brown), and the outline has been scored over with a hard point in transferring it.

[2] Among the opinions of his brother artists on Wolf's work, that of so great a veteran as Mr. Haag should find a place. For this I am indebted to Mr. Howard of Blackburn. Speaking of the black and white drawing "A Midnight Ramble," in his possession, Mr. Howard says, "At the time "I purchased the work, Mr. Wolf told me that he made a water-colour "drawing from this for Mr. Carl Haag ; and when I called on Mr. Haag

of the box, I grasp (much to our friend's astonishment) a little chalk design of " Wild Duck Shooting." This excellent drawing was intentionally hidden some time ago to avoid lending it on the application of an artist who proposed to paint the same subject much in the same way. Dropped into one of these boxes, it was nearly as much beyond recovery as a letter in a pillar-box : and short of a day's search, only a sheer accident such as this could lead to its exhumation. Another time, and in quite a different latitude, I come across the companion subject, " Wild Goose Shooting in a Fog " ; and the two drawings together are a goodly pair. It is noteworthy that, in both, the shooters are not at first seen at all. They are a gunshot off, and are nearly hidden, in one case by the long reeds, in the other by the fog. In the latter design we may see in perfection the quality of indefiniteness. It is this which gives the singular reality to the birds which approach in their panic out of the gloom.

We have not done with the first portfolio yet ; and when we have, there are others quite as interesting. There is no sort of arrangement, and among a quantity of uninteresting photographs, or a few quires of virgin paper, there may lurk one or two of Wolf's very best sketches, long mourned as lost. Far below and all but out of reach may glow even one of his little water-

"last autumn I saw it . . . Mr. Haag told me that, in his opinion, no
"man in the world could approach Mr. Wolf at his own class of work.
"I was delighted to hear this from Mr. Haag, for it is the opinion which
"I have long held."

colours, such as the Ring Dove of *The Poets of the Woods* series, or other works he describes as "the few crumbs of good things I have left."

Promising myself further exploration of these rich artistic catacombs another day, I glance hurriedly over the book-cases holding a few books of reference (but very few), and some of the works our friend has illustrated; from Knox's little volumes, to the huge folios which it is almost impossible to handle with any comfort; books such as Gould's *Birds of Great Britain* and Elliott's monographs, fit only for the scientific athlete. Thus, by degrees, I find myself facing the easels.

The foremost holds one of those large charcoal designs so many of which have gone (as this will go) from the studio direct to the purchaser, without exhibition. Apart from its beauty as a work of art, it is notable as representing a rare and singular scene. A Snow Leopard has stalked some of the gigantic sheep which Marco Polo discovered; "twelve and a "half hands high, the horns (each some six feet long) "forming a wide, open curve." It is a critical moment, for they have winded their enemy, hidden behind a snow-drift. He hears their abrupt movement, and raises his head to reconnoitre. "The Aggressor shall "not succeed. I always disappoint my animal of "prey." So says my host as he draws away a curtain which veils the second easel. Here I see, in an early stage, a life-size oil-picture which is striking from its

vigour, originality, and draughtsmanship. A hungry
Golden Eagle, sailing down from the neighbouring
peaks, launches from the mist and vainly strikes at an
Alpine Hare which leaps madly towards us. The
huge bird is enraged at his failure, and the force of
the swoop is shown by his extended wings and tail,
and the outstretched foot which viciously grips the
heather instead of the Hare.[1] It is the aggressor
foiled again with a vengeance. The artist has painted
a somewhat similar subject in water-colour, and has the
first charcoal sketch. Here the Eagle has struck one
of a pack of Ptarmigan, and grasps the tail-feathers on
the ground while the bird flies off otherwise unscathed.
This Eagle is even more vigorous in design than the
other; but not the least interesting point in the
finished drawing was the gradual discovery of the
rest of the Ptarmigan, concealed by the artist much
as they would be in nature. This, I believe, created
quite a sensation in the purchaser's family when the
picture was sent home. "I've found one!" "Here's
another!" and so on.

In the oil subject, part of the single-primed canvas
is still bare, and the painting is in an early stage.
The life and soul of the picture is yet to come,
but there is nothing tentative about the preliminary
work. Before he put charcoal to paper, the precon-
ception in the artist's mind was definite. "It

---

[1] It was a study for this Hare which received such complimentary
care from the Basset-hounds.

PTEROMYS GRANDIS.

must be here, you know," says Wolf, touching his forehead, " before it comes out there "—holding up his fingers. There is so much painting (art it can hardly be called), that shows the inability of the brain to create a subject, or to keep pace with the exquisite manipulative skill, that an opinion such as this is refreshing.

Unfortunately, the prospects of this fine work are not bright. Wolf says, " I couldn't venture to finish " it. I should go mad over it. The rheumatism has " stood a good deal in my way. I have had it now " for fifteen years." Sometimes, for weeks together, he is not able to put pencil or pen to paper, knowing that if he did so the wearisome pain would begin in the affected arm ; and from the same cause he dreads the vibration of a cab and many other things. It is the one black spot in an otherwise singularly healthy, painless life.

He tells me that a rich merchant was once brought to see this picture. " Why," he asked, " is the Eagle " sitting on its haunches in such an undignified way ? " " He has just struck at the Hare and missed her." " Does it want the Hare then ? " " Yes, of course." " Then why," said the critic triumphantly, as he turned away, " doesn't it peck at it with its beak ? " " The " thing I have most suffered from," continues the painter, " is the general ignorance about my subjects, " not only with purchasers, but with hanging-com- " mittees ; and my greatest difficulty has been to

" fathom the depth of this ignorance. Landscape
" painters have alluded to my work as ' *Natural*
" *History and that sort of thing.*' I have been
" continually swimming against the stream, chiefly
" with regard to the choice of subjects. I always
" found that the popular subjects were utterly im-
" possible for me, and against my nature. This was
" a great disadvantage in the world."

Speaking of his works having been sometimes condemned as mere transcripts from nature, he says : " If
" you paint a dead Redpoll or Linnet it is admissible
" at the Royal Academy. If you paint it alive it is a
" Transcript of an object of Natural History, ' *and that*
" *sort of thing,*' unfit for exhibition. Artists have been
" known to congratulate themselves that they have
" no knowledge of natural history. . . . In fact natural-
" history subjects do not go down unless they are very
" badly done." These are opinions which may sound
exaggerated, but the truth of them can be proved,
and is proved by the walls of our chief exhibitions
every year. Yet there is hope for the glorious art of
which Wolf was the pioneer ; for, as he says, it is
still in its infancy.

Near the easels hang a few oil studies of heads
from the life, which were done at Antwerp ; and they
show much more freedom of execution than I should
have expected to find at that period. There are not
many canvases in the studio, but there is one standing
against the wall which, in my opinion, helps to show

THE SIAMANG.
(A Water-colour Sketch from Life.)

that although oil is certainly not the material best
suited to the artist, it is one in the use of which he
has attained the greatest freedom and rapidity. This
sketch was painted in a day, and is called "Come down
in the World." A chained Golden Eagle, melancholy,
savage, and banished to a pig-sty, mopes away his
life, envying the impudent Sparrows which hop in
and out of his prison.

Another notable instance of rapidity resulting not
only from exhaustive knowledge but from perfect
technical mastery, involving all the refinements of perspective, foreshortening, modelling, and light and
shade, is dragged out from a dark corner. It is a life-
size charcoal study, made in a day and a half, for a
picture which was never painted, "The Lion and the
Wasp." The little insect has accidentally invaded the
cave, upon the floor of which some bones lie scattered,
and buzzes busily about in its anxiety to get out again.
As for the owner, he cringes down upon the ground, a
perfect picture of power and fear—fear at the sound he
cannot account for. His head is, perhaps, one of the
best examples of Wolf's almost incredible skill in
catching the exact expression of animals. There is
something here which separates this representation of
a Lion from all others I have seen ; and what that
something is, it is not easy to say.

Some of the works which are stacked against the
walls of the studio are highly-finished charcoal drawings
which were done for the meetings of The German

Athenæum (the chief of which drawings I have already described) ; and conspicuous among the remainder is a large and important water-colour. It is called "A Row in the Jungle," and a tremendous row it is. A Tiger creeps through the dense undergrowth towards the spectator, his lithe body flattened down, and his hide and massive limbs harmonizing in colour but contrasting in form with the tangled, flaunting vegetation which half conceals the skull of a Gaur. Overhead, a crowd of Rhesus Macaques follow their enemy's movements, with hideous uproar and every expression of fear and hatred. This subject has given the artist scope for the exercise of his love for rich, harmonious colour ; and like several smaller works, it shows how he prefers to represent the Tiger. One of them, in fact, gives us little more than the ferocious head framed by the exotic foliage.

"A Row in the Jungle" was exhibited at the Royal Academy of 1863, and thus has been more than thirty years on the painter's hands. I dare say he is not very anxious to part with it, for it is almost the solitary example he has left of his larger water-colour works.

Next, he shows me an unfinished water-colour version rather than replica of the *Ovis poli* subject, for he very rarely allows himself to paint a replica in the ordinary sense. So completely do some of the best of his black and white drawings convey the sense of colour, that this version does not strike me as new. I was prepared by the black and white for the rosy snow with its pearly shadows, and for the rich colour of the animals.

Never ceasing to strive after truth and the highest possible ideal, he points out that the expressions and characters of the animals in the water-colour are more ovine, and therefore more true, than they are in the other version, perfect as that appears to be.

A SKETCH OF OVIS POLI IN SNOW

The method by which these water-colours are done I shall briefly describe ; but for the present it will suffice to say that it is distinguished by order, and by conscientious, patient workmanship, in which the skill is far too great to suggest labour. There is no symptom of niggle, no littleness, no slobber, and no slapdash. But, nevertheless, his method is not quite so simple as it looks, and when the washing in of a sky is in progress, or any other delicate piece of manipulation that requires " the whole man," visitors at No. 2, The Studios may tinkle the bell in vain.

I ask him if he has ever kept any kind of record of his work, and he answered :—" Sometimes I did two " or three things in a day—What a record it would be ! " I have done many works of which I should be ashamed " to have a record. When you undertake a lot of work, " you may like part of it, but a vast quantity of it is " rubbish to you. As a rule, when I got something to " do which I didn't like, I tackled it at once, in order " to get rid of it." This strikes me as being one of the most important elements of his success ; and it reminds me of the advice of a certain successful drawing-master to his pupils, " Do the most disagreeable thing first."

On a chair opposite the lofty north window I discover a peculiar-looking long, narrow skull, with a label attached to it. Our friend introduces this as part of a new species of Antelope sent to him by the Secretary of The Zoological Society, who wishes for a drawing of the animal. I suggest that the material is perhaps a little scanty, but he says he has the hide in the next room. There I find that, on a kind of wooden horse, the crumpled skin of the new species displays its stiffness. This interpretation, as the reader will remember, is familiar work. Granted that Wolf has

THE SIAMANG.
(*Unfinished Water-Colour Sketch from Life.*)

known the relatives of the animals (and there are very few animals of which he does not know the relatives), he has many and many a time evolved from the skull and the tanned hide a highly-finished and beautiful drawing; or (if we prefer so to call it), a "correct figure." It is not a power which has come from mere repetition, but a power derived chiefly from the altogether remarkable faculty of observation and memory, and from the same sound and extensive knowledge that enabled him to make you an impromptu sketch of any beast or bird you wished, in the most difficult attitude you could suggest. This is the knowledge that guided the charcoal so well as to entrance the veteran Oswell, while he was transferring by word of mouth the stirring scenes of his African life from his own powerful imagination to one even more powerful. The artist's numberless studies of the structure and detail of mammals and birds have been a means to this end.

In the room where the hide hangs on its stand there are more box-portfolios; and who knows what they contain? Probably even their owner has forgotten; for a man who keeps no record whatever of the hard work of sixty years must needs have a memory if he can recall the details.

Among the studio furniture, but standing back in a recess, is a large, comfortable-looking, old-fashioned sofa, covered with the skins of beasts. It seems a sofa, pure and simple, but when we have tugged off the heavy cushion, behold the handle of a lid! I raise this

R

lid and reveal untold treasure, the discovery of which
makes an epoch in the life of a lover of art and of
animals. Hidden away here for years, in the bowels
of an unobtrusive piece of furniture, innumerable rolls
of paper composed of the first sketches of the cream of
a life's work have reposed.

Some of the designs are so beautiful and perfect in
the higher qualities of light and shade, and composition,
and *expression*, that, to a lover of sketches like myself,
they are far more interesting than the more elaborate
works of which they were the precursors. To make
use of the musical simile once more, they resemble an
infinitely touching, infinitely simple air, rather than the
complex, scientific, instrumental display. And yet they
show rare mastery, because they are the true offspring
of a cultured mind ; and the extraordinary knowledge
which has called them into being is mental as well as
manipulative. They show no trick of execution, no
mannerism, no sameness. In every case they bring us
face to face with nature without an effort and without
technical display ; and yet to the trained eye it is easy
to see that the technique is of the highest order. What
the hand has caused the chalk to express with a few
touches in as many seconds, it has taken years of hard,
devoted study to master. Indeed, if we believe the
evidence of some of the best judges in existence, sup-
ported in a humble way by the evidence of our own
senses, only one man has mastered it.

The sketches, for the most part, are in black chalk

upon plain "whity-brown," or "continuous cartoon" paper. They include, in the first place, the whole series of the designs which were reproduced in lithography for Mr. Elliott's monographs of the Cats, the Birds of Paradise, and the Pheasants ; and however much the lithographs might be preferred to the sketches for scientific purposes by scientific men, no trained artist would hesitate one instant in his choice between the two. They prove again, with irresistible evidence, the rule to which there seem to be no exceptions, that the bloom, so to speak, of Wolf's work—its more subtle refinements, and that which isolates it, inevitably die under other hands than his own, a death violent or gentle as the case may be.

The search in this great treasure-chest is too exciting and important to be compassed in a day, for no Egyptologist has unrolled the papyri that revealed the history of some unknown king, with more painful excitement and suspense than I feel as I read the inscription and strip off the grimy cover of each package. There are surprises too, not only for me, but for the artist. As usual, his pipe goes out as the old friends of his prime, with all their associations, greet him once more ; from some little Tiger-cat a few inches long, to a nearly life-size Elk bayed by Wolves. He recalls his valiant efforts, by means of skilfully placed twigs or flower-stems, to bend the tails of Pheasants aside, so that they shall come within the prescribed boundaries (and those no narrow ones) of an *édition de luxe* and yet look natural. A good deal besides the mere names and habitats of the species returns to his memory, and at last he says quietly, " I have done a good deal of work in my time."

Some of the sketches are for life-size Eagle pictures ; but the birds have a whole prairie of paper round them, and merely the marginal lines of the subjects are shown, or a few indications of the backgrounds. Touching the large margin the artist said, " An Eagle in a con-" fined space looks wretched—where he can't move, " you know. It went rather against me in painting " bird pictures, that very idea, to say nothing of the " enormous canvases life-size Eagles and Falcons " require. We are accustomed to see birds in plenty " of space." As a protest against the opposite, he has sometimes painted a subject such as " Come down in the World," just referred to, or " Spring in Seven Dials," where a poor Skylark in a tiny cage, pours forth to the sky of St. Martin's-in-the-Fields, the song he longs to sing once more in fields of a different kind.

Scarcely anything in the studio is locked up, but a small oaken cabinet is an exception. On being opened, the drawers are found to be crammed with plethoric little portfolios about the size of an octavo book ; and into these, again, are crushed hundreds of carefully classified sketches in all materials, of mammals, birds, reptiles, trees, foreground and other foliage, landscapes, mountains, and even wild-flowers. Each portfolio bears its own German inscription, such as " Falcons,"

THE SIAMANG.

(From an Unfinished Water-Colour Sketch from Life.)

" Eagles," " Grouse and Partridges,' " Small Cats," " Large Cats," " Antelopes," &c. ; and each lies in its own appointed place. There are no surprises here, for every sketch in the multitude, and every incident attending it are known to the author, to say nothing of the life history of every subject. He knows them as well as a carpenter knows his own bradawls and gimlets from his mate's ; and, indeed, these sketches may not inaptly be termed Wolf's well-worn bradawls, gimlets, and chisels. They have been used so often in his work that most of them are vignetted with the grime of a thousand thumbings, from the thumbs not only of himself, but of his friends. Some of the sketches are highly finished, and many of these are the originals of the auto-lithographs which were done for *The Proceedings* of The Zoological Society. In a separate division of their own are those early miniatures I have so often referred to, sparkling, glowing, and inexplicable as ever, after nearly half a century has passed.

The first feeling on looking at the contents of this cabinet is one of deep regret that they have not been more carefully preserved. They have been rubbed together and shuffled like cards ; exposed to the soot which gently falls without ceasing inside a London drawer ; held by the same fingers which were revelling in the magical smudges of the large charcoal drawings, and generally evilly entreated. They show, in fact, the signs of constant use which the implements of all hard workers bear upon them. The next thing to strike me is the literally enormous power of drawing, and of seizing upon the essential points and characters peculiar to each in a thousand animate and inanimate objects. As to the lovely art of expression—of conveying the appearance of much finish and modelling . by slight work, we find it here in perfection, and numbers of instances might be given. As an example of elaboration, showing how the power I have alluded to has been acquired, I may mention the feet and tarsi of a Goshawk, Buzzard, Heron, and others. The object of these drawings was to learn thoroughly the anatomy, and the arrangement and detail of the scales and scutellæ. So Wolf sat himself down (in the same dogged spirit as when he began to copy the engraving of the Queen of Prussia) and drew an elaborate map, giving the individual shape of each scale, and its exact relative position.

Touching the small number of people who can tell at a glance the right foot of a bird from the left, if not attached to the body, he gives a ready method. " The inner toe has one joint only, the one next the " tarsus without the nail. The middle toe has two " joints and the nail ; the outer toe has one more. And " with regard to the claws, particularly with the Birds of " Prey, the inner toe has a claw as strong as the claw " on the hind toe. These two toes meet in clutching."

It is always a good sign when the opposite poles of the artistic globe can be discovered in an artist's portfolios, showing equal mastery—the utmost freedom and learned slightness, and the utmost elaboration which brush or pencil can convey to paper. " I don't " admire a man," says Pascal, " that enjoyeth a Vertue " in its full perfection, unless he does at the same time " possess in the like degree the opposite Vertue. . . . " One does not show his Greatness by being in an " extream, but by touching þoth extreams at once, and " filling up the vacant space."

But now, overhead in the gallery my host added to the studio, for the purpose I described before, a mysterious kettle begins to sing its cheery summons to an evening meal. Mounting a narrow staircase which takes me by the insect cases, I have a bird's-eye view of all below, and can return the stare of the great Moose. It is up here that the essentially bachelor and essentially simple character of Wolf's life reveal themselves. There is a small gas-stove ; and on this, for many years, he has cooked an omelette for breakfast, and for dinner, a piece of stewed beef large enough for the Starlings and Sparrows to share with him. For many years he has daily divided his omelette into a certain number of pieces, and washed down his beef with a strict ration of bottled beer or whiskey and water. There is an attendant or two about the studios of course, but our friend finds it much more satisfactory to be independent as we are here to-day. Mellow claret and ancient whiskey can be produced from a dark recess (mysteriously connected with a store of his favourite anthracite coal), for the old friends who often come to smoke the pipe of peace ; but we are both fond of plain living, and are content with simpler fare.

I see that for several hours every day the sun pours in through a small window upon some frames which hang close to us, holding row upon row of experiments in the permanency of colours ; and I find that these experiments (and others in different trying positions) were carried out so long ago, so neatly and systematically that they are more interesting than many I have seen. Indigo, of course, was soon found wanting, and Wolf discarded it many years ago. As a substitute, he has adopted Newman's cyanide blue and lamp-black.

Over our coffee we talk, as usual, of a great variety of subjects, but there is a remarkable absence from my host of the garrulity of age, and several other points strike me in his conversation. Chief among them are the singular pertinence and vigour of his remarks (the hammer falling fair and square upon the nail time after time), his quickness of perception, and his innate love of fairness ; shown, for instance, in such matters as his criticism of other zoological artists. Of these we discuss several, and he points out their respective strong points (also giving his opinion as to where they fail), as fairly as he points out his own deficiencies. He speaks highly of a rising zoological artist, whose skill, exactness, and unmercenary industry, sometimes remind me of Wolf,

OSPREYS.
(A Charcoal Drawing.)

"—— *did* work hard to get his birds right, I can
" tell you. He used to come here very often, and I
" would tell him where he was wrong." Then he
speaks as follows of an ornithological draughtsman :—
" With regard to knowledge of detail —— stands
" very high indeed. He knows all the detail of feather-
" ing. Where he is wrong is that he has not done
" enough from nature. He excuses himself by saying
" that they don't pay him sufficient to enable him to
" spend the time. If anything looks extraordinary in
" nature he gets shy of it—declares that it is ugly, and
" that people will not like it. In drawing the Osprey,
" which is entirely different from all other Birds of
" Prey—a stupid, silly thing, he is afraid to show that.
" The people he works for will not like that be-
" cause they don't know it. I lent him studies of
" Ospreys, and pointed out the characters, but ——
" produced a thing with a Buzzard's outline and
" Osprey's markings. He may possibly draw from
" life such things as Herons which stand like a post ;
" but he does not consult living things sufficiently."

Of a very popular painter of the *Felidæ* whose
works he is unable to admire, he says, " His markings
are *sown* without natural order or arrangement."
He mentions how easy it is to draw a Tiger, till the
markings have to be added with all their complexities
of perspective and modelling, " However well you
" model and perfect the drawing, directly you put the
" stripes in and happen to make the least mistake, all

"goes wrong.   They get so narrow in the fore-
"shortening as the surface goes away from you, that
"they are hardly seen at all."   With regard to his own
consummate skill in this respect, and the admirable
result, I have heard another zoological artist speak
with enthusiasm.   A notable example will be found in
Col. Campbell's *Indian Journal.*

He says, "The chief fault among the modern
"zoological draughtsmen is the want of artistic feeling
"on the one hand; and on the other hand, insufficient
'study of the structure and detail of animals.   The
"artists who paint pictures from wild animals do not
"pay sufficient regard to the truth.   Their main aim is
"to produce a *picture ;* and the better and more truthful
"it is the less likely it is to sell.   Grotesque things
"will sell, and caricatures will sell—the only branch of
"art which some people think worth looking at.   The
"principle of 'shoddy' in cloth—of *good enough to sell,*
"goes through everything nowadays.   If a thing is
"worth doing it is worth doing *well ;* but nowadays
"the poor fellows are glad to earn a few shillings by
"doing anything."   "They have come to the conclu-
"sion," he adds, with an expression of disgust, "that
"subject is nothing in a picture.   The chief thing is
"'*how it looks.*'   What it means is beside the mark."

Touching some modern painters' apparent indifference to much of the loveliness of nature he says, "If
"it were a clown's cap, you know, that was worn in
'Shakespeare's time, they would be most careful to

"get the markings perfectly true, and they would go to
"the British Museum to study the subject. But here,
"in the case of the way Nature has ornamented these
"things for thousands of generations, they are in-
"different.   I believe that if a typical landscape-
"painter were to settle down to paint on the coast,
"near the breeding-place of the sea-fowl, and there
"were thousands and thousands of them about him,
"he would hardly look up.   Perhaps he would say, ' I
"wonder what all those birds are there for.' "   "How
"few," he adds, "know the language of Nature; and
"yet it is a most eloquent language. . . . How very
"seldom you find anybody who can interpret truly
"what he sees, and how seldom you will find even an
"artist who will stand still and admire beautiful
"foliage, or picturesque arrangements of leaves."

This leads us to talk, as we have often done, of
the backgrounds or accessories with which zoological
draughtsmen are wont to pack in their animals—the
"*appropriate scenery all coloured with great care by
hand*," of the prospectus.   I remark that the appalling
composition and draughtsmanship of some of these
accessories,[1] in works well known to both of us, seem
to have been received, both by scientific men and by
the public, with quite as much favour as the carefully
pondered work abounding in knowledge of composition
and detail, and in the knowledge that subdues and

---

[1] Some of these accessories have been applied to copies of Wolf's own
animals ! See Brehm's *Tierleben*.

harmonizes that detail. Deploring this state of things, Wolf mentions as an example, how naturalists will often perplex artists by making them put in a large expanse of landscape, or trees, or some other large object, as a background to a small bird. He asks the pertinent question, " When you look down upon a little Wagtail what landscape can you see ? " Let the reader try the experiment for himself.

In answer to a question as to what were his favourite subjects, he says, " I had periods when " Falcons were favourite subjects, and periods when " other things were favourites. There were so many " things I enjoyed doing. At different times through- " out life you make the acquaintance of different animals, " and change your favourites. At one time Deer were " my favourites. Like every boy I was fond of " Leopards and that sort of thing. You take to that " kind of thing as a kind of duty when you know " that your life is to be that of an animal-painter. I " liked Monkeys very well, but I also liked Antelopes, " besides all Animals of Prey. These will always be " favourites of mine. Domestic cattle I never could " take to somehow or other, because my father had " worried me too much with our horses. And yet it " was a jolly time then. I used to attend to the cattle " (or did not attend to them), and we used to steal the " potatoes, and cook them in the ashes of our bon- " fires." In birds he considers his strongest point the Birds of Prey and the Gallinaceous order. " Ducks," he says, "are nice things too—in fact all birds have a charm for me."

In connection with the subject of his favourites, he gives me a brief list of some works which he himself considers as among his best and most characteristic, as follows. A water-colour version of the *Ovis poli* drawing, done originally for Sir Victor Brooke. "Age," an old Red Deer stag lagging behind the rest which have passed through the forest in the snow, with a few gleams of light seen between the tree-trunks. This he regards as one of the best black and white designs that he has ever done. "A Midnight Ramble," the Wild Boar subject in charcoal, also painted in water-colour for his friend Mr. Carl Haag. "A Storm in the Alps," representing some Chamois sheltering under dwarf firs, with an Alpine Hare and Ptarmigan. Among his best water-colours he includes "Inquisitive Neighbours"; "Grave and Gay"; "Ospreys Fishing" (a water-colour companion to the *Ovis poli* design); and last, but not least, a drawing of a Labrador Jerfalcon painted for his friend Mr. H. E. Dresser, of which more hereafter. Of his oil pictures he mentions the "Jerfalcons and Kite" which I have alluded to already, and a life-size picture of an Ibex and Lammergeyer painted for Mr. J. H. Gurney. The artist has, of course, his own definite reasons for these preferences (into which it will not be profitable to enquire in the absence of the works in question), and sometimes, no doubt, pleasant associations have had their weight.

In the list of his most attractive, if not, perhaps, his best works, I should be tempted to include two or three that I have myself seen, beginning with a large water-colour drawing, "Arctic Summer,"[1] touching which its owner, Mr. H. E. Dresser, gave me some interesting particulars. At The Junior Athenæum some artists were talking of the alleged difficulty of painting white upon white; a white figure upon a white background; and, in consequence, he suggested an experiment to Wolf. The result was this drawing of Jerfalcons painted in 1875. The male bird sits upon a foreground rock on the left, his white plumage in a delicate and perfectly natural relief against the glacier in the distance, rosy in the sun. A gentle shadow from the high rock behind the spectator falls over part of the bird and the foreground, subduing the beautiful colours of the flowers. It steals also over a portion of the middle distance, where the full-fledged young sit together, their hungry eyes fixed upon a Ptarmigan, with which their mother, flying near them, lures them to an early lesson in their craft. That everything might be true to nature, down to the flowers and other vegetation, Mr. Dresser consulted the notes Mr. Edward Whymper had made in Greenland.

I was giving Wolf his friend's account of the origin of this drawing, the discussion as to the difficulty of painting white upon white, and he said,

Another version of "Arctic Summer" (by no means a replica) shows the young Falcons alone.

EQUALS.

" It is not difficult at all. White models very strongly.
" For instance, the round form of a bird, a Ptarmigan
" we will say, is sure to have a shadow on one side.
" Then there is always a difference of tone. The
" snow will be cold white, and the Ptarmigan creamy
" —a lovely white, you know. The fact is, if you see
" a dead Ptarmigan lying on the ground with its wings
" slightly separated from its body, the colour between
" the wings and the body is quite salmon-colour. In
" this instance the Falcon sits on a rock, but high
" above him the rock goes up, and throws a shadow
" over the lower part of his body. If the snow back-
" ground were near him, he would relieve warm
" against it ; but, being distant, it appears rosy in the
" sun."

The solution of problems such as these, so dear to
the mind of a colourist, has been favourite work with
our friend, ever since the days when, as a lad, he
stumbled on the mystery of the complementary
colours, and the way to give the brilliancy of his first
Goldfinch. Possibly all the owners of his finest water-
colours are not aware that they are colour harmonies
as beautiful and skilful and delicately fingered as any
ever awakened by a musician's hands.

I should also include among Wolf's finest works
another large black and white drawing. Two mighty
Boars, roaming the forest in the snow, have met by
chance at night ; and full of envy, hatred and all un-
charitableness, make up their minds that discretion, per-

haps, is the better part of valour on that particular
occasion. Gnashing their tusks, they pass one another,
every bristle raised, and every great muscle quivering
with rage. It is a subject after Wolf's own heart,
for it is nocturnal and mysterious—the romance of
natural history, and a little more than a mere accurate
figure of two adult ♂ specimens of *Sus scrofa.*

Remembering the many drawings of ugly animals he
has had to make for scientific purposes, I ask my host
whether he found them very irksome. He answers,
" When a thing is ugly in itself it is very wearisome to
" have to draw it carefully, but at last one ceases to
" see that it is ugly." [1]   No doubt he has found this
discipline useful, like another artist I knew, who would
sit down sometimes and "go to school to a potato," or
draw some equally ugly object as if his life depended
on it.

Asked which class of purchasers he has found most
common, the genuine admirers of the works, or those
who thought it just as well to have a " Wolf " in their
collection, he replies that he has found those most frequent who bought a work because they liked it, and he
thinks that his being a foreigner has made no difference.
" But, generally, before a gentleman buys a picture he
" asks his wife. She comes to see it, and says after-
" wards, ' My dear, I have not seen anything like that
" ' in our friends' houses. Do you think we had better

---

[1] Among the very ugliest of his sitters were the Manatee and a promising young Walrus. This animal he rightly likened to a sack of potatoes.

" 'have it ? ' He does not have it." " To what class " of the public have you most appealed," I ask. " I " have not the slightest idea," he replies.

He tells me that though he has been longer in England than most Englishmen, he has never gone through the formality of naturalization, and is still a German subject. He says it makes no difference in practical affairs, and that the shopkeepers would have cheated him just the same if he had been naturalized. He has preserved a warm attachment to his little village and his countrymen ; but although he is at heart, perhaps, a German, and thinks very little of a man who loves not his country and kindred, he has also a natural affection for his adopted land, where he has achieved so much, and for the friends he has made there. When they have died, he has always paid a visit to their graves, when he could.

It is no doubt owing to his forbearance and good sense that he does not convey the impression of being a foreigner, and it is easy to forget that he is one. He tells me that he has got so used to our language that he thinks in English, not in German. No doubt with his own countrymen he seems a true German, but to me he rarely conveys that impression by speech or manner. His friend, Mr. H. E. Dresser, however, writes to me thus :—" I think in your Life of " Wolf you should lay stress on the fact that, though " he has lived so long in England, he has remained " German in his ideas and to a large extent in his

s

" habits, and has never become an Englishman ;
" being, as you know, still as true a German as
" ever." Mr. Dresser is so familiar with the German
people and language, and so old and intimate a friend
of Wolf's, that this opinion carries great weight. The
point, however, is not a very important one.

As we rise from the table, it occurs to me that all
the most interesting information I have gathered about
Wolf and his works has generally arisen out of sheer
accident, not by cross-questioning. Most incongruous
remarks, or incidents, or questions, have awakened a
train of thought in his mind, much to my benefit. " I
" have found it," he says, "just the same in art. You
" may think and think, but nothing comes. All at
" once, by accident, you get a beautiful subject. I have
" noticed that when I have been sitting with a friend
" downstairs of an evening, talking of different things
" altogether, but always with an eye to the picture on
" the easel, that, all at once, I saw something which I
" had never seen before."

By this time the Blackbird outside is singing his
evening song, and London dines. Before I leave,
we arrange that my friend shall pay us a country visit
to renew his acquaintance with the Swallows and Sedge
Warblers. He chooses a fresh pipe from a large collection, to smoke while he waters his garden ; and as
he does so he says emphatically, " *There is nothing like
smoking a pipe in the world.*" All the most enthusiastic things that smokers have ever said or written he

would doubly endorse, and it was therefore inevitable that he should design a pipe-bowl or two. Of one of these designs, intended for execution in meerschaum, he says, what I have heard him say of very few other works of his, " I wouldn't part with that for anything." Even for his old tobacco-pouches he finds a use ; for sometimes he fills them with cocoa-fibre and drops them on an unfrequented pavement. Watching from afar, sooner or later he sees the pouch picked up. Sometimes the finder slips it furtively into his pocket, sometimes he opens it (with amusing results), and on one occasion the trap was carefully re-set.

As we pass the porter's lodge on the way out, a little baby-boy,[1] in his father's arms recognises Wolf as a special favourite, and screams to go to him. "Of "late years I have become very fond of children, and " I like to hear their young voices and their jolly laugh- "ter," says my stalwart friend. As he stands at the private entrance of the studios, I see him, as he waves an adieu, nursing one of the tiny puppies, while its mother wags her tail by his side, and the fragrant smoke of his pipe wreathes about his head.

.   .   :   .

[1] The tour of this faithful little friend of the artist's round his studio is an amusing sight. One after another, he greets the various works on the walls, and easels, and chairs, with a shout of recognition and delight, toddling to each in turn with outstretched arm. He knows each "dicky," "bunny," and " pussy " in the room, and claps his hands with joy. He even tries to frighten away the Eagles with his pinafore. Finally he pats the seat of his friend's favourite chair, as a hint for him to sit down, and that accomplished climbs upon his knee.

It is hot June weather, and Wolf has kept his promise to spare me a few days, far away in the remotest part of Surrey, a neighbourhood remarkable for its

PÈRE DAVID'S DEER

richness in bird life.[1]   It was rather difficult to persuade

It is on the commons in this neighbourhood, as related by Gould, that Mr. Smither, that most original man and keen naturalist, collected in the spring of 1859 no less than sixty-five nests of the Dartford Warbler.   I

him to leave his little garden and many tender seedlings
to the care of the porter at the studios ; but now that
he has unpacked his pipe and tobacco, and a favourite
pair of pistols (designed by himself many years ago),
he resigns himself to his fate, to the intense joy of the
children, with whom he is a very special favourite.

On meeting fairly early the next morning we find
that our guest has been up for at least three hours. He
says " As one can't add to the number of one's days,
one must add to the length of them." As he concocts
with his own hands the invariable omelette, he tells us
all about an unsuspected Goldfinch's nest he has discovered, and how he has been watching the old birds
feeding their young. In the course of the day, as he
roams about with his pipe, he finds out another nest
or two, which have escaped even boyish eyes ; but
he is especially pleased with the chorus of Swallows
and Martins which is kept up all day round
the old eaves and chimneys ; their dainty little songs
always reminding him of the remote days when he
watched so anxiously for their return.

We plant a comfortable garden chair in the shade
of a horse-chestnut, and here he alternately listens to
the music all round him, and studies the modelling of
a muscular Fox Terrier. " Trim," like the kittens,

was introduced to him some twenty years later, and remember being struck
by his originality and enthusiasm. He was in bed (I think with a broken
leg), and had been blowing a nest-full of Dartford's eggs, which lay on the
quilt. His house was full of the trophies of his gun ; a most interesting
collection, still treasured by his family.

becomes a fast friend with him in a moment, and vibrates his two-inch tail in a way which altogether belies his usual uncharitable opinion of strangers. As Wolf smokes and looks about him, he holds in his hand a box of matches, and gradually but surely the ground in front of him is besprinkled with the ends.

First on our programme for the day come some photographs I have to take, and he changes his white Leghorn hat for his favourite " Tam o' Shanter," the successor of a whole series of the Turkish fez. As I wish to use a slow lens at first, which, in the light of the studio, will require a long exposure, I am rather doubtful whether my sitter will be able to keep firm without supports of any kind. " Try me," he says, as he places himself instinctively in a good position. The result the reader will see in the frontispiece.

As the day is a calm one, we make up our minds to indulge in a little shooting, and having hung up a small target on the butts, we go back to a considerable range. There, again, his steadiness astonishes me, for he puts shot after shot from my ·295 Holland rifle into or near the bull's-eye. He complains a little about the haziness of the rear sight, nevertheless ; and it is rather a relief to him when he takes up his small-bore, hair-trigger pistols, the rear-sight of which he can get farther from his eye. It is easy to see from the way he handles his weapons and sets to work, not only that he thoroughly enjoys it, but that he must have had a large experience.

It is hot work in the sun, and he feels that the
effort of keeping steady is bringing on a twinge or two
of his old enemy, the nervous rheumatism ; so we
adjourn to the shady seat by the river. He has just
settled down on the cushions with his usual expression
of satisfaction—" By Jove! *Cap*-ital! " when he holds
up his finger with the words, " Lesser Whitethroat! "
He is right, for though the bird is far distant, it presently comes along the alders, and there is no doubt
about it. He scarcely ever boasts of anything, but he
does boast that he knows not only the striking distinctive notes of many of the European birds, but most of
the varieties of their language. Being well able to
realize what such knowledge involves, as far as England
is concerned, I was, perhaps, a little sceptical at first ;
but, from time to time, I have had ample proof that he
is right. The slightest glimpse of a moving bird,
even half concealed by foliage—the slightest utterance
of that bird's voice, enables him to tell you the species.
He says, " If you were to put me in prison for some
" years, then blindfold me, and bring me out into the
" country, I could tell you what time of year it was by
" the bird's notes." I admit that much that I have told
sounds incredible, but I have proved the truth of it
for myself; and I must leave others to believe or reject,
as they like.

You would not suspect that behind the great, round
spectacles there existed such keen vision. But the
unassisted vision, keen though it be, would be futile

without the knowledge which has been acquired by years of study. He says that his quickness of sight was gained through constantly watching things in movement, and continually sketching them from memory. The power of grasping the characters of moving objects or of giving the appearance of movement is, in fact, seldom found existing in very great perfection in the artist who relies much on photography. The perpetual struggle to do by memory and hand *and mind*, what another man prefers to do by means of his camera and proportional compasses leads in time—perhaps a long time, to a great superiority.

As we sit in the shade by the river, he gives me a rough outline of his methods of working. It is not very comprehensive, but it is very interesting as far as it goes. He says, "You get into a way of working " which you can't describe. *The great thing is to keep* " *on working*." Jointly with his habit of attacking the most disagreeable or difficult thing first, this seems to me to be one of the most important elements of success in art or in life. Theorize as much as you like, try endless experiments if need be, but keep on working.

I find that Wolf deprecates the tentative way some artists go to work to piece their pictures together, either by the aid of photographs or otherwise; and contrasts it with composing *con amore* from a distinct mental vision or conception of the subject. He thinks that such vital points as composition and the arrangement of colour and light and shade should be carefully thought out in the first instance. He thinks also (as other intellectual artists have done), that a picture should be a homogeneous creation of the intellect and the imagination ; not a more or less fortuitous selection of facts patched and pieced together, partly out of doors, partly in the studio, with a dash of photography and a rummage in the property-box. This being his belief, he has escaped those incongruities of perspective and light and shade which are often found in works of the opposite kind, beautiful though they may be with a rule-of-thumb beauty.

"I find," says my guest, speaking low for the sake of an inquisitive Moorhen a few yards away, " that the " landscape studies I have done will never form a " proper background or foreground, and I have always " to modify and adapt them. When you see a nice " thing in nature, you sit down and make a study ; and " when it is finished there is no room left for any animal " which you had intended to put in. It is a composi- " tion in itself. As a rule I find that everything has to " be simplified. If you want to do justice to your " principal animal or figure, you ought to put the back- " ground, as it were, out of focus. According to the " figure of the animal which forms the principal object " in the picture, you must avoid getting into your " accessories similar forms and objects of the same " degree of solidity. For instance, in 'Strength and " Weakness' [Rhinoceroses and Indian Axis Deer]

" I avoided anything in the shape of a tree-trunk or
" rock—anything which would rival the solidity of
" the Rhinoceroses. Instead of that, I chose loose,
" feathery stuff, and bamboo with elegant willow-like
" leaves. . . . In doing birds—simply a bird on a twig,[1]
" I always used to avoid getting the same size of leaf as
" the bird, or the same shape. The fact is that ninety-
" nine per cent. of what you see in nature is of no use
" to you, and should be avoided." He learned composition, he says, by illustrating. " The thing has to
" be finished by a certain time, and you go far more
" free and easy to work than in the case of a commis-
" sion." He disliked illustrations so arranged that the
book had to be turned round to look at them, and so
he gradually got into the way of composing, and I think
preferring, upright subjects.

He says, " Excessive knowledge of detail hampers
" me very often in doing things picturesquely, and in
" trying to work broadly. It has a tendency to inter-
" fere very often in art. For instance, in the case of
" Hippopotami, I know very well that they come up
" with hardly a ripple—yet everybody thinks there
" would be a great commotion in the water. It is
" far more difficult to get breadth in a composition
" when you are hampered by detail, than if you
" do not know the detail, and slur it over." The troublesome nature of excessive knowledge of detail is one

---

[1] Wolf's "bird on a twig" is often a perfect paragon of skilful arrangement and grace.

A MIDNIGHT RAMBLE.

reason why he likes nocturnal subjects. " My preference
" for night scenes is due to there being more poetry
" about them than when everything is seen clearly.
" At night the detail disappears altogether. An ugly
" animal, particularly, like a Wild Boar, makes a far
" better picture by moonlight." He even avoids
representing a clear moon in a picture, and prefers a
clouded one ; and for the same reason, he has preferred
northern subjects (such as Scandinavian) to Oriental.
He once made a water-colour landscape study of a
Wild Boar by moonlight [1] for his friend Mr. Carl Haag,
whose natural bent, he says, is to prefer things clear
and sharp as seen in the East by daylight. He omitted
the eyes which, save for a glint or two, as he had
proved, could not be seen by moonlight. He had,
however, considerable difficulty to convince his friend
that he was right. " It is of great importance to
know what to leave out in nocturnal subjects."

Light and shade, he thinks, are quite as important
as local colour. " In my case I cannot choose the local
" colour of the creatures. They have their own, and I
" am tied to that ; and in order to make that local colour
" tell I have to introduce as near as possible the com-
" plementary colour in the accessories. I want to be
" truthful in colour as well as in drawing ; and when I
" do a picture I am tied down by the local colour, and
" cannot put in the combination as well as I would

---

[1] " A Midnight Ramble."

"choose ; so, except in the background, there is very
"little choice."

Touching size it is interesting to find how he has
changed since the early days when he did miniatures,
partly from the inability to cover a larger surface.
"The size of a water-colour," he says, "has nothing to
"do with the time it takes. In a large one you go to
"work more boldly and use larger brushes. I would
"rather do a drawing large than small."[1]

I asked him why, as he was so fond of black and
white, he had done so little in pen and ink. He
answered, "Pen and ink work did not suit the detail
"which I knew. When you know a thing it takes you
"much longer to satisfy yourself than if you do not
"know it much. My knowledge has often stood in
"my way."

When an artist has arrived at such a pitch of
mastery over technique and materials as Wolf has
done ; when he can take up a bit of charcoal and a
certain magical, superannuated brush, and turn out
such a work as the first sketch for " Captivity " (where
a pair of kittens filch a Pigeon from beneath a hooded
Falcon's perch) ; when he can work wonders by simply
flinging his wash-leather at a sky, as he did in the
beautiful drawing of a dead Lion with Vultures called
" Morning "—when he can do all this, it is quite as useless to ask him to describe how he does it, as it would

---

[1] Some of these remarks may appear to the trained artist self-evident,
but I have inserted them for the benefit of the inexperienced.

CAPTIVITY.

be to ask Joachim how he fingers his violin, or a first-rate gun-maker how he bores a pair of barrels.

It is interesting, nevertheless, to learn that in some of his black and white work Wolf rubs in his backgrounds (clouds for instance) with a pocket-handkerchief or cotton-wool, or "anything"; taking out the lights with bread, or a mezzotint scraper. Sometimes he grinds the point of this scraper round for putting in his favourite reeds, and it is easily seen that he has used the same tool in his lithographs. For glitter, such as that of dew-drops on vegetation, he scratches into the surface of the paper.

Charcoal, and its water-colour relative charcoal-grey are, above all others, his favourite materials. His charcoal is not in the form of the ordinary slender twigs, but of good sturdy stakes that fill the fingers and will not snap under the strain of sudden inspiration. I have known this great affection for charcoal to exist very strongly in another artist who also aimed at the more abstruse qualities in art; a man to whose imagination the realms of the Indefinite were instinct with suggestive beauty and poetry. He called charcoal, aptly enough, "the artist's divining-rod"; and certainly, of all materials it seems to convey most freely that potent current which flows from the brain to the fingers of the poet-painter. Wolf might sharpen up his mezzotint scraper, or put a needle-point upon a 3-H pencil if he liked, for certain purposes; but it was when he resorted to the all-powerful, all-suggestive smudge, of finger, brush, wash-leather or cotton-wool, that one of his greatest mental as well as manual powers was shown.

It might be supposed, at first sight, that many of our friend's black and white drawings, especially moon-lights, were done on paper of a blue tinge, the moon being painted in body-colour ; but this is not so. He says, " After my drawings are finished and properly " fixed (a point, of course, of vital importance), and " particularly if the paper has become yellow and dirty, " I wash them over with very faint Prussian blue, or " cobalt, or both—a washer-woman dodge, you know ; " but of course if any high lights have been scratched " out, the colour would settle in the scratches." A good example of the effect of this treatment is the exceed-ingly fine drawing I have already described, " A Night Attack." In this case the moon is represented by white paper.

In reply to a few rather hopeless questions about his water-colour method, he tells me that he wipes out a good deal ; wetting the paper, and wiping out the colour with a handkerchief, small sponge, or piece of wash-leather ; and sometimes blotting it up with blot-ting-paper. After this, and while the drawing is damp, he takes out the sharp high lights with India-rubber.

Mr. H. E. Dresser has in his collection an exceed-ingly fine water-colour drawing of a Labrador Jerfalcon painted by Wolf in 1875, and remarkable for artistic quality, harmonious colouring and freedom of execution, and also for the short time it took to execute. The rich brown bird, which is small for the size of the drawing, sits in the foreground with the remains of a Rock Ptarmigan he has been devouring lying round him. His mate sails in the misty sky, through which we see portions of the great mountains so beloved by the artist. Wolf thus describes his *modus operandi* in this and parallel cases. First of all a very delicate outline of the principal object is drawn on the paper in Indian ink, or other indelible material. The paper is then thoroughly wetted and laid upon a wet board, or sheet of glass, so that it lies absolutely flat. The sky is then put in, and the drawing is finished, as far as possible, while it is wet. When dry, it is mounted upon another sheet of strained paper. Probably it is found that the drawing is lighter than it was intended to be. It is therefore emphasized here and there, and then the principal object is finished. This process, says Wolf, is particularly suitable for clouds, as the colours blend so well into one another on the wet paper.

This Jerfalcon subject was completed in about one day and a half, and the background and sky were done in a few hours, except the snowy mountains, which were elaborated. Mr. Dresser recently gave me some interesting additional particulars concerning this lovely work. He happened to call on Wolf when the drawing was finished with the exception of the bird, which was in outline only. The artist was in a difficulty because nearly all the Falcons were not suited in

colour to the background. He described what he
wanted, and said, " I wonder what I can do." " I have
the only bird that will do," said his friend, " the
" Labrador Jerfalcon ; the only specimen of the fully
adult in England." Mr. Dresser took the skin, and
directly Wolf saw it he said, " That's exactly what I
want." The result was a work that takes the highest
rank in water-colour art, and has been considered by
accomplished artists to be one of Wolf's very best
achievements.

I was lately recalling these circumstances to his
mind when he said, " I wonder whether that skin *was*
" the adult." " Dresser says so." " Yes, but you can't
" get the register of its birth, you know." Here crops
up once more the artist's indifference to authority, if
he has not quite satisfied himself of a fact.

He does much of his water-colour work with hog-
hair brushes, from half an inch wide or so, and with
good length of bristle, so as to hold plenty of colour.
For skies he uses large sables, for some purposes an
old brush irregularly cut, and for others a brush whose
hair is split or divided with the fingers when it is wet.
Rough rocks he calls into existence with a sponge, and
for glitter he scratches into the paper, just as he does
in black and white. When his water-colours are
finished he sometimes applies in places what he calls
Carl Haag's medium, that is gum tragacanth dissolved
in chloroform. This has the same effect as varnish in
oil painting, particularly in the dark parts. He says,

" I sometimes put the colour out of the tube direct
" upon the paper, to get its full depth and purity, and
" richness."

As for the material upon which he has worked, he
has preferred for his studies smooth, toned paper to
Whatman, but has always painted his finished drawings
on the latter. His sketches for the most part have
been made in charcoal on ordinary whity-brown paper,
a great favourite of his. I fancy that, with this exception, he has been somewhat indifferent, as I have
seen sketches of his on all kinds, and tints, and textures
of paper, the only material conspicuously absent being
Bristol or London board in spite of its great "bearing out" quality.

The processes of which I have given an outline are,
of course, easy enough to the painter as a rule ; but
even he comes to a dead lock sometimes. He says,
" I am always very particular, when I find a thing will
" not go as I intended, not to bother myself. I let it
" dry and put it aside, perhaps for a day or two." Unlike another artist who also knew the importance of
stopping short and not working for work's sake, he
does not go to the length of packing up the drawing
in much paper and string, to reduce the temptation to
touch on it ; but such a veteran knows the importance
of humouring the enemy—of swift attack and "masterly
inactivity," each in its own time.

Some of his most important work has been done
while he has been apparently idling away an hour or

T

two over a social pipe, and chatting with his friends
before his easels about anything but art. More still,
and probably the most important of all, has been done
with locked doors and intense concentration, and deep
thought.

In his opinions on art, as in his practice, Wolf is
thoroughly eclectic. He does not pin his faith to one
particular school, nor has he dogged the footsteps of
any particular hero. He hardly understands those
who have. " I cannot understand," he says, " the
" narrow-mindedness of many of the English school.
" They are full of —— or full of someone else, and will
" pay no regard to anybody besides." As for himself,
he admires with unaffected cordiality really fine work
of any date, or nation, or style, or individual artist,
wherever he encounters it, and hates with equal vehe-
mence work which is specious, impudent, or wanting in
conscientiousness. I have never heard a word come
from his lips conveying the impression that he considered himself a judge, but I have never heard more
pertinent criticism than his, or seen greater quickness
in artistic diagnosis.

I once heard it contended by a fellow-countryman
of his (whose knowledge of his works was not very
extensive), that his art is essentially German. That
whether he has drawn an English stubble, a Scotch
loch, the African veldt, or even " Spring in Seven
Dials," all have been treated in an essentially German
way. Waxing warmer, the gentleman said that

none of our nation can appreciate or understand Wolf's achievements, while The Fatherland, to a man, would receive them with acclamation. My own acquaintance with my friend's work and with some weighty English opinion of it being considerable, I ventured to demur to these statements. I thought that with the exception of some of his Darmstadt studies, if his art was essentially anything, it was essentially eclectic and, so to speak, cosmopolitan. From the first, he avoided falling under the influence of any academy or school, or of any great artist ; and he was chiefly self-taught when he left Germany as a youth to continue his studies in England for a period of forty-seven years, self-taught to the end. When he was making foreground studies near Darmstadt, toiling up Foinaven, sketching on Handa or the Bass Rock, or labouring till he was giddy with fatigue at the drawings for the Zoological Society, I did not think that he was brooding over German art, any more than he was brooding over the achievements of Landseer, or Snyders, or James Ward. He endeavoured, I said, and endeavoured successfully, to throw himself into the spirit of the object or the scene which he happened to be representing ; charming equally, either by extreme truthfulness, absence of mannerism, or great artistic skill, such dissimilar critics, (among a host of others) as Darwin, H. E. Dresser, Gould, Carl Haag, Landseer, Mitchell, Newton, Oswell, Owen, Rossetti, Rüppell, Schlegel, Sclater, A. Thorburn, Charles Whymper, Woolner, and the baby-boy at the

lodge. This, too, whether it was a German forest, a
Scotch mountain, an American wilderness, or a fine
" adult specimen of so and so in breeding plumage"
which he represented. All through this profitable
discussion, our friend sat peacefully puffing away
behind his spectacles, the picture of comfortable
indifference. When we had done, he removed his pipe
from his mouth and said these words : " I worked as
" I thought best, without any intention to appear
" English or to appear German. I always tried to
" avoid copying other men's style or subjects." Here
then, in Wolf's own words, I am content to leave the
question of the nationality of his style.

As for his knowledge, though immensely wide it
is not desultory. It is well classified, and is always
the result of the orderly evolution of principles from
phenomena ; of the humble, painstaking wrestle with
elements as a preliminary to all real proficiency. If
he wonders at the want of toleration and eclecticism in
some of the modern school, he is simply astounded at
their contempt for these elements. A young painter,
having been appointed to some art mastership, Wolf
was chatting with him one day on the subject of teach-
ing, and alluded to the importance to the pupil of some
knowledge of perspective and anatomy. " Perspective!
" Anatomy !" said the newly-fledged Professor. "That
" is not *Art*." " There is no such thing as a finishing
" school for an artist," says Wolf, as he tells me the
anecdote. " One remains a student all through life."

Himself the most unmercenary of men, Wolf deprecates the sordid spirit of certain painters who, even
after they have become rich, behave like tradesmen,
and paint just for the pounds, shillings and pence. Save
for a few early pot-boilers (such as the Woodcock
pictures), he himself has resolutely and loyally striven
for a certain ideal, well knowing it to be as far removed
from the ideal of the British public as from the ideal
of Councils and Hanging-committees.

At the time when, with the most seductive alchemy,
he could turn all his pencil touched to gold, he resolutely set apart a large proportion of his time to the
patient, unostentatious acquisition of facts and principles;
labouring (for that is the true word), in his search for
truth. As we have seen, this was not due to a mis-
taken belief that his labours would be appreciated. It
was simply the unmercenary, unswerving devotion of
the true artist and the scrupulously honest man. If,
with all his resources, such as his eye for colour, profound knowledge of detail, lively invention, draughtsmanship, and attractive, rapid technique, he had
painted thoroughly popular subjects—kittens, say, or
cattle, or Fox Terriers, or anything equally far
removed from the despised "Objects of Natural
History," he might have grovelled in gold and become
a fetich of the dealers. Even "shooting-coat" pictures,
as he calls them, with such power as his, might have
made him a baronet. But alas! He had a certain
definite ideal; and again alas! He had imagination.

By means of inflexible purpose, but flexibility in achieving that purpose, combined with ceaseless industry, he has succeeded in his aim ; so, at the age of seventy-five, he remains plain Joseph Wolf, utterly unknown, it seems, to the editors of any biographical dictionary ; forgotten, I fear, by some who once admired him ; but much beloved as an artist and as a man by a circle of enthusiasts to whom it is no slight honour to belong. Contentedly he smokes his pipe down by this little Surrey river where we have been talking, or divides his morning omelette into eight segments, rejoicing in that quiet mind and healthy body that he has been blessed with.

As the shadows of the alders above us grow longer, and the baby Owls in the neighbouring elms bethink them of their supper, I tell him how greatly I hope that some day his talent will be more widely recognised, if not here, at all events in his own land. I find he is neither very keen nor very sanguine about it. He has achieved that quiet philosophy which neither believes in nor desires popularity. He has lived into the age of high pressure and nine-day wonders in art, in literature, and all else—in art " Impressionism," in Literature the daily batch of novels. He may even have heard (as I have lately done, and that from a shrewd, educated man) the best picture defined as that which gives the greatest pleasure to the greatest number !

" As to my life," he says, " I was always very busy ;

"never was in debt ; and didn't know what extrava-
"gance meant. I believe that if I had ever so much
"money I should never become extravagant. Here, at
"the present time, a jolly blue sky and the green fields
"have the same charm for me as when I was young.
"I don't feel that I have grown old."

    .   .   .   .   .   .

I do not myself intend to compare Joseph Wolf's
works with those of any other artist living or dead.
His achievements, his artistic mastery, his ideal, and his
manly loyalty appeal to me so strongly, and fill me with
such overpowering admiration and respect, that I should
fight against prejudice in vain. It would be difficult,
moreover, to make a fair comparison. Few of the
most successful animal painters have had to struggle
against every conceivable disadvantage which could
beset them as beginners. They have excelled not alone
through their genius, but by constant practice within a
limited range of subjects—Deer and Horses, or Dogs
and game ; or the *Felidæ*, for instance. Wolf, on the
other hand, has had to fight his way upward, inch by
inch, from his boyhood; and yet has excelled in representing almost all orders of the warm-blooded animals
in the world, from an English Mouse to an African
Elephant, and from a Humming-bird to the Moa.
There is not a family of mammals or birds in existence
that he has not studied more or less deeply. For
example, as a zoological artist pure and simple, he
has, in the single instance of *The Proceedings* of The

Zoological Society, drawn nearly 350 different species from all regions of the earth.   Among mammals he has drawn most of the Primates, Carnivora, Ungulata, Edentata and Marsupialia, to say nothing of many representatives of the other orders, save the Cetacea. He has also drawn nearly all the Gallinaceous and Accipitrine birds, and numbers of the Passerine.

Moreover (to make comparison with other artists still more impossible), he has not stopped at the halting-place of the Zoological draughtsmen (though some of these, as far as numbers go, have been much more prolific) or even of the average animal-painter, but has proved himself to be an accomplished and poetical artist in the widest and highest sense of that word. Accomplished in landscape, and a perfect master of the more abstruse branches of art, such, for instance, as composition and chiaroscuro, he has worthily rendered some of the grandest and most lovely aspects of nature. As a painter in oil he has achieved success ; in water-colour, I think, still greater success ; and in black and white he has distinguished himself greatly.   In nearly all materials his capability is proven.   Modelling came natural to him, and as a lithographer he stands in the first rank.[1]

Lastly, he was a frontiersman and pioneer, and he has taken a distinct line of his own.   While some artists have endeavoured to humanize their animals and to surround them with human associations, Wolf, for

[1] " I hated etching," he says, " it was too much scratching for me '

the most part, has aimed at eliminating that element. His beasts and birds are such as might have walked and climbed and flown in an unpeopled earth, where even the flint arrow-head was unchipped, and the hide had never covered the broad shoulders of pre-historic man.

Comparison would not only be unfair; it would be futile. It is generally useless to endeavour to convince anyone that an artist whose work he knows not—whose fame is not backed by the authority of the Press of the last decade (to say the least of it), is worthy of being mentioned within a day's march of the favourites.

I also avoid comparison because I am one of those who, as surely as they know their own existence, *know* that in some of his achievements Wolf stands utterly alone. Believing it can be proved that nobody has approached him in times past, and having deeply studied his genius in its various aspects, I must be pardoned if I believe also that he will never be equalled in times to come.

I am aware of his few faults. There are works of his which I dislike, and there are others to which I am perfectly indifferent. I hold, however, that only mediocrity and machinery work uniformly up to one standard. The twenty-millionth pin is perfect, but not more perfect than the first. Real, worthy Mediocrity works up to its standard year after year, rarely falling below and never exceeding it. It is not disappointing, because it never fails to fulfil every expectation, and so it comes to be regarded as reliable and honest. This achieved, other virtues which it does not possess are added to it by its admirers; and in the end there sometimes comes substantial recognition by the State.

There are mainly three kinds of art; the art that asserts everything dogmatically, the art that obfuscates, and the art that, besides asserting here and there, suggests and teaches and allures, thus calling into play the best qualities of the minds of the beholders. Those who look at Wolf's works superficially, or (as I have sometimes seen), with the supercilious, envious scrutiny of hypercriticism, may consider them over-rated. They will be sure to miss the wealth of suggestion, the point of each story the artist has tried to tell, and naturally the consummate excellence of his way of telling it. Those, on the other hand, who love to dwell on these works month after month, ever seeking for new beauties and never seeking vainly, will inevitably be rewarded, and rewarded most richly. It is only those, however, who have had the advantage of his own comments and kindly but modest guidance—the advantage of leisure to explore his portfolios, who can fully realize the rare attributes of his workmanship. They are the attributes which have given vitality and dignity to art since those days of old when the lips of the marble Galatea warmed at Pygmalion's kiss.

. . . . .

In bringing to an end one of the happiest tasks

that can fall to a man's lot, in chronicling the life and
work of a friend who is enthusiastically reverenced
and admired. I bethought me that I would not close
with my own words, but would ask four old friends of
Wolf's (who by reason of their own attainments are
far more worthy than I could be to speak of his), if
they would give their reasons for their admiration.
I chose two representative ornithologists, and two
representative zoological artists, who all, with much
courtesy and kindness, complied with my request ; and
I print these passages, taking the names of the writers
alphabetically.

Mr. H. E. Dresser, the author of *The Birds of
Europe*, writes :—

" As regards Wolf, he is certainly best as far as the Raptores are
" concerned, . . . but where he excels and surpasses any animal painter
" I know of, is that not only is he an excellent *artist*, but he so
" thoroughly understands the pose and characteristic points of the
" animals he paints, whether mammals or birds. There are certain
" characteristic peculiarities in every species which can only be dis-
" tinguished by anyone who has made a life study of them ; and
" these Wolf has an inborn power of transmitting to his canvas. I
" can best describe this by referring to old shepherds, who can recog-
" nise each individual sheep in their flock. The late Sir Edwin
" Landseer once, speaking to me of Wolf, laid great stress on this
" power of his, and said that he considered Wolf to be, *without ex-*
" *ception*, the best all-round animal painter that ever lived. 'When
" 'a good many artists of the present day are forgotten,' Landseer
" added, 'Wolf will be remembered.' "

Professor Newton was so good as to write me the
following letter :—

Magdalene College, Cambridge : March 9. 1895.

" DEAR SIR,   With every wish to comply with your request, it is
" no easy thing to do so.   My admiration of the works of my old
" friend Mr. Wolf is almost unbounded, and has been often publicly
" expressed ; but to give my ' reasons ' for it might lead me into the
" domain of the 'art critic,' where I should be a trespasser.   I can
" only suppose his excellence to lie in his knowledge not merely of
" what an animal looks like, can do, and is ; but primarily in his
" acquaintance with its structure, derived from intelligent observation
" and close study, and when a bird is concerned, with its *pterylosis* –
" to use a very technical word—of which last most great masters, from
" Hondekoeter, Savery and others of old to those of our own time,
" have been absolutely ignorant.   Then there is an absence of any
" attempt to humanize the expression, as is so commonly, though per-
" haps unconsciously, done by many good artists.   Whether the animal
" be mammal, bird, or reptile, Mr. Wolf gives it its own expression.
" Landseer's dogs and horses frequently have, so to speak, human
" faces, and his deer hardly less so.   To my eye there is a trace of
" this in his birds, though that is by no means their chief defect.
" I remember the late Mr. D. W. Mitchell, himself a good artist,
" remarking to me that Mr. Wolf's figures of animals were not only
" portraits of the species they represent ; but, when taken from life,
" of the particular individuals, and this I think is perfectly true.   I
" know no one else of whom the same can be said, though of course
" one does not know the subjects of some of his predecessors, and it
" is possible that when they drew from life they at least tried to render
" personal peculiarities.   It follows from this that Mr. Wolf has never
" been guilty of exaggeration such as disfigures the designs of some other
" draughtsmen from Snyders to Audubon—the last having been more
" highly lauded in his time than anyone else.   It may be that in what
" is, I suppose, called ' feeling ' some of the moderns, such as Swainson,
" Lear and Mitchell, when at their best, may have equalled Mr. Wolf,
" and in accuracy both the Naumanns and Schlegel are often serious
" rivals, leaving little to be desired.   Certainly all these men, and
" some others, have produced beautiful things, but in the best of them
' there is nearly always a want of vitality which rarely fails in Mr.
" Wolf's work and is sometimes so strong as to bear translation by a

"copyist without any serious loss of force. Moreover the men just
" mentioned seldom or never attempted such grouping and accessories
"as he introduces so as to make a picture. On the other hand, he
" never sacrifices peculiarities of structure or coloration for pictorial
"effect, as I have known many another artist do ; but, giving, as a
" true Naturalist should, due prominence to the chief zoological
"character of his subjects, he brings all the surrounding scene into
" harmony with them, and thus represents Nature with the utmost
"fidelity. As might be expected, the result is almost invariably
" pleasing ; but it is a result that only genius of a very high order
"can attain. Trusting that this long explanation may satisfy your
" enquiries. I remain, Dear Sir, Yours faithfully,

"ALFRED NEWTON."

Having ventured to demur at what I imagined
Professor Newton to say with regard to the equality
in the matter of "feeling" of certain artists with
Wolf, judging from what I know of their work, he
was kind enough to add the following :—

"I do not put Mr. Mitchell and the others in the same category
"as Mr. Wolf, but you especially asked me to compare his work with
"that of his chief predecessors. What I wrote as to the ignorance of
" *Pterylosis* shewn by other artists was, perhaps, too sweeping ; for
"there are men now living who are aware of the need of studying in
"it though I quite believe they have been led thereto by Mr.
" Wolf's example. . . . I am not surprised at your being in doubt as
" to the meaning of *Pterylosis*. I should think the only dictionary
"which contains the word is my own. Therein it is defined as
" ' Plumage considered in regard to the distribution of its growth.'
" In only a few birds do the feathers grow over the whole body, but
"they are generally restricted to well-defined patches or tracts, which
"in 1833 received from Nitzsch (*Pterylographiæ Avium, pars prima,*
" p. 11) the name of *pteryla* or feather forests, in opposition to *apteria*
" or featherless spaces, which intervene. The article is of some
"length and gives several illustrations (some from Nitzsch and
" others original) of the pterylosis of various birds ; but a very large

"number of figures is wanted to do complete justice to the subject.
" Mr. Wolf had no doubt, in his younger days, seen Nitzsch's great
" work of which there is now an English translation containing the
"original plates [1] but so, I dare say, had many other artists, only
" they neglected the hints while he did not, and that makes all the
" difference between his work and theirs."

As I have said before, although it seems likely that
Mr. Wolf had seen Nitzsch's work, yet it is a fact that
he saw neither that nor the translation. His study
of pterylography was entirely independent of all help
either from books or otherwise.

Mr. A. Thorburn sent me the following :—

" Wolf's work is not only faultless as regards truth to nature, but
"there is, besides, an indescribable feeling of life and movement
"never attained by any other artist.

" The best aspect of it, to my mind, is his power of representing
"the pathetic side of animal life, in which he shows his sympathy
"for the suffering bird or beast. This is especially noticeable in
"such pictures as the wounded Hare hunted down by Hooded
" Crows, or the water-colour drawing in the South Kensington
" Museum of the terror-stricken Ptarmigan striving to escape the
"glance of the marauding Eagle. . . . I suppose you asked Wolf
" the other day about the little incident that occurred the first time
" he visited his father's grave. This shows not only his great power
"of observation, but also how much poetry there is in his nature.
" Many a man would never have noticed the Red Admiral butterfly
"sunning itself on the tomb-stone, but Wolf at once saw in it a
" beautiful emblem of the resurrection."

Mr. Charles Whymper, the artist, has not only
known Wolf intimately for many years, but has enjoyed the rare privilege of working in his studio for a
long period. He may therefore be said to be more

[1] *Pterylography.* Translated from the German by W. S. Dallas, and
edited by P. L. Sclater. Ten plates of figures, folio. Ray Society, 1867.
A.H.P.

or less of a disciple ; and, in response to my request, this is what he says :—

"Asked to put into concisest form the ground of one's admiration "for the work of Mr. J. Wolf, I think there can be but one way of "answering the question. It is because of the vast and exact know-"ledge, always exhibited, of the life history of the particular animal "shown ; and of the subtle drawing which, though based on precise "anatomical science, is never obtrusively scholarly ; whilst, best of "all, he always imparts a romantic or poetic view of his subject. "Pictures so carried out, of animal life, may be said to have been "really the invention of Wolf alone.

"Prior to the advent of this remarkable and most original man, "painters had never regarded wild animal life as a field to work in. "Of course there had been many works illustrated by more or less "inexact pictures of animals, from a very early date. But no single "man had ever portrayed the life of bird and beast with its ever "varying incidents. Rubens, it is true, had painted Lions, and "Snyders had painted Boar hunts, but the slightest knowledge of "natural history would show anyone that neither of these great "painters knew anything more than the mere picturesque outside of "their subject, and they were content to make their work rest on "its masterly painting. As real, accurate representations of the "animals their pictures are not of much value.

"Not one painter, apparently, had ever given that study, or "attained that knowledge, which would have enabled him to portray "truly the wild creatures around him. The nightmares of pictures "which do in any way show animals other than domestic, are "evidence that there was little or no knowledge. . . . None of these "show any knowledge beyond the mere form of the dead body. "They show no knowledge of the life. You may search your "galleries and your libraries as you will. There is a complete "blank.

"Wolf, therefore, must have credit for absolutely discovering a "new field for art. His knowledge is so vast and varied that he "can give you the minutest details of the life of the Moose and Elk "from the far North, or the Lion or the Koodoo from southern "Africa, as truly as he can of the brooding Woodcock on her nest

" in our own country, or the roaming Wild Boar of his own Fatherland.
" No bird or mammal, whether great or small, but he understands it
" as completely as if he had made just that one creature his entire
" study.

" These are not merely idle words. For six years I worked with
" Wolf—for three, actually in his own studio ; and I can honestly say
" that every hour of those years added steadily to my wonder for and
" admiration of the depth and exactness of his marvellous knowledge
" of the whole realm of animal creation. This it is that makes his
" work so distinct and individual. It is saturated with the most
" scientific exactness.

" Wolf would have succeeded in any branch of art that he might
" have taken up, because of his fine sense of form and power of
" drawing it, but it is doubtful if he could possibly have done more
" for the art world at large. No doubt a great deal of his power is
" in some way intuitive ; but, in the main, it is owing to his constant
" and painstaking study—study such as most men would not attempt.
" From very earliest years he has insisted on the need of always
" working direct from life ; and his untiring habit of never slurring
" over the slightest detail but always going straight to nature for the
" smallest matter is the grand secret of his power. . . .

" He has shown us how rich the animal world is in poetic and
" picturesque subjects ; and moreover his animals are always animal,
" as opposed to human. Although a true lover of animals, he never
" commits that folly of trying to make them other than what they
" are ' beasts of the field.' A large section of the public, reared
" on pictures of pet Dogs with interesting faces as like man's as
" possible, and noble Stags and Eagles of conventional beauty,
" do not therefore all at once see the charm of his completely natural
" animals. But the verdict of every single naturalist and sports-
" man is that no pictures of wild animal life could possibly be better
" and truer.

" In technique Wolf's methods are admirably simple. Often
" have I watched him putting in with a big, flat brush those tender
" washes of warm colour that form the base of so many of his
" pictures. Painstaking to a degree in every detail, he would sit and
" watch the effect of the colour till it was sufficiently dry ; and then,
" with unerring certainty, he would take the complementary colour,

"and dexterously laying it on over the first wash, instantly produce
"the most perfect pearly grey mist. Then, with a well thought out
"plan, he would wipe out lights, and deepen shadows; but always,
"between each stage, he would sit down, pipe in hand, and quietly
"survey his work, his whole mind concentrated on it, till at the right
"moment he would again rise to his feet, and with a few touches
"put in some new forms. His work was never muddled or sloppy.
"Hence his drawings are always very pure in their tones. Often he
"would tell me, 'You are in too great a hurry. Have patience, and
"'smoke a pipe over it. Think what you are going to do before you
"'do it.' He had no patience with slapdash work, and he himself
"never did hurried work, but always with deliberate, loving careful-
"ness. Indeed it is this loving carefulness of his that gives the hall-
"mark to all he does. . . . His whole heart is in his work.

"Personally I think that it is the poetry of Wolf's mind which
"places him far beyond any ordinary animal painter, and gives him
"the title to be placed amongst the great artists. His knowledge,
"his care, his accuracy and dexterity, all would have been vain with-
"out it; but with it (and he has it in every fibre of his nature), his
"work must for all time rank with the very highest."

LION CUBS

(A sketch from life)   U

A

CATALOGUE OF

SOME OF THE PRINCIPAL WORKS

ILLUSTRATED ENTIRELY OR PARTLY

BY JOSEPH WOLF

NOTE.

In addition to the works in the Appendix, there are a number of books, published from the fifties onwards, to which Mr. Wolf contributed one or more of the illustrations, including Mr. Whymper's 'The Great Andes of the Equator' and Mr. Selous' last work. I have seen proofs of many of these illustrations, but up to the time of going to press I have not been able to trace the titles of the works themselves

A. H. PALMER.

TURTLE DOVES

APPENDIX

———

IN THE PROCEEDINGS
OF THE ZOOLOGICAL SOCIETY

		No.			*Paper.*
1848.	MAMMALS.	2.	*Ptilocercus lowii.* Borneo	.	J. E. GRAY
		3.	*Ceropithecus pluto.* Angola .	.	„
		8.	*Herpestes ochraceus.* Abyssinia	.	„
	BIRDS.	4.	*Podica personata.* Malacca .	.	G. R. GRAY
		5.	*Psittacus rüppellii.* R. Nunez. Africa		„
1849.	MAMMALS.	9.	*Ceropithecus melanogenys.* W. Africa.		
		„	*ludio.* W. Africa		J. E. GRAY
		12.	*Capreolus leucotis.* Valparaiso	.	„
		13.	*Tupaia ellioti.* Eastern Ghats,		G. R. WATER-
			India .	. . . .	HOUSE

* U 3

	No.		Paper.
1849. MAMMALS.	14.	The young Hippopotamus presented to the Society by H.H. Abbas Pasha	
BIRDS.	7.	*Gallus temminckii.* Batavia	G. R. GRAY
	8.	„ *æneus*	„
	9.	*Glareola nuchalis.* Fifth Cataract of the Nile	„
	10.	*Cultrides rufipennis.* Mexico	„
	13.	Hybrid Crown Pigeon. Hatched in the Menagerie	D. W. MITCHELL
1850. MAMMALS.	16.	*Presbytes albigena*	J. E. GRAY
	17.	*Phacochœrus æthiopicus.* Juv. Natal	„
	18.	*Thalacinus cynocephalus* ♂ ♀. Van Diemen's Land	„
	19.	The newly arrived Hippopotamus taking his first bath	„
	20.	*Adenota leché.* S. Africa	„
	22.	*Coassus nemorivagus* ♂	„
	23.	„ „ ♀	„
	24.	„ *rufus*	„
	25.	„ *superciliaris*	„
	26.	„ *auritus*	„
	27.	1.3.5. Heads of *C. nemorivagus.* 2, *C. rufus.* 4, *C. superciliaris.* 6, *C. auritus*	„
	28.	*Cariacus punctulatus*	„
BIRDS.	14.	*Eos cyanogenia*	LUCIEN BUONAPARTE
	15.	„ *semilarvata*	„
	16.	*Chalcopsitta rubiginosa*	„
	17.	*Garrulus lidthi.* Remote China?	„
	18.	*Oriolus broderipii.* Island of Sumbava	„
	19.	*Aquila audax.* Eggs laid in the Gardens	„
	22.	*Buteo rufipennis.* Kordofan	H. E. STRICKLAND
	23.	*Mirafra cordofanica* „	„
	24.	*Alauda erythropygia* „	„
	25.	*Palæornis derbianus.* New species in the collection at Knowsley	LOUIS FRASER
	26.	*Palæornis erythrogenys.* Ditto	„
	27.	*Crax alberti* ♂. Ditto	„

		No.	*Paper.*

BIRDS.   28. *Crax alberti* ♀. New species in the collection at Knowsley . LOUIS FRASER

29. *Penelope niger* ♂ ♀. Ditto.   „

30. 1.2. *Apteryx australis*
3.4. „ *mantelli* . . . A. D. BARTLETT

31. 1. *A. australis* (Foot). 2. *A. mantelli* (Foot) . . . „

32. *Turdus vulpinus.* Caraccas . HARTLAUB

33. *Machærirhynchus flaviventer.* N. Australia . . . . . „

34. *Plilotis filigera.* N. Australia . JOHN GOULD

1851. MAMMALS. 30. *Herpestes smithii.* Ceylon . . J. E. GRAY

31. *Cynictis maccarthiæ.* Ceylon . „

BIRDS. 35. *Balœniceps rex.* Upper White Nile . . . . . . JOHN GOULD

36. *Saurophagus derbianus.* Mexico. KAUP

37. *Psaris fraserii* ♂ Mexico . „

38. „ „ ♀ Mexico . . „

39. *Magapodius cumingii.* Island of Labuan . . . . . L. L. DILLWYN

40. *Francolinus yemensis.* Arabia . NICHOLSON

41. *Tænioptera erythropygia.* Republica Equatoriana . . . P. L. SCLATER

42. *Tænioptera striaticollis.* Republica Equatoriana . . . „

43. *Artamus cucullatus.* India. . NICHOLSON

44. *Sagmatorrhina lathami* . . L. BUONAPARTE

1852. MAMMALS. 32. *Anomalurus beecrofti.* Fernando Po . . . . . L. FRASER

33. *Hyrax dorsalis.* Fernando Po . „

34. *Potamochærus pencillatus.* Camaroons . . . . J. E. GRAY

BIRDS. 46. (Eggs.) 1. *Apteryx mantelli.* 2. *Sterna.* ? 3. *Strigops habroptilus.* 4. *Ocydromus australis.*

47. *Culicivora boliviana.* Bolivia . P. L. SCLATER

48. *Pipra flavo-tincta.* Santa Fé de Bogota . . . . . „

49. *Suthora webbiana.* Shang Hai . G. R. GRAY

1853. MAMMALS. 35. *Poëphagus grunnieus.* Juv. India. J. E. GRAY

36. *Budorcas taxicolor.* ♂ Ad. India. „

37. *Porcula salvania.* India . . „

38. *Felis macrosceloides.* India. . „

	No.		Paper.
1853. BIRDS.	50.	*Bucco radiatus.* New Granada .	P. L. SCLATER
	51.	*Malacoptila substriata.* New Granada	
	52.	*Dendrocolaptes cytoni.* Para .	
	53.	Nest and Eggs of *Menura alberti.* Australia	J. GOULD
	54.	*Ptilonopus chrysogaster*	„
	55.	„ *purpurœcinctus* .	G. R. GRAY
	56.	Eggs. 1. *Otogyps auritus.* 2. *Prosthemadera novæ-zealandiæ.*	H. F. WALTER
1854. MAMMALS.	39.	*Petrogale xanthopus.* Australia .	J. E. GRAY
BIRDS.	57.	*Ruticilla phænicuroides.* N. India.	F. MOORE
	58.	„ *hodgsoni,* ♂ ♀. Nepal.	„
	59.	„ *rufogularis,* ♂ ♀. India.	„
	60.	„ *vigorsi.* ♂. India.	„
	61.	„ *nigrogularis,* ♂. India.	„
	62.	*Nemura hodgsoni,* ♂ ♀. Nepal.	„
	63.	*Delichon nipalensis.* Nepal .	„
	64.	*Buthraupis chloronota* . . .	P. L. SCLATER
	65.	1. *Euphonia hirundinacea.* Guatemala. 2. *Euphonia concinna.* New Granada	„
	66.	*Tyrannula phænicura.* Ecuador.	„
	67.	*Arremon spectabilis.* Ecuador .	„
	68.	*Chlorospingus melanotis.* New Granada	„
	69.	*Tachyphonus xanthopygius.* New Granada	„
	70.	*Myrmeciza leucaspis.* Rio Negro.	„
	71.	„ *margaritata.* Peru .	„
	72.	*Pithys erythrophrys.* New Granada	„
		Hypocnemis melanolæma. Peru .	„
	73.	„ *melanostica.* New Granada	„
	74.	*Formicivora caudata.* New Granada	„
	75.	*Melacocichla dryas.* Guatemala .	JOHN GOULD
	76.	*Orthotomus derbianus.* Philippines?	F. MOORE
1855. BIRDS.	77.	*Galbula fuscicapilla.* New Granada	P. L. SCLATER
	79.	*Thamnophilus leuchauchen.* E. Peru . . .	

	No.		Paper.
BIRDS.	80.	*Thamnophilus melannonotus.* Para	P. L. SCLATER
	81.	*Thamnophilus nigrocinereus.* Para	„
	82.	„ *cæsius.* B. Guiana	„
	83.	„ *melanurus.* Brazil.	JOHN GOULD
	84.	*Todirostrum nigriceps.* Santa Martha	P. L. SCLATER
		Todirostrum spiciferum. N.E. Peru	„
	85.	*Conirostrum ferrugineiventre.* Bolivia	„
	86.	*Synallaxis erythrothorax.* Honduras	„
	87.	*Rhamphocænus cinerciventris.* New Granada . . .	„
	88.	*Cyphorinus albigularis.* Isthmus of Panama	„
	89.	*Arremon erythrohynchus.* Bogata.	„
	90.	*Tachyphonus xanthopygius.* Bogota	„
	91.	*Tanagra notabilis.* In Republica Equatoriana	„
	92.	*Saltator arremonops.* Ditto .	„
	93.	*Prion brevirostris.* Madeira .	„
	94.	*Grallaria modesta.* Santa Fé de Bogota	„
	95.	*Chamæza mollisima.* Ditto .	„
	96.	*Formicivora callinota.* Ditto .	„
	97.	*Dysithamnus semicinereus.* Ditto.	„
	98.	*Pyriglena tyrannina.* Ditto	„
	99.	*Nemosia albigularis.* Ditto	„
	100.	*Pyriglena ellisiana.* Ditto	„
	101.	*Anthus bogotensis.* Ditto	„
	102.	*Octocorys peregrina.* Ditto .	„
	103.	*Vireolanius icterophrys.* Ditto .	
	104.	*Ampelion rubricristatus* . .	
	105.	*Bucco hyperrhynchus.* Upper Amazon	„
	106.	*Bucco pulmentum.* Upper Amazon and E. Peru . . .	„
	107.	*Somateria v.-nigra.* Kotzebue Sound	G. R. GRAY
	108.	*Lampronetta fischeri* ♂. Norton Sound	„

		No.		*Paper.*

1855. BIRDS.   109. *Buarremon leucopterus.* In
                     Republica Equatoriana   .   .   P. L. SCLATER
                110. *Iridornis porphyrocephala* .   .   „
                111. *Octocoris longirostris.* Agra   .   F. MOORE
                112. *Emberiza stracheyi.* Kumaon,
                     India   .   .   .   .   .   „
                113. *Propasser thura* ♂. Nepal   .   „
                114.   „   „   ♀.   .   „

1856. MAMMALS. 41. *Mus musculus*   .   .   .   JOHN GASCOIN
                46. *Sciurus macrotis.* Sarawak   .   J. E. GRAY
                47. *Paradoxurus strictus.* Plains of
                     Nepal   .   .   .   .   T. HORSFIELD
                48. *Paradoxurus quadriscriptus.*
                     Hills of Nepal   .   .   .   „
                49. *Mustela strigidorsa.* Sikim   .   „
                50. *Arctonyx isonyx.* Nepal .   .   „
         BIRDS. 115. *Calænas stairi.* Samoan Islands   G. R. GRAY
                116. *Margarornis brunnescens.*
                     Bogota   .   .   .   .   P. L. SCLATER
                117. *Octhoëca funicolor.* Bogota   „
                118. *Euscarthmus agilis.* Bogota .   „
                119. *Conopophaga cucullata.* Bogota   „
                120. *Granatellus sallæi.* Cordova, S.
                     Mexico .   .   .   .   „
                121. *Pipra mentalis.* Cordova, S.
                     Mexico .   .   .   .   „

1857. MAMMALS. 51. Shanghai Sheep .   .   .   .   A. D. BARTLETT
                55. *Oryx beatrix.* Bombay   .   .   J. E. GRAY
                56. *Lepus nigripes.* Himalayas?   .   A. D. BARTLETT
                57. *Cephalophus grimmi* .   .   .   J. E. GRAY
                     „   *burchelli*   .   .   „
                58. *Leopardus hernandesii.* Mazatlan   „
         BIRDS. 123. *Cotinga amabilis.* Guatemala   .   JOHN GOULD
                124. *Euphonia gouldi.* Mexico   .   P. L. SCLATER
                125. (1 *Todirostrum calopterum.* In
                     Republica Equatoriana   .   „
                     (2) *Todirostrum capitale.* Ditto   „
                125. *Todirostrum exile.* Ditto   .   „
                126. (1) *Formicivora urosticta.* E.
                     Brazil .   .   .   .   .   „
                     (2 *Formicivora hauxwelli.* Ditto   „
                127. *Polychlorus westermanni.* Island
                     of St. Domingo .   .   „

		No.		*Paper.*

1858. MAMMALS.   59. *Potamochœrus africanus* .   .   J. E. GRAY

     61. *Cuscus orientalis.* ♂ ♀. Island of
         Ula   .   .   .

     62. *Cuscus celebensis.* Celebes   .

     63. *Dactylopsila trivirgata.* Aru
         Islands .   .   .   ,,

     64. *Myoictis wallacii* ♂. Ditto   .   ,,

BIRDS.   131. *Melanerpes rubrigularis.* Cali-
         fornia   .   .   .   .   . T. BRIDGES

     132. (1) *Euchœtes coccineus.* Ecuador. P. L. SCLATER
         (2) *Creurgops verticalis* ,,   .   ,,

     133. *Dacelo tyro.* Aru Islands .   . G. R. GRAY

     134. *Todospis cyanocephala.* Aru
         Islands .   .   .   .   ,,

     135. *Chalcopsitta rubrifrons.* Aru
         Islands .   .   .   .   ,,

     136. *Ptilonopus wallacii.* Aru
         Islands .   .   .   .   ,,

     137.   ,,   *aurantiifrons*   Ditto   ,,
     138.   ,,   *coronulatus*   Ditto   ,,

     139. *Thamnophilus amazonicus.*
         Upper Amazon   .   .   . P. L. SCLATER

     140. *Dysithamnus leucosticus.* Ecu-
         ador   .   .   .   .

     141. *Myrmotherula surinamensis.* ♂.
         Rio Negro   .   .   .   ,,
         Myrmotherula multostriata. ♂ ♀.
         Upper Amazon   .   .   ,,

     142. *Formicivora erythrocera.* Brazil.   ,,

     143. *Myrmelastes plumbeus.* ♂ ♀.
         Upper Amazon   .   .   ,,

     145. *Phrygilus ocularis.* ♂ ♀. Ecu-
         ador   .   .   .   .   ,,

     146. *Elainia griseigularis.* Ecuador
         ,,   *strictoptera*   ,,

     147. Young of *Catreus wallichii* and
         Lophophorus impeyanus. [Li-
         thographed by J. Jennens.]
         India   .   .   .   .   . D. W. MITCHELL

     148. Young of *Gallophasis albocri-
         status.* India   .   .   .,
         Young of *Gallophasis horsfeldii.*
         India   .   .   .   .   ,,

	No.		Paper.
1859 MAMMALS.	73.	*Equus kiang*	W. E. HAY
BIRDS.	150.	*Dendrocincla anabatina.* South America	T. J. MOORE
	151.	*Chloronerpes sanguinolentus.* S. America	,,
	152.	*Otothryx hodgsoni.* N. India .	G. R. GRAY
	153.	*Plectoperus gambensis* . .	P. L. SCLATER
		,, *ruppellii* . . .	,,
	154.	*Vireo josephæ.* Ecuador . .	,,
	155.	*Carpophaga goliath.* New Caledonia	G. R. GRAY
	156.	*Montifringilla adamsi.* Cashmere	A. L. ADAMS
	157.	*Laimodon albiventris.* West Africa	JULES VERREAUX
	158.	Hybrid between *Tadorna vulpansa* and *Casarsca cana* .	P. L. SCLATER
1860. MAMMALS.	76.	*Didelphis waterhousii.* Ecuador.	F. R. TOMES
BIRDS.	169.	*Aquila gurneyi.* [Lithographed by Jennens.] Molucca Islands.	G. R. GRAY
	170.	*Tanysiptera sabrina* ,,	,
	171.	*Megapodius wallacii* ,,	,,
	172.	*Habroptila* ,, ,,	,,

	Plate.		Paper.
1861. MAMMALS.	4.	*Lepus cuniculus.* Var. (See June 23, 1867.)	A. D. BARTLETT
	12.	*Potamochœrus pencillatus.* Fœm. et Juv.	P. L. SCLATER
	16.	*Sciurus gerrardi.* New Granada.	J. E. GRAY
	21.	*Hylobates pileatus.* Camboja .	,,
	22.	*Felis concolor.* Juv. . .	A. D. BARTLETT
	27.	*Cervus pseudaxis.* Pekin . .	J. E. GRAY
	31.	*Myoxomys salvinii.* Guatemala .	R. F. TOMES
BIRDS.	32.	*Megapodius quoyii.* Juv. Gilolo	G. R. GRAY
	33.	,, *reinwardtii.* Juv. New Guinea	,,
	34.	*Megapodius tumulus.* N. Australia	,,
	35.	*Grus montignesia.* Juv. China	A. D. BARTLETT
	40.	Heads of *Meleagris ocellata.* 1 ♂, 2 ♀. Honduras . . .	P. L. SCLATER
	42.	*Podargus superciliaris.* Waigiou.	G. R. GRAY

	Plate.		*Paper.*
BIRDS.	43.	Fig. 1. *Machærirhynchus albifrons* Waigiou and Mysol . .	G. R. GRAY
		Fig. 2. *Tudopsis wallacii*. Mysol.	„
	44.	*Henicophaps albifrons*. Waigiou.	„
1862. MAMMALS.	16.	*Cervus taëvanus*. Formosa .	P. L. SCLATER
	17.	„ *swinhoii* „ .	„
	24.	*Sciurus isabella*. Camaroon Mountains . . .	„
	32.	*Ursus japonicus*	„
	33.	*Leopardus japonensis* . . .	J. E. GRAY
	34.	*Cephalophus bicolor*. Natal .	„
	35.	*Capricornis swinhoii* . . .	„
	37.	*Pithecia monachus*	W. H. FLOWER
	41.	*Lemur leucomystax*. Madagascar.	A. D. BARTLETT
	42.	*Macacus cyclopis*. Formosa .	R. SWINHOE
	43.	*Leopardus brachyurus* „ . .	„
	44.	*Helictis subaurantiaca* „ . .	„
	45.	*Pteromys grandis* „ . .	„
BIRDS.	3.	*Harporhynchus ocellatus*. Oaxaca.	P. L. SCLATER
	8.	*Melacoptila poliopis*. West Ecuador	„
	11.	*Urochroma strictoptera*. New Granada	„
	14.	*Cacatua ophthalmica*. Sydney .	„
	18.	*Tylas eduardi*. Madagascar .	G. HARTLAUB
	19.	*Halcyon nigrocyanea*. New Guinea	A. R. WALLACE
	20.	*Gracula pectoralis*. Sorong .	,
	21.	*Ptilonopus humeralis*. Salwatty.	„
	30.	*Rhinochetus jubatus* . . .	A. D. BARTLETT
	38.	*Loriculus sclateri* . . .	A. R. WALLACE
	39.	*Trichoglossus flavoviridis* . .	„
	40.	*Oriolus frontalis*	„
1863. MAMMALS.	8.	*Hyracodon fuliginosus*. Ecuador	R. F TOMES
	17.	*Prosimia xanthomystax*. Madagascar	J. E. GRAY
	18.	*Prosimia melanocephala*. Madagascar	„
	19.	*Octogale pallida*. Fernando Po .	„
	22.	*Orcas derbianus*	W. W. READE
	28.	*Galago monteiri*. Angola . .	A. D. BARTLETT
	31.	*Lagothrix humboldtii*. Rio Negro	P. L. SCLATER
	32.	*Galago alleni*. West Africa .	„
	35.	„ *demidoffi*. Senegal? .	WILLIAM PETERS

		Plate.		*Paper.*
1863. BIRDS.		4. *Falco rubricollis.* Island of Bouru	A. R. WALLACE
		5. *Ceyx cajeli* „ „	„
		6. *Monarcha loricata* „ „	„
		9. *Perdix barbata*	J. VERREAUX
		10. *Pipra leucorrhoa.* New Granada	P. L. SCLATER
		13. *Hypherpes corallirostris.* Madagascar	A. NEWTON
		16. *Euplocamus nobilis.* Borneo .	P. L. SCLATER
		23. *Panyptila sancti - hieronymi.* Guatemala	„
		24. (1) *Cardellina versicolor.* Central America. (2) *Dendroeca niveiventris.* Central America .	O. SALVIN
		33. *Bubo fasciolatus.* Africa . .	P. L. SCLATER
		34. *Phloganas bartletti.* Philippine Islands?	„
		42. *Casuarius bennettii.* Juv. . .	„
1864. MAMMALS.		1. *Sciurus ornatus.* Natal . .	J. E. GRAY
		8. *Mustela aureoventris.* Ecuador .	„
		10. *Zorilla albinucha* . . .	„
		12. *Tragelaphus spekii.* E. Africa .	P. L. SCLATER
		13. *Golunda pulchella.* W. Coast of Africa	„
		28. *Arctocebus calabarensis.* Old Calabar	T. H. HUXLEY
		40. *Galago garnetti* . . .	P. L. SCLATER
		41. *Pithecia satanas.* Para . .	„
	BIRDS.	6. *Megapodius pritchardi.* Island of Nina Fou ♀ . . .	G. R. GRAY
		11. *Chauna nigricollis.* New Granada	P. L. SCLATER
		14. *Psalidoprocne albiceps.* Uzinza .	„
		16. *Smithornis rufo-lateralis* . .	G. R. GRAY
		17. *Cacatua ducorpsii.* Island of Guadalcanar	P. L. SCLATER
		18. *Tadorna tadornoides.* Tasmania	„
		19. „ *variegata.* New Zealand	„
		20 *Pucrasia xanthospila.* China .	G. R. GRAY
		24. *Cornurus rhodogaster.* Brazils .	P. L. SCLATER
		30. *Eucometis cassini.* Panama .	„
		34. *Anas melleri.* Madagascar .	„
		35. *Myadestes melanops.* Turrique .	O. SALVIN
		36. *Carpodectes nitidus.* Costa Rica.	„
1865. MAMMALS.		3. *Antilocapra americana* ♂. Juv. .	P. L. SCLATER

	Plate.	Paper.
MAMMALS.	7. *Enhydris lutris.* California	J. E. GRAY
	11. *Erithizon rufescens.* Columbia	„
	12. *Tupaia splendidula.* Borneo	„
	16. *Hystrix malabarica*	P. L. SCLATER
	17. *Pholidotus africanus.* W. Africa	J. E. GRAY
	18. *Dasypus vellerosus.* Santa Cruz	„
	19. *Cyclothurus dorsalis.* Costa Rica	„
	22. *Equus burchelli*	E. L. LAYARD
	45. *Cebus leucogenys.* Brazil	J. E. GRAY
BIRDS.	1. (1 and 2) *Foudia flavicans.* (2) *Drymœca* (?) *rodericana.* Island of Rodriguez	
	4. *Toccus elegans.* Angola	G. HARTLAUB
	5. „ *monteiri* „	„
	6. *Otis picturata* „	„
	24. *Leucopternis princeps.* Costa Rica	P. L. SCLATER
	28. *Rhipidura torrida.* Ternate	A. R. WALLACE
	29. (1) *Prionochilus aureolimbatus.* N. Celebes. (2) *Nectarinia flavo-striata.* Celebes	„
	33. *Cypselus squamatus.* Brazil. 'J. Wolf and J. W. Wood. Del. and lith.'	P. L. SCLATER
	34. *Chœtura biscutata.* Brazil. Ditto	„
	35. *Nasiturna pusio.* Saloman Islands. (Natural size)	„
	44. *Circus wolfi.* New Caledonia	J. H. GURNEY
1866. MAMMALS.	19. *Macacus inornatus.* ♀. Borneo	J. E. GRAY
	20. *Cephalophus breviceps.* W. Coast of Africa	„
1867. MAMMALS.	17. *Saiga tartarica,* ♂	P. L. SCLATER
	24. *Pardalina warwickii.* Himalaya	J. E. GRAY
	25. *Gueparda guttata.* Juv. Cape of Good. Hope	„
	31. *Prosimia flavifrons.* Madagascar	„
	35. *Phascolomys platyrhinus.* New South Wales	J. MURIE
	36. *Felis aurata.* Sumatra. Ad.	P. L. SCLATER
	37. *Gazella swmmerringi*	
	42. *Elasmognathus bairdi*	J. E. GRAY
	47. *Ateles bartletti.* River Amazons	„
BIRDS.	16. *Lorius chlorocercus.* Saloman Islands	P. L. SCLATER

		Plate.		*Paper.*

1867. BIRDS.   22. *Coracopsis barklyi.* Seychelles Islands . . . . .   EDWARD NEWTON

1868. MAMMALS.   6. *Macacus lasiotus.* China .   . J. E. GRAY
              7. *Pteromura sandbachii.* Demerara . . . . .   „
              8. *Ursus nasutus.* West Indies .   P. L. SCLATER
            15. *Colobus kirki.* Zanzibar .   . J. E. GRAY
            24. *Mico sericeus.* America .   . „

BIRDS.   13. (1) *Euscarthmus impiger.* Venezuela . . . . .   P. L. SCLATER
            (2) *Sublegatus glaber.* Ditto .   „

1870. MAMMALS.   6. *Hydropotes inermis.* China. (Lithographed by Smit.) . .   R. SWINHOE

1871. MAMMALS.   39. *Tragelaphus euryceros.* (Lithographed by Smit.) . . .   SIR VICTOR BROOKE
           76. *Felis euptilura.* N. W. Siberia. Ditto . . . .   D. G. ELLIOTT

1873. MAMMALS.   37. *Pteromys tephromelas.* Pienang. Ditto . . . .   A. GÜNTHER
           38. *Sciururopterus pulverulentus.* Penang. Ditto . . .   „

1874. MAMMALS.   6. *Chaus caudatus.* Bokhara. Ditto   J. E. GRAY
           8. *Cervulus sclateri.* Ditto .   . SIR VICTOR BROOKE
           28. *Rhinoceros sondiacus.* Java. Ditto   P. L. SCLATER
           49. *Felis badia.* Sarawak. Ditto .   J. E. GRAY

1875. MAMMALS.   15. *Chirogaleus trichotis.* Madagascar. Ditto . .   . A. GÜNTHER
           16. *Brachytarsomys albicauda* .   .
           37. *Cervus mesopotamicus.* Ditto .   SIR VICTOR BROOKE
           54. *Bubalus pumilis.* Africa. Ditto   „

1877. MAMMALS.   8. *Cervus philippinus.* Philippine Islands. Ditto . . .   „
           35. *Troglodytes gorilla.* Ditto .   P. L. SCLATER
           81. *Canis jubatus.* South America. Ditto . . . .   „

1878. MAMMALS.   39. *Tapirus roulini.* Ditto . .   „
1880. MAMMALS.   44. *Tragelaphus gratus.* Gaboon .   „

TRANSACTIONS OF THE ZOOLOGICAL SOCIETY.

	Plate.	*Paper.*
VOL. 4.	*Notornis mantelli.* New Zealand.	
	58. *Urubitinga schistacea,* ½. Bolivia.	P. L. SCLATER
	59. *Buteo zonocercus,* ½. Guatemala.	,,
	60. *Syrnium albitarse,* ½. S. America.	,,
	61. *Scops usta,* ¼. Upper Amazon .	..
	62. *Buteo fuliginosus,* ½. Mexico .	,,
	63. *Ciccaba nigrolineata,* ½. Mexico.	,,
	64. *Balæniceps rex.* (Lithographed by	
	J. Jury.)	W. K. PARKER
VOL. 5.	14. Female Aye Aye, ½. (From Life.	
	Lithographed by Erxleben.)	
	15. Male Aye Aye, ¼. (Specimen in	
	spirits.)	
	16. ,, ,, ,, ½. (Front.)	
	17. ,, ,, ,, ½. (Back.)	
	18. Male Aye Aye. Head and limbs, ¼	PROFESSOR OWEN
	43. Adult male Gorilla from M. du	
	Chaillu's collection . . .	
	44. (1) Adult male, showing the or-	
	dinary quadrupedal mode of	
	progression . . .	
	(2) Adult female Gorilla . .	
	(3) Young male Gorilla, from M.	
	du Chaillu's collection. (Pre-	
	served in spirits.) . .	
	46. (1) Sketches of the same speci-	
	men	
	(2-6) Sketches of the details .	PROFESSOR OWEN
VOL. 6.	1. *Potamogale velox,* ½. Old Cala-	
	bar	G. J. ALLMAN
	29. *Machærhamphus alcinus.* Da-	
	maraland	J. H. GURNEY
VOL. 7.	1. (1) *Galago crassicaudatus,* ♀ ⅔.	
	From a photograph by Dr. Murie	J. MURIE
	(2) *Galago garnetti* . .	,,
	31. *Cervus mantchuricus* . . .	P. L. SCLATER
VOL. 9.	95. *Rhinoceros unicornis.* Litho-	
	graphed by Smit. . .	,,
	96. *Rhinoceros sondaicus.* Ditto	..
	97. *Rhinoceros sumatrensis.* Ditto .	.,
	98. *Rhinoceros lasiotis.* Ditto .	,,

X

IN THE IBIS

Plate. *Paper.*

1. *Gymnoglaux nudipes* St. Croix . A. & E. NEWTON

1859. 3. *Cephralopterus pendulicer.* Ecuador

6. *Falco barbarus.* Eastern Atlas . O. SALVIN

7. *Gallinula pumila.* Natal . . J. H. GURNEY

8. *Accipiter haplochrous.* New Caledonia . . . . . P. L. SCLATER

15. *Scotopelia peli* . . . . J. H. GURNEY

1860. 4. *Syrrhaptes paradoxus* . . . T. J. MOORE

6. *Accipiter collaris.* New Granada P. L. SCLATER

10. „ *poliocephalus* . . „

1861. 7. *Falco babylonicus* . . . L. HOWARD

9. (1) *Basilornis corythaix* . .
(2) „ *celebensis* . . A. R. WALLACE

10. *Accipiter pectoralis.* S. America.
(Lithographed by J. Jennens.) . P. L. SCLATER

1862. 3. *Circaëtus fasciolatus.* Natal.
Ditto . . . J. H. GURNEY

4. *Spizaëtus ayresii.* Natal . . „

7. *Circaëtus beaudouini.* Nubia . J. VERREAUX

8. *Buteo brachypterus.* Madagascar. S. ROCH

9. *Atelornis pittoides* . . .

10. *Hirundo monteiri.* Angola . J. J. MONTEIRO

13. *Psarophotus ardens.* Formosa . R. SWINHOE

1863. 2. *Tinnunculus newtoni.* Madagascar.

3. *Oreocetes gularis* Northern
China . . . . . „

4. *Circus maillardi.* Bourbon . P. L. SCLATER

5. *Circus spilonotus.* Formosa . R. SWINHOE

6. *Pomatorhinus musicus.* Formosa. „

8. Fig. 1. *Camaroptera natalensis.*
Natal . . . . . J. H. GURNEY
Fig. 2. *Cisticolor ayresii.* Natal . „

9. *Megalophonus rostratus.*

11. *Accipiter stevensoni.* China . „

12. *Calliste dowii* . . . . P. L. SCLATER

1864. 1. *Acrocephalus stentorius.* Egypt . S. S. ALLEN

2. *Caprimulgus vexillarius* . . P. L. SCLATER

5. *Astur griceiceps.* Celebes . A. R. WALLACE

7. *Accipiter francesi.* Comoro Islands . . . . P. L. SCLATER

	Plate.	Paper.
1864.	8. *Falco dickinsoni.* Zambesi	
	9. *Turdus gurneyi.* Natal . .	J. H. GURNEY
	10. *Tetragonops frantzii.* Costa Rica	P. L. SCLATER
1865.	2. *Nectarinea osea.* Palestine .	H. B. TRISTRAM
	3. *Chasmorhynchus tricarunculatus.*	O. SALVIN
	4. *Orites tephronotus.* Asia Minor .	A. GÜNTHER
	5. *Aquila nævioides* . . .	LORD LILFORD
	6. *Fratercula glacialis.* Spitzbergen	A. NEWTON
	7. *Sitta krueperi.* Asia Minor .	P. L. SCLATER
	8. *Copsychus sechellarum.* Sey-	
	chelles	A. NEWTON
	9. *Phlegœnas tristigmata*, ⅓. Malay	
	Archipelago	A. R. WALLACE
	10. *Chætusia leucura.* Islands of	
	Malta and Gozo . . .	C. A. WRIGHT
	11. *Iridornis reinhardti.* Peru . .	P. L. SCLATER
1866.	1. *Sula bassana*	R. O. CUNNINGHAM
	2. *Caprimulgus tamaricis*, ⅓. Dead	
	Sea	H. B. TRISTRAM
	3. *Pyrrhula murina.* The Azores .	F. DU CANE
	4. *Sibia auricularis.* Formosa .	
	5. *Turdus albiceps* ,, .	
	6. *Phlexis layardi.* (After O. Finsch.)	
	Africa	G. HARTLAUB
	7. *Oxynotus typicus*, ⅓. Reunion (3	
	figs.)	F. POLLEN
	8. *Oxynotus newtoni*, } . . .	,,
	9. *Suthora bulomachus.* Formosa .	R. SWINHOE
	11. *Cyornis vivida* ,, .	,,
1867.	1. *Bessornis albigularis.* Palestine .	H. B. TRISTRAM
	2. *Cinclus ardesiacus.* Veragua .	O. SALVIN
	3. *Garrulus brandti.* Northern Japan	H. WHITELY, JUN.
	4. *Tchitrea corvina.* Seychelles Ar-	
	chipelago	E. NEWTON
	5. Fig. 1. *Lanius isabellinus.*	
	2. ,, *phœnicurus* . .	VISC. WALDEN
	6. *Lanius magnirostris* . . .	,,
	7. *Passer moabiticus*	H. B. TRISTRAM
	10. *Piprisoma agile.* (Ad., nest, and	
	young.) India	R. C. BEAVAN
1868.	1. *Spizaetus nanus.* Borneo . .	A. R. WALLACE
	2. *Erythropus amurensis* ♂ ♀. Juv.	J. H. GURNEY
	4. *Hirundo alfredi.* S. Africa .	

	Plate		*Paper.*
1868.	6.	*Petronia brachydactyla*	H. B. TRISTRAM
	7.	*Serinus aurifrons*	„
	8.	*Glareola nordmanni.* S. Africa	J. H. GURNEY
	9.	(1) *Cichladusa arquata.* After Henglin	M. T. VON HENGLIN
		(2) *Cichladusa guttata.* Ditto	„
	10.	*Hyphantornis mariquensis.* Natal	J. H. GURNEY
1869.	9.	*Campithera capricorni*	EDITOR
	16	*Hypotriorchis eleonora,* ♂. Madagascar	J. H. GURNEY

OTHER ILLUSTRATED WORKS.

IN THE FORTIES.

1845. RÜPPELL, DR. EDUARD. *Systematische Uebersicht der Vögel Nord-Ost Afrikas.* Frankfurt a/M. [Auto-lithographs.]

1. Gypaëtus meridionalis.
2. Nisus sphenurus.
3. Caprimulgus poliocephalus.
4. ,, tetrastygma.
5. Cecropis melanocrissus.
6. ,, striolata.
7. Acedo semitorquata.
8. Epimachus minor.
9. Nectarinea cruentata.
10. Drimoica mistacea.
11. ,, lugubris.
12. ,, erythrogenis.
13. ,, robusta.
14. Curruca chocolatina.
15. Salicaria leucoptera.
16. Saxicolor albofasciata.
17. ,, albifrons.
18. Parus dorsatus.
19. Crateropus rubigenosus.
20. Musicapa chocolatina.
21. Bessonoris semirufa.
22. Parisomus frontalis.
23. Telopherus aethiopicus.
24. Melaconotus chrysogaster.
25. Lamprotornis purpuroptera.

26. Lamprotornis superba.
27. Eurocephalus augintimeus.
28. Euplectes xanthomelas.
29. Textor flavoviridis.
30. ,, dinemelli.
31. Pionus flavifrons.
32. ,, rufiventris.
33. Dendrobates scaensis.
34. ,, poicephalus.
35. ,, hemprichii.
36. Dendromus aethiopicus.
37. Jyns aequatorialis.
38. Peristera chalcospilos.
39. Numidia-ptilorhyncha.
40. Francolinus gutturalis.
41. Otis melanogaster.
42. Œdicnemus affinis.
43. Glareola limbata.
44. Lobivanellus melanocephalus.
45. Ibis comata, ♯
46. Rallus abyssinicus.
47. Beanicla cyanoptera.
48. Anas leucostygma.
49. Onocrotalus minor.
50. Phalacrocorax lugubris.

1833-50. SIEBOLD P. FRANTZ. *Fauna Japonica.* Animalia vertebrata elaborantibus C. H. Temminck et H. Schlegel. [Auto-lithographs.]

AVES

Falco tinnunculus japonicus, ♀.
Astur (nisus) gularis.
Spizaëtus orientalis, ♀.
Haliëtos palagicus, ♀.
Milvus melanotis, ♀.
Buteo vulgaris japonicus, ♀.
,, hemilasius, ♀.
Otus semitorgues.
Scops japonicus.
Stryx fuscescens.

Hirundo alpestris japonica.
Caprimulgus jotaka, ♂
,, ,, ♀
Lanius bucephalus.
Muscicapa cinereo-alba.
,, gularis.
,, hylocharis.
Ficedula coronata.
Salicaria cantans.
,, cantillans.

1844 53. PROFESSOR H. SCHLEGEL AND H. WULVERHORST. *Traité de Fauconnerie.* Düsseldorf. [Auto-lithographs.]

Plate.
V. Le Groënlandias Faucon Blanc Mue.
VI. Le Tiercelet Hagard de Faucon D'Island.
VII. Le Tiercelet Hagard de Gerfaut.
VIII. Le Gerfaut Sors.
IX. Le Sacre Hagard.
X. Le Faucon Hagard.
XI. Le Tiercelet Sors de Fau-

Plate.
con au plumage de Cresserelle.
XII. L'Emérillon Hagard, Le Tiercelet, Sors, et Hagard D'Emérillon.
XIII. L'Autom Hagard.
XIV. Le Tiercelet, Sors de l'Autom.
XV. L'Eperirer Sors et le Mouchet Hagard.

[All life size.]

1846 52. SÜSEMIHL, J. C. und EDUARD. *Abbildungen der Vögel Europas.* Stuttgart. [Auto-lithographs.]

Taf. 6A. Der weisse Falke (*Falco candicans*), Group.
,, 44. Der sibirische Uhu (*Strix sibirica*).
,, 47. Der Stein-Kauz. 1, Alt. 2, Jung. (*Strix noctua*). Group.
,, 54. Eleonoren's Fa ke. 1, Männchen. 2, Weibchen. 3, Schwarze Var. 4, Grane Var. Group.
II Taf. 6. Der schwarzköpfige Hacher (*Garrulus melanocephalus*).
,, 14. Der schwarzstirnige Würger. 1, Alt, m. 2, Jung, m. (*Lanius minor*).
17. Der Masken - Würger (*Lanius personatus*). Alt. Fig. 1.

II Taf. 17. Der gehaubte Würger (*Lanius cucullatus*). Alt. Fig. 2.
,, 20. Der bunte Staar (*Sturnus vulgaris*). 1, M. im Herbst. 2, M. im Frühl. 3, Jung. Vog. Group.
IX Taf. 5. Das Feld-Rebhuhn (*Perdix cinerea*). 1, Männchen. 2, Weibchen. Group.
,, 6. Das Birkwaldhuhn (*Tetra tetrix*). 1, Männchen. 2, Weibchen. Group.

1846. J. WOLF AND F. FRISCH. *Jagdstücke der hohen und niederen Jagd.* Darmstadt. Ernst Kern. [Among J. Wolf's are Auto-lithographs of Badgers, Capercailzie, Partridges, Blackgame, Woodcock, &c.]

1844-49. GRAY, G. R. *The Genera of Birds.* Longmans & Co. [Auto-lithographs.]

Vol. I.
XXXV. *Phaëtornis petrei* (Wedge-tailed Humming-bird.)
XXXVI. *Polytmus aquila* (Humming-bird.)
XXXVII. *Melisuga mirabilis.*
XLVIII. *Myalurus citrinus.*
XLIX. *Calamodyta affinis.*
XLX. *Vireo virescens.*
And twenty-eight plates of detail.

Vol. II.
CXX. *Didunculus strigirostris.*
CLVIII. *Phalaropus wilsonii.*
CLXXI. *Colymbus arcticus.*
CLXXVII. *Brachyramphus antiquus.*
CLXXXIV. *Plotus nova-hollandiæ.*
And eleven plates of detail.

Vol. III.
Twenty plates of detail.

IN THE FIFTIES.

1850. KNOX, A. E. *Game Birds and Wild Fowl, their Friends and their Foes.* Van Voorst. [Auto-lithographs.]

Frontispiece : The Death of the Mallard.

Page 68. Off at Last.

Page 150. The Old Poacher's Springe.

,, 205. Grouse and 'Seaul Crows.'

1852. BURTON, RICHARD F. *Falconry in the Valley of the Indus.* Van Voorst. Frontispiece : Goshawk and Gazelle. Auto-lithograph.]

1853. ARNOLD, J. T. *Reynard the Fox.* After the German version of Goethe, with Illustrations by J. Wolf. Pickering. Twelve designs etched by A. Fox and R. H. Roe.

1853. *The Poets of the Woods.* Twelve pictures of English Song Birds. Printed in colours by M. and N. Hanhart. Bosworth. [Chromo-lithographs.] 4to.

Turtle Doves.	Bullfinch.	Goldfinch.
Robin.	Thrush.	Cuckoo.
Chaffinch.	Linnet.	Ring Dove.
Skylark.	Blackbird.	

1854. *Feathered Favourites.* Twelve coloured pictures of British Birds from drawings by Joseph Wolf. Bosworth. [Chromo-lithographs.] 4to.

House Sparrow.	Woodpecker.	Wood Lark.
Wren.	Water Wagtail.	The Swan.
Blackcap.	Titmouse.	The Eagle.
Swallow.	Kingfisher.	The Wild Duck.

1855. KNOX, A. E. *Ornithological Rambles in Sussex.* Third edition. Van Voorst. [Auto-lithographs]

Frontispiece : The Osprey.
Page 31. Heron and Water Rat.
,, 110. Falcon and Teal.

Page 136. Othello's occupation's gone.

1856. ANDERSSON, C. J. *Lake NGami.* Hurst and Blackett. [Auto-lithographs.] 8vo.

Frontispiece : Lions pulling down a Giraffe.
Page 110. The lucky Escape.
,, 126. Shooting Trap.
,, 213. Unwelcome hunting Companions.
,, 253. Coursing young Ostriches.
,, 279. Oryx and Gemsbok.
,, 381. Chasing the Eland.
,, 414. The approach of Elephants.

Page 422. More close than agreeable.
,, 424. Desperate situation.
,, 448. Nakong and Leche Antelopes.
,, 484. The Koodoo.
,, 521. Hippopotamus harpooned.
,, 528. (Woodcut) The Downfall.

1857. LIVINGSTONE, DAVID. *Missionary Travels and Researches in South Africa.* Murray. [Woodcuts.] 8vo.

Page 13. Missionary's escape from the Lion.	Page 210. A new or striped variety of Eland.
,, 26. The Hopo, or Trap for driving Game.	,, 242. Mode in which the female Hippopotamus carries her Calf.
,, 27. The Pit at the extremity of the Hopo.	,, 498. Boat capsized by a female Hippopotamus robbed of her Young.
,, 56. Hottentot Women returning from the Water.	,, 562. Female Elephant, pursued with javelins, protecting her Young.
,, 71. New African Antelopes (Pokne and Leche).	,, 588. The travelling Procession interrupted.
,, 140. Three Lions attempting to drag down a Buffalo.	
,, 142. Buffalo Cow defending her Calf.	

[Another Edition was published in 1861.]

1857. *The Book of Job.* 'Illustrated with fifty engravings from drawings by John Gilbert.' Of these J. Wolf's designs are :

Page 25. The Dead Lion.	Page 140. The Unicorn.
,, 72. The Cobra [altered].	,, 141. The Ostrich.
,, 137. The Den.	,, 145. Behemoth.
,, 139. The Wild Ass.	,, 147. Leviathan at play. Nisbet.

[Another Edition, 1880.]

1858. JAMES, T., M.A. *Æsop's Fables.* A new version. 'With more than one hundred illustrations designed by John Tenniel.' Of these the following are J. Wolf's. Murray. [Woodcuts.]

Page 1. The Fox and Grapes.	Page 51. The Hares and Frogs.
,, 4. The Wolf and the Crane.	,, 65. The Oak and the Reed.
,, 5. The Vain Jackdaw.	,, 89. The Birds, Beasts, and Bat.
,, 9. The Eagle and the Fox.	,, 104. The Fox and the Mask.
,, 16. The Dog and the Shadow.	,, 106. The Lion and the Bulls.
,, 23. The House-dog and the Wolf.	,, 110. The Fox and the Stork.
,, 27. The Tortoise and the Eagle.	,, 111. The Ass in the Lion's Skin.
,, 49. The Fox without a Tail.	,, 115. The Quack Frog.
	,, 120. The Stag at the Pool.
	,, 126. The Wild Boar and the Fox.
	,, 133. The Old Lion.

[Another Edition, 1882.]

1858. KING, THE REV. S. W. *The Italian Valleys of the Pennine Alps.* Murray. Page 340, 'The Steinbok.' [Woodcut.]

1858. DRAYSON, CAPT. A. W., *Sporting Scenes amongst the Kaffirs of South Africa.* 'Illustrated by Harrison Weir from

designs by the Author.' The whole of these illustrations
are by J. Wolf. Routledge. [Woodcuts.] 8vo.

Frontispiece : Buffalo Hunting.
Page 109. Eland Hunting.
  ,, 127. Wild Boar Hunt-
      ing.
  ,, 131. Hunting the Hart-
      beest.

Page 174. Elephant Hunting in the
      Bush.
  ,, 195. Sharp Practice.
  ,, 248. The Run.
  ,, 291. The Red Buck and the
      Sporting Leopard.

[The List of Illustrations does not correspond.]

1859.   FREEMAN, G. E., and CAPT. F. H. SALVIN. *Falconry: its
      Claims, History, and Practice.* Longmans. [Woodcuts.]

Frontispiece: Magpie Hawking.
Page 50. Hawk Furniture.
  ,, 223. Female Goshawk
      and Hare.

Page 317. Hook. 320. Swivel.
  ,, 327. Cormorant Fishing.
  ,, 339. Cormorant Palaquin.

1859.   *Zoological Diagrams.* Prepared for the Department of Science
      and Art. R. Patterson. Chapman and Hall.

SHEET A	SHEET B	SHEET C
2. Spider Mon-	2. Hippopotamus.	1. Peregrine Falcon.
key.	3. Red Deer.	2. Magpie.
3. Bat.	4. Sloth.	3. Silver Pheasant.
4. Hedgehog.	5. Squirrel.	4. Heron.
5. Tiger.	6. Red Kangaroo.	5. Wild Duck.

1859.   THOMPSON, JAMES. *The Seasons.* Illustrated by Birket Foster,
      F. R. Pickersgill, R.A., J. Wolf, &c. Nisbet. [Woodcuts.
      Engraved by Dalziel Bros.] Small 4to.

Page 5. Bittern.
  ,, 49. Blackbird in Nest.
  ,, 69. Tiger and Antelope.
  ,, 139. Partridges.

Page 187. Cormorant and Gulls.
  ,, 197. Wolves attacking a Tra-
      veller.
  ,, 213. Deer sheltering in Snow.

1859.   WORDSWORTH, WILLIAM. *Poems.* Selected by R. A. Willmott.
      Illustrated by Birket Foster, J. Wolf, John Gilbert, &c.
      Routledge. [Woodcuts.]

Page 9. Swans and Young.
  ,, 25. Eagle in a Storm.
  ,, 159. Hares playing.
  ,, 167. Linnets.
  ,, 189. Robin and Rookery.
  ,, 221. A Sheep by a Lake.

Page 226. Wild Fowl.
  ,, 249. Peregrines.
  ,, *265. Lambs.
  ,, 301. Kite and Nest.
  ,, 317. Poultry, Sparrows, &c.
  ,, 327.   ,,   Chickens, &c.

    * Also in Routledge's ' British Spelling Book,' p. 95.

1859.   WOOD, THE REV. J. G. *The Illustrated Natural History.*
      With 1700 illustrations by Wolf and others. Routledge.
      4to. 3 vols. [Woodcuts.]

Vol. 1 : MAMMALIA.

Frontispiece.
Page 11. Group of Monkeys.

Page 15. Gorilla.
  ,, 20. Chimpanzee.

Vol. 1 : MAMMALIA *continued.*

Page 26. Orang-outan.
,, 31. Siamang.
,, 44. Ceropithici.
,, 60. Wanderoo.
,, 62. Group of Chaemas.
,, 64. Gelada.
,, 67. The Chaema.
,, 71. The Baboon.
,, 73. The Papion.
,, 75. The Mandril.
,, 78. The Drill.
,, 109. (1) Galagos. (2) The Tarsier.

Page 112. The Colugo.
,, 133. The Lion.
,, 136. Lion and Zebras.
,, 144. Gambian Lion.
,, 148. Maneless Lion.
,, 151. Tiger.
,, 178. Serval.
,, 192. Egyptian Cat.
,, 193. Wild Cat.
,, 212. European Lynx.
,, 663. Koodoo.
,, 669. Ibex.

Vol. 2 : BIRDS.

Frontispiece.
Page 1. Group of Vultures.
,, 67. ,, Falcons.
,, 128. ,, Swallows.
,, 168. ,, Kingfishers.
,, 278. ,, Warblers.
,, 312. ,, Wagtails.
,, 373. ,, Shrikes.
,, 463. ,, Finches.
,, 504. ,, Hornbills.
,, 596. Crested Curasso.

Page 601. Brush Turkey.
,, 614. Veillot's Fireback.
,, 642. White Sheathbill.
,, 657. Apteryx.
,, 672. Crane.
,, 673. Demoiselle and Crowned Cranes.
,, 675. Egret, Heron, and Bittern.
,, 725. Group of Swans.
,, 751. ,, Gulls.
,, 762. Pelican.

Vol. 3 : REPTILES.

Page 27. African Crocodiles at Home.

See also a few plates in Routledge's smaller Natural Histories.

IN THE SIXTIES.

1860. BENNETT, GEORGE, M.D. *Gatherings of a Naturalist in Australia.* Van Voorst. 8vo. [Lithographs.]

Frontispiece : Australian Jabiru. (After F. Angas.)
Page 135. Australian Water-mole (Platypus). (Auto-lithograph.)
,, 264. The Mooruk. (Auto-lithograph.)

1860. DUNLOP, R. H. W. *Hunting in the Himalaya.* Demy 8vo. Bentley. [Lithographs.]

Frontispiece : Bunchowr brought to Bay.
Page 86. Addressing a Stranger without an Introduction.

Page 108. A Prompt and Public Execution.
,, 286. Heemachul and its Inhabitants.

1860. ATKINSON, T. W. *Travels in the Region of the Lower and Upper Amoor.* Hurst and Blackett. [Woodcuts.] 8vo.

Page 114. The Maral's Leap.
,, 352. The Tiger and its Victim.

Page 147. Bearcoots and Wolves.
,, 347. The Bearded Eagle and Steinbok.

1860.   MONTGOMERY, JAMES. *Poems.* Selected and edited by Robert
        A. Willmott. Illustrated by John Gilbert, J. Wolf, Birket
        Foster, &c. Routledge. 4to. [Woodcuts.]

Page 67. Giraffes.   Page 315. Flamingoes.
  ,, 216. Swan.   ,, 323 Tiger seizing a Zebu.
  ,, 309. Pelicans.   ,, 369. House Martin and Nest.
  ,, 311. Pelicans and Young. |

1861.   *Traits and Anecdotes of Animals.* With illustrations by Wolf.
        Bentley. 8vo. [Two of the illustrations are by Zwecker.
        Woodcuts]

Frontispiece: An Unpleasant   Page 69. The Bull and the Bear.
  Predicament.   ,,   96. An uncalled-for Assault.
Page 26. Retreat of the Leo-   ,, 151. The Briton and his Beef.
  nidæ.   ,, 238. Starved to Death.

[Reprinted under the title of *Curious and Instructive Stories about Wild
  Animals and Birds.* Nimmo. 1873.]

1861.   TENNENT, SIR JAMES EMERSON.   *Sketches of the Natural
        History of Ceylon.* Longmans. [Woodcuts.]

Page *5. Ceylon Monkeys.   Page 184. Mode of Tying an Ele-
  ,, *14. Group of Flying Foxes.   phant.
  ,, 23. Indian Bear.   ,, 185. His Struggles for Free-
  ,, *26. Ceylon Leopard and   dom.
         Cheetah.   ,, 188. Impotent Fury.
  ,, *38. Mongoose.   ,, 189. Obstinate Resistance.
  ,, 41. Flying Squirrel.   ,, 203. Attitude for Defence.
  ,, *44. Coffee Rat.   ,, 204. Singular Contortions.
  ,, *58. Mouse Deer.   ,, 243. The Hornbill.
  ,, 69. The Dugong.   ,, 247. The Devil Bird.

  * These cuts also appear in Hartwig's *Tropical World.* Longmans. 1863.

1861.   *The Alphabet of Birds,* with pictures by Wolf, Weir, Zwecker,
        &c. Engraved by Brothers Dalziel. Routledge. [1 Wood-
        cut. The Apteryx.]

1861.   P. H. GOSSE.   *The Romance of Natural History.* Nisbet. 8vo.
        [Woodcuts.]

Frontispiece: The Gorilla.   Page 118. The African Elephant.
Page 42. The Hyæna in the   ,, 200. Wildfowl   on   Solitary
  Deserted City.   River.
  ,, 60. A Brazilian Forest   ,, 208. A Moose Yard.
         Scene.   ,, 250. Encounter with a Rhino-
  ,, 82. A Tropical Bird Sta-   ceros.
         tion.

1861.   *The Romance of Natural History.*   Second Series.

Frontispiece: Fascination.   Page 310. Mourning   the   Dead
Page 36. Encounter with a Moa.   Cuckoo.
  ,, 304. Antelopes.   ,, 326. Peacock Shooting.

1861.   ELIZA COOK. *Poems.* Selected and edited by the Author. Illustrated by John Gilbert, J. Wolf, H. Weir, J. D. Watson, &c. [Woodcuts. Engraved by Dalziel Brothers.] Routledge. 4to.

Page 55. 'Song of the Sea-   Page 215. 'The Rook sits high.'
gulls.'   ,, 241. 'To the Robin.'
,, 195. 'Birds.'   ,, 402. 'Not as I used to do.'
,, 197. ,,

1861.   *English Sacred Poetry.* Selected by R. A. Willmott. Illustrated by Holman Hunt, J. D. Watson, John Gilbert, J. Wolf, &c. [Woodcuts engraved by Dalziel Brothers.] Routledge. 4to.

Page 40. Search after God.   Page 127. The Garden.
,, 59. Decay of Earthly   ,, 160. God s Argument with Job.
Pomp.   ,, 347. The Truant Hour.
,, 119. The Bird.   ,, 356. Wisdom Unapplied.
[Another Edition was published in 1877.]

1861.   *Zoological Sketches by Joseph Wolf.* Made for the Zoological Society of London from Animals in their Vivarium in the Regent's Park.   Edited with notes by Philip L. Sclater, M.A. Graves. [Lithographs by Mr. Smit. Coloured by hand after the original water-colour drawings.]

MAMMALS.

1. The Chimpanzee	. . . .	Troglodytes niger.
2. The Pluto Monkey .	. . .	Ceropithecus pluto.
3. The Lion	. . . .	Felis leo.
4. The Leopard .	. . .	,, leopardus.
5. The Painted Ocelot .	. . .	,, picta.
6. The Eyra .	. . .	,, eyra.
7. The Clouded Tiger .	. . .	,, macrocelis.
8. The Serval	. . .	,, serval
9. The Egyptian Cat .	. . .	,, chaus.
10. The Caracal .	. . .	,, caracal.
11. The Red Caracal .	. . .	,,
12. The Canadian Lynx	. . .	,, canadensis.
13. The Cheetah .	. . .	,, jubata.
14. The Bassaris .	. . .	Bassaris astuta.
15. The Patagonian Skunk	. . .	Mephitis humboldtii.
16. The Grey Fox .	. . .	Canis azarae.
17. The Syrian Bear	. . .	Ursus syriacus.
18. The Walrus .	. . .	Trichecus rosmarus.
19. The Wapiti Deer .	. . .	Cervus canadensis.
20. The White-tailed deer	. . .	,, leucurus.
21. The Eland .	. . .	Oreas canna.
22. The Persian Gazelle	. . .	Gazella subgutturosa.
23. The Leucoryx Antelope .	. . .	Oryx leucoryx.
24. The Punjaub Sheep .	. . .	Ovis cycloceros.
25. The Thar Goat	. . .	Capra jemlaica.
26. The Alpaca .	. . .	Auchenia pacos.
27. The Hippopotamus .	. . .	Hippotamus amphibius.
28. The Bosch Vark	. . .	Potomochœrus africanus.
29. The Red River Hog	. . .	,, pencillatus.
30. The Great Anteater .	. . .	Myrmecophaga jubata.
31. The Thylacine .	. . .	Thylacinus cynocephalus.
32. The Tasmanian Wombat	. . .	Phascolomys wombat.

BIRDS.

33. The Saker Falcon	. .	Falco sacer.
34. The Greenland Falcon	. .	,, greenlandicus.
35. The Iceland ,,	. .	,, islandicus.
36. The Angoloan Vulture	. .	,, Gypohie ?
37. The Chinese Pheasant	. .	Phasianus torquatus.
38. The Japan ,,	. .	,, versicolor.
39. Horsfield's Kaleege .	. .	Gallophasis horsfeildii.
40. The Caspian Snow Partridge	. .	Tetrogallus caspius.
41. The Painted Spur-Fowl	. .	Galloperdix lunulosa.
42. The American Rhea	. .	Rhea americana.
43. The Mooruk	. .	Casuarius benetti.
44. Mantel's Apteryx	. .	Apteryx mantelli.
45. The Great Bustard	. .	Otis tarda.
46. The Mantchurian Crane	. .	Grus montignesia.
47. The Australian mycteria	. .	Mycteria australis.
48. The Black-necked Swan	. .	Cignus nigricollis.
49. The Ashy-headed Goose	. .	Chloëphaga poliocephala.

REPTILES.

50. The Green Boa	. . .	Xiphosoma caninum.

1862.   JOHNS, THE REV. B. A. *British Birds in their Haunts.* S.P.C.K. 8vo. [One hundred and ninety woodcuts. There were subsequent Editions.]

1863.   BALDWIN, W. C. *African Hunting.* 'Illustrated by James Wolf and J. B. Zwecker.' Bentley. 8vo. [Auto-lithographs.

Page 79. River Scene.   Page 372. An African Serenade.
,, 92. Inyalas.   ,, 410. Night Shooting.
,, 187. Chasing Harris Buck.   ,, 424. A Narrow Escape.
[Third Edition, 1895.]

1863.   READE, W. W. *Savage Africa.* Smith, Elder. 8vo. [Three Woodcuts.]

Page 220. Gorilla and Nest.   Page 463. A Flood in Senegambia.
,, 397. The Djikikunka.
[Second Edition, 1854.

1863.   BATES, H. W. *The Naturalist on the River Amazons.* Murray. 2 vols. 8vo. [4 Woodcuts.]

Vol. 1. Frontispiece : Adventure with Curl - crested Toucans.
Page 177. Ant-Eater grappling with Dog.

Page 232. Flat-topped Mountains of Parauáquára.
Vol. 2. Page 306. Scarlet-faced and Parauacu Monkeys.

[There were subsequent Editions.]

1864.   CAMPBELL, COL. WALTER. *My Indian Journal.* Edmonston & Douglas. 8vo. [Auto-lithographs.]

Frontispiece : The Tiger in Ambush.
Page 101. Indian Bison.

Page 369. Ibex of the Neilgherries.
,, 377. Sambar.

1864.   *Quarterly Journal of Science.* Pages 214-219. P. L. Sclater. The Mammals of Madagascar. [Auto-lithographs.]

1864.   *The Illustrated Penny Almanack.*   Vickers, 172 Strand
[Twelve wood-cut bird designs.]

1864.   *The Golden Harp.* Hymns, Rhymes, and Songs for the Young.
Adapted by H. W. Dulcken. Illustrated by J. D. Watson,
T. Dalziel, and J. Wolf. [Woodcuts. Engraved by the
Brothers Dalziel.] Routledge. 4to.

Page 29. Joy Everywhere.
 ,,   67. Live in Peace.
 ,,   74. Morning Song in the
          Country.
 ,, 115. The Little Lamb.

Page 125. The Chickens and the
           Hawk.
 ,, 130. The Four Seasons.
 ,, 159. The Lion and the Wolf.

1864.   *Oötheca Wolleyana.* Edited by Alfred Newton, M.A.   Part 1.
Accipitres. Van Voorst. [Lithographs.]

Tab. C. Falco gyrfalco. | Tab. F. Eagle's Nest.
          Tab. G. Eagle's Nest.

1866.   STEVENSON, HENRY, F.L.S.   *The Birds of Norfolk.* Van
Voorst. 8vo.

Vol. 1. Frontispiece : Bargate,
   Surlingham   Broad.
       'Lithographed   by
   J. Wolf and J. Jury.'
Page 376. Pallas's Sand Grouse.
   [Auto-lithograph.]
Vol. 2. Frontispiece : Great

Bustard. Lithographed by
   Smit. After J. Wolf.
Vol. 3. Frontispiece : Scoulton Mere.
   The Breeding Place of the
   Blackheaded Gull. [' Litho-
   graphed by J. Wolf and
   J. Jury.'

1866.   HARTING, J. E. *The Birds of Middlesex.* Van Voorst. Frontispiece : ' The Head of Kingsbury Reservoir.' [Auto-litho-
graph.]

1867.   TENNENT, SIR JAMES EMERSON. *The Wild Elephant, and the
Method of Capturing and Taming it in Ceylon.* Longmans.
Post 8vo. [Woodcuts.]

Page 124. Noosing Wild Ele-
          phants.   (Full
          page.)
 ,, 126. Mode of Tying an
          Elephant.
 ,, 127. His Struggles for
          Freedom.

Page 130. Impotent Fury.
 ,, 132. Singular Contortions of an
          Elephant.
 ,, 134. Attitudes of   Captives.
          (Full page.)
 ,, 135. Obstinate Resistance.
 ,, 147. Attitude for Defence.

There is an earlier edition.]

1867.   *Æsop's Fables.* A new edition edited by Edward Garrett, M.A.
With 100 illustrations by J. Wolf, J. B. Zwecker, and
T. Dalziel. Strahan. 32mo. [Woodcuts.]

Page 1. The Cock and the
         Jewel.
 13. The Eagle and the
         Fox.
 95. The Jackdaw and the
         Peacocks.

Page 95. The Fighting Cocks and
         the Eagle.
 ,, 119. The Eagle and the Crow.
 ,, 143. The Tortoise and the
         Eagle.

1867. TRISTRAM, THE REV. H. B. *The Natural History of the Bible.*
S.P.C.K. 12mo. [About 20 woodcuts, mostly taken from
Johns' *British Birds in their Haunts.*]

1867. LLOYD, L. *The Game Birds and Wild Fowl of Sweden and
Norway.* Day & Son. Royal 8vo. [Full-page woodcuts.]

Page 37. The Capercaillie Lek. | Page 370. The Bird Cloud.
,, 241. The Ruff Lek. | ,, 457. Walrus and Polar Bear.

1867. ARGYLL, THE DUKE OF. *The Reign of Law.* Strahan. 8vo.
[Woodcuts illustrating the flight of birds.]

Page 154. The Swift. Page 166. Sparrow-hawk, Merlin,
,, 162. Wing of Gannet. and Kestril hovering.
,, 164. Wing of Golden
Plover.

1867. *Maunders' Treasury of Geography.* Hughes' edition. Longmans.
Frontispiece, line engraving : ' Animal Life in South Africa
in its Native State, from an original drawing by J. Wolf,
under the direction of C. J. Andersson.'

1867. *Zoological Sketches,* by JOSEPH WOLF. Made for the Zoological
Society of London. Edited with notes by Philip L.
Sclater, &c. Second series. Graves. [Lithographed
by Mr. Smit after the original water-colour drawings.
Coloured by hand.]

MAMMALS.

1. Ashy-black Macaque	. . .	Macacus ocreatus.
2. Black-fronted Lemur		Lemur nigrifrons.
3. Aye Aye .	. . .	Chiromys madagascariensis.
4. Fennec Fox	. . .	Canis cerdo.
5. Yaguarundi Cat		Felis yaguarundi.
6. Norwegian Lynx		,, lynx.
7. Viverrine Cat .		,, viverrina.
8. Rasse	. . .	Viverricula malaccensis.
9. The Ratels	. . .	Mellivora capensis and Melli-vora indica.
10. Binturong .		Arctictis binturong.
11. The Sea Bear .		Otaria hookeri.
12. Persian Deer .		Cervus maral.
13. Mantchurian Deer .		,, mantchuricus.
14. Formosan Deer .		,, tiavanus.
15. Japanese Deer .		,, sika.
16. Rusa Deer .		,, rusa.
17. Swinhoe's Deer .		,, swinhoii.
18. Pudu Deer .		,, humulis.
19. Leucoryx .		Oryx leucoryx.
20. Markhore .		Capra megaceros.
21. Aoudad .		Ovis tragelaphus.
22. Andaman Pig .		Sus andamanensis.
23. Collared Peccary .		Dycotyles torquatus.
24. African Elephant .		Elephas africanus.
25. Three-toed Sloth .		Bradypus tridactylus.
26. Red Kangaroo .		Macropus rufus.
27. Hairy-nosed Wombat		Phascolomys latifrons.

BIRDS.

28. Satin Bower Bird	. .	Ptilonorhyncus holosericeus.
29. Concave-casqued Hornbill		Buceros bicornis.
30. Rhinoceros Hornbill	.	,, rhinoceros.
31. Spotted Eagle	. . .	Aquila nævia.
32. Soemmerring's Pheasant .	.	Phasianus sœmmerringii.
33. Reeves' Pheasant	. . .	,, reevsii.
34. Rufous-tailed Pheasant .	.	Euplocamus erythropthalmus.
35. Siamese Pheasant	.	,, prælatus.
36. Viellot's Fireback	. .	,, viellotti.
37. Swinhoe's Pheasant	.	,, swinhoii.
38. Lineated ,,	.	,, lineatus.
39. Horned Tragopan .	. .	Ceriornis satyra.
40. Talegalla	. . .	Talegalla lathami.
41. Ostrich	. . .	Struthio camelus.
42. Weka Rail	. . .	Ocydromus australis.
43. Saddle billed Stork .	.	Ciconia senegalensis.
44. Shoe-bill .	. . .	Balæniceps rex.
45. Kagu	. . .	Rhinochetus jubatus.
46. African Wood Ibis .	.	Tantalus ibis.
47. Indian Wood Ibis .	.	,, leucocephalus.
48. Upland Goose	. .	Chloëphaga magellanica.
49. Shielded Duck	.	Anas scutulata.

REPTILES.

50. The Clotho	. .	Clotho nasicornis.

1868.   BUCHANAN, ROBERT W. *North Coast, and Other Poems.* Rout-ledge.   Small 4to.   [Four woodcuts at pp. 189, 191, and 213.]

1868.   *My Pet's Picture Book.*   Routledge.   [A few electrotypes from Wood's Natural History, in 'The Alphabet of Animals.']

1869.   WALLACE, A. R.   The *Malay Archipelago, The Land of the Orang-utan and the Bird of Paradise.*   Macmillan. Frontispiece : 'Orang-utan attacked by Dyaks.'
    On the title-page and at p. 41 : 'Female Orang-utan,' from a photograph.   [Woodcuts.]
    [Also in subsequent editions.]

1869.   EWING, J. H. *Mrs. Overtheway's Remembrances.*   Bell & Daldy. 4to.   Frontispiece only : 'The Albatross's Nest.'
    [Another edition 1885.]

IN THE SEVENTIES.

1872.   KNOX, A. E. *Autumns on the Spey.* Van Voorst. [Lithographs after J. Wolf.]

Frontispiece : 'Otherwise En-   Page 93. The Black Informer.'
        gaged.'   ,, 138. Ortgarr.
Page 46. The Last Chance.

1872.   DARWIN, CHARLES. *The Expressions of the Emotions in Man and Animals.* Murray.
[Page 136, 2 woodcuts. *Cynopithecus niger.*]

1872.   ELLIOT, D. G., F.L.S., F.Z.S., &c. *A Monograph of the Phasianidæ.* 2 vols. Folio. Published by the Author. New York. [Lithographs by Smit & Keulemans, after J. Wolf. Coloured by hand.]

Vol. 1.

1.	Generic Characters.	18.	Crossoptilon auritum.
2.	,, ,,	19.	Lophophorus impeyanus.
3.	Pavo cristatus.	20.	,, lhuysi.
4.	,, nigripennis.	21.	,, sclateri.
5.	,, muticus.	22.	Tetraophasis obscurus.
6.	Polyplectron thibetanum.	23.	Ceriornis satyra.
7.	,, bicalcaratum.	24.	,, melanocephala.
8.	,, germaini.	25.	,, temminckii.
9.	,, emphanum.	26.	,, caboti.
10.	,, chalcurum.	27.	,, blythi.
11.	Argus giganteus.	28.	Pucrasia macrolopha.
12.	,, grayi.	29.	,, darwaueli.
13.	,, ocellatus.	30.	,, xanthospila.
14.	,, bipunctatus.	30 bis.	,, darwini.
15.	Crossoptilon thibetanum.	31.	Meleagris gallopavo.
16.	,, drouyni.	32.	,, mexicana.
17.	,, mantchuricum.	33.	,, ocellata.

Vol. 2.

1.	Phasianus shawi.	24.	Euplocamus prælatus.
2.	,, cholchicus.	25.	,, swinhoii.
3.	,, insignis.	26.	,, ignitus.
4.	,, mongolicus.	27.	,, nobilis.
5.	,, torquatus.	28.	,, erythrophthal-
6.	,, formosanus.		mus.
7.	,, decollatus.	29.	,, pyronotus.
8.	,, elegans.	30.	Ithaginis cruentus.
9.	,, versicolor.	31.	,, geoffroyi.
10.	,, wallichi.	32.	Gallus ferrugineus.
11.	,, reevesi.	33.	,, lafayetti.
12.	,, sœmmerringi.	34.	,, sonnerati.
13.	,, sœmmerringi.	35.	,, varius.
	var. scintillans.	36.	Phasidus niger.
13 bis.	Calophasis ellioti.	37.	Agelastes meleagrides.
14.	Thanmalea amherstiæ.	38.	Acryllium.
15.	,, pieta.	39.	Numida meleagris.
16.	,, obscura.	40.	,, coronata.
17.	Hybrid pheasant.	41.	,, mitrata.
18.	Euplocamus albocristatus.	42.	,, ptilorhynca.
19.	,, melanotus.	43.	,, granti.
20.	,, horsfeildi.	44.	,, verrauxi.
21.	,, nycthemerus.	45.	,, cristata.
22.	,, andersoni.	46.	,, pucherani.
23.	,, lineatus.	47.	,, plumifera.

Y

1873. *Lyrics of Ancient Palestine.* With illustrations by A. de Neuville, P. Skelton, J. Wolf, J. D. Watson, &c. Religious Tract Society. 8vo. (Page 86, 'Samson's Riddle.') [Woodcut.]

1873. GOULD, JOHN. *The Birds of Great Britain.* Published by the Author, at 26 Charlotte Street, Bedford Square, W.C. 5 vols. Atlas folio. [Lithographs by Richter, after J. Wolf, of the following species. Coloured by hand.]

Vol. 1.

Egyptian Vulture.
Golden Eagle.
Spotted Eagle.
Sea Eagle.
Osprey.
Common Buzzard.
Rough-legged Buzzard.
Goshawk.
Sparrow-hawk.
Iceland Falcon.
Iceland Falcon, Young.
Greenland Falcon.
Greenland Falcon, Dark.
Gyr Falcon.
Peregrine.
Hobby.
Merlin.
Kestril.
Kite.
Black Kite.
Tawny Owl.
Eagle Owl.
Long-eared Owl.
Snowy Owl.
Little Owl.

Vol. 3.

Hooded Crow attacking eggs of Black Game.

Vol. 4.

Capercailzie.
Black Game.
Red Grouse.
Ptarmigan in Winter.
Ptarmigan in Summer, with young.
Ptarmigan in Autumn.
Red-legged Partridge.
Great Bustard.
Little Bustard.
Common Crane.
Grey Plover.
Golden Plover.
Woodcock.
Coot.
Moorhen.

Vol. 5.

Grey Lag Goose.
Bernicle Goose.
Mute Swan.
Whooper.
Bewick's Swan.
Shoveller Duck.
Mallard.
Ferruginous Duck.
Stella's Duck.
Scoter.
Smew.
Gannet.
Iceland Gull.
Herring Gull.
Blackheaded Gull.
Pomatorhine Skua.

1873. ELLIOT, D. G., F.L.S., &c. *A Monograph of the Birds of Paradise.* Published by the Author. Atlas folio. [Lithographs by Smit, after J. Wolf. Coloured by hand.]

1. Generic Characters.	20. Epimachus ellioti.
2. Paradisea apoda.	21. Depranornis albertisi.
3. ,, raggiana.	22. Seleucides alba.
4. ,, minor.	23. Ptiloris magnificus.
5. ,, sanguinea.	24. ,, alberti.
6. Manucodia atra.	25. ,, paradiseus.
7-8. ,, keraudreni.	26. ,, victoriæ.
9. Astrapia nigra.	27. Sericulus melinus.
10. Parotia sexpennis.	28. Ptilonorhynchis violaceus.
11. Lophorina atra.	29. ,, rawnsleyi.
12. Diphyllodes speciosa.	30. Chlamydodera maculata.
13. ,, chrysoptera.	31. ,, nuchalis.
14. ,, respublica.	32. ,, cerviniventris.
15. Xanthomelus aureus.	33. ,, xanthogastra.
16. Cicinnurus regius.	34. Æluredus crassirostris.
17. Paradigalla carunculata.	35. ,, melanotis.
18. Semioptera wallacii.	36. ,, buccoides.
19. Epimachus speciosus.	37. Amblyornis inornata.

1873. *The Life and Habits of Wild Animals.* Illustrated with designs by Joseph Wolf. Engraved by J. W. and Edward Whymper, with descriptive letterpress by D. G. Elliot, F.L.S., &c. Macmillan. Super royal 4to.

Who comes here?	Hunted Down.
A Hairbreadth Escape.	A Race for Life.
The Struggle.	A Happy Family.
Bruin at Bay.	Maternal Courage.
The Island Sanctuary.	Rival Monarchs.
At Close Quarters.	The King of Beasts.
Strategy versus Strength.	The Shadow Dance.
Gleaners of the Sea.	Catching a Tartar.
The Siesta.	The Ambuscade.
A Tropical Bathing Place.	The Avalanche.

1874. *Picture Posies.* Poems chiefly by living authors, and drawings by F. Walker, J. D. Watson, Birket Foster, J. Wolf, and others. Engraved by Dalziel Brothers. Routledge. 4to.
     [These woodcuts had for the most part appeared in other works such as 'A Round of Days,' published by Routledge.] J. Wolf's are as follows :—

Page 172. Live in Peace.	Page 209. The First Spring Day.
,, 173. Morning Song in the Country.	,, 213. The Death of the Deer, I.
	,, 214. ,, ,, II.
,, 191. The Four Seasons.	,, 227. The Quail and her Young.
,, 194. Joy Everywhere.	,, 233. By the River.
205. The Chickens and the Hawk.	

1879. DRESSER, H. E., F.L.S., &c. *The Birds of Europe.* Published by the Author. 8 vols. [The following are lithographs, after J. Wolf, coloured by hand.]

The designs for the title-pages :

Plate 308.	Lapp Owl .	. Syrnium lapponicum.
,, 319.	Griffon Vulture	. Gyps fulvus.
,, 322.	Egyptian ,.	. Neophron percnopterus.
,, 326.	Marsh Harrier	. Circus æruginosus ♂ Juv. ♀ Ad.
,, 327.	Marsh Harrier .	. Ad. ♂
,, 328.	Montagu's Harrier	. Circus cineraceus.
,, 329.	Hen Harrier .	. Circus cyaneus.
,, 330.	Pallid Harrier .	. ,, Swainsoni.
,, 345.	Golden Eagle	. Aquila chrysaetus.
,, 375.	Lanner .	. Falco feldeggi.
,, 370.	Saker . .	. ,, sacer.
,, 381.	Merlin	. ,, æsalon.
,, 466.	Black-bellied Sand Grouse .	. Pterocles arenarius.
,, 468.	Pallas's Sand Grouse .	. Syrrhaptes paradoxus.
,, 618.	Capped Petrel . .	. Œstrelata hæsitata.

1876. *Thierleben. Kriegs- und Friedensbilder aus der Thierwelt.* Von B. TÜMLER. Mit 20 Illustrationen von JOSEPH WOLF. Einsiedeln, New York, Cincinnati und St. Louis : Gebr. Karl und Nikolaus Benziger. [This is a reprint of the *Wild Animals* blocks.]

1876. BREHM'S *Thierleben: allgemeine Kunde des Thierreichs.* Leipzig. [In these volumes will be found a considerable number of woodcuts copied from Wolf's designs in *The Proceedings of the Zoological Society*, or in other works. The animals have in some cases been slightly altered, and other backgrounds and accessories have been introduced. The following are instances from among the mammals :—

Vol. 1.

Page 151.	Cynocephalus porcarius.	Page 265.	Arctocebus calabarensis.
,, 166.	Cynocephalus gelada.	,, 269.	Otolicnus galago.
		,, 278.	Chiromys madagascariensis.
,, 189.	Ateles bartletti.	,, 389.	Felis eyra.
,, 212.	Pithecia hirsuta.	,, 390.	Tigris regalis.
,, 215.	Brachyurus calvul.	,, 481.	Felis viverrina.
,, 251.	Lemur macaco.	,, 509.	Lynx canadensis.
,, 254.	Hapalemur griseus.		

Vol. 2.

Page 28.	Bassaris astuta.	Page 215.	Arctitis binturong.
,, 126.	Enhydris lutris.	,, 611.	Ornithorhyncus paradoxus.
,, 133.	Mephitis suffocans.		

Vol. 3.

334. Capra jemlaica.

There are also some Birds in the succeeding volumes.]

Golden Thoughts from Golden Fountains, illustrated by eminent artists. Engraved by the Brothers Dalziel. Warne.

Page 19. My Doves.   Page 207. Linnets and Nest.
 ,, 113. The Birds that awake
         the Morning.
     In an earlier Edition the designs are printed in brown ink.

IN THE EIGHTIES.

1880.   HARTING, J. E., F.L.S., &c. *British Animals extinct within Historic Times.* Trübner. Demy 8vo.

Page 11. The Bear. | Page 115. The Wolf.
 ,, 77. ,, Wild Boar. |

1882.   WILSON, DR. *Wild Animals and Birds: their Haunts and Habits.* With illustrations by Wolf and Specht. Cassell. 4to.

   [These illustrations by Wolf are reprints of the whole of the *Wild Animals* series with different titles; and, in addition, there are four other subjects.]

The Gorilla at Home	Who comes here?
Bonnet Monkeys	A Happy Family.
The Lion and his Prey	The King of Beasts.
A Fight for Life	The Struggle.
The Jaguar on the Watch	The Siesta.
Unconscious Victims	The Ambuscade.
Strategy versus Strength	
A Shadow Dance	The Same.
An Unequal Contest	Catching a Tartar.
Bruin at Bay	The Same.
Bison and Grizzly Bear	Rival Monarchs.
An Intruder Baffled	Maternal Courage.
Just Saved	A Race for Life.
In the Snow Drift	The Avalanche.
The Wild Boar at Bay	At Close Quarters.
A Favourite Watering Place	A Tropical Bathing Place.
Hunted Down	The Same.
The Island Sanctuary	The Same
Only just Caught	A Hairbreadth Escape.
The Harvest of the Sea	Gleaners of the Sea.

Also

An Arctic Scene	Polar Bear and Snowy Owls.
A Marauder	Golden Eagle and Ptarmigan.
A Midnight Attack	Wild Cat and Ring Dove.
The Home of the Heron	A Lake with many Herons.

1883.   ELLIOT, D. G., F.L.S., &c. *A Monograph of the Felidæ.* Published by the Author for the Subscribers. [Forty-three lithographs by Smit after J. Wolf. Coloured by hand.]

1.	Felis leo	Lion.
2.	,, concolor	Puma.
3.	,, tigris	Tiger.
4.	,, uncia	Snow Leopard.
5.	,, onca	Jaguar.
6–7.	,, pardus	Leopard.
8.	,, diardi	Clouded Leopard.
c.	,, marmorata	Marbled Cat.
10.	,, manul	Pallas's Cat.
11.	,, pageros	Pampas Cat.
12.	,, colocolo	The Colocollo.
13.	,, jaguarondi	The Jaguarondi.
14.	,, eyra	The Eyra.
15.	,, badia.	
16.	,, temminckii	Golden Cat.
17.	,, planiceps	Flat-headed Cat.
18.	,, pardalis	Ocelot.
19.	,, tigrina	Margay.
20.	,, geoffroyi.	
21.	,, bengalensis	. Leopard Cat.
22.	,, viverrina	. Fishing Cat.
23.	,, tristris.	
24.	,, scripta.	
25.	,, chrysothrix.	
26.	,, serval	The Serval.
27.	,, euplilura.	
28.	,, javensis.	
29.	,, rubignosa	Rusty-spotted Cat.
30.	,, catus	Wild Cat.
31.	,, caffra	Egyptian Cat.
32.	,, ornata	Indian Desert Cat.
33.	,, chaus	Jungle Cat.
34.	,, caudata.	
35.	,, shawiana	. Shaw's Cat.
36.	,, cervaria.	
37.	,, canadensis	. Canada Lynx.
38.	,, pardina	. Pardine Lynx.
39.	,, lynx	. The Lynx.
40.	,, rufa	. Red Cat.
41.	,, caracal	. The Caracal.
42.	,, domestica.	
43.	Cynailurus jubatus	Hunting Leopard.

1883. GOULD, JOHN. *The Birds of Asia.* Published by the Author and continued after his death. 1850 to 1883. 7 vols. Atlas fol. [The following are lithographs by Richter, after J. Wolf. Coloured by Hand.]

Vol. 1.

Plate 1.	Black Vulture	Otogyps calvus.
,, 4.	Red-naped Falcon	Falco babylonicus.
,, 5.	Saker Falcon	,, sacer.
,, 6.	Lanner ,,	,, lanarius.
,, 7.	Jugger	,, jugger.
,, 9.	Rufous-breasted Spilornis	Spilornis rufipectus.
,, 10.		Spizaetus alboniger.
,, 11.	Govinda Kite	. Milvus govinda.

Vol. 6.

Plate 74. Thibet Partridge	Perdix hodgsoniae.

Vol. 7.

,, 13. Bulwer's Pheasant .	Lobiophasis bulweri.
,, 15. Viellot's Fireback .	Euplocamus viellotti.
,, 18. Cheer . . .	Catreus wallichi.
,, 29. Caspian Snow Partridge .	Tetraogallus caspius.
,, 30. Himalayan Snow Partridge	,, h'malayensis.
,, 31. Altaic Snow Partridge	,, altaicus.
,, 32. Thibetan Snow Partridge .	,, tibetanus.
,, 34. Common Pheasant . .	Phasianus colchicus.
,, 37. Soemmerring's Pheasant .	,, soemmerringi.
,, 38. Sparkling Pheasant .	,, scintillans.
,, 40. Japanese Pheasant . .	,, versicolor.
,, 41. Mongolian Pheasant .	,, mongolicus.
,, 47. Blythe's Horned Pheasant .	,, Ceriornis blythii.
,, 62. Zic Zac . . .	,, Pluranus ægyptus.
,, 69. Mandarin Duck .	,, Aix galericulata.

1883. HARTING, J. E., F.L.S., &c. *Sketches of Bird Life from Twenty Years' Observations on their Haunts and Habits.* Illustrated by Whymper, Wolf, and others. Allen. Demy 8vo.

IN THE NINETIES.

1892. BUXTON, E. N. *Short Stalks or Hunting Camps: North, South, East, and West.* Illustrated by Lodge, Whymper, Wolf, &c. Stamford. 8vo. ⌐Woodcuts.¬

Page 174. 'Skræmt.'	Page 208. 'The Capra ægarus.'

RICHARD LYDEKKER. *The Royal Natural History.* Illustrated by Specht, Mützel, Wolf, &c. Warne. In progress.

The illustrations copied from Wolf are confined for the most part to reprints of the cuts in Brehm's *Thierleben* already given, but without the acknowledgment of their authorship. They are here signed 'G. M.' Among other instances in the first volume (for example) in which Wolf's work has been made use of, the following may be mentioned :—

Page 150. White-cheeked Sapajou . .	See *Proceedings* of the Zoological Society, 1865, plate 45.
,, 164. Variegated Spider Monkey .	See Ditto 1867, plate 47.
,, 176. Humboldt's Saki . .	See Bates' *Naturalist on the River Amazons*, vol. 2, p. 306.
Bald Uakari . .	See Ditto.
,, 192. The Silver Marmoset .	See *Proceedings* of the Zoological Society, 1868, plate 24.
,, 226. The Senegal Galago	See Ditto 1863, plate 28.
,, 217. The Gentle Lemur .	See Ditto 1863, plate 17.
,, 235. The Awantibo . .	See Ditto 1864, plate 28.

Page 261. The Red-necked Fruit Bat. Signed 'J. Wolf' .   See Tennent's *Sketches of the Natural History of Ceylon*, p. 14.

The Pen-tailed Tree-shrew. Signed 'J. Smit.'   See *Proceedings* of the Zoological Society. Mammalia 2.

,, 345. The Potomogale .   From a lithograph signed by J. Wolf, and natural size.

'The Struggle in the Stream' .   Part only of 'The Struggle' in *Wild Animals*.

,, 353. The Lion at the Pool.

,, 410. The Fishing Cat. 'After Wolf.'   See Elliot's *Monograph of the Felidæ*, plate 22.

,, 489. The Eyra .   See Ditto, plate 14.

,, 437. The Northern Lynx .   See Ditto.

,, 550. An Interesting Discovery .   Part only of 'The Shadow Dance' in *Wild Animals*.

1895.   Badminton Library, *Big Game Shooting*. Longmans. 1895. 2 vols. In Vol. 1. Eleven reproductions of the drawings which were made to illustrate Mr. W. C. Oswell's African Adventures.

Page 40. Molopo River.

,, 90. Odds—3 to 1.

,, 116. Feeling both Horns of a Dilemma.

,, 120. The Drop Scene.

,, 128. Elephants -- Zouga Flats.

, 140. Threatening of Elephantiasis.

Page 52. Death of Superior.

,, 66. A Night Attack, Lupapi.

,, 70. 'Post equitem sedet "fulva" cura.' The Lioness does the scansion.

,, 103. Death of Stael.

,, 131. Maneless Lions.

PRINTED BY

SPOTTISWOODE AND CO., NEW-STREET SQUARE

LONDON

www.ingramcontent.com/pod-product-compliance
Lightning Source LLC
Chambersburg PA
CBHW031055110726
47900CB00003B/940